For permission, inquiries, or information on bulk purchases, please visit the author's website: www.steveblinder.com
Published in the United States by Raindance.

This book is a work of fiction. With the exception of historical and public figures, any resemblance to actual persons living or dead is entirely coincidental.

LIBRARY OF CONGRESS CATALOGING-IN-PUBLICATION DATA
Blinder, Steve, 1955- author.
The Last City : a novel / by Steve Blinder
First Edition: August 2019
LCCN: 2019911022
ISBN (paperback) 978-0-578-54957-6
ISBN (ebook) 978-0-578-54958-3

Printed in the United States of America

10 9 8 7 6 5 4 3 2 1

Published By:

The
LAST CITY

Acknowledgements

I'd like to express my sincere gratitude to the following people who have contributed in ways both large and small in helping me turn the concept of this novel into a reality:

Eve Wittenmyer, Jeff Haller, Shep Zebberman,
Harry Elston, Lamonte McLemore, Angela Houle,
Mark Schwartz, Kathy Lombard, Julie Brown,
Annie Luu, Ariel Kosover, Gideon Rosman,
Eyal Kanitz, Steven Sherman, Robert Roth,
Renee, Elana, Alyssa & Josh…

This book is dedicated to my Mom & Dad.

They were pioneers, coming from out of the cold to settle in the West. I am in awe of their courage—making it all the way to the farthest outpost of Western Civilization—Los Angeles, California. It was 100 years after the Gold Rush—so they did not travel by covered wagon, but, the closest thing: a 1949 Buick Convertible.

They made the enormous commitment back in 1954 to buy a brand new house in the shiny new suburb of Inglewood for $11,000. Not $11,000 down—$11,000 total. Though most of the gold had already been discovered—they provided the golden years of my childhood. They also provided a great deal of the inspiration for this book, as, the lion's share of the thought processes, experiences and environment can be traced directly back to them.

This book is also for my one and only brother Bob.

Someday, I'm hoping he forgives me for setting fire to his fort. Uh... with him in it. Bro—in case you're reading this and I never told you—I'm glad you made it out OK.
I think that on a given day—if the Santa Ana wind is blowing right—Bobby & I might be quite proud to be able to say that we once hailed from Inglewood...

Steve Blinder
2019

Contents

THE LAST CITY

By Steve Blinder

CHAPTER 1 - The Fires

April 29, 1992
Santa Catalina Island, California

It was still there—her fear of drowning. She thought of that most basic of primal instincts, to breathe, being suppressed by cold, heartless seawater. The terror of that death, the gasping, the panic—the *knowing*. Her fear was far from being unfounded—it was solidified by the awful news, when she was just a kid, that her best friend from school, Leslie, had drowned. Snorkeling with her family in Jamaica, she heard that Leslie got caught in the current—struggling madly and yelling for help—but nobody could get to her. Renee's folks allowed her to procrastinate learning how to swim until she was well into her teens. She often visualized her friend's terror—couldn't imagine anything worse. That was before she met Eddie.

Now, standing at the aft rail of their boat, she looked down into the water and with a giant stride, punched that fear in the face. The explosion of bubbles was blinding. Both divers plunged into the teal blue waters off the backside of Catalina Island, left hands holding their buoyancy control buttons, right hands covering mask and regulator. The hot adrenaline rush was instantly extinguished by the impact of the cold Pacific, where ten thousand chrome spheres of various sizes raced to the surface as if to avoid the bodies plummeting in the opposite direction.

With all air in the vests expelled, the weight belts dictated the fall. For Renee, this was the best part—a free fall through inner space. She was flying. She was free. Remembering after numerous previous dives that she was going to challenge herself on the next one; she wanted to test her own brain power to see if she had the ability to think of something else during this moment of the fall. Could she distract herself, could she flash—if only for a millisecond—on a telephone ringing somewhere, a pager sounding its wiggly beep, a small item that needed attention around the house, or something a professor had said this week during one of her law classes? Could she even think of Leslie? She couldn't. That she could bring herself, with a 40 pound steel tank strapped to her back and another 18 pounds of lead weights buckled to her waist, to step off the boat into the dark water, was something her parents never believed. The bubbles raced by her, tickling her even, as she embraced the chilly sensation, while marveling at the visual wonders that unfolded before her. She failed her own test, becoming consumed both physically and spiritually by the cool, blissful descent. Her brain could not wander—it would not accept distraction, as she hypnotically slid deeper and deeper into the depths.

Eddie had different reasons for scuba diving. The absence of sound was in big contrast to the frenzied office and warehouse of his apparel manufacturing company. He embraced the total submersion into the strange and silent world undersea. But there was more: the glorious variation in colors and sheer weirdness of the creatures had long ago captivated him. He spent years honing fine underwater photographic skills, checking off his bucket list by logging dives in the world's premier spots: the coral reefs of the Red Sea, Tahiti, and the Great Barrier Reef in Australia. These were all unique and fantastic—but perhaps his favorites were the many dives exploring the Palancar Reef off the Northern coast of Honduras.

It had been quite some time since he spent money on a birthday or wedding present; gifts of his enchanting reef photos capturing the impossibly strange shapes, psychedelic colors and exotic critters were welcomed without exception by friends and family members. Plus, he was beginning to receive interest from a handful of galleries who were eager to display his work. Additionally, he thought, selling a few pieces wouldn't hurt to defray the costs of his ridiculously expensive underwater camera gear and incessant film developing.

Eddie had shared in the underwater thrill with dozens of novice divers—amusing himself—while studying their facial expressions: eyes bulging out from behind the magnifying glass of their face masks as they spotted a menacing toothy eel, or giant Manta Ray for the first time. He wondered if it would sell—pictures of divers—a coffee table book with his photos of their cartoonish masked faces. Two years ago, while filming a shark dive off the coast of Moorea, Eddie had, as his diving buddy, a retired pro defensive back for the Philadelphia Eagles. He nearly choked with laughter on his regulator as he observed a bright yellow cloud of urine appear around the swim trunks of the former tough guy on seeing his first seven foot tiger shark.

The seawater in Southern California, relative to tropical dive sites, was too cold for coral to live. The large kelp beds, however, were unique to the Channel Islands. There were few spots in the world where these magnificent golden trees of seaweed thrived as they did in Eddie's own backyard. It was as if these strange rubbery flora were inverted, appearing to grow backwards from normal earthly trees—almost as though they grew downward—starting from a clump of bronze leaves flopping harmlessly on the surface, and then plunging straight down to the ocean floor, often exceeding 100 feet in length.

Eddie was enchanted by the sun rays through the forest phenomenon created by the lasers of sunlight streaking through the kelp. The intense light and dark chiaroscuro effect would have certainly been the subject of many black and white photographs had Ansel Adams been a diver. He also likened the warm sunny spots and the cool shadows of the kelp to a walk, or, a *fly* through the woods. Eddie was sure that had Naturalist John Muir owned a scuba tank instead of a hiking stick, he would have forsaken his famous long walks through Yosemite and the Pacific Crest Trail in favor of flying through these woods. He felt he knew what blue-jays and hawks must feel soaring through the redwoods and giant Sequoias. In fact, thought Eddie, this might just be superior to the birds' feeling—for they had to work; they had to flap their wings or they would fall—whereas he could hover effortlessly in a desired spot—floating 70 feet or more under the surface; he could maintain neutral buoyancy by adding or subtracting air from his vest with the mere push of either of two buttons.

On a calm day, when there was little or no current, the tall trees of kelp were spectacular. Still. Silent. But when the sea turned rough—the kelp could be hell. He had experienced actual heart-pounding fear on a couple of occasions, becoming entangled in the vines when conditions quickly changed from calm to treacherous. Just last year, in Baja California, off the island of Ispiritu Santu—he thought he was in real trouble as in minutes the sea transformed. He was in fairly shallow water when the surge of the tide seemed to increase in power with impossible rapidity. The waves began to pummel the deadly rocks as tranquility gave way to terror. The ocean boiled, as the kelp became a live thrashing animal, with tentacles and arms of thick rubber rope coiling around his arms and legs, while multiple nooses wound around his neck. Only moments before, what were beautifully still hundred foot long strands of golden kelp, had morphed quickly into a chaos of thousands of ugly brown flags, surrounding him—slapping, whipping, cutting him and impairing his vision—seemingly intent on entangling him beyond hope—tying him up long enough so that the remaining air in his oxygen cylinder would dwindle until he drew his final breath. An hour later, pulse returning to normal while safe on the warm Mexican beach, the only item in his mental damage report that couldn't be remedied by a couple of quick cold beers was one lost flipper.

It was a Zen sort of training to remain calm when things got crazy. Feeling the tendrils of kelp winding around the ankles, intuitively, people were inclined to begin thrashing furiously—in attempt to kick out of the foreign entanglement. But this is the exact opposite of the preferred technique of slowing down—to an almost effortless glide of miniscule movement, wherein the kelp tended to harmlessly slip off the legs and ankles.

Eddie was lucky. He was well aware of tragic stories where people panicked in the kelp and lost infinitely more than a $30 swim fin. Eddie often reminded himself of his training—and knew that it applied to much more than diving.

For him, the biggest thrill from scuba diving was not the beauty or the weirdness or the silence. It was the hunt. He felt it was symbolic of his life, the life he had built and was always striving to improve. Eddie often debated his fisherman friends that spearfishing was the superior sport. 'With a rod and reel,' he would say, 'you drop the line and wait. It's too passive. You can only sit there and hope the fish jumps on your hook. Spearfishing is more like hunting; you can swim into a school of fish and pick out the one you want for dinner.'

Eddie's life was anything but passive. He regularly charged himself with tasks, or goals, and worked or figured out what needed to be done to achieve them. In his business, he was driven to land bigger orders, or make his manufacturing operation more efficient; he experimented with new techniques in his photography; he designed new landscaping with drip irrigation for his house. Even when sailing—he couldn't relax—he needed to alter the course, or trim the sails to achieve optimum boat speed. He read books to improve his chess game. He was a perfectionist. It was necessary in being a successful entrepreneur. The last time he had a boss—that creepy old man who paid him 25 cents an hour for delivering newspapers on his bicycle—he was twelve years old. Eddie vowed at that young age to never have to work for anybody but himself.

The kelp beds made terrific hiding places and were home to countless game fish—Perch, Sheepshead, Calico Bass, Halibut and Eddie's favorite: Red Snapper. Eddie loved the look of this fish. He loved the beautiful red-coral coloring and wide caricature mouth, and most of all, the taste of this delicious fish. He even loved hearing the sound of its name—especially the Spanish translation of snapper: *Huachinango!* Though he had a self-proclaimed proficiency in Spanish equivalent to that of a six year-old kid, he had learned the Spanish names for most Pacific saltwater creatures he encountered underwater—as well as in restaurants. Without seriously studying Spanish, Eddie learned the nouns from dozens of trips driving and sailing around Baja and the Sea of Cortez. To him, *huachinango* sounded like a dance. Or a party.

The hunt didn't hold nearly the same thrill for Renee—at least at first. She hated the killing of these fish. She hated the stalking. She hated the gruesome spearing, and she especially hated the disgusting cleaning. She couldn't stand the imagery: their pristine white fiberglass boat—awash with bones and fish guts. She detested the scales and rivulets of blood spilling down the deck and rails like something out of a horror movie. But she couldn't deny that these were necessary steps if she were to enjoy her number one fantasy: lying at anchor with her new husband under a star splashed sky, boat rocking to an intoxicating rhythm, candles flickering in the fraction of the steady sea breeze that found its way below decks—and Eddie serving up a fried Red Snapper or Calico as the heads and tails drooped lazily over opposite ends of the plastic green plates.

Renee chuckled to herself, reflecting back on those earlier dates when he romanced her—bringing her here—to drop anchor in a hidden cove at one of his 'secret spots' on the island. She had begged him not to serve the fish with the heads—but he insisted. Eddie offered long-winded ethereal explanations of the totality of the experience—the methodical sequence of necessary steps—from sharpening the spear tips, to preparing the gear, to tribal hunt, all the way to the obligatory after dinner belch; he gently admonished her that the ritual did not include the humiliating decapitation of the fish. He tried to get her to feel as he did— about how the honor of the creature would be compromised. He sold it to her in such a way that, like so many things that made up Eddie's personality, she often didn't know if he was being serious.

At first, on those earlier weekends, she protested the wanton spearing and murder of these beautiful fish. But slowly she acquiesced to his rationale, and now, looking down at her plate, she admitted, albeit to herself, that there was a twisted pleasure in staring into the small hologram created by the dead blue-black eyeball.

Eddie had fallen more in love with Renee since they were married. But he also marveled at his luck, because that fact notwithstanding—in spite of her earlier days as an absolute beginner with no desire to even go near the water, let alone put on weights and jump into the ocean—she had evolved into a heck of a diving buddy.

****

A spark jumped as one of the steel points of Eddie's treble pronged Hawaiian Sling grazed the rock. He had missed his shot at a 6 pound Sheepshead. God had played a cruel trick in the design of this Pacific fish, as, between the dorsal and pectoral fins of their mid-section, the males sported a bright red patch—this, painted against the contrasting charcoal grey field, while clearly attractive to the females and necessary for the procreation of the species—ironically made a neat target for the spear-hunter.

It was a rare miss for Eddie. Cursing a garbled obscenity into his regulator, he switched the pole spear to his right hand, dropped his left hand down, slightly behind his back, and found the familiar black hose of his pressure gauge. He held it up in front of his face—Depth: 85 feet. Air Pressure: 1000 Pounds. He signaled Renee by turning the gauge toward her, tapping the dial. She understood his query—checking on how much air she had left. Already holding her gauge, she signaled back to him that she had 750 p.s.i. remaining. Time enough for a five minute look back inside the periphery of the kelp beds. Eddie signaled her to follow him back into the forest, to which she answered with a barely perceptible nod.

Out of the corner of Eddie's left eye he registered a flash of movement. A white and tan Calico Bass had darted from the kelp shadow, through the light rays, and then back into the shadow.

His weapon was cocked. The surgical tube rubber band dug into Eddie's right hand at the crook between his thumb and forefinger. With his remaining fingers, Eddie made a tight fist around the yellow pole. He glided forward through the kelp—circling to the right of where he had seen the bass. He passed three long stalks of kelp on his left, and then turned into the shadows. The kill zone for his spear was anything within fifteen feet. The fish was about twenty feet away, facing him head on. That was good as far as his approach was concerned; with eyes on the sides of his head, the Calico could not clearly see him—but it presented an almost impossibly narrow target. Eddie had to guess a direction the fish would turn, so he aimed his weapon about six inches to the left of the face of the fish. It was a calculated guess; with the kelp slightly darker and thicker in that direction, he figured the fish would dart toward greater cover.

Flippers propelling him into the radius of the kill zone, he made one powerful scissor kick from the hips. Simultaneously, he opened his right fist. The simple, but deadly tool, vaulted forward as the taught tension of the surgical tubing released all of its energy. His guess was correct. There was a barely audible low-pitched *thwack*, as a flash of several silvery scales flew off the fourteen inch Calico. Two of the three spear tips found their mark, impaling the fish at a point midway between the gills and pectoral fin. Though the third missed any meat, it effectually pinned the top of the fish—backbone and entire fan of dorsal fin—to the other two prongs. The victim was frozen and could not move.

Renee had seen the shot—impressed once again at his deadly accuracy. Swimming directly over Eddie, she had already ripped open the Velcro top of her game bag, and with a neat economy of movements, slipped the red mesh over the three spear tips as well as the entire paralyzed fish. Squeezing the top of the bag closed, she nodded at Eddie. The stunned Calico fell into the bag as Eddie pulled back on the pole. The spear came out clean with the exception of three or four white scales wedged between the points. Free from the impaling skewers, the bagged fish immediately began to wiggle frantically, bumping wildly yet harmlessly against Renee's hip. They gave each other a neoprene gloved underwater high five, and then the thumbs up signal to begin their victorious ascent to the surface.

****

Renee sat back in the cockpit, enjoying the sizzle of the frying pan as the lovely aromas of garlic, butter and lemon wafted up from the galley. She stared up at their tall black mast, tickling the brand new crescent moon rising above the cactus covered hills. She thought back fondly to an encounter from the first time he brought her to Catalina. He impressed her in so many ways—but the moment she realized she had fallen for him was his reference to some historical trivia about Los Angeles—the city where he had lived his entire life.

"Do you know the real name of L.A? The Spanish name?" he had asked her.

"My Spanish is fairly dreadful," she answered, "but I'm pretty sure it's something about angels."

"Not bad. But the original name happens to be, 'El Pueblo de Nuestra Señora de los Angeles del Rio Porciúncula'."

"You're kidding! That's quite a mouthful."

"It sure is. Eleven words! How would you like to put that as your return address every time you write a letter, or fill out a form? Only a tiny percentage of people I've ever met know the real name. Even people who have lived here their whole lives don't know it. And absolutely nobody from the East Coast."

"What does it mean?" she asked.

"The English translation is, 'The Town of Our Lady, the Queen of the Angels of the River Porciúncula'."

"I'm kinda glad they shortened it to Los Angeles."

"Yep. People who just say 'L.A.' don't really appreciate how much time they now have on their hands."

"And what did you say—about a river? I'm sure I've never heard that before."

"Right, the Rio Porciúncula. It was the original Spanish name of the L.A. River—named by two Franciscan priests and explorers, Juan Crespi and Junipero Serra.

"Father Serra I've heard of. He's the guy who founded all the missions, right?"

"Right, when he wasn't robbing the various California Indian tribes such as the Chumash or the Gabrielino of their culture, or torturing them, I guess he was doing them a favor by introducing them to Jesus."

"Such a tradeoff," she said sarcastically. "I heard they are considering him for sainthood."

"That's true. Hero or horror. You decide."

"I'm glad it's not up to me. But the L.A. River? Whatever happened to that?"

"It's still here. It kind of flows into L.A. Harbor, near Long Beach—after a hard rain anyway. People used to drink from it, and catch fish in it. Now it's just a big cement storm drain. Guess we're all lucky Junipero Serra didn't stumble upon it now, 'Our Lady, the Queen of Concrete,' doesn't quite roll off the tongue as nicely."

"I agree. So if you didn't have your boat, instead of sailing to Catalina, would you be taking me down for romantic hikes along the river with a spear?"

"I don't think you'd want to be eating fish coming out of the L.A. River."

That conversation was a few years back, before they were married. It was in fact a moment before their first kiss. This trip marked an even dozen times that they had come to the island together, and she took pleasure in the fact that, unlike some of her married friends, friends who warned her about the inevitable changes in a serious relationship, she still enjoyed listening to Eddie's answers to her questions and the many tangents they would lead to.

****

"One of your best efforts yet, Eddie. I liked the addition of the cilantro."

"Evolve or die, they say."

She stared up at the moon again, thought for a second about asking him—it had been several months since they last spoke about it. She wanted a baby. Wanted it more than anything. Maybe a little girl—she could name Leslie. Eddie was successful, he was driven. She knew he was the perfect person for her, and would make the perfect father. But previous discussions on the topic had made him agitated. He assured her that he wanted it as well, a family. But he defended the procrastination by explaining his dream, and how close he was to realizing that dream; how his company was growing rapidly, and the opportunities now before him, to create his 'mini-empire' were at hand. How, if she were just a little patient, this foundation he was laying would greatly pay off. Other than saying, 'the time will be right...soon...' he never quantified exactly when, how long it would take, or what it would take, to make the commitment of having a kid.

The days surrounding the tranquility of the island had been too perfect: five beautiful dives, incredible fresh fish dinners, expensive wine, glorious weather, and a nice break from her studies. Most of all, though, she enjoyed spending time alone with the man she loved. So, once again, she suppressed the urge to broach the subject of children.

"Gosh I love it here," she said. "Are you sure we're only 26 miles from Los Angeles—like the song says?"

Eddie grabbed the old Ibanez guitar that he kept on the boat, strummed a couple of C major chords, and started singing.

"Twenty Six miles across the sea, Santa Catalina is a waitin' for me. Santa Catalina—the island of romance, romance, drop your pants for romance."

"Something tells me that those are not the correct lyrics."

"Actually, from the slip in Marina Del Rey, to the exact spot where we dropped anchor is 28.2 miles. My Loran tells me so," he informed, tapping the blinking green L.E.D. numbers on the faceplate of the device.

"You promised you would teach me to navigate someday," she said.

"That's before I bought Loran here. Or as we pirates call her—when we've been at sea and away from our women for too long—'Lorraine.' Old fashioned navigation is almost a lost art. People don't know about celestial bodies and sextants and almanacs. All you have to do now is ask the computer."

"I still want to know," she said.

Eddie put down the guitar and propped open the top of the nav-station table; he pulled out the charts, the parallel rule, and a pencil. Renee silently watched his methodical whittling as he grabbed his large diving knife and slowly honed the lead to a fine point.

After the purchase of his boat, the very first addition, right before he bought the Loran, was a small ninety dollar compass. He mounted it directly over the nav-station below deck. This served as a backup to the big compass in front of the wheel topside. From here, he plotted courses, and, equally as important, he could make quick checks on the current course of the helmsman above.

He brushed the yellow and wood pencil shavings off the chart and onto the mahogany floorboards, where they joined some of the garlic and lemon peels from the earlier feast.

"OK, try to keep in mind," Eddie said, tapping the black compass with the eraser end of his pencil, "that the compass is not what's turning. The boat in fact is turning around the compass."

"You've got my interest already," she said.

He smiled and continued, "So, when you look at a chart, or any map for that matter, always position it with North at the top. If we know one direction, we can figure out all of the others. For example, if we are facing North, West is always to the left."

"Even below the equator?" she asked.

He chuckled. "You must be thinking about how the water in a toilet bowl is supposed to spin opposite—it spirals counter-clockwise south of the equator. I forgot to check that the last time I was in Tahiti. Too busy with other things, I guess."

They both had a little laugh recalling a quick second of their blissful 10-day honeymoon in Bora Bora.

"But, in this case, always means always. When facing North, West is *always* 90 degrees to the left."

"OK," she said, "let's say we're sailing home from here but visibility is bad—it's real foggy."

"If we know where we are, it's easy." Eddie made a small dot with the pencil in the middle of a tiny inlet on the chart. "This is 'Eddie's Cove.' Now we can't sail through the island, so we must go around the farthest westerly point." Eddie made another dot at the West End of the island, and then drew a line connecting that dot to a third dot just outside the mouth of his cove.

"The first rule of any successful navigation is to always keep a little water under your keel. It doesn't have to be much—even two inches will do, but it does have to be there, or it tends to put a slight damper on your day."

Eddie paused momentarily as his minds' eye brought forth the terrifying vision of the submerged rock he hit that night with his uncle 30 years ago. He was only eight at the time. It was a very rough sea, so he was frightened to begin with, but when they slammed into the reef, he was sure by the look on his uncle's face that they were going down. One of the worst imaginable sounds on the entire planet is the crunching of the fiberglass of the boat you happen to be on. That rock was not shown on the chart, and wasn't more than a mile from where they now lay peacefully at anchor. He considered for a moment—but knowing the story of her friend that drowned—decided to share his memory of running aground another time...

"Now the way we figure the compass course is by "walking" the parallel rule over to where it intersects the little 'x' in the center of the compass printed on the chart. That little 'x' is called the "compass rose.""

"Why are there two different sets of numbers in the circles around the compass on the chart?"

"Excellent question; the outer numbers pertain to '*true* North.' The inner circle of headings refers to '*magnetic* North.' Remember when you were a kid in geography class and the teacher taught you that the North Pole was a few degrees away from magnetic North?"

"I think I was sick that day."

"Well that's OK, 'cause you can forget about anything but magnetic North, as that's what the compass is all about."

"So if I only look at the inner ring of numbers..."

She carefully manipulated the parallel rule as Eddie taught her, until it intersected the compass rose. He was impressed but not surprised. In the same way she had mastered the essence of diving so quickly—he was impressed once again at what a quick study she was.

"... the course tomorrow morning, from where we now sit at anchor to round the first rocks will be... 265 degrees?"

"Perfect!"

"And then, let's see... we'll bear off to starboard at the West End to a course of... 360 degrees... or would that be zero degrees?"

"Exactly right, either one works. But actually you'd probably say 'due North.' And if you steer due North for about 4-6 hours, depending on the wind, you'll see the flag on the Marina Del Rey breakwater."

"I got it!"

"You got it all right baby. Now let's see if I can navigate my way into those tight jeans of yours."

****

"We'd better head out soon or we won't be home till midnight," Eddie said.

"Anchor drill?"

"Sì querida. Anchor drill. You want the bow or the helm?" he asked.

"I'll take the wheel," she answered, without hesitation.

"Somehow, I knew you'd say that. After last night with you, do you really think I have the strength to lift the anchor?"

She smirked, "I thought pirates were supposed to be tough."

Eddie went forward and hauled the hinged Danforth anchor and heavy chain up onto the bow. It came up clean from the sandy bottom. Neatly coiling the anchor line in the forward locker, he shackled the anchor to the bow pulpit, and they were adrift. Most Southern California cruisers tended to leave the island no later than noon, for a daylight sail back home, but a nighttime spinnaker run had become somewhat of a ritual for them. With the wind out of the West at a steady fourteen knots—together with that beautiful silver fingernail of a moon—this had the makings of a memorable night.

Setting the main and jib, they pulled out of Eddie's Cove at sunset. An hour later passing Eagle Rock to starboard, they set the spinnaker gear. Heading South, six Brown Pelicans cruised single file, inches off the water. Renee went forward and dropped the jib as Eddie turned a few degrees downwind. The huge balloon sail filled, and the boat responded by quickly accelerating through the black water, throwing off silver jets of phosphorescent spray from the bow and stern wakes. In the distance, the low glow of Los Angeles appeared above the last rocks at the end of the island. And, as Renee had correctly calculated in her first navigation lesson after last night's dinner, they were sailing a perfect due North.

But there was something different tonight. Eddie had navigated this right turn around the West End rocks a hundred times. Ever since he was a kid too small to wrap both hands around the tiller of his uncle's boat, he remembered this turn and the first view of the twinkling lights of L.A. As he grew older, he always likened it to flying into Las Vegas at night from the blackened desert. It was one of the great contrasts—a billion watts of man-made electricity bursting out of nature's vast void. Tonight, though, something was strange; there was no fog, and due to the fresh breeze, visibility was excellent—but now—they both clearly saw many great plumes of white, grey and black smoke billowing skyward.

Renee took the wheel as Eddie jumped down the companionway. He dialed up channel 28 on the single side band radio, pulled the microphone to his mouth, and held in the small white button with his thumb.

"Redondo Marine Operator. Redondo Marine Operator. This is the vessel Lazy Lightning. Whisky-Roger-Zulu-Five-Two-Two-Eight. Come in please."

"This is Redondo. We read you Lazy Lightning. Go ahead skipper."

He gave the operator his radio call letters again, the phone number he wanted to reach, and waited...

"Hello."

"Harry, this is Eddie. We can see smoke all over the city. What the hell's going on? Over."

"Man, where the hell have you been, Mars?"

"We've been underwater all day, diving. Over."

"Must be nice. You should have stayed underwater man. The bastards did it. Over."

"What do you mean dammit? It looks like Beirut from out here—over."

"The King verdict came back today. They let them all off."

Eddie could hear sirens from the background of his receiver. His heart-rate increased as he flashed back to when he was a kid—and the terror of the 1965 Watts Riots.

"What were those people on the jury thinking? Over."

"That's a good question buddy. But I thought you could answer that one better than me—you bein' of the superior race and all. They're breaking windows and looting every store in the city! Look, I gotta go. My parents are on call waiting from Detroit. They're freaking out right now; they know how close I live to the Crenshaw District. Man! It's getting *hot* around here! Every trash can in the alley is on fire! I can feel the heat from my balcony!"

"Jesus! Take care man. I'll call as soon as we get in. Over."

"Right. Happy sailing, motherfucker."

"This is Redondo. Are you through skipper?"

"I apologize for the profanity operator. Over."

"No problem skipper. I understand."

"This is the vessel Lazy Lightning. Whisky-Roger-Zulu-Five-Two-Two-Eight. Over and out."

****

Occasionally they looked up at the spinnaker, strangely backlit by the weird light. Occasionally they glanced down at the wobbling black disc of the compass, white capital letter "N" undulating slightly to either side of the red course indicator arrow. An eerie orange glow reflected off the glass dome. Mostly they held each other in chilled silence—unable to break out of the trance—staring straight ahead at the growing columns of smoke which made up the surreal landfall off the bow.

They inched their way over the waves—no longer enchanted by the silvery beauty of the stern wake. Curiously, Eddie recalled the old Crosby, Stills, & Nash song, *"Wooden*

Ships." In the song, the survivors were escaping the fires and destruction of the war in small boats.

But this was reversed. They were not escaping.

They were heading due North, but with the disturbing visual off the bow, they no longer needed the compass. With the wind out of the West, now having dwindled to under ten knots, they glided along the course agonizingly, slowly, rolling up the crests and then sliding down the troughs—hypnotically almost—as they crawled toward their city, The City of Angels, in flames.

CHAPTER 2 - The Summons

July 29, 1993
Los Angeles, California

Armored military vehicles began rolling down the freeways, establishing positions in key intersections, especially in South Central L.A, in attempt to quell the uprising. Thousands of fires that burned for days spread throughout the city, two being directly across the street from Eddie's warehouse on Vernon, while one inferno completely destroyed the building next door to him. Eddie's attorney called on the second day of the riots—informing him he was not insured against the civil unrest that engulfed Los Angeles. He had heard that Daryl Gates, the Chief of Police, who was white, was not on speaking terms with Mayor Bradley, who was black. Television reports, and newspaper editorials were rife with stories and opinions of just how precipitously the precarious racial balance of Los Angeles had foundered.

How could it all be happening again? Especially in L.A? Nobody even needs to buy a jacket or raincoat. I've never owned a damn umbrella! Every season is summer, and there are beaches everywhere. But—with the ugliness of racism, everybody lost. Didn't people evolve—learn from their mistakes? Yet, here it was again, only 27 years later, on the very same streets: the incessant blaring of sirens, fires, looting and killing. Harry intimated that I should know what the people on the Rodney King jury were thinking... Like hell, I know!

All he had worked for, all he had built, was now at risk. Unlike several of his neighbors, Eddie elected not to take to his warehouse rooftop with a rifle. Instead, he began making hasty plans to set sail for the South Pacific. How far would the riots spread? He had to be ready. He began buying 2.5 gallon jugs of drinking water and taking them to his boat. He purchased a portable filtration system that converted saltwater to freshwater. He bought fish hooks. He went to his bank and withdrew $20,000 in cash. He hid the money— methodically rolling up 200 one hundred dollar bills—hiding them on his boat by neatly tucking $2,000 into each of 10 empty cassette tape cases. Santana's *Abraxas* held $2,000. The Grateful Dead's *Europe '72*, $2,000.

I'm sorry, Jimmy Page. Led Zeppelin II will no longer hold 'Whole Lotta Love.' It'll hold a whole lotta cash.

Friends were calling, wanting to talk about the riots and how they were glued to their TV sets. Eddie didn't want to watch TV. He had no time to talk on the phone; he was making preparations. He began buying boxes of canned goods. Somewhere along the way, he had heard that canned Vienna Sausages left unopened, could last for 100 years. He bought two cases and stowed them in the anchor locker in the bow of his boat.

Renee and Eddie even agreed on a secret code—should they be in separate locations—and the unthinkable had begun. It was sort of a play on the Japanese code "Tora Tora Tora," which initiated the attack on Pearl Harbor. Each of them was to drop everything, and get to their sailboat in Marina Del Rey, upon hearing the words from the other, "Bora Bora Bora."

They talked about the fine line between being paranoid and being prepared.

But within a week, a semblance of calm was restored to the city with the deployment of over 12,000 soldiers from the National Guard and the Marines. Unlike many of his neighbors, except for the closing of his business for two weeks, he had no losses.

Eddie realized he was lucky. Not just lucky in his cognizance that his skills and talents were allowing him to lead a meaningful and interesting life, but more specifically, he knew he was fortunate to have come through the riots unscathed. Eddie parlayed that luck into an even more aggressive business style—but retained a cautious feeling in the back of his mind. It was an underlying feeling that—now having lived through both the Rodney King Riots and '65 Watts Riots—the fate of Los Angeles was always one matchstick away…

It was Eddie's entrepreneurial skills in business that enabled him to pay for his beautiful home perched on the cliffs of Palos Verdes, his annual exotic vacations, and his new Corvette. He was nearly 38 years old, and by almost anyone's metric, successful. He had a 40 foot yacht in a prime slip in the marina and took great pleasure in the fact that his beautiful wife of three years enjoyed sailing nearly as much as he did. His stock portfolio was strong, and he was even beginning to dabble in real estate investments.

Eddie was driven. He constantly reminded himself of the small house he grew up in—the only house his parents could afford in a lower middle class neighborhood in Inglewood.

He grew up eating macaroni and cheese for almost every meal, Friday being the night wherein his mom would throw in some sliced Farmer John hot dogs to make the meal special. Fresh fruit never made an appearance on the table, unless it came from their peach tree in the backyard. Eddie liked to say that he was ten years old before learning that tomatoes were not something that grew in cans. He saw his parents working hard to make ends meet, going to work each day, bringing home just enough money to pay the mortgage, and feed him and his little brother. After dinner, and on weekends, he'd watch his dad sweating in the yard, mowing, weeding, or painting something. There was no money for gardeners or fix-it men. But there was pride. His parents had come a long way from their humble beginnings in a tiny village somewhere near the border of Russia and Poland, where a can of tomatoes would have been looked at as a small miracle.

In time, the old neighborhood changed. Being a bi-product of gentrification, lower income families who were displaced from the growing, thriving communities of surrounding L.A, were forced to move to places like Inglewood. The neighborhood became rough, as the crime-rate increased. Where others saw the value of their homes appreciating, in Inglewood, home prices started falling. Eddie began to feel the daily racial tension in the mixed neighborhood, witnessed by all during the horror of the Watts riots.

Eddie used the memory of his childhood environment as a motivator. He needed to make enough money to live in a nice neighborhood, where he could afford a gardener, where weekends meant something other than additional time to work. He didn't want his wife to have to wait for the coins in the kitchen jar to reach the crayon line so she could buy a chicken or some ground beef. He wanted to be able to walk down the street without having to think of getting mugged. It drove him. He wanted to be able to buy a house for his parents in a safe neighborhood. He wanted them to have baskets overflowing with fresh oranges and bananas. He wanted them to have the incredible luxury—to be able to throw into the garbage an apple that had gone bad—instead of trying to cut around the rotten parts.

****

He had just signed the contract authorizing his $47,000 commitment to the 'speed rail' system. Eddie's company was growing fast. Possibly too fast. He was worried about cash flow, but not as worried about that as he was over losing customers to his competition. The new system would enable him to streamline his entire warehouse so that merchandise would be available virtually at the push of a button—in much the same way a tiny neighborhood dry cleaners could deliver a freshly pressed suit to the front counter in a few seconds.

"There is no 'pretty good' job done around here," Eddie would lecture. "It's either perfect, or its trash." In time, workers who would not produce finished goods up to his standards of excellence were weeded out. He had a habit of relaying metaphors to his subordinates of how wolves would hunt, patrolling the forest, at the edge of the meadows, and how weak animals would be naturally culled from their herds.

During the early years of his business—Eddie drove himself crazy trying to make the *best* pockets, or sewing the *best* quality buttonholes. He learned to swear both in Spanish and in Vietnamese so he could communicate with—or curse at—his sewing contractors who delivered less-than-perfect garments to him. But once these seemingly mundane problems were solved—being able to get the goods into the customers' hands became the real challenge; delivery was the great equalizer in the garment business. The number of things that could go wrong was mindboggling. Eddie's production manager, Bella, had a saying, "We don't need anybody's help to do wrong." She implied that internal problems were inevitable. That was the nature of the beast. It was the screw-ups by *outside* forces that caused hair to be pulled out. *These* were what shortened the life expectancy of owners and managers in the garment business—or, as Eddie referred to it—the *'garmental'* business.

Eddie could lose $10,000 in a single day if buttons were dyed the wrong shade of purple. He didn't even like to be in the same room as "John the Cutter." John worked all day with a machine that could cut through 100 layers of fabric as easily as a sharp kitchen knife sliced through a head of lettuce. He shuddered when considering what that twelve inch blade could do to fingers. Or a wrist. In addition to the physical danger of the machine, a cutter following the wrong lines on the marker, or blueprint, covering the top layer of fabric, could ruin $5,000 worth of fabric in under ten seconds.

Eddie was an entrepreneur. He was an entrepreneur from a young age, possessing that rare ability to use—and switch between—right and left brain skills almost seamlessly. He encouraged creativity from his employees. But, when misapplied, it could prove costly. He hated it when, during production, the sewing contractors got creative...

Please... I pay a lot of money for designers. Just follow the instructions—make the production just like the samples...

****

Eddie's office staff cheered wildly as the fax machine kept spitting out curled pages onto the floor. It was the large order they had been trying to land from Nordstrom for over a year. Eddie agreed to make matching tops and bottoms for their kids' department; the buyer had loved the samples shown to her by the sales rep—cute matching shorts and shirts sets for little boys—available with either dinosaur or cowboy prints. The upside potential was exciting: new styles, new fabrics, lots of units, and terrific profit margins. It was the biggest order Eddie had ever received, requiring much planning, forecasting and calculating. All of these skills came naturally to Eddie, to the point that, he tended to micro-manage the huge amount of details necessary to help ensure a flawless outcome.

Thinking back, to be fair to himself, even with all that calculating, Eddie could not have foreseen the eighteen year old girl, Annie Luu, playing such a key role in the equation—in the botching of the order—turning a tremendous opportunity into rubbish. A Vietnamese refugee, as manager of the small sewing factory, and also the daughter of the sewing contractor, she had the job of sorting through the huge bags produced by John the Cutter. She separated the cut pieces into piles for her sewing machine operators—right sleeves in one pile, left in another; medium pockets in one pile, large collars in another. Unfortunately, despite Bella's careful instructions, Annie Luu didn't pay much attention to the design printed on the fabric.

His phone beeped.

"Eddie, you'd better take this. It's Sally from Nordstrom on line 2. She doesn't sound happy."

Eddie took a deep breath, picked up the phone. "Hi Sally, how are you today?"

"I've been better, Eddie."

"Talk to me."

"The shipment just arrived for our end-of-summer special. As you know, we've spent money on photographers and models and graphic artists creating advertising to promote *your* new styles. These ads are set to appear in several magazines this Sunday..."

Eddie felt his pulse quicken at her emphasis on the word '*your.*'

"That's great, Sally. I appreciate the commitment you guys have made here. I think we'll both do well with..."

"You're not letting me finish. On the samples I approved..."

Sally, his most important buyer, now spoke slowly and methodically, almost as if she had rehearsed her next line, "I don't recall the samples having cowboys and dinosaurs intermingled within the same garment."

On hearing this, the restraint Eddie showed by not unleashing a stream of profanity was in fact impressive. At least the restraint lasted until after he hung up. Several years prior, in Eddie's first year of apparel manufacturing, one of his workers wasn't careful to separate the different cut bundles according to the printed fabric, so that the sleeves of one garment were switched with the sleeves of another. But that was a small order, affecting only about 50 pieces.

Eddie was forced to calculate the loss. Figuring it to be in the vicinity of $35,000, he drove to the contractor's shop in Gardena. He was fuming. When he was able to directly trace the huge mistake to her, he began yelling at Annie Luu. He could not suppress his selective knowledge of key Vietnamese words, and used them. Annie Luu's father, Pham, the owner of the small sewing factory, stood back and let Eddie finish his tirade against his crying daughter. He then invited Eddie back into his office, poured him a cup of tea, and began a story.

It was of the night Pham and his family made the bold decision to attempt escaping the slaughter surrounding the fall of Saigon. They shoved off in a 24 foot leaky wooden boat with 30 terrified cousins, five gallons of water, and a bag of rice between them. They had no outboard motor, and no oars. Exhaustingly, they paddled with their hands. After seven days of misery, adrift in the South China Sea, only half of them survived the ordeal, being picked up by a Philippine freighter. Four days before the rescue, Pham's wife, Annie Luu's mother, died. On the day before the rescue, the last of her three little brothers died, and like the mother, had to be cast overboard. In a long series of convoluted turns for the refugees, Pham and Annie Luu eventually made it to Gardena, California, where they were able to buy one sewing machine and begin their new life.

Though the man offered to sew Eddie's merchandise on future orders for free for as long as it took to recoup the loss on the Nordstrom order, Eddie declined. He left Pham's office and walked back into the sweat-shop, amongst all of the rows of noisy sewing machines, to seek out the daughter. Annie Luu was frightened when she saw him approaching her—but in better than adequate Vietnamese—'*Toy sin loy nyeh, toy lon ting voy ban,*' he apologized for yelling at her, gave her a quick hug, and got in his car to drive back to his office.

After hearing the father's story, Eddie found himself unable to be troubled about cowboys and dinosaurs for little rich kids in Beverly Hills and Santa Monica.

****

"Hi Judy, how's my favorite fe-mail man?"

"Just fine, thanks. I hope there are some nice checks in this stack for you today, Eddie."

"That makes two of us. You have more power over me than anybody I know."

"I wish that were true. See you tomorrow... and... good luck!"

Eddie smiled, optimistic that today would be a better day than yesterday. He still got a kick out of opening the mail.

First the big ones. Here's a good check from Macys. $11,000 from Oshman's for those jerseys. $1250 from that small chain in Philly...

"Thank you Jesus," he whispered, on seeing a $735 check from a store in Florida that was six months late; Eddie had already mentally written it off as a bad debt.

There were about a half-dozen payments from smaller customers. Tossing aside a few of the usual bills, he came across something different from the norm. It was a notice from the Los Angeles County court system—a summons to appear for Jury Duty. He had been excused from jury duty three times in the past few years. "Too Busy. Self Employed. Severe Financial Hardship," he would write on the form, "please excuse me." But this one was different. Maybe he felt grateful for being spared a huge loss during the King Riots. Maybe he felt he had to pay a price—perhaps it was how awful he felt yesterday after yelling at Annie Luu. More than the yelling, it might have been the guilt that he felt, comparing his life, and all that he had built, to people who had to face real challenges—challenges vastly greater than losing some money—challenges where they saw their family members dying of starvation right in front of their eyes.

He immediately began filling out the summons, committing to his availability to serve.

****

His secretary beeped. "Harry on line one, Eddie."

"Whassup Dog?"

"Hey home-boy, you playin' hoops tonight?"

"You know I wouldn't miss the chance to guard your black ass."

"Oh man... you must have just opened your mail. You always get uppity after you open your mail and see all those checks."

"It's been a weird couple of days. How do you always know when to call?"

"You must have forgotten: I met her last month when I was in your office. The mail lady and I are very close."

"Dream on bruddah. Actually, she just brought me a summons to jury duty today."

"What's your excuse gonna be this time, Eddie?"

"No excuse, I think I'm gonna do it."

"Jury duty? You? I did it two years ago. The most boring two weeks of my life."

"It'll probably be boring, but right now I could use the four bucks a day."

"Hah! I remember my check. Forty-eight dollars for two weeks time," Harry said.

"Plus gas? I need a new mainsail for my boat."

"Then I think your boat's a little too big. They pay mileage—one way."

"Such a deal. I'll see you tonight."

"Maybe the ball will bounce off of somebody's big head—you'll get lucky and get your first rebound of the season."

****

Eddie loved Thursday nights. This had certainly been a difficult couple of days, but no matter how bad the week was, once he stepped into the gym, his mind snapped into another mode. Much like diving, or spear-fishing, it was impossible to think of anything else. Problems with cash-flow or cowboys and dinosaurs disappeared. Basketball with the fellahs. The running. The sweating. The banging. The cursing. Basketball: the great equalizer of men. Al was a commodities broker at Merrill Lynch. He made $250,000 a year, but he dribbled with his head down. Rick had 60 people working under him at Hughes, but he couldn't go to his left. Jason was the lead singer in his own band, popular among the many Hermosa Beach clubs and bars along Pier Avenue. He was with a different beautiful woman every month; didn't they know how often he misses layups?

Eddie liked passing. He liked scooting a bounce pass between two or three defenders to his man for an easy basket. He was an adequate shooter, and as Harry liked to constantly remind him—a poor rebounder. But he could pass. Passing took more of an understanding of the game: the speed, the spacing, and the abilities of the other players all had to be considered. He loved continuously assessing and adjusting to the defense and that special chemistry when another player understood what he had in mind. The funny thing was—talking about it never worked. He had to convey the concept with his eyes.

Make eye contact with your team mate. Hold the pick for two beats. Nod. Roll off your man through the key and to the basket. The ball will be there. Trust me. Deliberate blink. The signal. Now! Bucket!

The unique sounds of the gym were an integral part of the experience. The slap of the authentic leather Spalding against the varnished wooden floor—bouncing to different rhythms. The high pitched screech of rubber from $90.00 high-tops as players slammed on the brakes from a dead sprint and changed direction. The war cries of "Foul!" and, "Bullshit! All ball!" and "I didn't touch you—you pussy!" were all part of it.

Harry excelled at trash talk while he dribbled. "You can't guard me, man. Park benches are full of white guys who have tried to guard me."

"Where have I heard that before?" asked Al, sarcastically.

"Maybe every Thursday night for the past eight years," answered Jason in a tired voice, while jockeying for an improved rebound position under the basket.

Harry slapped the ball down methodically—moving slowly toward the right wing. Sudden crossover dribble to his left. Head fake. Pump once. Pump twice. He pulls the trigger from seventeen feet near the right elbow. Swish. "That's *two* baby! Too bad that scoreboard only has space for three digits. I think I'll score a thousand tonight if this skinny white boy keeps guarding me."

****

Pitchers of beer at the bar following the game were as much a ritual of Thursday nights as the game itself. The waitresses all knew the basketball gang. Despite an occasional sweaty hand on the leg or lewd suggestions as the evening wore on and the beer soaked in and began to take hold, the girls waiting tables actually looked forward to this group as entertaining.

"Hey Harry, you foul anybody tonight?" asked Shelly, a red-haired college cutie dressed in an extremely tight black Lycra mini-skirt and dangerously low-cut top. To the delight of the customers, the pink tube-top became yet even more revealing when she bent down to serve or clear the cramped quarters of the small table.

"Oh baby, you know I never foul anybody. That's why you should put that tray down and come over here and sit on my lap."

Shrieks of laughter and protest rang out from the guys.

"Don't do it Shelly!" yelled Eddie over the crowd. "Look what he did to me tonight," pointing to a patch of dried blood over his left eyebrow.

"Look at this," shouted Jason pulling up his Celtics jersey and twisting to reveal a massive purple bruise below his ribs on the right side.

"That Harry's a criminal, my dear," added Al. "The way he plays basketball would be considered a felony in some states."

"Fellahs, fellahs—I am a tender, loving, sentimental black man. I enjoy classical music and poetry and historical novels."

"You'll say anything as long as it improves your chances of sleeping with a sexy white woman!" shouted Al.

Harry let out a yelp of laughter, sloshing the beer in his mug, causing a good dose of it to spill onto his tank top and gym shorts.

"I'll interpret that as you guys needing another pitcher," said Shelly.

"Yes, that, and see if you got a first-aid kit behind the bar or at least a couple of band-aids for us," said Jason. "Harry's buyin' this round. In fact it's been his turn for months!"

There was more clinking of the heavy glass mugs and shrieks of laughter from the rowdy group at the table.

"OK, sweet darlin' angel baby," Harry said to Shelly, holding up his large left hand with the two smallest crooked fingers tied together with white adhesive tape, "just put it on my tab."

"Tab hell," replied Shelly. "I need to see green pieces of paper—six and a quarter inches long by two and a half inches wide with pictures of dead presidents on 'em."

"No problem baby—I was just tryin' to make it easier on *you*! You know I gots *lots* of cash."

Impossibly, the roars of laughter became louder.

"OK, OK. I'll buy. But speaking of criminals," Harry said, changing the tone, "how about old Eddie here going on jury duty?"

"Jury duty?" asked Al. "You, Eddie, Mr. Businessman giving up your valuable time to be part of the system?"

"Why bother?"

"What's your excuse to get out of it gonna be this time, dude?" asked Jason. "That the brass hardware on your yacht needs buffing?"

While waiting for the initial wave of sarcasm to fade, Eddie slowly poured out the last of the second pitcher of Heineken into his mug. One of the television monitors above them in the sports bar played the tape of the Reginald Denny beating from the L.A. Riots a year earlier. It was a bizarre juxtaposition with the adjacent screen, which simultaneously showed a fight in the Kings-Blackhawks hockey game, while the bar patrons went wild. Eddie had a fleeting thought— wondering to himself which of the brawls the cheering was for.

"Yo, Eddie, they're picking jurors for the Denny trial this week. Maybe you'll get selected," Rick said.

"Hey man," said Al, "they don't need a jury for that trial. They got the videotape clear as day. There it is," holding a fistful of oozing nachos up toward the screen.

"How much you want to bet those guys get off?" asked Dave.

"You've got to be kidding me man," answered Harry. "A bunch of black guys kicking the shit out of a white man? Another pitcher of beer says they all go to jail."

"That's not much of a bet bro," said Rick. "We've talked about this before. This Denny thing is just the opposite of the King beating from last year."

"Right," said Rick. "That was white guys beating up a black man."

"And those cocksuckers all got off!" said Harry.

"These guys aren't cops," said Al. "You've got a bet dude."

Harry turned serious, "That truck driver got what he deserved. That videotape doesn't prove shit."

"How can you say that, man?" demanded Al.

"The black people of Los Angeles were responding to an injustice. Denny was simply in the wrong place at the wrong time. Besides, how do you know he didn't provoke them?"

"Provoke them?" asked Al, increasing the decibel level of his voice. "Is there one shred of evidence showing that

Denny *provoked* them? Are you saying the riots were justified? I guess I don't know you as well as I thought."

"Well dude, maybe you don't know me. You live in a world of white privilege. You make tons of money off of white people making investments and trading in the stock market. You can't even begin to see the big picture. The *real* picture. You are totally unaware of the lives of the black man in America today. It's the same way you play basketball—with your head down. I don't own any shares of AT&T or IBM. Black people don't have stock brokers, motherfucker!"

In a few seconds, Al mentally ran through his list of over 150 clients. He had never thought about it before, but realized Harry was right. He looked down into his glass.

"You're damn right you don't know me," Harry continued. "Did it turn out you also didn't know the white people on the Rodney King jury as well as you thought?"

"Which brings us back to Eddie," Rick interrupted, partly because his earlier question was never answered, but mostly to diffuse the tension between Harry and Al. "Are you so naive to think you can actually do some good in this fucked up system of ours?"

Eddie finished another glass from the new pitcher before answering. "It seems to me that for the most part, our only contributions to the system occur when we pay taxes and when we vote every other election and when we stop at red lights. Maybe I just feel like putting a little energy *in* for a change."

"You're not thinking of selling your business and running for mayor are you Eddie?" asked Al.

Even Harry chuckled at that idea.

Eddie thought for a second of relaying the story of the poor Vietnamese refugees in the sinking boat, but kept it to himself. "I just want to see how it feels to do some good.

Maybe it'll be boring, maybe it'll be interesting. I just don't know. But aren't we arguing here about how people don't do the right thing anymore? Besides, that's why they call it a 'duty'."

"Your patriotism is refreshing Eddie," Rick raised the pitcher. "Here's to Eddie—out to make the world a better place for all of us schmucks."

They all raised their glasses and chanted in unison, "To Eddie."

****

Harry turned and blew a kiss back to Shelly as they walked out of the noisy bar. She balanced the drink tray with one hand and feigned excitement, as she held a fist up to her ear—exaggerating the extended thumb and baby finger symbol for a phone, while silently mouthing the words, "Call me."

At this, the guys all hooted again and said their good nights.

In the parking lot, Harry offered Al a peace-pipe in the form of a fist bump and a quick hug and then turned to Eddie as Al got in his immaculately restored yellow '65 Mustang and drove away.

Eddie and Harry stood watching the path of the beautiful vintage ride rolling out of the parking lot—chrome bumpers gleaming under the streetlights.

"You were kinda rough on young Al in there tonight," said Eddie.

With a big gap tooth smile Harry responded, "I do some of my best thinking after three pitchers of beer. Forget about Al. I think I've got *you* figured out—this new Jury Duty Jones you're on."

"Oh yeah, Harristotle?" asked Eddie. "How's that?"

"You just want the chance to send some black dude to prison."

Eddie laughed and gently stroked the fresh scratch over his left eyebrow—courtesy of a couple of Harry's fingernails two hours earlier in the gym. It was a failed attempt, with the clock winding down in their final game, Harry swiping wildly to try and block one of Eddie's shots.

"Better hope it's not you buddy."

CHAPTER 3 - Raul & Oliver

October 15, 1992
Compton, California

The two security guards had been on duty only twenty minutes when they heard the shot. Raul Hernandez and Oliver Jefferson had drawn what was generally considered by the staff to be the easiest shift: a weekday, 10 PM to 6 AM. They had been briefed by the two guards retiring from the earlier shift at the Century Palms Apartments in Compton—except for the usual raucous bunch of teenagers in front of Building 2—the grounds were quiet.

Hernandez, at five foot two, 230 pounds, did not have the physical makeup to be an actual police officer. It's not that he learned and accepted it from the reflection in the mirror. He knew it because ever since he was eight years old, his father repeatedly told him so.

"Hey niño," he would chide rhetorically, "do you really think the L.A.P.D. wants someone like you?"

A cop was all Raul wanted to be, but he acquiesced to rejection five years before he was even old enough to apply to the academy.

He spent the better part of his youth—most of his teens, and all of his twenties—rolling burritos at Tito's Tacos in Culver City. Often, he would spend an entire day making chips, repetitively cutting corn tortillas into little triangles and dropping them into vats of hot oil for deep frying. One day, determined to count how many he made, Raul started counting out loud right after punching the time clock in the morning. He had to put his hand up several times to stop curious co-workers from interrupting his task. He reached 7,650 by lunchtime, but thought about it, and became too depressed to resume the count after his break.

In all those years, was that my only accomplishment? Wasting the prime of my youth making several million tortilla chips?

When Javier, an old schoolmate from the brass section of the Dorsey High Band, called Raul to join him in applying for a job as security guard at the Century Palms, Raul, now 33, embraced the opportunity. It was a welcome change for him. He loved the freedom, loved being outside most of the day, as opposed to the stifling kitchen of the fast food restaurant. Even long nights spent walking the dimly lit grounds, sometimes rehashing the same stories from high school, were enjoyable. No matter how many times Javier told the story of the expression on Raul's face, when, right before halftime of a football game against Venice High, Raul pulled a dead mouse out of the bell of his trumpet—put there by a couple of mischievous bandmates—they would both laugh.

However, Javier's girlfriend became pregnant, and he needed to move in with her, into a cheaper place. Within a few months of them having started the security gig together, his buddy moved away to Nevada, to the outskirts of Reno. Raul spoke with him once on the phone to congratulate him on the birth of his daughter, but never heard from him again.

Raul remained on the job, and was introduced to his new partner, Sergeant Oliver Jefferson. Until that time, Raul had never really known a black man. He wasn't quite sure how to refer to him, and it made him uneasy. Black? African American? Colored? Negro? He knew it kept changing: the names that used to be acceptable, often, in time, came to be considered derogatory. Of course he had lots of interactions throughout the years, as was inevitable in the sprawling melting pot of Los Angeles, but even back in high school he certainly never had any he considered friends. He was reserved at first, a bit aloof and sometimes even bordering cold—but it was impossible to spurn Oliver's amiable spirit for long.

When he was little, Oliver, on the other hand, had no interest in law enforcement. He had other notions, and kept waffling between wanting to be an astronaut or an announcer. One year, the only uncle he ever knew visited from Chicago. The uncle bought him a telescope for a Christmas present. Staring at the stars and planets became a perfect otherworldly escape from his difficult childhood growing up in a tiny studio apartment in Inglewood with no father, no siblings and no money. Oliver's lifetime dream was to one day see a total lunar eclipse. Over time, worried about the many solitary hours Oliver would spend in his room straining his eyes to focus on some fantastical far away galaxy—his mother saved a few extra dollars and was able to buy him a microphone kit for his 10th birthday. It was a small black and silver microphone and came complete with a mic stand, six feet of cable, a speaker and a five watt amplifier. But more importantly—it was the perfect catalyst to help Oliver come out of his lonely shell.

He would watch the neighborhood kids play ball, but instead of grabbing a glove or a bat, he would set up his kit and try to be the announcer. Whenever needed, he would string several long extension cords together to bring power to his amp. There was a running neighborhood joke: 'If you ever need to find Oliver—just follow all the orange extension cords.'

The neighborhood kids loved hearing Oliver call their games and considered him as much a part of the game as the players. He once found it necessary to run his cords across all four busy lanes of Van Ness, so he got his friends to hold up traffic while he could make his duct tape connections. When there was nowhere to plug-in he eventually rigged up a battery for the small P.A. system. His mother was thrilled with the development, and even encouraged Oliver to consider moving away from his boyhood dreams of planets and rocket ships to perhaps think of something more earthly—like becoming a reporter or sports announcer.

He practiced imitating Vin Scully. Baseball became a thing of beauty. He didn't feel comfortable with the quickness demanded in calling a basketball game, like Chick Hearn; the required rapid flowing combinations of words, would constantly lead to "wangles." It was the term Oliver coined for "word tangles." So he found himself listening to every Dodger game, becoming enchanted with Scully's ability to tell a story. He became the beloved high school DJ through his junior and senior years—spinning tunes and making clever commentary to the delight of the entire student body during lunch break. A popular kid on campus, he was rarely seen without proudly wearing his royal blue Dodger cap.

Sadly, in time, reality tended to fade the dreams of most kids growing up on the inner city streets of Los Angeles. Streets with names such as Western, Vermont, Normandie, Crenshaw, Imperial, Alameda, Hawthorne, Florence, and Figueroa. These street names alone had connotations which filled the mind, the local mind, the knowing mind, with the myriad thoughts covering the widest possible range from life, hope, fun and joy to sadness, despair, crime and death. Oliver was no exception, and as with countless kids both before and after him—the dreams eventually faded until even the memory of the dreams had evaporated completely.

His mother had a favorite neighborhood store in Hawthorne she would frequent to buy groceries. She loved looking through the magazines, especially *Better Homes & Gardens*. One Saturday morning, standing in front of the newspaper rack, she leafed through the new issue, wondering if she would ever get to see one of those beautiful houses in person. She did not realize the store had just been held-up until she looked up to see a man running out the front door. The man, thinking she had gotten a good look at his face, stuffed the $91 in his front pocket and turned back into the tiny store. He fired two shots, the first bullet hitting her in the shoulder, while the second ripped through the large blue hydrangea on the magazine cover, lodging in her belly. She died at Centinela Hospital the next morning. She was 34.

Oliver had been taking broadcasting classes downtown, at a well-regarded trade-school. But with his mother gone, he could no longer afford the tuition. So at the age of 20 he enlisted in the army; it was 1968. After performing well at the Fort Irwin training base in the Mojave Desert, he made sergeant, and was promptly sent over to Vietnam. His brief army career came to an end when one night on patrol, during the Tet Offensive, his unit came under fire. A VC mortar round exploded ten yards behind him and he took a piece of shrapnel in the leg. Oliver was lucky; he was a scout, on point that day. Two of the soldiers in his platoon who were behind him didn't live through the blast. He was sent back to California, where, outside of a large scar, and a small limp, he recovered nicely. Shortly after being discharged from the army, he saw an ad in a newspaper, and interviewed for a security job at The Palms. With his upbeat personality, combined with his military experience, he was hired. That was almost 25 years ago.

All of the children at the Century Palms loved Oliver; his broad smile was infectious and, perhaps from all those hours announcing and studying Vin Scully, he still had that soothing tonal quality to his voice.

Oliver knew almost every kid in The Palms' six building complex by name. He was always happy to pick up a fallen bicycle or shag and throw back an errant toss of a baseball. Several of the young boys regularly came up to him after school or on weekends to get a quick lesson on the proper technique for throwing a curveball.

"Drysdale would hold it this way," he demonstrated, twisting the ball so all of the kids could see—drawing particular attention to the way his bony fingers sat along the dirty red seams. Impressing as well as delighting the kids with his details—he would then exaggerate flipping the ball high into the air and then catching it with flair in his left hand, "while Koufax, the greatest southpaw of them all, would shift one long finger across the seam like this…"

"Was Colefax a black man, Oliver?" asked one of the kids.

"Of course he was, stupid!" answered another. "Otherwise he wouldn't be Oliver's favorite player."

"I think he was a white boy." said a third.

While the smallest kid, named Lamont, no older than seven, and one of Oliver's favorites, softly said, "I heard he wasn't either black or white. I heard Colefax was Jewish."

Oliver laughed and put up his hand to calm down the excited group of future all-stars.

"OK, quickly—two important things and then I've got to get back to work.

"Number One. I like Sandy Koufax because he was the best. Period. For five straight seasons, starting in the early 60's it seemed like nobody could even get a base hit off of him. He knew the hitters weak spots and could put the ball in or just out of the strike zone—exactly where he wanted. He was unhittable! His fastball was as accurate as a laser beam.

"And his curveball? Forget about it! He'd simply embarrass the hitters with that nasty Uncle Charlie because they were so worried about his fastball! And I don't care if he was black or white or Jewish or Mexican or Japanese. And, if you kids are smart, you won't care either."

"Wow. That's one thing?" said the oldest kid. "What's number two?"

"Oh yes, number two," replied Oliver, thinking he'd already made his two points. He opened the glove of little Lamont and placed the hardball gently in the pocket, "… the second most important thing to know… is…." he paused dramatically for effect, turning to make eye contact with each individual kid, "there's no 'L' in Koufax."

Raul saw that Oliver was able to somehow calculate that when there was little risk or threat of being reprimanded by The Palms manager, they found themselves increasingly spending more time with the kids than making the repetitious circles of the grounds. Raul walked alongside his partner and learned. He was also amazed that Oliver could remember the names of nearly a hundred kids.

"How do you do it, Oliver? There's so many of them."

"Oh, it's just a little trick, I guess. Each time I meet a kid, I just think to myself: 'this kid might grow up to be president.'"

In a short time, an unlikely, but strong friendship formed between the two security guards. The job was not without inherent dangers. They would joke about it, but the truth was, they couldn't deny it. Raul rationalized the risk by telling himself that the alternative, facing 40 years standing over a boiling hot stainless steel grease bin in a taco stand, was more terrifying than anything the Bloods or Crips could throw at him. They both were trained and authorized to carry weapons; but even though the apartment complex was in the heart of Compton, they had only one occasion in their four year partnership to draw them—that being two summers ago—when they answered a call from a tenant to check out a domestic quarrel in one of the upstairs apartments.

Following the sound of the yelling, scampering up the wooden stairs, they arrived at a wide open door of the unit in the far corner of Building 4. There, they saw the stunning nineteen year-old black woman wearing a miniscule neon pink bikini top and hot pants in the form of frayed cutoff Levis. Oliver knew her as "D." On her feet were turquoise colored flip-flops, while a massive headful of tightly woven bronze cornrows covered her scalp. The braids transitioned into numerous plastic bead studded strands of hair wildly spilling down and clicking together around her shoulders. It was uncanny what a perfect color match the turquoise beads made with the rubber flip-flops.

She was standing over her husband, who was seated in a metal folding chair. But the item that demanded the focus of the guards' attention was not how spectacular she looked in that outfit or how strong the skinny spaghetti-straps had to be to hold up her large, perfect, mocha colored breasts. It was her right hand—where two fingers curled around both triggers of a 12-gauge double-barreled shotgun. The huge old gun was pressed firmly against the head of her unfaithful husband. It was another twisted juxtaposition of the scene, as, like the pink bikini top, it was impressive how steady this slender girl held the heavy load of the Remington. Unrelenting in applying constant pressure from the large bore barrels—a visible indentation was formed by the last two inches of the deadly tubes being buried into her husband's afro. Neck and head tilted at quite an awkward angle, the pressure from the barrels pushed in hard on his skull ending at a point a bit below the temple—between the man's right ear and eyebrow.

After five excruciating minutes of half intelligible ranting by D, the two guards attempted to somehow mitigate the intense situation. Jefferson did most of the talking. With his silky voice, he was able to calmly concentrate all his persuasive reasoning to get her to slowly remove her index finger away from the forward trigger which powered the right barrel. Beginning again, tediously, patiently, like Scully describing the limp flags in centerfield on a balmy August night in Dodger Stadium, he got D to release her middle finger from the rear trigger. The three males in the room exhaled audibly as she finally set the weapon down on the pine coffee table in the middle of the tiny living room.

The couple had been married just over three months. The young bride went up to Oliver first, to give him an emotional hug. She then turned away suddenly to sledgehammer a rock-hard fist into her husband's chest. Hernandez quickly moved to the table, broke open the shotgun and removed the two fat red cartridges from the breech. Raul considered for a moment what 200 pellets of No. 4 size steel shot would do to a human head at point blank range. He looked up at the humming ceiling fan, then across, at the floral wallpaper behind the husband, imagined what might have been—and shuddered.

Raul and Oliver were rewarded with a case of Budweiser that Christmas by the grateful husband.

****

"Hey! Throw me that basketball, boy!" ordered Jimmy, the ring-leader of the group gathered out in front of the apartment complex.

"What do you think will happen if I shoot at that ball? Will it pop, or will the bullet bounce off?"

"I bet the bullet ricochets off the B-ball and hits Leon here in the leg."

"Fuck you, motherfucker," said Leon.

"Or maybe it'll bounce off and hit you between the eyes."

"Hey! Quit fucking around. That belongs to Lamont— that's my little brother's ball," said Marcus, moving into the middle of the pack.

"Your little brother should learn to pick up his toys," said Jimmy.

Jimmy had been expelled from Compton High last May, near the end of his freshman year. A teacher on yard duty had reported him after spotting Jimmy putting what looked like a handgun into his locker. The principal, Mr. Williams, called an emergency meeting that afternoon with Jimmy, his school counselor, the Vice Principal, the assistant supervisor of the school board, and Jimmy's aunt. Mr. Williams went into the meeting with an open mind, telling himself he would delay any decision until he heard all parties speak. He knew that Jimmy had never met his father, and that he had been living with his aunt since his mom had died of complications following a crystal meth overdose at a party in Lynwood when he was just eleven. Being aware of the numerous hardships, coupled with Jimmy being only fifteen years old, the freshman counselor wanted to give him another chance. Mr. Conners, the V.P, wanted his head.

Mr. Williams began the closed-door meeting by introducing everybody to the aunt. He then asked Conners to begin.

"As I'm sure by now most of you are aware, earlier today, at approximately 1:10 PM, we opened locker number 1377, which is absolutely within our authority. That locker is assigned to James Bradley."

Conners paused, turned, and opened the middle drawer of a yellow metal filing cabinet. He reached in and pulled out a black Sig Sauer .22 caliber pistol. "Where we found this."

Jimmy's aunt's sobbing, which started as soon as the principal began the introductions, grew louder.

"Furthermore, we have a reliable witness who reported seeing James Bradley placing the weapon inside the locker, near the end of lunch hour, at approximately 12:50."

"Mr. Bradley," Conners walked slowly toward Jimmy. Holding the gun high, he stopped less than eighteen inches from where Jimmy was seated, bent over, and looked him directly in the eyes, "this is about as serious a violation of school regulations as there can be. And though you are a minor, it is also a felony. This committee has discussed our options, and would first like to give you a chance to explain yourself. Son?"

Jimmy shifted his weight in the scarred old wooden chair. He didn't realize that—before he opened his mouth—he had at least three people in the principal's office in that meeting who were in his corner. Jimmy's aunt had been gently tapping her right hand on Jimmy's left knee. Jimmy forcefully slapped her hand away and began speaking.

"This is fucked up."

"Excuse me?" asked Mr. Williams.

A bit louder, Jimmy answered, "I said this is fucked up."

"I'm warning you," said the principal.

"This is fucked up because that's just a crummy old .22. You said so yourself, right Conners?"

"If you know what's good for you, young man, you will address me as 'Mr. Conners.' And yes, it is a .22 caliber pistol. I did not mention earlier that there were eight live rounds in the magazine."

"Do you people even know that a .22 aint shit?" said Jimmy.

Mr. Williams, who had 17 years' experience as principal, was held in very high regard by the school board. The multitude, and magnitude, of problems associated with Compton High—running one of L.A.'s poorest and most difficult inner city schools—was something that would boggle the mind of most principals in other school districts, no matter how seasoned they were.

Mr. Williams prided himself on his ability to calculate various possible outcomes to different high school scenarios. However, he did not predict this one correctly.

Incredibly, Jimmy kept on talking, "I couldn't even hurt anybody with that little thing if I wanted to. It's barely bigger than a BB gun. You people are so fucked up."

The aunt's sobs turned shrill.

Jimmy shifted to a much higher pitched voice; he also increased the decibel level to be heard over his aunt. "It's a motherfuckin' .22! I don't think that little piece of shit could cap anybody. Shit. It couldn't even kill one of those rats running around behind the cafeteria."

Mr. Williams abruptly slammed his fist down hard on his desk. It startled all three members of the school administration personnel; it also brought an immediate end to the aunt's awful wailing as well as the idiotic monologue by Jimmy.

In spite of his earlier willingness to give careful consideration to what Jimmy had to say, Mr. Williams had heard enough. In his head he had already begun the tedious process of filling out the expulsion papers. Maybe it was the repeated mention of the caliber of the weapon; his mind conjured up the tragic events of June 1968 at the Ambassador Hotel in L.A.—where in a chaotic few moments—celebration and light and hope turned black. He believed it was the darkest day in his life, and possibly for America as well. It was almost exactly 25 years ago and happened up on Wilshire Boulevard, only 16 miles from where he now sat. He remembered for quite a while, because of it, being embarrassed to be from Los Angeles. He attempted to compose himself. Slowly, the principal removed his glasses with his left hand, while his right index finger extended from his fist and honed in on Jimmy.

"You might encounter some difficulty explaining that to Bobby Kennedy."

****

"I said throw me that fuckin' basketball! I got a hundred bucks says the ball doesn't pop. Any takers?" challenged Jimmy.

"You gotta bet, niggah!" said Leon.

"And I said quit fucking around. Gimme that ball!" shouted Marcus.

"Hey Marcus, why don't you hold it on top of your head and run over there—by Reggie's Cadillac? See if I can shoot it off—sort-a-like William Tell."

"Why don't I ram this basketball up your black William Tell ass?"

"Go for it, bitch!"

Marcus palmed the ball in his huge right hand. He cocked his elbow like a quarterback, in attempt to sling the ball into the quad—the direction of his apartment unit— away from the group.

He thought his world had ended as the point-blank blast from Jimmy's .38 exploded into the orange ball. The leather sphere instantly went flaccid in his still upraised hand, drooping sickeningly over his wrist.

"You owe me a 'c-note' Jimmy," said Leon.

"I guess I do. I guess I do," said their leader, as he stuffed the warm gun into the front of his overalls. He reached into one of several bulging denim pockets, deftly snapped open a green rubber-band and peeled off a crisp $100 bill from a half inch thick roll.

"Who says growing up a nigger in South Central ain't no fun?" said Leon.

"Dig that home-boy," said Jimmy. "Somebody find some more basketballs! I just love scientific experiments!"

Except for Marcus, the six gang-bangers let out high pitched shrieks of laughter.

****

Hernandez and Jefferson broke off their conversation with the unemployed tenant in Building 6. They had now heard the man's theory on the solution to the recession every other night for six weeks. Realizing reluctantly that it was time to address the nagging complaints about the loud rap music, they bid him goodnight and continued their rounds. They had taken only a few steps when they heard the shot. Unsnapping their holsters, they each broke into a run. Even with the limp, Oliver was faster than Raul. Rounding the corner onto the cement and grass quad formed by the intersection of Buildings 1,2,4, and 5, they spotted the group by the sidewalk in front of Building 2.

Jefferson's experience had taught him to quickly grasp the often fine-lined distinction between trouble and a party. Seeing no victim, Oliver holstered his weapon. Hernandez followed suit. From a boom box on the hood of a closely parked yellow Datsun, the intense "gangsta rap" was blaring.

"Why if it ain't the Lone Ranger and Tonto!" Jimmy shouted in mock friendly greeting. "Our favorite rent-a-cops."

"Which is which Jimmy?" asked Leon, Jimmy's six foot six shadow.

At the age of 14 Leon could do 20 reps—pressing a 350 pound barbell. Along with the strength, by 15, he had blazing speed—being clocked at 4.7 in the forty yard dash. Like Jimmy, he also was expelled from Compton High, but he lasted a year longer due to some persuasive lobbying by the head football coach. He never received a 'C' or even a 'D' on his report cards, getting all 'F's and Incompletes. He could have greatly helped the team at tight end or outside linebacker, and then, perhaps with his size and skills, he might have attracted some interest from a few college scouts.

That almost certainly would have led to a future with more opportunities than being Jimmy's right-hand-man.

"Come on Leon! Didn't you learn *anything* in your two long years of high school? Obviously Hernandez is Tonto, and Jefferson here is the Lone Ranger. Only *his* black mask is permanent. Whassup Oreo Cookie Man?"

"Hey wait Jimmy, wasn't Tonto an Indian?" asked another of Jimmy's followers.

"An Indian and a fat-ass Mexican is the same fucking thing."

"Give it a rest fellahs," offered Jefferson in a mellow voice. "We've got a few complaints about the music. Now turn the shit down—please."

"Oh man that's N.W.A! You can't call that shit! This ain't the '50s. This is 1992 Oliver. John Coltrane is dead, and so is that Jazz jive you listen to. This is the music of the city. This is the music of the 'toe. Don't you be walkin' up on us callin' our sounds shit."

"The point is, Jimmy," Oliver said calmly, "not that it's the music of the ghetto, or that it's shit or not shit. The point is—it's too damn loud."

"Sure, I'll turn the shit down," said Leon. He went over to the boom box and exaggerated turning the volume knob to the left, but his fingers touched only air. With his massive, powerful frame, he broke into an incredibly athletic and erotic performance of the Butterfly dance move. Responding to the encouraging shouts from his homeys, Leon flipped his Raider cap around backwards, yelled out "Fuck it!" and turned the volume louder.

"Go Lee-on! Go Lee-on!"

"And who's got the piece?" Oliver inquired, losing his calm demeanor. "Let's knock that crap off now or we're gonna call the police."

"First of all Sergeant Jefferson," responded Jimmy, "we *all* got pieces. And we're not afraid of the fuckin' Po-Lease. Truth be told: those motherfuckers—they're afraid of us."

"This is our hood and we're takin' it back!" A new voice bellowed from the tan El Dorado parked across the narrow street.

"Like the song says: Fuck the Police."

A sixteen ounce long neck beer bottle flew from the car, in the direction of Jefferson, but landed intact on the dead grass just beyond the near curb.

Hernandez had been watching in nervous silence behind his partner. He had trusted Oliver's judgement and handling of the situation up until now—in fact he had trusted his judgement completely these past four years—but his heart rate told him that this was more than a party.

"Oliver, come over here a second," Hernandez said.

"I got things under control, Raul."

"Oliver!"

Jefferson backed away from the group to speak with his partner, out of earshot of the group. Whispering was not necessary, as the 200 watt boom-box was now pumping out a different rap tune at an even louder volume. Several of Jimmy's gang now joined Leon, dancing in the street.

"Oliver, let's call the police. This thing is a little out of our jurisdiction anyway with that guy across the street and all."

"Come on Raul, they're just a bunch of punks having some beers. Calling the cops will just escalate things."

Another beer bottle was launched from the El Dorado. This one exploded at the base of the curb. Jefferson's shoes and cuffs were splashed with foam, while a small piece of brown glass grazed the front crease of Raul's khaki pants.

"Come on fellas, take the party elsewhere," Jefferson pleaded. "We don't want trouble and you don't either."

"We told you—we're takin' back our hood. And we're not afraid of the police," came the voice from the Cadillac again. The driver made a mock gun out of his thumb and forefinger, and pointed it with disturbing seriousness at the two guards. "The Lone Ranger and Tonto. The Oreo Cookie Man and the Fat Ass Mexican tellin' us to break up our party. Ain't that some shit."

Hernandez now focused on the car—recognized the voice of the driver wearing the red bandanna. It was Reggie. Reggie's reputation was made a half-year earlier, when it was rumored, during the riots, he killed a cop. The story was, on the second day of the riots, Reggie had spotted him sitting alone, without a partner, parked in his patrol car on Imperial. Reggie pulled up alongside, to ask the young officer a question, and executed him.

"Come on Oliver. This dude's bad news."

"I know who it is."

"Well then, let's call it in."

"Raul, you know that piece of shit radio you're wearin' doesn't work. I requisitioned a new one over six months ago, but these cheap bastard landlords keep telling me to be patient."

Raul listened nervously. He knew his partner was right about the radio. He wore it on his belt only because he felt it made him look more official. He was angry at himself for not at least having tried new batteries in the thing.

"So the radio isn't an option," stated Oliver flatly.

To which Hernandez replied, "Walking away now, and getting to a phone *is* an option! Vamos! Let's get the hell out of here."

Looking up, Raul noticed that, like cells multiplying from under a microscope slide, the group on their side of the street had doubled in size. There were also at least four more big dudes on the other side of the street—drinking and passing bottles in and out of the Cadillac. He also spotted what appeared to be a glowing glass pipe moving among the group. He couldn't smell from this distance, but gave it odds that it was crack cocaine.

"These guys are all jacked! Please Oliver!"

"Go make the call then. I'll talk to Marcus over there. I know his family. He's a good kid."

Hernandez took off running between the dark buildings—toward the guard's office in the bungalow at the end of Building 6. He cursed himself for being so out of shape. Sucking air, he scampered clumsily up the six steps to the small room, and hit the phone keys "#3," which speed-dialed the Compton Sheriff.

****

The engine cranked to life on the classic old '67 Caddy. Reggie threw it into drive, stomped on the accelerator pedal. At first, it looked as though he was speeding away—heading East down 128th until, after about 30 yards, he swung the wheel hard to the left in attempt to negotiate a U-turn. But the limited turning radius of the huge beast of a car would not allow such a maneuver. The left front tire slammed into and up over the curb. As Reggie jerked the vehicle into reverse, a horrible screeching sound of metal dragging against the sidewalk could be heard; the bottom of the front bumper and inside edge of the front fender scraped like industrial strength fingernails on a concrete blackboard. Sparks flew, tires smoked, and parts from the 429 cubic inch engine screamed as the possessed driver again attempted to reverse direction before the transmission was ready.

Jimmy, and the rest of the crowd from both sides of the street, could not predict what would happen next; Leon's circle of dancer's instinctively inched back—retreating out of the street. The Cadillac went into a ten yard skid, beginning in front of the tiny Datsun, which seemed like a toy compared to the enormous and powerful machine taking orders from a beer and crack infused brain. The El Dorado jerked to an abrupt halt directly in front of Oliver. More than two dozen pairs of nostrils flared slightly, as toxic fumes from burning rubber permeated the warm night air of the neighborhood. The smoked glass power window of the passenger side lowered with a perverted slowness. The blaring rap song had not diminished a single decibel, but, in spite of the volume level pushed to the painful point of distortion, a twisted silence cut the air. Two shots rang out in quick succession from the nine millimeter semi-automatic handgun. Both missed their mark high and to the left before Reggie adjusted his aim. The third bullet ripped through Oliver's right forearm, causing him to drop the pistol he had just removed from its' holster. The shooter took his time to further recalibrate his aim before pulling the trigger for the fourth time. This last shot struck Oliver in the left clavicle, and again the high velocity ammo passed through his body. It probably would not have been a fatal shot, had Oliver's collar bone not splintered. The razor-like shards of bone sliced the internal carotid artery. One three inch section of bone burst up and into Oliver's windpipe. Bloody right hand dangling useless, his left hand instinctively reached up for his neck but his fingers found only the jagged edges of ivory white bone protruding sickeningly through his own brown throat. Oliver teetered and fell backwards. From the cold pavement of the quad, he stared up at the lone streetlight.

His childhood fascination with the secrets of the solar system offered up a final memory of the trick he would play with his eyes as a small boy. Without blinking, he would keep them open to the point of tears and stare at the streetlights. By purposely blurring his focus, he could form moon beams and lasers which would shoot to far away galaxies. The ability to see planets and stars and enjoy clear nights above Los Angeles was somewhat of a rarity, although the smog from the sixties had decreased appreciably since the advent of unleaded gasoline. Still, Oliver always manufactured his own version of celestial phenomena. He thought fondly, for a split-second, about his old telescope. Tonight, his watery eyes allowed the familiar illusion of an amber ring of light around the single lamp in the sky—like the magnificent icy rings around Saturn.

It's incredible! Could I be that lucky? Is that a full lunar eclipse?

****

Raul heard the shots during his phone call to the police.

"No! No! Por favor Dios! No!"

Dropping the phone, he stumbled back out the door and down the bungalow steps. He had never fully caught his breath from his earlier run and frantic phone call. Panting wildly he began running back out to the street scene in front of the complex. As he rounded the corner of Building 2, into the quad, he moved through the mystical golden light. He approached the body of his partner—no, not his partner, but the man who had become his best friend. He was lying there—half on the sidewalk and half on the crabgrass. Raul registered immediately that something was very wrong; Oliver's black pistol was lying in the grass by his feet. But more disturbing was the sight of the slippery white object protruding out of the dark skin of Oliver's throat from where his Adam's apple should have been.

Raul was sickened.

It would haunt him the rest of his life…

Did he see me before he died? Did I get to him in time? His eyes were open—but did he see me?

Perhaps, it would have provided a miniscule bit of solace for Raul. But it remained unknown to him how his own face—the same round fat face that was subject to so much ridicule by his father—the dark silhouette of his own head moving into the field of vision of his dying friend looking skyward—looking up into the circle of light from the lone amber streetlamp above—actually provided the lovely image of what Oliver enjoyed as a perfect, glorious eclipse. Perhaps Raul would have taken some comfort to know that his own head provided the beauty—the final and eternal image captured by the death stare of Oliver.

CHAPTER 4 - Crystal & China

October 16, 1993
Palos Verdes, California

Renee just finished pouring a chilled Chardonnay into one of two tall crystal goblets. It was from one of her favorite wineries in Napa. She was about to fill the other, when the phone rang. Seeing the 614 area code, Columbus, she drank half the glass in one shot.

"Hi sweetie, it's mom."

"I recognize your voice, mother," said Renee. "How are you? How's dad?"

"We're fine, but we miss you. Already getting excited to see you and your husband for Thanksgiving."

"I miss you too. And his name's Eddie, mom. Has it started getting cold there yet?"

"Let's not talk about the weather. I know his name. I've got nothing against him, except for the fact that he's from California."

"Well, good luck changing that. Say his name, mom."

"Edward," she said after a slight pause.

"Close enough, I guess."

"Thank you. Now tell me about school, dear."

They chatted for several minutes, filling her in on her classes, and the excitement surrounding Eddie's thriving business. Plus the news that he just sold a photograph of an octopus for $900.

"An octopus? Why would anyone want a photograph of an octopus?"

"Because it's beautiful, mom."

"I'll never understand people from California. Please don't tell me they actually had it framed."

"As a matter of fact, they did. And it was from a gallery in New York."

"Even worse. Liberals."

Renee knew enough not to comment, knowing her silence would signal a shift in topics. But then it came—the inevitable dreaded question from her mother...

"Are you pregnant yet?"

Renee gulped down the second half of the wine.

She had spent her entire life in Ohio, getting nearly perfect grades in school, scoring 1320 on the SAT test, while also winning several writing awards. She received a full scholarship to do her English undergrad work at USC, breaking her parents' hearts that she would be moving out to California. To them, the most important thing in life, since the wedding, had become their desire to be grandparents. It had always seemed a little selfish to Renee—the pressure they put on her—until she realized that, even more than excelling in school and getting her career started, the thing she desired most was to have a baby. But with Eddie's mantra, of his dream being within reach, she acquiesced to the waiting. Knowing full well that the constant pressure to start a family would only increase, she could not share this frustration with her mother. She found herself being forced to defend Eddie—often stealing his lines—the key word in most of her answers to her mother being: *soon*.

As one of the greatest distractions imaginable, she had applied, and was accepted, to USC law school.

As usual, after hanging up, she felt crappy—poured another glass of wine—and began preparing dinner. The combination of the phone call and the wine made her emotional; she thought back fondly to the first time she met Eddie, and how, at that moment, life in Columbus began to fade from memory. It was at a party, one Saturday of her junior year, after the big cross-town rivalry USC-UCLA football game. They were introduced by a mutual friend, and it wasn't long before Eddie invited her to go sailing.

"Tomorrow—Sunday? she asked. "We just met 20 minutes ago."

"I can come back 20 minutes later and ask you again if you like."

"Are people from UCLA always this persistent?" she asked.

"We tend to get a little aggressive whenever the Bruins lose to the Trojans."

"Sorry about that. You guys could use a quarterback. The game was kind of a massacre."

"Yes it was. I'm depressed," he said.

"You don't quite strike me as the type to get depressed."

"Which is why this loss is so devastating. You're an English major; I'm sure you'll come up with the right things to say. You can help me get over it."

"By going sailing with you?"

"Yep."

"But I've never been on a boat before. It's somewhat of a badge of honor with people from Ohio—which, now that I think about it—is kind of curious, since my hometown was named after a sailor."

"See that? You might be a natural."

"So you're talking about going out in the ocean? The Pacific Ocean?"

"We'll start in the Pacific. If we hit it off, we can continue on South to the Tasman Sea. Then maybe West to the Indian Ocean."

"Sounds a little ambitious for a first date."

"Maybe you're right," said Eddie. "That is a lot for a Sunday."

"What if I get seasick and throw up on your boat?"

"Just remember: always barf to leeward."

Renee scrunched up the muscles in her forehead. "As an English major, I'm embarrassed to say I don't know what that means."

"Nautical terms are really a different language. I'll teach you everything you need to know. Besides—tomorrow is supposed to be a very calm day."

"Have you ever gotten seasick?" she asked.

"No, but they say everybody has got their sea condition…"

"So… what's your condition?"

"A very calm day."

They were married twelve months later. She recalled with clarity, the split second when her heart jumped upon him saying the word 'sailing.' Maybe it was her immediate attraction to Eddie—he had *something*—something that intrigued her that allowed her to delete the synapse in her brain that fired, bringing up a picture of her friend Leslie's face, and suppress her fear of the water. Renee smiled, thinking back that she had long ago learned what 'leeward' meant, more importantly, that she had never gotten seasick.

Eddie liked her cooking—not loved, but liked. Maybe it was her great taste in wine that made the meals better. He did make note, however, that the trend had been improving in the past year. The meals were getting more interesting: spicier, more creative. His mom happened to be a terrific cook. He thought for a moment—he might be embarrassed to admit this to anyone—but his top five favorite dishes were probably all made by his mother. She could make anything, and make it delicious, leaving the choice between going out to a restaurant and going to his parent's house for dinner an easy one. Eddie's dad often talked about how bad his mother was at first. It was, without fail, entertaining, no matter how many times he heard their stories from the early days.

"Yes," his pop would say, faking a pensive display of far off recollection, "I suppose I must think back on it now as having been a low point in my life. But then I had a great epiphany: I realized—she couldn't get worse."

This always brought roars of laughter as well as attacks from all who were ever present. The reaction generally divided straight along male-female lines.

"You should be so lucky!"

"You're an animal, Sid!"

"You lived through two wars yet considered Shirley's cooking the low point?"

Playing to the crowd, he would put his hand up to calm the audience. "Oh the early days with Shirley… It took her awhile to learn that potatoes take a *long* time to cook. A raw potato is gosh dang inedible! A human being simply cannot eat a raw potato! A raw apple or carrot—fine. But a potato? Maybe if you're living in Russia in the 1800's—under the Czar," Eddie's dad would roll, "when Trotsky or Lenin were in power and controlled what we bought, what we thought, what we wore and what we ate. But this was America! California even! Plus: *potatoes need salt!* Lots and lots of salt. Not to mention: she didn't realize that 'burnt' was not a seasoning. Now don't get me started!"

Multiple voices inevitably rang out, "Don't get you started?"

"It's too late for that, Sidney!"

But more than the fun reflection on his mom and dad, Eddie was optimistic that in time, Renee would become a great cook.

On Sunday nights, even if it was just the two of them, Renee liked to use the china they received as wedding gifts. But the thought of cracking or chipping one of these plates or saucers put him in a constant state of anxiety during these meals. Whenever they had people over, and Renee wanted to bring out the good stuff, Eddie became particularly tuned in to the sounds of forks or knives against the china. Any contact by the silverware from a heavy handed relative would make Eddie cringe. And two pieces of china plinking together? A potential double whammy—and therefore absolute pain. She became aware of his phobia, and purposely let him have the volume of the music a bit higher than she normally liked it, as it tended to mask some of the inevitable little clicks and clinks that bothered him. But he knew it made her happy, and, unlike the chandelier lit dining room he now sat in, he mused that at least he could control *his* domain—that being the galley of his boat—where he could serve everything on paper or plastic plates.

Still, he thought he'd never forgive himself if he didn't at least try.

"Aren't these dishes better left packed away in the garage, in the original boxes with the bubble wrap? I've got the perfect space on the new racks and the boxes will be easy to get to and use if we have a really special occasion."

"Oh, a really special occasion?" she mocked. "Like when? When the Messiah comes?"

"Yeah. That would be an excellent time. Count me in! Or, when we have our first grandchild. Isn't it a tradition to leave the fine china to your grandchildren?"

"Shut up and drink your wine," she teased, "and maybe you'll loosen up and get in the mood a little later to work on making some grandchildren."

He did take a sip, realizing that they were teetering on the edge of another heavy conversation about kids.

"You picked out the pattern," she said. "Remember? Besides, I thought you loved the good stuff."

"I think it's beautiful and I do love it… which is exactly why I want to keep it in perfect condition for our offspring. And don't give me the old, 'What's the point in having them… blah… blah speech.' Just think, what if there's an earthquake in the middle of dinner?"

He grabbed the thick edge of the glass dining room table with both hands. "In fact I think I'm beginning to feel a minor temblor now," shaking the table gently, so that all of the items in front of them began to slightly vibrate. "That big hanging chandelier could crash down and smash all of this to hell. Then, how will you feel that you have ruined the inheritance for all future generations because you wanted the table to look pretty tonight?"

"Now you're beginning to make *me* nervous," she said. "Please stop shaking the table."

"OK, but do you know that the San Andreas Fault practically runs through our living room?"

"Oh Eddie, relax. I know this is just another one of your tactics to get out of doing the dishes."

"Gosh honey, I hadn't thought of that! But you know—you're right! You handle them so much more carefully than I do, and it would be such a damn shame if I should stumble over my shoelaces while carrying—"

"Cut the crap Eddie," she interrupted. "You know you always eat barefoot at home—I have a theory that it somehow makes you feel like you're still bopping around on your boat—so stumbling over your shoelaces would certainly be a neat trick. Stumbling over your disgusting long toenails because you haven't trimmed them in over a month would be more likely."

He looked down at his toes, and saw that she was right. He made a mental note to trim them—next weekend for sure.

"I heard you talking on the phone earlier," he said. "Was it your mom's usual Sunday night check-in?"

"Yep," she answered.

"How are they? What did you talk about?"

She looked down into her glass. "Mostly the weather."

"We'll be there in four weeks—I can hardly wait. By then the temperature will probably be a balmy two degrees."

Renee knew Eddie's sarcasm—knew how much he hated Ohio. He got along fine with her dad, but her mother was another story. She loved him for the restraint and good behavior he always displayed. She thought of talking about the tension between him and her mother, but decided against it, in favor of changing the subject.

She raised her glass.

"Let's have a toast on this special occasion—even though the Messiah hasn't ridden down off the Hollywood Hills on his donkey yet."

"Special occasion?" he inquired. "Birthday? No. Anniversary? No. Valentine's Day? Not in October. Did I forget something?"

"Yes. In fact you did. The occasion is the eve of your entering the world of the court system—albeit only for two weeks." She raised her glass a tad higher. "May you get selected to be on the jury. And—may it be the jury of an exciting murder trial—as I know you want so badly."

"Oh that. Thank you. That was beautiful," he said, raising his own glass.

She continued, "I'm not done. Just don't do anything stupid like volunteer to be the foreman. I know you."

"Now that was *really* beautiful. I'm getting all choked up. The part about the toenails was especially touching."

She took a small sip of the nice wine and set her glass down. A hint of rose colored lipstick was left behind on the thin crystal rim.

"Seriously—please don't be too disappointed if you don't even make the panel on an actual trial. Only about one prospective juror in five gets selected. The rest are excused for one reason or another and go back into the jurors' pool, just to get excused again the next time their name comes up and the attorneys get a good look at them."

"Thanks for the vote of confidence my dear—but tomorrow morning I'll shave off this scruff. I'll wear a coat and tie and look like the intelligent and fair young citizen that I am. Hell, I might even wear shoes!"

She chuckled, "That might be advisable."

"What attorney in their right mind would excuse a juror like me?"

"You feel pretty strongly that you are going to make such a huge impact, being one person on one small insignificant trial. You are a little naive my dear Eddie, but that is one of the reasons I married you."

"How can you say that? You, who have been going to law school for two years? You think you can change the system for the better?"

"Oh Eddie, we've talked about this before. No, I don't think I can change the system for the better. I just want to try and have a positive impact on those I come in contact with. I don't know where you got the idea that you will be able to do so much good. By far, most of jury duty is incredibly boring, just as much of law is full of dull technicalities—a courtroom can be quite the cure for insomnia. I just don't want to see you disappointed."

"Well, I've considered that it could possibly be dull as hell. I just think one or two college grads on a jury could be a good thing. People who are educated as we are should give a little of our input into the system for a change. If the jury system is all made up of unemployed people who are excited to get off their front porch or couch and put down their T.V. remotes for ten days because they are the only ones who do have the time—aren't we in a bit of trouble?"

"Well yes, we are in a bit of trouble," Renee answered, "but that happens to be the reality."

Eddie reached across the table and held her left hand, turning it gently; he loved the way the marquis diamond refracted the light and threw off minuscule rainbow rays from the facets when he rotated the band.

"You know, a single burnt refried bean would look good on these dishes."

"Aw—that is sweet. I'm so glad you approve Captain Edward. Maybe next Sunday night I'll just make refried beans for dinner."

"What would my father say?"

"He'd probably love the new material as the perfect lead-in to his stories of your mom's cooking!" she retorted quickly. "I can practically hear it from Sid now, '... *are you trying to tell me she served you a romantic dinner that featured refried beans? That reminds me of a story... I believe the year was 1896... it was a brutally cold winter in Leningrad... the Cossacks had begun confiscating all of the beans for the Russian Army...*'"

They both laughed.

"Not a bad imitation of my dad!" he said.

"I've been listening to him now for several years," she said. "But thankfully—you're not Sid."

"They say you always end up marrying your father-in-law," said Eddie.

"Shut up!"

They laughed some more.

"Hey," she continued, after they both had taken a few bites, "today in Ralph's, when I was in the checkout line, I saw an article in the Enquirer about how a couple gave birth to grandchildren without having any children. Maybe I'll tell you all about their secret after you finish the dishes."

CHAPTER 5 - Voir Dire

October 17, 1993
Compton, California

The hot Santa Ana winds of October were blowing. It left the view of the mountains to the North clearer than the view over the ocean behind him. Driving East on the Artesia Freeway, Eddie seized the opportunity to make the cruise with the top down on his Corvette. He had been uncertain of how to dress; the jurors' handbook said 'dress as if you were going to a business meeting.' Eddie smiled on first reading that recommendation, as often, he wore shorts and sneakers to his own meetings. This morning, he wore a grey suit and multi-colored tie. He was feeling good, high with excitement, looking forward to his first day in court, while simultaneously looking back to last night's session in bed with his wife.

He smiled upon hearing the opening harmonica chords of the Rolling Stones' classic anthem *"Midnight Rambler,"* and cranked a few more decibels out of his new Blaupunkt CD player. He considered with amusement the possibility of a subliminal message in the song—that Mick Jagger and Keith Richards were able to remotely trigger an implant in the brain—wherein listeners were commanded to move their fingers toward the volume knob, and their toes to the accelerator pedal. Eddie felt the increased pressure of his back against the black leather bucket seat as the 'Vette responded. He had already planned his response to the potential pullover by a cop. "It wasn't me officer. Really. It was Jagger!" Grinning at the thought, he turned the volume even higher.

South Central Los Angeles was made up of miles and miles of tiny old single family residences and rundown apartment buildings. There were hardly any trees. Gardeners were not needed, as now, by October, months of the baking sun had rendered the majority of lawns dead. Welders, on the other hand, were in high demand: they were needed to install all of those wrought iron security bars on tens of thousands of doors and windows. In this part of town, the landscape was flat as far as the eye could see. It was flat save for one exception; visible from all directions, visible even from several of the South Bay freeways, the Harbor, San Diego, Long Beach, and of course Artesia Freeway, arose a giant white monolith: The Compton Courthouse.

Eddie turned North on the Wilmington off-ramp. He had always heard jokes about Compton. The poverty. The gangs.

Could I have gone my whole life living 12 miles away without ever driving through? Actually, there was that time in high school after that football game against Centennial, when the guys went to a BBQ rib joint. It was fantastic...

In fact one of his buddies made a commitment right then and there that he would open a barbecue place serving ribs and sausages down near the beach, when he got out of high school. But, inevitably, any attempt by a white man to introduce BBQ in Hermosa, Redondo or Manhattan met with quick failure, as apparently there was some sort of natural law wherein it just couldn't compare with the sauces and soul food preparation offered up in South Central.

The last time I was here, could that have been 22 years ago? How could the city look so different so close to home?

He had only been off the freeway eight blocks yet had already seen three fried chicken places and four tiny neighborhood churches with tacky pastel paint jobs. Eddie wondered what happened to all the gleaming new cars he usually saw flying down the freeways; there wasn't a single vehicle post 1986. At eight thirty in the morning, clusters of people on the sidewalk were drinking booze out of paper bags. A young kid yelled something at Eddie that he did not quite understand, but the tone was not welcoming.

Sitting at a stoplight, a huge green Pontiac pulled alongside on his right. Three black men eyed Eddie. He was immediately sorry he had not driven his wife's Mazda. It was agonizing trying not to make eye contact; somewhere he flashed on that tip as a good general rule...

... or, was it better to look at them and smile? God Damn you Jagger—what are you trying to tell me?

"Fuck," he whispered.

Dropping his left hand down from the steering wheel, he unbuckled his Rolex, slipping it under the seat. Eddie relaxed a bit when the Pontiac turned right. Still, he immediately hit the button to raise the top on his convertible. As the tan canvas accordion of the rag-top moved into position, he hit a second button which turned off the music—aware of the fact that he was violating one of his own rules; Renee referred to them as *'The Edweirdo Rules.'* It was sort of in-line with his thing about spearing, and the fish heads; Eddie had made his own list, back when he was in his teens, of ten songs you just could not turn off once they had started playing. *Midnight Rambler* was one of them. It was legal to turn the volume lower—but off? Never. Renee almost always acquiesced to his many quirks such as this. She generally had no choice, as Eddie had made her understand his feeling—it was a feeling that a deviation would generally be a precursor to something bad happening. Acknowledging the violation, he nonetheless ejected the disc and removed the faceplate from his CD player. It hadn't been five minutes, but the high from his delightful morning cruise was long gone.

A few painfully slow streetlights later, Eddie pulled up to the courthouse. Glad to see an armed guard on the sidewalk standing a few yards away from the parking structure attendant, he pulled up to the booth and showed the man the juror badge he had received in the mail.

"Put this on your dash." The man handed Eddie a small yellow card and said without emotion, "Free parking for jurors on Level 4. Welcome to Compton."

Eddie found a spot in the dark concrete structure, mulling over his dilemma...

Some decisions simply had no right answers unless you had a crystal ball. Or hindsight. Should I keep the watch with me, or leave it hidden in the car?

He tucked the watch deeper under the driver's seat, set the alarm, and started across the parking structure. Instead of the elevator, he decided to walk the three flights, down to the courthouse level. Graffiti covered the concrete stairwell walls. Littering the area were lots of empty cans, crumpled up newspapers and burger wrappers, as well as broken glass of differing sizes and colors. He was stung by the strong smell of urine. Two middle aged ladies came through an opening in the stairwell on Level 3, right ahead of him. They smiled at him briefly, continuing their conversation. He wondered if they were as affected by the pungent piss as he was, decided they weren't—and sadly—that they might be used to it.

He was already sorry he'd worn a tie.

At the main entrance, Eddie showed his juror badge again, and passed through the door on the right. People who lined up to enter the door on the left, anyone who was not a prospective juror, were being searched by armed guards. Inside the old building, Eddie was immediately struck by the flurry of activity; people huddled together, pushing and waddling, like Antarctic penguins, to make the elevators. One huge room had at least 500 people in it. Eddie conjectured that there must be some kind of food stamp, or special unemployment seminar going on from the haggard looks of the people in that room. He continued on past the stale smelling cafeteria, trying to dodge attorneys, clients, and family members, all rushing to make their court appearances. He found a guard who appeared to have a break in fielding repetitive questions. "Excuse me sir, where do I report for jury duty?"

Without looking up, the guard answered impatiently, "You passed it. Room 102 back down the hall."

It was the massive hall crammed with the mob of people.

Shit. This is no food stamp program... these are the potential jurors.

They were stuffed to the window panes. It more closely resembled a bus terminal. Some people were trying to peer over shoulders to watch an inane morning talk-show on a laughably small television set. Others had already begun games of Scrabble or dominoes. Many were reading newspapers or cheap paperbacks. Most were seated at the long pew-like wooden benches, doing nothing; they stared aimlessly across the room. Along the side wall, he saw a glass window with three ladies quickly shuffling papers. He stood in line under a small hand-lettered sign: *'ALL PROSPECTIVE JURORS CHECK IN HEAR.'* Eddie chuckled and pointed to the sign while gently tapping the shoulder of the Hispanic man in front of him.

"I guess spelling isn't a prerequisite for this job."

The man stared blankly at Eddie for two long seconds, and turned away silently.

"I'm here to report for jury duty," said Eddie, when he reached the window.

"Badge and picture I.D. please." The young woman ran Eddie's badge through a scanner. "Please wait to be called. Next please."

"Wait," said Eddie. "What do I do now?"

"Anything you want sir, just as long as it's in this room. Next please."

"But how long till I get called?"

"I can't answer that sir. Kindly step away from the window. *Next!*"

Finding a space on a hard bench in the far end of the room, Eddie was unable to identify the source of a foul smell somewhere in the immediate vicinity. He loosened his tie. After several minutes of shifting his gaze in all directions to study the unusual scene, he turned his left wrist to check the time, but saw only the pale tan-line.

****

Eddie had been sitting for three hours. In that time, he grabbed a home improvement magazine out of a large wooden bin. He thought maybe he'd be inspired to take on a project around the house, or see a neat new artsy approach to a job, maybe in the garden, but the magazine didn't have many articles. It was filled mostly with ads for saws and drills. He visualized the work bench in his garage and his collection of power tools…

If I live to be a hundred will I ever need to buy a saw or drill again?

He tried to kill time by reading an old paperback he found in a different bin. He ultimately had no idea what the story was about or whether it was good or bad, as he couldn't concentrate. He got up to get a drink of water. On the way back to his seat, he saw two middle aged black men engaged in a spirited game of checkers. He decided to challenge the winner. He stood over them for a minute, watching their fast paced game. But his confidence in proposing the match waned when one of them, the man playing red, who was down two pieces, looked up with a confronting scowl. Embarrassed, Eddie made his way slowly back to his seat.

A burst of sour feedback from a microphone pierced a thousand ears. "Lunchtime. All prospective jurors must be back in the jury room by 1:30. Thank you."

Eddie knew Renee would be home studying. He found a payphone and called her.

"So, has the jury reached a verdict?" she asked with mock enthusiasm.

"Very funny. Actually, I've reached a verdict. This absolutely sucks. You were right, it's boring as hell. The

88

T.V. area is too crowded to get near. People either stink from not taking showers, or from too much perfume. And I can't even get into a checkers or Scrabble game.

"So that's it? Nothing's happened?"

"They called out the names of about a hundred people an hour ago to report to a courtroom on the 5th floor. Maybe I should have just gone with them. After three hours, of absolute zero—we are breaking for lunch. Can you believe it? Anything would be better than this."

"Yes, I believe it," she said. "That's how it works. There's a lot of stuff that goes on in the courtroom before they call the prospective jurors in. And you can't go running off with any group of people unless they specifically call your name. I bet they'll be calling you after lunch."

"Speaking of lunch, wanna join me? I hear the courthouse cafeteria is supposed to be incredible. It got 5 stars in the Michelin guide and is supposed to be one of the top places for fine dining in all of L.A."

"Sounds like a line to me, mister. I can smell that bad food through the phone. Besides, I'm trying to see if I can go my whole life without ever going to Compton."

"Oh honey, but it's beautiful here. I'm at a window, and I can see a palm tree from where I'm standing. It's just like Bora Bora."

"Sorry sailor. I've got work to do. Bye."

Eddie had a strange sensation after he hung up. He didn't often experience the feeling of needing to kill time—this slightly unsettled him. He had so much going on in his life, with his booming business and his house and his boat. Basketball, photography listening to music, and planning the next trip to a remote tropical island for some fantastic scuba diving, took up much of his spare time. Then, of course, there were just fun little outings with his wife when she was able to take a break from her studying. But this—this gap in the constant stream of action that made up his life—was a bit unnerving. He had to fill a 50 minute gap until he could begin his walk back to the jury pool room.

What should I do? Guess I better bring a paperback tomorrow...

He sat on a cold grey concrete bench in a relatively clean area outside the courthouse and stared out. He found himself hoping somebody would come by and sit down next to him, before his mind drifted to thoughts of drills and saws...

****

"Will the following jurors please report immediately to Superior Court in Department A on the sixth floor: Anita Andujar, Roberto Bonilla, James Campbell, Edward Curtain, Arlene..."

Eddie had been back from lunch for less than ten minutes. He felt as if he had won an award upon hearing his name. He wanted to yell out "Goodbye suckers!" to the more than three hundred remaining prospective jurors who were still stuck waiting in the pool, and then was sobered, upon remembering Renee's comment from last night about how only one in five end up making it onto the jury panel. It took seven elevator loads to carry them up to the sixth floor, where they all silently and respectfully filed into Department A, nearly filling the courtroom gallery. Eddie quickly counted—three rows of ten on the right, two in the middle, and three on the left—eighty people. From eighty, only twelve would get selected. Eddie did some math in his head...

Only about one chance in 6 point 5. Damn.

Bailiff Cedric Ellis was a huge black man. He stood six five. Thick brown horn rimmed glasses wrapped around his completely bald head. Eddie, reminded of Queequeg from Melville's *Moby Dick*, tried to picture the bailiff with a harpoon.

Ellis' voice resonated off the courtroom walls, "Please rise for the honorable Judge Sherman."

Wondering if his menacing bellow was simply for effect to intimidate prospective jurors, Eddie learned in the days to come that it was his normal courtroom tone.

"Please remain standing and raise your right hand. Do you understand and agree that you will accurately and truthfully answer, under penalty of perjury, all questions propounded to you concerning your qualifications and competency to serve as a trial juror in the matter pending before this court, and that failure to do so may subject you to criminal prosecution? Please acknowledge by saying 'I do.'

"You may be seated."

Markedly, the intensity in the room rose as the judge began to speak. In contrast to the bailiff, Judge Sherman seemed to whisper, though his enunciation was impeccable.

"Good afternoon ladies and gentlemen. You are here in this courtroom to serve as a potential juror in the matter of *The People of the State of California versus Reginald Washington*. A man sits before you accused of the crime of first degree murder." Eddie's heart began to pound. "If selected, you will be given the task of deciding guilt or innocence based solely on the testimony and evidence presented in this courtroom. Furthermore, if you are selected to be part of this jury, you are ordered not to discuss this case with anyone. Your discussions regarding this case are limited exclusively to the jury room during deliberations. You may be excused for any one of a variety of reasons. If you are excused please do not take it personally. A juror excused from one trial may make an excellent and conscientious juror in another trial. If you are excused, please report immediately back to the jurors' pool in Room 102 down on the first floor. Bailiff."

Ellis commanded, "Please fill in each seat as your name is called."

"Juror number one, Anita Andujar."

Oh God, don't be in alphabetical order! I don't want to go so early... I can see the reactions to the judge or attorneys' questions and quickly learn from their mistakes... But—if I got called later—in the sixties, or seventies, they might have already decided on twelve good ones... I just realized that these other jurors are my adversaries!

He wanted so desperately to get selected, but couldn't put his finger on exactly why. Perhaps it was growing up in a poor neighborhood in Inglewood and connecting the dots to where he was now in life. Or, his awareness of the blessed path he seemed to be on, and though it sounded cliché—he really wanted to give something back. He was keenly aware of the many racial injustices that existed in everyday life in Los Angeles, the memories of the riots being quite fresh. But it was his home, and the city he loved. He saw how hard his wife worked at studying law, and thought perhaps he could better relate to the commitment she was making. Perhaps there was some guilt, for having always been able to get out of serving on jury duty—leaving the task to others. Maybe it was that comment by Jason in the bar the other night, about how the hardware on his yacht needed polishing.

He was proud of all he had worked to achieve, knew there was more to come. He was profoundly touched by that episode with Annie Luu, how she had to have suffered watching her dead mother and brothers being cast overboard into the sea—so there was more than a hint of guilt there. But now, ever since he received that summons in the mail, he wanted this. He wanted to serve on the jury of a real trial, to help figure and reveal the truth. Today was his chance.

"Juror number two, Roberto Bonilla. Juror number three, James Campbell. Juror number four, Edward Curtain. Juror number five Arlene Donaldson. Juror number six...

Damn! Looks like Plan A just went out the window.

Within three minutes, the jury box was full. There were subtle smiles and nods between the occupants—almost as if they had just achieved something. Eddie was surprised; he was immediately struck by how comfortable the seat was, especially as contrasted with that awful wooden bench in the jury pool room downstairs. The base and seatback was made out of contoured fiberglass and had thick blue foam cushioning in all the right places. He loved the swivel action. However long he lasted up here, he had to admit he was enjoying it. Suddenly, he noticed the defendant for the first time, as earlier, when he was in the gallery, he could only see the man's back.

Reggie Washington was wearing a dark brown blazer with a burgundy colored tie. His shirt was a yellowish white. The blazer seemed a bit too small for him as too much of the cuffs poked through the sleeves. Eddie could not tell how tall he was, as Reggie was seated—additionally, he was slightly slumped over the table. His stooped shoulders were wide, however, and he appeared to have massive hands. Even from his seat in the jury box, which was at least 40 feet away, Eddie could make out several purple-black scars on the knuckles of the brown hands. Eddie looked at Reggie's face. The eyes. Eddie could never tell with people who had a glass eye which was the good one, and which was the bad one— only that something was—off.

Does he even have a glass eye? Or is there some old injury or birth defect making them asymmetrical? Cousin Maddie has a lazy eye... she always looks sleepy.
This guy, Reggie Washington, does not look sleepy...

Even hunched over a bit, he seemed acutely aware of his entire surroundings. Eddie watched for a sign of nervousness from the defendant. There was none. Eddie hated the fact that he could not control his own brain; he kept thinking and conjecturing about the defendant—asking questions of innocence or guilt. He welcomed the interruption of his thought pattern by the judge.

"Juror number one, Ms. Andujar, do you understand that you are under oath?"

"Si señor. I mean yes."

"Please tell us your occupation, the occupation of your immediate family members, and your place of residence."

"I live in Carson. On 120th Street. I work at the Post Office. My husband is unemployed at the moment, and I have four children."

"Do you know the defendant before you, myself, or either of the attorneys, Ms. Andujar?"

"No."

Judge Sherman asked, "Do you have any relatives who are police officers or security guards?"

"Yes. I have a brother who is a cop in Philadelphia."

"Does he ever tell you cop-type stories Ms. Andujar?"

She paused, before answering, "Sure, lots of times." Eddie noticed the district attorney writing frantically as the first potential juror was speaking. The defense attorney and defendant were watching together carefully. At one point, Reggie leaned over and whispered something in her ear.

The judge continued, "Some of the witnesses you will hear in this trial are police officers, Ms. Andujar. Do you think having a brother as a policeman will affect your ability to listen with an open mind to what they have to say?"

"Yes," she answered.

For the first time the Judge's voice rose out of monotone mode, "It *will* affect your ability, Ms. Andujar?"

She giggled. "I mean no."

"Do you think policemen are basically good, or basically bad Ms. Andujar?"

"I think they work pretty hard."

"Thank you Ms. Andujar. Good Afternoon Mr. Bonilla. Do you understand that you are under oath?"

"Yes I do your honor."

"Please tell us about your job and your family."

Bonilla was visibly nervous. He stuttered slightly. "My wife and I got divorced three years ago. We ain't got no kids. I work for a machine shop in L.A."

"Where do you live Mr. Bonilla?"

"Right now I'm stayin' with my cousin Alberto."

"But where does your cousin live, Mr. Bonilla?"

"Oh, he lives in an apartment in Wilmington."

"Do you know any policemen or security guards Mr. Bonilla?"

"Yes."

"Have you ever been arrested, Mr. Bonilla?"

"Sure, who hasn't?" Bonilla smiled, as a moderate burst of laughter filled the courtroom.

"Well," the judge answered with a smile of his own, "I'd like to think there are one or two of us left who haven't yet had the pleasure. Please tell us about some of your experiences, involving the legal system, or the police."

"I was arrested during the riots, last year in '92, but I got off."

"What was the charge?"

"To be honest, there were two charges."

"We only want you to be honest with us Mr. Bonilla," said the judge. "Please tell us the two charges."

"Arson. Arson and looting."

"Was there anything else?" asked the judge.

"You mean during the riots?"

"During the riots, or any other time."

"A couple of months ago, in August, I hit a driver of another car."

"You mean you were in a car accident?" asked the judge.

"Well, yes, I was in an accident, but what I meant was, I literally hit him. I mean I punched him. This black guy ran a red light and smashed into my front fender. It was over on Alameda Street. They hauled me in for that. So I spent the night at Compton P.D.—the station on Willowbrook. I just paid a fine and that was it."

"You paid a fine for punching him?" asked Judge Sherman.

"I guess," answered Bonilla, "I don't quite understand the legal stuff. I think he didn't press charges because he didn't have insurance."

"Anything else?"

"Yeah, but they were all a long time ago."

What's a 'long time ago' in this guy's mind?

"Do you have any feelings toward the police which might impact whether you believe or disbelieve them if you were to hear them testify?"

"I don't think so."

"So just to be sure, do you feel you can be a fair and impartial juror when weighing the testimony and evidence even when it's given by a police officer?"

"Yes I can."

"Thank you Mr. Bonilla. Juror number three," the judge looked down at his list, to read the next name, "James Campbell. Please tell us about your family, occupation, and residence."

"I've lived two blocks from the courthouse here in Compton my whole life. I work at the Shell station on Avalon. My wife stays home with the kids. There's Bobby 9, Theresa 8, Jessica 5, Michelle 2, and she's pregnant with another. My oldest, James Junior, died last year."

"Have you had any experience with the police, Mr. Campbell?"

"Well, yeah, when James, the one I told you about, was killed, they were over the house a lot."

"Go on."

"It was on Normandie, during the riots, and they asked a bunch of questions about friends he hung out with, and if he had any enemies, if he was part of a gang, and got in fights and stuff. They showed us lots of pictures."

"Did your son belong to a gang, sir?"

"No, he did not."

"We're all very sorry to hear about your loss. Did they find who killed your son, Mr. Campbell?"

"They said they knew what gang it was, the Bloods, but they couldn't pinpoint the exact guy who pulled the trigger."

"And how do you feel towards the police now, Mr. Campbell?"

"Well, I wish they could make an arrest. I wish somebody would pay for what happened to Junior. I guess they tried."

Eddie attempted to put himself in the shoes of the attorneys.

The defense attorney probably wants this guy because he doesn't like the police. The D.A. probably wants this guy because his kid was murdered by a gang member... on the other hand, he seems awfully calm for someone who had his son gunned down so recently... maybe he would be considered a risky juror for both sides...

"Do you think your unfortunate experience will affect your ability to impartially weigh all of the evidence, and to give the defendant a fair trial, Mr. Campbell?"

"I think I can be fair."

Wow! How can the guy say that? Some gang guys murdered his son 18 months ago, the cops didn't catch the killers, and...

"Thank you Mr. Campbell. Juror number four, Mr. Edward Curtain—good afternoon." Eddie was slightly jolted; he was so caught up in his analysis he didn't even realize he was next.

"Can you please tell us about yourself? Please remember that you are under oath."

"My name is Ed Curtain. I am self-employed in the garment industry, and live in Palos Verdes. I have been married for just over three years, and have no children." Eddie wanted to interject that he had 10 grandchildren, and list all of their names and ages, however his private joke was better left stifled.

"What are your tasks in the business, Mr. Curtain?"

"Well, on a given day it could be any number of things. Talking on the phone with key customers. Buying fabric for production. Dealing with sales reps. Or reviewing the accounting. I also spend lots of time going over designs and samples for each upcoming season." He was glad the judge did not force him to answer a question pertaining to his wife's profession. Her being in law school, he conjectured, would certainly be a negative in *someone's* eyes.

"Please tell us, Mr. Curtain, about any unsatisfactory interactions you may have had with police officers, security guards, or anyone in law-enforcement."

Eddie wondered why the judge had worded his question so differently to him, but quickly began relating the first story that came to mind.

"I had a situation with a couple of cops about nine or ten years ago after my car was broken into."

"Please tell us about it Mr. Curtain."

"It was after a Grateful Dead concert at Winterland, in San Francisco. I had parked on the street. As I walked up to my car after the show, I saw that a window was smashed and a few things were stolen. Somebody yelled and pointed to the two guys running away—down the street, and between two houses. A cop car was driving by at that moment. I flagged them down and hurriedly explained the theft and pointed to where they went, fully expecting them to hit the gas and take off after them. Instead, they parked the car and got out. I frantically explained about my new stereo, and something like, 'Come on, this just happened a minute ago! You can catch them!' But they remained stationary. One of them pulled out a notepad and asked my name. He then asked where I worked and to spell the name of the company for him. In short, it was pretty frustrating."

"Do you feel the police did a poor job in handling your situation?"

Eddie swallowed. "Yes I do your honor."

"Do you still harbor ill feelings toward the police?"

"There is little doubt that they didn't seize the opportunity to increase the chances of me getting my belongings back. I don't know. But that was a long time ago, and I've since had a few positive experiences with the police."

"Do you feel, Mr. Curtain, that these and other experiences you may have had might influence your ability to hear the case at hand without bias?"

"I feel I can listen with an open mind your honor."

"Thank you Mr. Curtain. Juror number five, Arlene Donaldson. Please tell us about yourself Ms. Donaldson, and remember that you are under oath."

The intensity was staggering. Eddie felt like *he* was on trial—if only for two minutes. The district attorney was standing a few feet in front of him, tapping her pencil in her palm. Judge Sherman, though he often rotated his neck to look at some distant random spec on the far wall, did not miss a single syllable. But during most of this strange confession, that Eddie had never before given, his eyes were in direct contact with the disturbing glare of the defendant. Relieved by the judge's new questions to the next prospective juror, Eddie had a moment to reflect on his bizarre dissertation.

Idiot! Why did it have to be a Grateful Dead concert? Why not just a concert? Hell! Why a concert at all? Why not a darn movie! I might as well have said I partied backstage with Jerry Garcia!

Eddie was familiar with the fact that witnesses often said too much in response to a question. Eddie now realized that even a *juror* could say too much. He was sure he had dashed his hopes of making the final panel, as, the *'Dead'* have always been inextricably linked with drugs—especially hallucinogens. He fought the urge to yell out...

'Excuse me for interrupting, juror number five. Excuse me your honor. I would like to add that I never inhaled.'

But the focus of all in the courtroom had already passed him by. All eyes and ears were now dialed into the quick snapshot of existence offered up by the next prospective juror sitting to Eddie's right. All eyes except those of the defendant. Reggie Washington still stared at Eddie.

CHAPTER 6 - The Witness

October 18, 1993
Compton, California

The selection process continued, the tediousness of Judge Sherman's questions rarely broken. Upon completing the questioning of the twelfth person in the jury box, Judge Sherman asked, "Is counsel satisfied with the composition of this panel?"

The D.A. spoke first, "The People would like to thank and excuse juror number two."

In the second jury seat, in the front row, Mr. Bonilla offered a pained expression. He lingered nervously, uncertain of what to do next.

Judge Sherman spoke, "Again, ladies and gentlemen, please don't take an excusal by either of the attorneys personally. If you do happen to be excused, please report immediately back to the jury pool in Room 102 down on the first floor. Your services may very well be required in another trial. Thank you Mr. Bonilla, at this time you are excused."

As if savoring his last moment in the jury box, Bonilla sat another second; the delay was not lost on Eddie. Eddie conjectured that Bonilla had reveled in his temporary position of power—how it just may have been the first time in his life he was able to experience such a sensation—a marvelous feeling that complete strangers would look to him for his opinion on something that mattered.

Eddie thought back to this prospective juror's recap, just moments ago, of his recent auto accident. He could see the disappointment on the man's face.

By excusing him, this tiny redheaded woman just dashed this guy's hopes of being on the jury. Maybe... like with that unfortunate driver who had rammed his bumper, could Bonilla be thinking about jumping over the jury box and punching the District Attorney?

Now, Bonilla wondered if he would ever be given another chance. Swiveling in his seat, searching the courtroom for sympathetic eyes, he found none. Fumbling awkwardly with his windbreaker, he stood, and left the courtroom.

Eddie did not want to make the same embarrassed exit.

The tension was broken by the defense attorney, "The Defense would like to thank and excuse juror number five."

The two lawyers called out numbers like executioners. "The People would like to thank and excuse juror number six..."

"...juror number ten."

"...juror number three."

Only four people remained in the jury box. Cedric Ellis bellowed out eight new names to prospective jurors in the courtroom gallery, the empty seats were filled in, and the inquisition began again.

In this high stakes game of musical chairs, Eddie held onto seat number four. He felt a relieved confidence when the lawyers stopped excusing people, and the judge began questioning only the new jurors. He considered his coveted position now safe. But his relief soon faded, as, after the second round of questioning by Judge Sherman, the district attorney asked a question of Anita Andujar—juror number one—who had also made it through the first round.

"Juror number one," asked the D.A, "you stated earlier that..."

Crap. My position is never safe...

His anxiety returned when Eddie suddenly realized why there were so many prospective jurors.

The process continued for almost two hours. After seven rounds of questioning, excusing and subsequently filling in vacant seats, Eddie was one of only two people who remained from the original group of twelve.

"The People are satisfied with the makeup of this jury your honor."

"The Defense is also satisfied with this panel your honor."

There were a few subtle grins among the accepted jury members. Eddie wanted to shake everybody's hand.

Oh my God! I made it! Congratulations. My name is Edward Curtain. My friends call me Eddie.

But his cocky pride in enjoying the moment was quickly broken by the judge.

"Would the People like to make an opening statement?"

Sandra Levinthal was the District Attorney. She stood barely five feet tall. Her nickname both in the courthouse, and on the streets, was "MJB." More than a handful of new felons had spent their first night at the L.A. County Jail plotting painful ways to repay the Midget Jew Bitch.

She had known the defendant, Reggie Washington, for several years. Their paths crossing three times previously in the justice system—Reggie getting off on a technicality the first time due to a key omission in the arrest report by a second year officer, and with a plea bargain in the second instance—in the hopes of busting and forever removing from the South Central streets a major crack dealer. It was a hope that never materialized, as the dealer was able to afford a defense team and parade of highly paid expert witnesses that the city could not compete with. In the third instance, the D.A. had him nailed, but it was discovered that an ambitious detective from the Rampart Division of the L.A.P.D. had planted false evidence. With an abundance of evidence that would have put this high ranking member of the Bloods away for good, the overzealous detective's actions were entirely unnecessary. Upon seeing the handcuffs on this known cop-killer removed—Sandra was livid.

Sandra knew that Reggie had probably not gone more than a few days since he was ten years old without committing some sort of a crime. An avowed feminist since her college days at Cambridge, her blood curdled at the thought of the ritual rape—the one rape *required* as initiation into the twisted faction of the Cimarron Avenue Bloods to which Reggie belonged.

She vowed that the next interaction with Mr. Washington would be their last.

Stepping forward to make her opening statement, Ms. Levinthal wore a petite forest green pant suit. A rust colored silk blouse, which neatly set off her closely cropped red hair, puffed out from the top of the blazer collar as well as the cuffs. In the tense silence broken only by her tapping high heels while she stood and walked slowly to approach the jury box, an incongruous thought from his younger days as a designer surfaced to the awareness point of Eddie's brain...

It's true: redheads always wear green.

"Ladies and gentlemen of the jury, good afternoon. First off, let me thank you for your service here. I know that many of you are sacrificing a great deal of your valuable time—away from your jobs and your families. So again—thank you. Allow me to share with you something that strikes me as strange about this case. Please observe with me if you will: there are no T.V. cameras. There are no reporters. Nor are there people pushing to get a good seat in a crowded courtroom. In fact, now that all of the prospective jurors who have not made it through the 'voir dire'—the selection process—as you have, are in those elevators on their way downstairs to another trial—this courtroom seems rather empty, doesn't it? Let's count the people in this room: there's the judge, myself and the defense attorney, of course the defendant, the bailiff, the stenographer, two people there who might be family to one of the parties, that makes eight, and yourselves—the twelve of you who make up the jury, plus the two alternates. She waved her right hand at all the empty wooden seats. "To me, it is odd that this huge courtroom is so empty. There are only 22 of us here now, but you saw for yourselves that there is plenty of room for more! Perhaps, after I share with you my thoughts, you too will find it odd. To me, it is strange that this trial is not big headline news. You see, an innocent man was murdered because he was doing his job."

Sandra's voice had been calm—almost friendly. It now rose to an alarming level, shocking several members of the new jury, "An innocent man was murdered because he asked someone to turn down the volume on his radio!" She paused to make direct eye contact with several of the jurors. Eddie was one of them. She lowered her voice. "But it seems there is no interest in this crime because it has become commonplace. This case is not newsworthy. There is no celebrity involved. Not a politician, nor a movie star, nor a superstar athlete. A man had his life cruelly snatched away. A good man, and a man who was loved by all who knew him.

"Oliver Jefferson had a family. He had a wife and he had children and nieces and nephews. He played with the kids at the apartment complex where he worked. But he certainly wasn't famous. The closest thing to fame he ever experienced was being the high school DJ. Now take a look around you... look at all of these empty seats in the courtroom. Here's something else: the day after Oliver was killed, there wasn't a big story in the L.A. Times. There wasn't even a story in the local paper. There wasn't a picture of his face, or even a small paragraph."

She paused, this time scanning the faces of the entire jury. "Outside of a few people who know *him*, Reginald Washington is not famous either. Reginald," she hesitated, "Reggie, Washington, will never be in People Magazine. But Reggie Washington did an incredibly—famously—cowardly thing."

Sandra aimed her thin index finger at the defendant. "The man you see sitting there stole the life from Oliver Jefferson. For this, Reggie Washington is finally getting some attention. It is our job, ladies and gentlemen, to let people know that a life is indeed worth a headline. We cannot allow murder to become so commonplace that it is not even newsworthy. We cannot allow murder to become boring. I ask you all to listen carefully to the witnesses and evidence you will see and hear in the next few days. I trust that you too will feel the rage I feel inside when it becomes clear to you how easily—how matter of factly—Reggie Washington eliminated a precious human life. The evidence will show that he fired four shots from close range at a man who he probably didn't even know. The evidence will show that he fired with his powerful handgun and killed Oliver Jefferson as easily as if he were putting on his shoes.

"Oliver Jefferson won't get to tell you his story. Oliver needs to rely on us, ladies and gentlemen, to have his story be heard. Oliver is dead. He has in fact been buried for almost exactly a year now. You may not know this, but, directly across the street from the Forum, where the Lakers play basketball, is a small cemetery. Inglewood Park Cemetery. Just a few months ago, in April, Oliver got a tiny plaque unveiled over his grave. Do you know how many people were at that ceremony? I'll tell you: five. Think about that for a moment. Oliver Jefferson had a life. He had friends, classmates, birthday parties, a wedding. He fought for our country and was even wounded in Vietnam. He worked as a Security Guard, trying to protect children and families in a rather rough neighborhood, not far from where we are gathered today. But there are more than twice as many people sitting together with you in your small jury box right now than came to Oliver's final farewell.

"Oliver Jefferson's death is senseless almost beyond our comprehension. And I am asking you to get excited about his death. I am asking you to get worked up about the tragedy of this senseless murder. I am asking you to protest the fact that murder has become mundane. I am asking you to listen to the proof that the man sitting in front of you is guilty of this horrible crime so that together we may write our own headline.

"Thank you."

****

On the drive home that evening, Eddie was excited; the D.A. had requested he get excited, and he had to admit that it worked. He could not wait to get home to tell his wife about his day. He watched the orange speedometer needle veer to the right as the powerful V8 engine followed his command: 45...50... change lanes and pass a slow pickup on the right, 60, back to the fast lane and pass a lady in an old Ford on the left... 65, into the number three lane and around another woman driving a non-descript import. *Damn generic cars,* thought Eddie as he cut straight through to the second lane and immediately punched his way through to the daylight he saw back in the fast lane. Backing off the accelerator for the first time in this lane changing sequence... 80,79,78... he smiled.

****

"Honey," announced Eddie with his toothy Jack Nicholson impersonation from *'The Shining,'* "I'm home."

Renee met him at the top of the stairs.

"Tell me everything."

"Sure I will," responded Eddie, "just as soon as the trial is over."

"Oh don't give me that crap. Tell me!"

"Ladies and gentlemen of the jury," began Eddie, reciting Judge Sherman's oft repeated words, "I remind you that you are not to discuss this case with anyone."

"You really can be infuriating. Now come on!"

"Ladies and gentlemen of the jury—I especially admonish you not to discuss this case with spouses who may be second year law students."

"At the count of three," warned Renee, "you'll be eating a frozen T.V. dinner. One..."

"OK, OK."

"You certainly respond well to torture." she said.

"I guess I wouldn't have made a very good spy."

"No you wouldn't. I'm glad our military secrets aren't in your hands... now *talk!*"

"First of all," he began, "I was selected juror number four out of a possible ten thousand applicants."

"Yes, yes, I know that already. What did the man do?"

"How do you know it's a man?" he asked.

"It's always a man."

"Oh is that a fact?"

"Tell me I'm wrong," she offered.

"Well, it just so happens, this gentleman, is charged with murder."

"Oh my God!"

"Yep. It's a gang related killing. Bloods. Crips. Guns. The whole bit."

"Jesus, are you serious?"

"I'm sorry ma'am... we're out of time. Thank you for playing."

"Come on Eddie, tell me... black guy?"

Eddie paused, thought for a moment, but answered her anyway, "Yep."

"Black guy, Compton, gang related. He's guilty," she quipped.

"That's it. You blew it. I'm not saying another word."

"Oh come on!" she pleaded.

"Why would you say he's guilty? That's ridiculous, almost racist."

"No, it's not racist. It's just a statistic. No emotion whatsoever. I believe I first read it in Time magazine, and also, it was used by one of my professors, in a discussion last semester in a criminal law class: 90% of black males arrested are guilty."

"You really had a professor who said that? In law school?"

"Yep. Last semester. Mr. Gibbons."

"No shit. That's a weird thing for a law professor to say."

"Weird or not, he was a great teacher. He said it was just a fact from arrest records, coupled with what the verdict ended up being in their subsequent trial."

"Wow."

"Wow is right," she continued, "It was my Criminal Procedure class. Fascinating stuff. I wish he would have taught another class—I would have taken it whatever it was."

"I bet you would have. You've always liked hanging around with good looking men," he said.

"He actually was a real nerdy guy. Thick glasses and elbow patches on his sport coats. But interesting and brilliant. He really got some lively debates going. He got me thinking that Criminal Law might be something I should pursue."

"Nice when you get an inspirational teacher once in awhile," Eddie said.

"Let me tell you something else I remember from that class. But you're probably not going to like it…"

"If it's about my trial, I don't want to hear it."

"It's not about your trial."

"Should I trust you?" he asked.

"Well, if I remember it correctly, it's about all trials."

"Your professor said something that pertained to *all* trials?"

"Fact is, it wasn't him who said it. He was quoting somebody else, and it was a lead-in to a big discussion we had in class that day."

"I regret to say that you have my attention," he said.

"OK… now as I remember it, Mr. Gibbons was quoting some law professor from Harvard. It was over 10 years ago—I think I remember it being from 1982. I definitely remember his last name—Dershowitz. Oh yeah first name was Alan. Alan Dershowitz."

"Never heard of him," he said. "So what's the big deal with the quote?"

"I memorized it, as I thought it spoke volumes about our legal system. So this professor, Dershowitz, said, '*The defendant wants to hide the truth because he's generally guilty. The defense attorney's job is to make sure the jury does not arrive at that truth.*'"

"Well dammit to hell, Renee! This discussion just ended. I knew I shouldn't talk to you about this!"

"You asked me for the quote, Eddie. Besides, that's a well known quote in some circles. You easily could have found it or been aware of it without my help. Did any of the attorneys, during *voir dire*, ask you if you know the Dershowitz quote?"

"No."

"Well that's my point. If it was so inflammatory, and bias inducing, they would have asked and then excused you from serving. So just relax."

"Well that's some pretty heavy stuff. If he's right, what that means is—"

"What that means is just what I said earlier. Most arrests are justified. They got the right guy."

"Don't you think that—"

She interrupted him again, "At least 90% of the time they got the right guy. So as far as the jury goes—"

Now it was Eddie's turn to interrupt, "Forget it. I've said too much already. We're done here."

"Who are you kidding Eddie? What difference does it make?"

"Hey—it might make no difference, it might make a lot of difference. It's not for me to decide. The judge gave me instructions, and that's all there is to it."

"I'm glad you are taking this seriously. The system would work better if everybody did."

"Thank you. Besides, when you become a famous criminal attorney, would you want your jurors blabbing with their spouses?"

"No, I wouldn't. But this is just you and me talking here."

"Either way. Let's change the subject," he said. "How was your day?"

"I read about a hundred pages. I got up from my desk once—it was the highlight of the day—eating an avocado with a few crackers for lunch. I'm starving."

"Sounds delicious compared to my lunch at the courthouse. Let's throw something on the grill."

Renee wasn't quite ready to end the discussion, but took a step toward the kitchen. She turned back, doing a double-take.

"Hey—where's your watch? I know I saw you put it on this morning."

He held his left arm up, considered his naked wrist. His heart skipped. "Oh my gosh—I was so excited I forgot all about it."

"What the hell? You forgot your Rolex? Have you lost your mind?"

Running back down the stairs into the garage, he fished the watch out from beneath the bucket seat of his car with a smile.

****

The first witness called by the State of California, opening Day 2 of the trial, was a Latino man, a tenant in the Century Palms apartment complex. An interpreter stood next to the witness as he spoke no English. She was middle aged, and wore fake jewelry around her thick neck. Her shoes were badly scuffed.

"As an official court interpreter," instructed Judge Sherman, "you understand that it is your duty to exactly convey every question I ask the witness, and every question either of the attorneys may ask the witness. Do you understand?"

"Si señor."

"Answer in English please."

"Sorry, señor, yes."

At this, Judge Sherman tucked in his chin so he could more effectively glare over the top rim of his glasses at this woman.

"I mean yes sir," she corrected quickly.

"Furthermore," continued the judge, "you must repeat to the court precisely what is answered by the witness. You must not leave out any detail, and just as importantly you must not embellish on any detail. Is that understood?"

"Yes."

"Do you feel you have an adequate command of both English and Spanish to proceed?"

"Yes."

"Bailiff. Please swear in the interpreter."

Cedric Ellis stepped forward, stopping only two feet from the nervous lady. He bellowed, "Please raise your right hand and repeat after me..."

She raised her left hand.

"Excuse me ma'am," said the bailiff. "Your *right* hand."

The woman giggled nervously and switched hands. Judge Sherman winced.

Enrique Chavez answered many routine questions in the tedious, if not comical parroting of questions and answers between himself, the judge, the district attorney, and the interpreter. Eyes oscillated right and left as if the twelve jurors were box seat spectators sitting courtside at Wimbledon.

Chavez occupied a second story corner apartment of The Palms. He lived in Building 2, which overlooked the quad, as well as 128th Street. Crossing the border from Tijuana in the back of an old van when he was a teenager, he performed stoop labor, picking grapes, almonds, and tomatoes in the fields of Central California for nine years. Outside of fruits and vegetables, Enrique's understanding of English was mainly limited to numbers, colors, and automobile parts. But his understanding of survival was far greater. In the time between his initial statement made to the Compton police on the night of Oliver Jefferson's murder, and today's testimony as the first witness called by the prosecution, Enrique had a chance to reflect on the ramifications of being an eyewitness. His reflections were aided in no small part by the message given to him the previous week by a member of Reggie's gang. The subject of the message concerned Enrique's son, Pablo. It conveyed a detailed understanding of Pablo's school schedule and the daily route he took walking home from junior high. Enrique knew Oliver. His death upset him, and he excitedly relayed the details of what he saw that night a year ago to the Hispanic officer who had questioned him. But Enrique feared the Cimarron Avenue Bloods more than he feared the police or the court system. His love for his only son, and the fear instilled by the Bloods outweighed the guilt and outrage he felt over the dead security guard.

This morning, when he unlocked his car door to begin the drive to the courthouse, Enrique found a reminder of the gang's resolve, as well as their reach. There, draped over the bottom arc of the steering wheel of his grey Impala, was a red bandanna. Enrique quickly glanced about the street in all directions, but saw nothing. Nervously, he folded the bandanna, jamming it into his right front pocket. That was only two hours ago. Now, on the witness stand, under direct questioning by the prosecution, he became aware of his own hands sweating profusely. Attempting to dry them by patting his thighs, he felt the disturbing bulge of the bandanna. He caught himself making direct eye contact with the defendant, at which point his memory concerning all that he had witnessed that fateful night failed him.

"Mr. Chavez," pleaded a frustrated Sandra Levinthal, "I have a copy of the police report right here containing your description to the Compton Police of what you saw that night."

"No recuerdo," answered Enrique, after waiting patiently for the translation.

"He doesn't remember," offered the interpreter.

"Mr. Chavez," asked Sandra, "do you have a birth certificate?"

"No intiendo."

"Objection. Relevance," interrupted the Defense.

"Objection sustained," ruled Judge Sherman, as the interpreter frantically attempted translating the interplay to the witness. The judge pounded his gavel as his patience with the interpreter had come to an end. "You shall not repeat or translate objections. You will speak to the witness while translating only those questions asked by me, or by the attorneys. Nothing else. Is that understood?"

"Siento. I'm sorry your honor."

"Proceed, Ms. Levinthal."

"Mr. Chavez, do you remember what you were watching on television on the night in question?"

"Objection. Relevance!" came the immediate response from the defense.

"Overruled. I'll allow this one."

The translator giggled nervously until she was waived onward by the judge to relay the question.

"Si, señora. Fútbol," responded Chavez.

"Yes Madam. Soccer."

"Thank you Mr. Chavez. So you remember what you were watching on television... now please tell the court, what color was the Cadillac driven by the defendant, Reggie Washington, that night?"

Again, the jurors' eyes bounced from attorney to interpreter to witness. "No recuerdo," came the response from Chavez.

"He doesn't remember," repeated the interpreter in English.

"Thank you," said Sandra sarcastically, "I'm sure by this time we all have a pretty good idea what *'no recuerdo'* means. No further questions."

"Does the defense wish to question this witness?" asked Judge Sherman.

"The defense has no questions of this witness your honor."

"Very well. The interpreter is excused. Mr. Chavez, thank you, you are excused as well."

Enrique stepped down from the witness box. It was all the strength he could muster to not look at Reggie. He walked briskly through the courtroom, having already decided he would drive straight to Pablo's school and take him out, under the guise of a dental appointment. The bandanna in his pocket was burning—it was small, a simple 22 inch square of cotton, yet it felt like 10 pounds of molten iron. He spit in it, and discarded it in the first trash can he passed outside the courtroom doors.

"The People may call their next witness."

"Thank you your honor. The People wish to call Raul Hernandez."

Upon hearing the Latino name, Judge Sherman's eyebrows raised.

"Will counsel please approach the bench."

The judge removed his glasses as the two women walked briskly toward his sidebar. "Ms. Levinthal, I trust that we do not need an interpreter for this witness?"

"Mr. Hernandez is a security guard your Honor. He speaks excellent English."

"I'm certainly glad to hear that. I do not want to turn this courtroom into a remedial Spanish class. Is that understood?"

Sandra, reeling from the unexpected memory loss of her first witness, knew that Judge Sherman's comments went deeper than his superficially simple reprimand. Mindful that this judge demanded total control over his courtroom, she could see that he did not appreciate the two minor breakdowns engineered by the inept interpreter.

Sandra did not know that those two hiccups paled in comparison to Judge Sherman's fears that the prosecution had no case. He liked efficiency, while he hated waste. He detested attorneys who wasted the court's time. As a black man, as well as being a greatly experienced and highly respected judge, he was well aware of the troubled streets of inner city Los Angeles. He had zero patience for repeat offenders, even joking at cocktail parties that capital punishment was appropriate for taggers.

In his nightly walks out to his white Jag, the judge generally eschewed the courthouse provided security escort, trusting instead the freshly-oiled Glock and 15-round clip he kept in his shoulder holster.

He knew Sandra Levinthal, knew she was intelligent with a nice future as a trial attorney. He empathized with her current problem, having quickly sized up the situation that Washington's gang had probably gotten to the first witness, Enrique Chavez. But, Judge Sherman did not like surprises; he felt it was unacceptable for any attorney to be surprised.

"Understood your honor," responded Sandra.

Defense attorney Davis, in turn, nodded to the judge, who put his glasses back on. This was taken correctly as a sign for both women to return to their seats.

The district attorney was also correct in assuming that for the most part, the jury did not completely grasp the meaning of Chavez' testimony—and lack thereof.

Eddie Curtain, in seat number four, wasn't sure himself he knew what it meant, thinking it was odd for the prosecution to get such a small amount of information out of their very first witness.

A soccer game on TV? That's it?

His brain would not synthesize until several days later what the barely discernable smile on the face of Reggie Washington meant.

The district attorney knew that the testimony of the next witness was critical. It was very early in the trial, but this was indeed a crucial moment. She needed to let the jury know she had some ammunition to support her strong claims made in yesterday afternoon's opening statements. So far, they had heard only a re-read of a police report—a report which was later rescinded by the same man who offered the information in the first place. She needed to let the judge know immediately that she had a case. She also needed to make the defense fear her…

The defense attorney—that inexperienced court appointed attorney who thus far had skated on a boilerplate opening argument and the misguided conception that the fate of the accused rested in her hands…

But mostly, Sandra knew that the next witness was critical for herself. She needed to further realize her passion. She needed to purge Los Angeles. She needed to purge society of its' Reggie Washingtons.

****

Raul Hernandez had been dreading this day for a long time. He was eager to see justice done. He was eager for revenge—to punish Reggie for the murder of his friend and partner. But for over a year now, Raul could not help feeling that he perhaps was in some way at least partly responsible—that he was somehow negligent. Some small detail he overlooked, or some response on his part that was not up to code or by the book. He spent scores of restless nights, in his mind's eye, replaying the events of that terrible evening.

Sometimes the ending came out differently: Raul would rescue Oliver, jumping out in time to tackle him—pushing him out of harm's way. Sometimes all four of the bullets would miss. Sometimes, the bullets all ended up in his own shoulders and back as he protected his friend by shielding him with his own body. In one version, Raul was able to race out from between the buildings in time to shoot the driver of the Cadillac. In an extended version of that scenario, he stood proudly, side by side with his partner, he and Oliver surveying the spattered blood and brain matter that decorated the inside windshield of the El Dorado, after they had both emptied their pistol magazines into the face and head of Reggie.

But, on most of the particularly bad nights, the nights when he ultimately found himself unable to run fast enough to alter the ending, he drank Cuervo until he passed out.

This morning, while standing in the back of the elevator up to the courtroom, he wondered for the thousandth time...

Should I have left my partner alone when I ran to make that phone call to the Compton Police? Should we have gone together? Was I responsible for not being able to talk Oliver out of his naive attempt at reasoning with the gang members? Did Oliver die because I did not put new batteries in the walkie-talkie?

Raul was sure that some smart lawyer would question his actions. He was certain that in some small way, he must inevitably share in the blame for Oliver's death. He cursed his stupidity for ever wanting to be a security guard. He longed for the simplicity—the pleasant boredom—of working back in the old taco stand.

Hernandez held up quite well to the direct questioning put to him by the district attorney. At first, he was perceived by all who were present in the courtroom as being visibly nervous. But in the course of the two hour testimony he began to lose some of his intense self-consciousness. Mostly, this was due to the brilliant path he was led down by the prosecutor. The lawyer and witness were able to rehearse this part of the play in the weeks prior to the trial, but Sandra was well aware of the difference between question and answer sessions in a comfortable office, from that of an actual courtroom. Identical questions could often evoke entirely different answers with many intangible factors contributing to the changes. One was an intimidating judge. Another was when a wildly pounding heart was thrown into the mix. Even when the words in the answers were the same, the body language of a squirming, fidgeting, or very slightly stuttering witness could cause an astute juror to read between the lines. She had seen some very cool characters choke on simple questions such as the color of a house, or what they had for breakfast. She had seen seasoned businessmen unable to stop that one bead of sweat which unfortunately dripped down the left side—the jury's side—of their brow. Often, innocent defendants, even witnesses with nothing at stake whatsoever, could not control the foreign, nervous voice that emanated from out of the same chest that contained that fickle, palpitating heart.

The tedious rehearsals tended to mitigate the anxiety, albeit, not completely. As anxious as she was herself, Sandra walked over to her chair, and sat—pleased that she had come through under pressure. She did not feel the pressure as originating from the judge. It did not come from her superiors, or the L.A.P.D. police captain or the many detectives who were familiar with Reggie's resume. It came from within. She put this pressure on herself. And now, she was content that she was well on track toward a favorable outcome. She had been able to raise the confidence level of the witness by cleverly asking a pattern of simple and obvious questions followed by a question wherein Hernandez could channel his excitement into the testimony. She knew from fleeting glances at the jury that they were soaking up the testimony offered by Hernandez. She had achieved her goal in having this witness convey the absolute horror that culminated in his running up to and ultimately standing over his dying partner. She could not have transferred the knowledge any clearer, as through her questions and Hernandez' story, she achieved the perfect empathetic situation. The jury saw what he saw: the bewildered look in Oliver's eyes, as he looked up at Raul at the very last moment of his life, while the dark red blood gurgled out of his throat and onto the white concrete.

"I have no further questions for the witness at this time your honor," said the district attorney.

"Very well," replied Judge Sherman. "It's almost 12:30 now. Mr. Hernandez, I admonish you, as well as you, ladies and gentlemen of the jury not to discuss this case with anyone, including yourselves. Have a nice lunch, and we'll see you all back here at precisely 1:30."

Eddie sat motionless.

Jesus—I've just heard a true story of how a guy witnessed his buddy getting blown away—saw his partner's blood and bones coming out from his bullet wounds... and I can't talk about it to anybody! And now I'm supposed to go out and have a nice lunch? Sure Judge... whatever you say...

Seats in the jury box swiveled, and uncomfortable glances were exchanged for a brief moment until juror number two stood. Darryl Rollins had served on several other panels; he knew the drill, and had perfected the ability to switch gears.

"See everybody later. I'm off to the new Wendy's down the street."

Eddie stood and followed the others out of the courtroom. He suppressed the urge to call his wife to tell her about the morning. He already felt guilty about sharing the basic points of the trial with her last night.

****

At precisely 1:30, Judge Sherman began the afternoon session. "Mr. Hernandez, I'd like to remind you that you are under oath."

He nodded to Rosemary Davis in a signal for her to begin the cross examination. The defense attorney whispered something in the right ear of Reggie Washington, looked at her notes, and slowly approached the witness box where Raul anxiously waited.

"Good afternoon, Mr. Hernandez."

"Good afternoon."

"How old are you Mr. Hernandez?"

"46," answered Raul.

"And how tall are you?"

"About five two and a half."

"Mr. Hernandez, are you overweight?"

"Objection your honor," blurted out the district attorney.

"Sustained."

"Mr. Hernandez," she rephrased, "how much do you weigh?"

"A little over 200 pounds," answered Raul.

"Isn't it closer to 240 or 250?" asked Davis.

"Asked and answered, your honor," objected the prosecution.

"Sustained. Jury to disregard. Ms. Davis, please make your point."

"Thank you your honor. I'm just trying to establish the fact that Raul Hernandez is physically out of shape. The normal weight range for a man of his height and age is 140-160 pounds.

"Mr. Hernandez, would you consider yourself to be in top physical condition?"

"No, I guess I'm not. But who is?"

A few members of the jury chuckled audibly.

"I'll leave that unanswered for the moment, Mr. Hernandez. Please tell the court, if you will, are there certain guidelines for physical training of security guards such as yourself?"

"Yeah, there's a manual."

"Have you read it recently Mr. Hernandez?"

"I've read it."

"When did you read it?"

"When I got hired. There was a written test."

"Is it true that that was over 13 years ago Mr. Hernandez?"

"I guess."

"Is that a yes or no, sir?"

"I believe—uh—yes," answered Raul, getting visibly shook. Davis momentarily thought of pushing the point, but decided to wait. She picked up a small green pamphlet. "I have here a copy of the *'Security Guard's Handbook'* which I believe is the book you were given the test on—that was provided by the Century Palms. Does this booklet look familiar Mr. Hernandez?"

"Yes."

"Good. Now please allow me to read from the section on physical conditioning. *'...furthermore, all officers are required to maintain such reasonable physical conditioning so as to optimize the response times to various situations. Additionally, basic quickness, reaction, and strength must be maintained in order to increase the chances of properly executing the appropriate response depending on the situation...*

"Let's see," she continued, "it goes on to say, '...*the following weekly exercise routine is recommended in keeping with minimum physical conditioning standards...*'

"Does this sound familiar Mr. Hernandez?"

"Yes."

"The pamphlet lists here those minimum weekly requirements: '...*running 2 miles each week, 35 pushups every other day, 50 situps, chinups, toe touching...*' Mr. Hernandez, can you please tell the court—when was the last time you ran two miles?"

"I can't remember," he answered softly.

"Can you remember perhaps the last time you tried to touch your toes?"

"Objection! Your Honor, clearly she is badgering—"

The Defense Attorney responded before the judge, "We're not talking about training for the Marines or the Navy Seals here your honor—we are merely establishing the basic—"

"Sustained. It's been established. Now move along Ms. Davis."

"Thank you your honor." The defense attorney put down the pamphlet. "OK, let's switch gears a bit—back to the night in question, when you and Mr. Jefferson were on watch. Please tell the court your usual routine, and how that night was different."

As Hernandez began his recital, the district attorney was relieved at the open ended question. The prosecution knew there were no real skeletons that would surface in the testimony of Raul Hernandez. Sandra feared only that Raul might stumble from his own nervousness and create doubt in the minds of a few jurors as to his reliability. She felt the defense was beginning to break Raul—with the steady questions pertaining to the sensitive issue of his weight—but she also felt that Ms. Davis, with her latest query, had just made a huge mistake. And now, Davis would lose a point with the jury as she would be forced to interrupt Raul's gripping story.

"We were making our normal rounds that night," said Raul. "We had stopped to chat with the old man in Building 5—the tenant in apartment number 511. He often flagged us down to discuss a problem, with his apartment unit, or with the grounds, but it always turned out to be nothing. We pretty much ended every discussion with him by me and Oliver trying to explain the difference between security and maintenance. Then, I guess, we were alarmed at first, because the guys out front were shooting a basketball. We reacted by immediately running—"

Davis abruptly interrupted him, "Wait just a moment Mr. Hernandez—are you telling us that you reacted in this fashion just because some of the tenants were shooting baskets?"

"No. They weren't playing basketball. They were shooting basketballs."

"I don't understand."

"I mean really *shooting* the ball. You know—with a gun."

CHAPTER 7 - The Compass

October 19, 1993
Palos Verdes, California

That night, Renee again prodded Eddie for information about the trial.

"Come on," she begged, "tell me about the witnesses. Did you believe them?"

"Sorry ma'am. Can't do that."

"How about the judge? And the attorneys? Are they male or female?"

"Are you going to try and torture me again?" he asked.

"I hope for your sake it doesn't have to come to that."

"OK... Black judge. A man. Both attorneys are women. The D.A. is white, and the defense attorney is black."

"Two women lawyers," she mused. "I like that."

"I figured you would. They don't know it yet, but both of their jobs are in jeopardy as soon as you pass the bar."

"Don't get me thinking about the bar exam. It tends to put me in a bad mood. Now tell me about the trial. How did it start? What were their opening statements? Were they good? Who was the first witness?"

Looking at his watch, "Sorry folks—I know you've all been quite patient. But Air Force One is waiting. Now that I've found my Rolex, I realize we've only got time for one more question. Let's see, yes you—the pretty lady in the yellow dress in front..."

"How did the trial start, Mr. President?"

"It started with an interpreter."

"Really?" she asked.

"The first witness spoke only Spanish, so they swore in an interpreter. But the interpreter didn't seem to speak English all that well either. She didn't know her left hand from her right."

"You're kidding."

"Nope."

"That's ridiculous."

"It appears that the judge agrees with you."

****

The former Palms security guard, Raul Hernandez, returned to the stand to begin the second day of the trial. The judge reminded him that he was still under oath as the district attorney took another turn questioning the witness.

"Good morning, Mr. Hernandez," began Sandra Levinthal on redirect. "You made reference yesterday to the basketball incident. How many people were involved at this time?"

"Well, I recognized Marcus and Jimmy. They both live in Building 4. There was Big Leon—who didn't live at The Palms, but he hung out there all the time—so that's three. And maybe three or four others. So maybe only six or seven guys when we first got there, but real quickly it seemed that it became a much larger group."

"Can you describe what they were doing?" she asked.

"It was real loud. They were partying and carrying on..."

"Excuse me, please back up a second—what do you mean it was loud... from the earlier gunshots?"

"Well, the first shot was what made us start running to the area. We were sort of on our way to check it out anyway because we got a few reports of the noise."

"What kind of noise, Mr. Hernandez?"

"Real loud stereos blasting."

"You stated there were about six or seven people there—you said the names Marcus, Jimmy and Leon, but you didn't mention the defendant. Did you ever see Mr. Washington?"

"Sure I saw him. There were six or seven guys, Jimmy's gang, just on our side of the street. He—Reggie—was hanging out with all the gangbangers across the street."

"How do you know they were gang members?"

"I could see their colors. It was the Bloods." He pointed at the defendant. "I could see Reggie sittin' in his car wearing his red bandanna."

"I wear a bandanna to aerobics class, Mr. Hernandez. That doesn't make me a gang member."

"You wouldn't want to be wearing a bandanna in this neighborhood, ma'am."

"Thanks for the advice Mr. Hernandez. I'll keep that in mind."

Even Judge Sherman smiled.

"Let's back up a moment… please tell us more about when you and Oliver Jefferson arrived to the front of the property."

"Well, like I said—it was very loud and real confusing."

"Why was it confusing?"

"That music. It was getting everybody real riled up. The rap stuff."

"What was playing?"

Raul paused for a second before answering softly, "You know, typical rap songs."

"What songs specifically?"

Raul put his hand up to his face, in attempt to dampen the volume of his answer, "Niggers with an attitude."

The defense attorney bolted up from her seat. "I must object your honor. Obviously this witness—"

Judge Sherman's eyes bulged upon hearing the racial slur. The intensely derogatory phrase left him with his own objection. "Mr. Hernandez, let me remind you that you are in a court of law, and you should respect it as such when answering the—"

"But I do respect the court sir... I, I am answering the question, your honor."

Judge Sherman was caught in a rare moment of being incredulous. Plus—he had very little experience being interrupted in his own courtroom. "Excuse me?" queried the judge.

"N.W.A.—Niggers With an Attitude. That's the name of the group."

"You mean the gang, Mr. Hernandez?" asked the judge.

"No sir," answered Raul. "The group—the band."

Judge Sherman held his left hand over his own mouth and chin for a moment. He blinked forcefully, before he took his hand down. "You may proceed with redirect Ms. Levinthal."

"Thank you, your honor."

Two of the younger black jurors, who were familiar with the group and music of N.W.A., chuckled. Eddie, who was watching intently from the jury box, wanted to scream at the pure entertainment value of what he was watching.

"So, '*Niggers With an Attitude*' is the name of a *band*?" Sandra asked—her voice slightly unsteady, slightly softer—at the uncomfortable pronunciation of the word '*niggers*.'

"Is that correct?"

"Yeah. I guess they are a popular rap group with the gang guys."

"Why do you say that?" she asked.

"Well, it's the words they use," answered Raul. "There's a lot of profanity and stuff. It's straight outa Compton. It can get the guys pretty jacked up. I think they call it 'gangsta-rap'."

"Sorry," interrupted Sandra, "you just said *straight outa Compton.* ' What do you mean? Why did you say that?"

"Uh—I'm not 100% sure, but I think that's the name of the most popular song or maybe the album they keep playin' all the time."

"Were you able to hear the lyrics that were in the songs that night?"

"Yeah."

Rosemary Davis again rose from her chair. "I must object again your honor. Of what possible relevance do songs and bands and lyrics have to the case at hand?"

At this point, Judge Sherman's own curiosity was piqued. He needed to hear more of this bizarre testimony.

"I'll allow it."

The district attorney asked again, "Please tell the court what you were able to hear from the stereo Mr. Hernandez."

Afraid to offend the judge, Raul paused. He looked down at the microphone, but turned his mouth slightly to the side, muttering softly, "Fuck the police."

The previously incessant typing from the court stenographer stopped. When the rhythmic clicking of the keys was suddenly broken, the silence of the steno machine caught people's attention as much as what they thought they just heard.

The court reporter looked up. Eddie was unsure if it was because the lady hadn't heard Hernandez, or—that she had heard him—but was reluctant to type the profane phrase.

The prosecutor made quick eye-contact with the judge, who gave her a miniscule nod. "Excuse me," she said, "some of us couldn't hear you. Could you please repeat that for us?"

Now, Raul leaned forward, directly into the microphone, "Fuck the police." This time, he said it loudly and clearly. He looked around, surprised that nobody objected or interrupted him. "They were saying stuff like 'fuck the police.' Then they were sort of yelling—you know sort of chanting it together."

"And what else did you hear?" she asked.

"Well, like I said there was a lot going on. It was loud and confusing, and the rap sounds were coming from the guys in front, and from another stereo from the car across the street."

"What did you hear from across the street?"

"You mean the words?" he asked.

"Yes."

"You want me to tell you more of the actual words I heard?"

"Please, Mr. Hernandez."

Raul was shocked at the request. He was uncomfortable, but he understood they really wanted more. "It was more stuff like 'fuck the police,' and 'kill the cops.' Stuff about raping bitches and cock sizes."

Eddie thought back for a moment about what his wife had said the other night. Something about a courtroom often being the cure for insomnia.

I doubt anybody is sleeping through this…

"So was the same rap music coming from the car, as the stereo from the guys on the property—by property, I mean The Palms?"

"I don't know. That rap stuff is real confusing anyway. There was the boom box from the Datsun, that they kept turning louder, and also the sounds coming from the Cadillac. Plus, by this time a lot of the guys were singing and yelling along. So some of it was from one stereo, some from another across the street. A lot of it was hard to tell if it was the music from the tape—I mean the CD's, or real life—you know—the gang guys singing along and yelling."

"Wait just a moment Mr. Hernandez. Please back up a bit. You just said music was coming from a Cadillac as well as from a Datsun?"

"Oh, sorry—the big boom box was sitting on top of the roof of the yellow Datsun. Maybe it was orange. Everything looks orange under those weird streetlights. I think it belonged to Leon."

"You mean the car belonged to Leon?" asked Sandra.

"No. I think the Datsun belonged to Mrs. Jackson, the old lady who lives in 421. That's upstairs in Building 4. She was probably asleep. The boom box belonged to Leon."

"Objection your honor," announced the defense, "calls for speculation."

"Sustained," answered the judge.

Eddie wondered if the objection was over Mrs. Jackson's car, where she lived, that she was probably asleep, or Leon's boom box. At least for now, it went unclarified. The pace was furious, and he loved it.

"Back up again please, Mr. Hernandez. You said a moment ago, *'everything looks orange under those weird streetlights,'* correct?

"Yes."

"But, earlier you also said the driver of the Cadillac had on a red bandanna. Correct?"

"That's right," he answered.

"How can you be so sure?"

"It was a red bandanna." For perhaps the first time, Hernandez showed real confidence in his answer. "That dude, I mean Reggie, always wears a red bandanna. To tell the truth, yesterday and today here in this court, are the only times I've ever seen him without it."

"So you've seen him many times around the Century Palms Apartments?"

"Yes. Always in his car—that brown Cadillac."

"And you're absolutely certain it was the defendant?"

"Objection your honor!" blurted out defense attorney Davis again. "Asked and answered!"

"Sustained," ruled the judge. "Let's move on Ms. Levinthal."

Reluctantly complying, Sandra changed gears. "Were any of the guys from across the street talking to you or saying anything to you and Oliver?"

"Yeah."

"What were they saying?"

"Just a lot of stuff about 'fuck the police' and 'we're takin' back our 'hood.' Mostly just 'fuck the police' over and over. It got crazy, like I said, even telling the stuff on tape from the real stuff that the guys were yelling."

Ms. Davis stood again. "Your honor, I must object again to the relevance of this line of questioning. What does music have to do with this case? Haven't we heard enough of this profanity to get the idea?"

"I too am beginning to wonder if my courtroom has turned into a porn shop." The judge motioned to the district attorney. "Do *The People* wish to make a point?"

"Yes, thank you your honor," answered Levinthal. "I believe this testimony all goes directly to the state of mind of the defendant—to the specific atmosphere at the time of the killing. I do apologize to the court for the language."

"Very well," he said. "I'll allow you one more question along these lines, and then we'll move on."

"Thank you, your honor. Mr. Hernandez, you mentioned in your testimony yesterday that your partner, Oliver Jefferson, tried to be diplomatic in talking with the guys in front—some of whom were tenants who you knew—on your side of the street. You said he tried to talk them nicely into turning down the volume. How did they respond?"

"They said, 'Fuck you.'"

****

During a short recess, Eddie found a pay-phone and called his office. He talked to his production manager, Bella, who informed him of a couple of minor problems that needed his attention. Also, the sewing operators were behind schedule in finishing up a fairly large order for dresses. On another order, the color of the fabric was inconsistent from roll to roll.

"I'm telling you Eddie," she said, "you know the Garden print that we just got in from Japan?"

"Yeah..."

"Well, it's supposed to have bright red flowers—it does have bright red flowers, but..."

"Get to the point—please Bella—I don't have much time here."

"The rolls have red flowers some of the time, and then all of a sudden they kind of change to sort of orange-ish."

"What the hell do you mean 'change to orange-ish?' You know as well as I do that orange is the worst color in the entire world of fashion this season."

"Well, I guess it's not all of a sudden, that is unless you don't look up for a while."

"Isabella, you're driving me crazy. Speak English please."

"I'm trying. Please, just listen to me, Eddie." She had worked for him for eleven years, and knew he tended to switch to calling her Isabella when he was beginning to lose his patience. And for Eddie, losing his patience could sometimes be a precursor to him losing his temper. "It's more of a sort of a gradual change of the print that occurs in the middle of the roll. When we're spreading the fabric out along the cutting table, each roll starts out with bright red flowers. Then, after we get about 25 yards into the roll—after 10-15 layers are spread, the flowers look orange. But it's real gradual."

"Look, I can't pretend I'm following what the heck you are saying. And—I've really got to go. You'll just have to deal with it. Call the fabric rep, call the mill, do whatever. I know you can handle it."

"But Eddie there's—"

He cut her off, "They are waving the jury back in. I've got to hang up now. Handle it."

His mind could not manage shifting gears into his usual production problems. He was sorry he checked in.

Can't she solve a simple problem without me? Can't she just say, 'Everything's perfect. Have a nice day.'

At least they didn't cut the fabric yet. Now that would be a real disaster…

****

For nearly 40 minutes, the district attorney questioned Hernandez. Before finishing, she walked toward the front of the courtroom.

"I'd like to introduce People's Exhibit 1."

The petite woman carried a cumbersome white artboard and placed it on the easel next to the witness stand. Measuring 30 inches by 40 inches, the cardboard was a little too large for the flimsy aluminum easel. As Sandra turned to walk back to her notes at the attorney's table—the poster board silently fell face forward onto the floor.

"As we can plainly see from this exhibit..."

She swirled around quickly as the audible laughter from a few jurors startled her.

Eddie was starting to like Sandra, although at this moment, he felt embarrassed for her. He saw a large grin sweep across the defendant's face. He noted how perfect Reggie's teeth seemed to be, how incongruous they were—occupying the same face that displayed those menacing unbalanced eyes.

Sandra smiled at her own faux pas and walked back toward the fallen exhibit. Picking it up, she leaned it on the floor—against the easel.

"Can you see this from where you sit, Mr. Hernandez?"

Raul leaned far forward in his seat. A few members of the jury in the back row craned their necks to get a better vantage point of the exhibit—the first visual aid of the trial.

"I guess so," Raul stood up in the witness box, "from here."

Judge Sherman spoke. "Mr. Ellis, let's see if we can come up with some masking tape or something to help Ms. Levinthal here. I hope a small roll of tape is still in the County of Los Angeles' budget somewhere."

The bailiff looked through several drawers in a desk behind the stenographer. He didn't find any tape, but with a bit of string, some scissors to poke holes in the upper corners of the D.A.'s exhibit, and a few jumbo-sized binder clips, he was able to adequately hang the exhibit from the easel.

"Can the jury see the exhibit clearly?" Judge Sherman asked. A dozen heads nodded in affirmation—like bobbleheads jiggling their oversized heads in the rear window of cars from another era.

"Good work bailiff."

"All part of the job your honor," he bellowed.

The judge smiled as a moment of comic relief laughter filled the courtroom. Eddie was also amused—but more than that, he was impressed at the terrific relationship these two had obviously developed over the years.

The layout of the apartment complex dominated the board which also depicted the surrounding streets and neighborhood.

Sandra thanked the bailiff, and began again. "Mr. Hernandez, can you please describe for the jury what we are looking at?"

"Well, that looks like the Century Palms apartment complex where I used to work as a guard. There's the six buildings, and the quad that separates them. That's Regent Park—the park across the street from The Palms—and there's 128th Street, and of course Century Blvd."

"Mr. Hernandez, I wonder if you might step down and help mark a couple of key places for me..."

Raul looked up at the Judge, who nodded his approval for the request, and walked the few short steps to where Sandra stood by the exhibit.

Eddie noticed for the first time how overweight Raul seemed to be. The wrinkles between the buttons on his khaki shirt strained over his large belly—revealing a white t-shirt underneath. He waddled slowly into position.

"Mr. Hernandez, I'm going to ask you to place these little yellow stickers in various positions on the exhibit. Please place them as accurately as possible. Can you put this first sticker in the place where, when you initially arrived to the front of the property, you saw the group on your side of the street was gathered?"

Raul took the nickel sized yellow sticker, and positioned it carefully in front of Building 2.

"Thank you. Now please place this second sticker at the spot where you recall the defendant was sitting in his car."

Raul saw that the word 'Cadillac' was next to the small rectangle in the spot where he wanted to put the sticker. "Is that Reggie's Cadillac?" he asked.

"Objection," came the predictable outcry from the defense attorney. Ms. Davis rose from her seat and pointed sharply at the easel. "She is leading the witness with this exhibit."

"Sustained," ruled the judge.

"Allow me to rephrase. Does this look like the spot where you saw the brown Cadillac parked?" she asked.

"Yes."

"Was the defendant sitting in the driver's seat of the Cadillac?"

"Yes."

"Please place the yellow sticker in the spot where you recall first seeing him."

He placed the sticker in the center of the rectangle that represented the parked car.

PEOPLE'S EXHIBIT 1

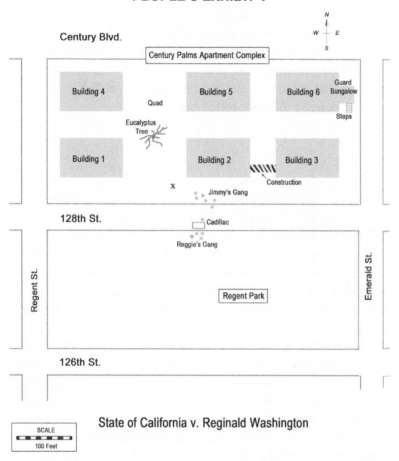

State of California v. Reginald Washington

There was a small black X marked on the sidewalk of the exhibit. Sandra did not know whether or not this X was visible to the jury. She glanced quickly up at the judge, and then back at her notes, thinking on the fly to carefully change the wording of her next question.

"Regardless of any markings whatsoever on this exhibit, will you please place this red sticker on the spot where Oliver Jefferson lay dead on the ground after being shot..."

Two jurors in the back row stood to improve their angle of view. Though he could see fine, Eddie also stood. Raul carefully placed the red dot right next to the small X.

The defense attorney rolled her eyes.

****

The prosecuting attorney had Raul place a total of nine stickers in various key positions on the exhibit. She had him answer dozens of carefully worded questions pertaining to the night of the killing. She methodically extracted testimony from him—having him pinpoint his position during various pivotal moments prior to the shooting—including exactly where he made the call in the bungalow, and hurried back out to his partner—how he broke into a sprint when hearing the first shot, and his vantage point after he turned the corner of Building 2 into the quad where he claimed he was able to see Oliver fall from the fatal fourth and final bullet. After answering her questions up to and including the time of arrival of the Compton Police, Sandra announced that she was done questioning the partner of the murdered man.

Raul was relieved. He began to follow her away from the witness box. Sheepish about making eye contact with the jury on his left, he instead focused on the escape offered by those large double doors at the rear of the courtroom. He walked briskly toward them, until he reached the low swinging gate separating the gallery. He stopped upon hearing the Judge's voice.

"Excuse me—Mr. Hernandez—I may be mistaken, but I have a feeling that the defense would like to ask you a question or two. Ms. Davis?"

"Thank you your honor. We would in fact like to cross examine Mr. Hernandez."

Raul took his hand from the low gate, turned, and pointed quizzically at the witness box. The judge nodded. This time, he made the mistake of looking directly at the faces of the jury as he passed. About half and half: male and female. Several blacks, a couple of whites and Latinos. Maybe an Asian or two. His severe self-consciousness surfaced once again.

All these strangers are looking at me! They better believe me—Oliver is dead—Reggie, shot him! Now they're all smiling at me! Even that bastardo, Reggie! I know what they are all thinking. 'Dumb Mexican.' I just know it...

Raul stepped up and took the familiar seat in the witness box.

What is this now—the third time I've been up here? The fourth? That cunt lawyer asking me all those stupid questions about exercise and my weight, yesterday...

In rehashing his testimony and the events of the day to his wife last night—he had omitted that part.

...now this bitch wants to ask me some more questions...

He could not go through it again. His many alternate endings to the tragic death of his friend flashed in jumbled sequences in his mind. Were they just dreams? Daydreams?

Nightmares? Reality—or—merely his version of it? He was tired of the complicated questions by everybody in this courtroom. He was tired of being confused. Mostly, he was tired from reliving the worst day of his life in such exhausting detail.

But the merciless onslaught began anew.

"Mr. Hernandez, you claim you had left your partner to make the call to the police... is that correct?"

Why the fuck do you phrase it like that? '...left your partner?' It's almost like I'm the one being accused! You weren't there—you don't know what it was like... I was there that night! These are real bad dudes. Jimmy's gang is bad enough. But Reggie's guys—The Bloods—they're the worst! And by now—there were like 20 of them! And they had guns!

He somehow suppressed the urge to curse at her. His mind left the courtroom. His eyes looked out at the defense attorney, but she was invisible; Raul looked right through her, toward the rear of the courtroom again. But those large wooden doors were part of a mirage; the doors had become the cupboards of his small apartment. He pictured himself standing in front of the broken tile countertop in his kitchen. Just as he saw through the defense attorney, he was able to see through the white painted cupboard—where, on the top left pine wood shelf, there rested a golden bottle of Tequila.

"Mr. Hernandez?" the attorney asked.

Judge Sherman also detected the uncomfortable delay in responding to the question, "Mr. Hernandez, are you all right?"

Like one of those Stereo Viewmaster 3D viewers from the '60's, hitting the big white lever to change the picture, Raul blinked his eyes deliberately as if to snap away the image of the bottle.

"…as I said, Oliver wanted to stay in front of the building. He thought he could..."

"Mr. Hernandez, please just answer yes or no," instructed Davis.

Raul could almost taste the soothing comfort of a small glass of Cuervo. One ice-cube to cool the entry of the alcohol into the bloodstream. That smell. That incredible fermented, musky agave smell. Nothing in the world smells like that.

He swallowed, imagining the cold tequila of his mirage swirling around the roof of his mouth and tongue, while hating the reality of the taste of his own sour saliva.

"Uhh, could you please repeat the question?" he asked meekly.

Methodically, Ms. Davis asked him again, "Did you leave your partner to make the call to the police?"

Raul preceded his answer with a slight cough, "Yes."

"So, Oliver Jefferson remained behind on the sidewalk in front of the building during this—what you referred to earlier in your testimony as—'confusion.' Is that correct?"

"Yes."

"Thank you. Now I'm asking you this because it's really important that we establish an accurate timeline. I know how you must feel going over and over these many details, and I'm truly sorry about your partner. But I want to be real clear about the events in question."

Eddie felt she was buttering him up for something. She was too sincere, too friendly, and it didn't fit. Plus, he had learned a long time ago, in business, and certainly in life, that whenever you hear either the word *'apologize'* or *'sorry,'* shortly followed by the word *'but,'* that you needed to be on your guard; something was insincere. Something was rotten.

Besides, what events are in question?

"Mr. Hernandez, the police report says the call came in at 10:35 that evening. Does that sound about right?"

"I remember—it was exactly 10:35."

"You sound quite certain. How can you be so sure?" asked Davis.

"The phone on the desk is right next to the time-clock in the bungalow—the guard office. I have a habit of sometimes punching the clock with a scrap of scratch paper while I'm on the phone..."

Now, for some reason, Raul's mind flashed to his many years punching time-clocks thousands of times, back at Tito's Tacos. He loved that quick thud—that jolt the little device made—like a nail gun. He had to use the Viewmaster again, to blink away that image as well. To refocus.

"Well—I did it that night—punch the time clock I mean. The stamp read: Twenty-Two-Thirty-Five and no seconds, in military time... Oliver taught me how to understand military time, he was a sergeant, in Vietnam, I mean, so... that's 10:35 PM exactly."

"Exactly 10:35. Thank you. Your honor, I'd like to enter into evidence Defense Exhibit A." The bailiff came over to take a clear bag containing the small yellow Post-It Note. It was stamped in blue ink with the date: 101592, while the time: 223500, was printed below in red ink. She continued, "We might as well use People's Exhibit 1, as long as it's up here.

Now the space between Building 2 and Building 3 is blocked off—as you explained earlier—due to the construction. In fact you placed a yellow dot there earlier—isn't that correct?"

"Yes."

"OK. So you couldn't run through the construction, correct?"

"That's right."

"So when you ran, after hearing the shots..."

"Objection," shouted the D.A. "She's putting words in his mouth."

"Words?" said the judge. "Exactly which words do we have a problem with?"

"He said he was already running—not running '*after*' the shots," answered Levinthal.

"Will the stenographer please read back the appropriate line," asked Judge Sherman.

Eddie leaned forward in his seat...

Jesus! I sure didn't catch that. And I thought I was following along pretty closely!

The stenographer began to carefully re-read the earlier transcript, "Question from the People by Ms. Levinthal: 'Please explain precisely what happened when you were on the phone with the Compton Sherriff.'

"Answer from the witness: 'I heard the shots and I began running, after, when I rounded the building...'

"Wait! Stop right there please," interrupted the district attorney.

But it could still be interpreted two ways!

"Let's please clarify, Mr. Hernandez," asked defense attorney Davis. "Were you already running, or did you begin running after the shots?"

"Your Honor! I must object again," said Sandra.

"Mr. Hernandez," asked the judge, "will you please explain?"

"OK... I think I started running after the first shot. Yeah... I'm sure I did. I definitely wasn't running before the first shot, because I was in the office—on the phone when I heard it."

"Go on."

"There were two quick shots in succession. Then a gap when I started running. Then the third shot. Then another little gap, and then the last shot when I rounded the corner of Building 2."

"*When* you rounded the corner, or *after* you rounded the corner?" asked Davis.

"Objection again your honor! She keeps putting words in the mouth of this witness."

"I'll allow this one, but be careful Ms. Davis," said Judge Sherman. "Mr. Hernandez?"

"Uh, what?" Raul was unable to follow.

"Mr. Hernandez," the defense attorney asked, "you still say you got to the quad area in time to see the fourth and final shot... is that correct?"

"Yeah. I saw Oliver go down."

"Are you saying that you witnessed Mr. Washington shoot Mr. Jefferson from the Cadillac?"

"Yes."

"And you are quite sure you didn't miss the fourth and final shot—that you didn't just assume it came from the Cadillac when you saw your partner fall—as you said yourself in earlier testimony that you already knew there was at least one other gun at the scene. Isn't it possible that the shot that killed Oliver Jefferson came from one of the boys in front of the building, and not from Reggie Washington's Cadillac?"

"No," said Raul.

"No, you're not sure?"

"No, I didn't miss the final shot. Yes I'm sure I saw it. It came from the Cadillac."

"But Mr. Hernandez, you also said earlier, that on your first patrol to check out the street scene, before you ran back to the guard bungalow, that you saw smoke. That there was white smoke from some substance the gang members were smoking by the Cadillac. Do you remember your testimony from yesterday? Do you want the stenographer to read for us your testimony again?"

"Yes."

"Yes, you want her to read it again?"

"No, she doesn't have to read it again. I remember—yes—I saw smoke earlier."

"Good. Now, then, isn't it possible that the smoke from a bong, or a crack pipe or even a cigar, for that matter, so whatever it was that you saw—that emanated from the windows of the car or from the men standing by the car—was actually what you saw—and not smoke from a gun?"

"Objection your honor! Asked and answered!" shouted Sandra.

"Overruled," said the Judge. "Mr. Hernandez, please answer…"

"I did see smoke earlier—from the car windows and the dope pipe across the street. Later, after the car moved, I saw different smoke. It was from the gun."

"What do you mean *'different'* smoke?"

"I don't know. Just different."

The defense attorney picked up the wooden pointer and started stabbing at the exhibit.

"The Compton Police said they stopped Reggie Washington in his vehicle at 10:39 PM at the corner of 126th and Vermont. Mr. Washington was driving a brown Cadillac. That has been so stipulated—it is not in dispute. But that huge car—a 1967 El Dorado—could not possibly negotiate two ninety degree turns at more than 40 miles per hour. Not in these narrow streets."

She smacked the tip of the pointer down on 126th & then Regent. "So, there were two full minutes between 10:35, and 10:37, when the vehicle traveled six tenths of a mile, from point A, driving West, in front of the apartment building, to point B, at the corner of 128th and Regent where he turned South—onto point C—one quarter of a mile away—where at point D he made the second turn—a right onto 126th Street. He was stopped just before Vermont, another half-mile away, by the police at a point about here—just outside the exhibit."

"I don't blame you if this is a lot of information, or if this is perhaps confusing to you. Let me simplify. What this means is this: the car could not have been going *slower* than 25 miles per hour at any point—Between A and B—the street in front of the apartment—or it would never have made it to where the police stopped him at 10:39!"

Miss Davis saw that she had achieved exactly what she wanted—which was the complete attention of each of the twelve jurors—but this was mitigated slightly as she also noted confused faces on a few of them. Anticipating this, she was already prepared to clarify.

"What all of this means, is that even if you, Mr. Hernandez, started running at the moment you heard the first shot, and even if that moment was as early as 10:35 on the nose—so you dropped that little scrap of yellow paper that is now Exhibit A—and started running as fast as you could—you would have had to cover the distance on foot—down the steps of the bungalow—running between the corridor formed by the four buildings—you said yourself you could not cut between Buildings 2 and 3 because of the construction... The distance from the steps of the bungalow to the absolute first point at the corner of the quad that allows a line of sight to the street is just over 100 yards. In fact, we have measured the distance to be 104 yards, and one foot...

"Mr. Hernandez, just a few years ago, in the 1984 Olympics at the Coliseum—right here in Los Angeles—in fact only a few miles away from this very courtroom where we are all gathered—Carl Lewis, the 'World's Fastest Human,' won the Gold Medal, by running the 100 meter dash in just under 10 seconds. And now are you are telling this jury that you—just last year at the age of 45—being more than 50 pounds overweight—covered a similar distance in 9 seconds?"

"Objection!" shouted the prosecution.

"Ms. Davis, you're out of line," said Judge Sherman. "The witness does not have to answer that last question."

To which, the defense attorney calmly responded, "The defense has no further questions of this witness your honor."

Davis unclenched her left fist. She set down the pointer, and walked back to her seat. Objection sustained or not, she knew she had made her point with the jury.

"Thank you Mr. Hernandez," said the Judge. "You are dismissed."

Raul wanted to vaporize.

Eddie had to admit that the defense attorney made a huge point with him. He was impressed at the delivery and ability of Rosemary Davis. Her presentation of those details was rather compelling, if not magnificent. He also had to admit that he had done a 180 degree turn—having underestimated the defense attorney. But, more importantly—he was beginning to have doubts that Hernandez did in fact witness the moment of the kill shot. It was no longer black and white. Eddie's quest to help in performing his duty—his hunt—to understand and reveal the truth, just became a bit more complicated.

****

The D.A. stood and announced, "The People would like to call to the stand: Officer Eric Allen."

Bailiff Ellis swore in the policeman, and the questions commenced.

"Good afternoon sir. Please state your name and occupation."

"My name is Rick Allen. I have been an officer for the Compton P.D. for eight years."

"Officer Allen, were you on duty the night of October 15th of last year?" Sandra asked.

"Yes ma'am. From eighteen hundred to twenty four hundred. That's 6 PM till midnight."

"And what was the area you patrolled that night?"

"The usual Compton-Inglewood border. About a 4-square mile area bordered by Imperial on the South, Century on the North, Normandie on the East, and Vermont to the West."

Eddie, having grown up in L.A., was familiar with all of the streets. He appreciated the meticulous enunciation by the cop. It was quite a contrast with the earlier witnesses.

The prosecution furnished a large blow-up of a page from the Thomas Guide—mounted on bright white foam core for Exhibit 2. Today, Ms. Levinthal brought along her own heavy duty easel. She then brought forth another large art-board. On it were mounted a series of six, eight by ten, color pictures, which she placed on an adjacent matching easel. A big compass was drawn neatly on the left, with a red arrow pointing to a large letter 'N.' Two pictures were of cars and street scenes. There also was a photograph of a wall, a picture of a tree, and what seemed to be a close-up of a curb, or sidewalk.

"The People would like to enter into evidence Exhibits 2 and 3 your honor."

The judge motioned to the bailiff, who made quick notes, and then attached something to the back of each board.

"Officer Allen. Do you recognize the property shown here—in picture number 1 of People's Exhibit 3?"

"Yes, I do."

"Please tell us what we are looking at sir..."

"It appears that we are looking North, across 128th street, at the front of the Century Palms apartment complex."

"Can you describe the complex for us?" she asked.

"Well, it's a rather typical apartment building for the area, perhaps a little older, and, maybe on the large side for this particular neighborhood. Six total buildings, all two story—three in front—and another three in back. Mostly blue collar families. Counting kids, roughly 300 people live there. It takes up almost the whole block bordered by Regent to the West, and Emerald to the East."

"And what are we looking at here, in picture number 2 of Exhibit 3?"

"We are looking East, down 128th Street, toward Regent."

Already Eddie was confused. He felt rather comfortable following that fantastic, but long winded scenario, put forth by the defense attorney earlier—all the turns and distances—but this was strange.

How can the cop say they are looking East, when the compass clearly indicated North?

"Mr. Allen, is Regent Park an area of concern to you as a police officer?"

"Well... it's a rather popular hangout—especially on Friday and Saturday nights—for some of the gang members in the neighborhood. We usually have at least one cruiser in the vicinity."

"But the night in question, the 15th was a Thursday night, was it not?" Sandra asked.

"Yes it was."

"Does that mean you would not necessarily have patrol cars close by?"

"Well, like I said, we never got out of our quadrant that night, so we never would have been more than two miles or so away from Regent Park, or The Palms complex the entire shift."

"Thank you. And do you know which gangs typically hang out there?"

"Sure. The Crips do roll through there on occasion. There are several smaller neighborhood gangs... but mostly it's the Bloods. The Bloods are who we try hardest to keep tabs on, as that neighborhood is really very much their turf."

"Thank you officer. Now tell us, please," Sandra continued, "what do you see in picture number 3?"

"That is Regent Park. We are looking South—from directly across the quad of the apartment complex in picture number 1."

Holy Shit! Either this cop doesn't really know, is blatantly lying, or the defense attorneys' scenario was totally screwed up this morning in an attempt to confuse us... us and Hernandez!

"...so a car driving West, at 25 miles per hour...," continued Sandra.

Hey wait a minute! They are obviously referring to Washington's Cadillac, and the path it was speeding away after the shooting... I KNOW that had to be going West... but the picture shows it as EAST! What the hell? Could it be the D.A.'s exhibit that's screwed up? Is that possible?

"So looking South, down Regent, in picture number 4..."

That's it! The compass on the exhibit cannot be right. How can someone take a picture, then turn ninety degrees to the right, take another picture... and have the directions—the compass coordinates—be the same?

After shuffling her notes for a moment, the district attorney looked up to the judge, "Your honor, it's nearly 5:00. I move that we recess until tomorrow morning."

"I agree Ms. Levinthal. It has indeed been a long day." Judge Sherman turned to the witness box. "Mr. Allen, I admonish you not to discuss this case with anyone. Ladies and gentlemen of the jury, please remember my previous instructions to you as well. You are not to discuss this case with anyone—not even amongst yourselves—until it is presented to you for deliberation. We are in recess until tomorrow morning at 9:00 am."

****

Eddie bounded into the house, towards his wife's study.

"Renee! We've got to talk—it's about the trial!"

She yelled from her office, "I'm busy."

"No, really… this is important," he said, as he appeared in the doorway.

"Aren't you breaking your sworn code of duty, my dear?" she said, taking off her glasses.

"Well, this is different. I've got a question for you."

"Oh you do—Mr. Conscientious Jury member—but I thought you were supposed to base all of your decisions on things you hear exclusively in the courtroom. I don't think I can participate in this sort of anti-duty activity. Now leave me alone. I have to study."

Putting her glasses back on, she turned away from him. He moved up behind her, brushed her dark hair aside, and gently started kissing the nape of her neck.

"OK, OK," she murmured in mock boredom. "Tell me everything."

"So, I guess you too respond to torture."

"I respond to the opposite of torture. But more on that subject a little later—if you're lucky. You've got five minutes. Now talk."

"Well," he began, "with all the trips to Catalina we've made—all the sailing we've done—what's the first thing you learned?"

"You ran up here to interrupt me, and your important thing to talk about is sailing?"

"Just answer me, please," he pleaded.

"Always barf to leeward?" she said, being half-serious.

"OK. The second thing."

"I don't know, Eddie, there's a thousand things... how to tie a good knot, a bowline, the wind, the sails—"

"Come on now—think!"

"OK... keep the boat away from the rocks, the compass, the—"

"Yes! The compass. If there's one thing we both know about it's the compass. Wind direction, course direction, navigation, charts, North, South, blah, blah, blah... it all has to do with the compass."

"So?"

"So... it seems that directions are a key part of what's happening in the trial. And—as I understand it, the shooter, in the getaway car, made all of these quick turns: West, then South, then West again."

"OK..."

"Well, the defense attorney has this theory that no more than two minutes went by from the shooting, till the time the killer was stopped by the police—a few blocks away. The direction he drove, and the turns he made all become critical, if this one guy, Hernandez, is truly an eyewitness. But the cop said that he was driving West, or actually East, as the picture showed, which makes the two minute theory—or rather the ten second theory—impossible. But... it might NOT be impossible because the pictures are screwed up..."

"Hold it! Two minute theory? Ten second theory? You are babbling like a madman."

"Let me backup," he said.

"I wish you would. And what does this have to do with a compass?"

"I'm trying to tell you—the prosecutor has this exhibit— Exhibit 3. It's got all these groovy color pictures on it, and a beautiful compass in the legend. The pictures were taken looking in all different directions—but there's only the one compass that refers to all of them!"

"You're kidding."

"No, I'm not, and it gets worse. She keeps referring to the pictures and how important it is: was the car traveling East, is the park to the South, was the gun shooting North... etc, etc... and the cop keeps answering these questions and explaining right along... They are making such a big deal that the directions are critical to the whole thing... and they are! If what the defense attorney is saying is true... it's coming down to counting seconds! Ten critical seconds. And it's all screwed up! It's meaningless garbage. I don't know how anybody on the jury can truly follow what's going on. The truth is, they can't, nobody can. But they all seem to be paying close attention. Am I the only one who sees it?"

"There's a pretty fair chance that you are. But what can you do Eddie?" she asked. "You're on the jury."

"Well, what I want to do is jump over the jury box, grab her stupid Exhibit 3, and throw it like a giant Frisbee right out of the courtroom. Then I'd give her a coupon for 10% off on Eddie's basic navigation course."

"I would like to advise you against doing that," she said, gently wagging her index finger back and forth.

He opened both palms, and held them out wide, "Well?"

"Do you think the *judge* knows it's screwed up?" she asked.

"I thought about that. I don't know. It's weird, this guy, Judge Sherman, is as sharp as they come. He doesn't miss *anything*—but I bet he doesn't." He paused to think to himself for a moment. "I'd like to at least ask the question... but... what if it has a critical impact on the whole trial... Jesus!"

"Eddie, you already said it has critical implications in terms of figuring out what really happened that night. Isn't it your job as a jury member to try to figure out the truth?"

"Absolutely. That's why I'm there. But, I'm not supposed to *directly* influence anything—not until deliberations anyway.

This is still the evidence phase—for God's sake—I'm just supposed to be listening and taking notes."

"But can't you ask a simple question?"

"I don't know. The judge did seem quite concerned at one or two points that we were able to clearly see the exhibits..."

"Didn't you get some sort of juror's handbook or something? Yeah, I remember you reading it to figure out what you were supposed to wear."

"You're right... where is that damn thing?" He looked around her office for a moment—thinking, really, more than looking. "Do you have the stopwatch in your drawer?"

"Yeah, it's right here," she answered. "Why?"

"Hit it."

He jumped up, ran out the door, down the hallway, up the stairs, into their bedroom, opened the bottom drawer to their oak nightstand, grabbed the green pamphlet, and reversed his tracks back to her office.

"Time," he said.

"Not bad," she answered. "Fifteen point five seconds. Not your best, but not bad."

It was a game they played. They used the stopwatch often—it came in handy for sailboat regattas, and sometimes for diving exercises—when they would practice holding their breath—but mostly it was just a neat thing to have for fun games like this one.

She grabbed the pamphlet from him. "Let's see... 'Conduct in the Jury Box'... page 9." She began reading, "On occasions when you can't see, or hear, raise your hand, and wait for the judge to acknowledge you. Generally the judge will order testimony to be reread, or a question to be asked again, so that you don't miss anything. On rare occasions, a juror may have a question regarding the proceedings. Do not ask your question out loud, as it may have an affect on the trial. Instead, please write down your question as neatly as possible on a blank page from your juror's notebook. Fold the paper, and raise it in your hand. The judge will read your question, and address it if he deems it appropriate. Do not be surprised, or insulted if the judge ignores your question completely. If this happens, it is up to you to pursue the question, should you so choose, on your own, during deliberations."

****

Eddie had just kissed his wife goodbye. As his hand reached for the door leading from the hallway to the garage, she called out from her office.

"Babe—I forgot to tell you—I had a note here on my desk, but we got all caught up last night on that stuff about the compass..."

He was anxious to get on the freeway. He was excited about what lay in store at the trial. "Yeah?" he answered a bit impatiently.

"Bella called here yesterday afternoon. She said she had just spoken to you and to tell you... something about a batch of fabric. That all the new Japan Garden print had already been cut. Is everything..."

"Oh my God! Aw hell!" She heard him curse as the door to the garage shut behind him.

How many times have I read the warnings on invoices that defective fabric could not be returned nor would any credit be given once the goods had been cut?

How much is this little screw-up going to cost me— $9,000? $10,000?

This is starting to get old, calculating how much money I'm going to lose...

Renee poked her head out of her office but vetoed the idea of chasing after him, when, again, from over the roar of his freshly started engine, she heard him scream, "Shit!"

CHAPTER 8 - Sirens & A White Rabbit

October 20, 1993
Compton, California

The Bailiff opened the courtroom doors at 8:55. All twelve jurors lolling about in the hallway quickly filled in the empty seats in the jury box. Eddie wondered how early the defendant and attorneys were allowed in, as they seemed to be fixtures in the courtroom. It was strange, he observed, sometimes the attorneys scrutinized the jurors quite closely as they walked in, nodding, or even smiling as they filed by. Other times, they ignored them completely.

At precisely 9:00, the black satin robed judge emerged from his chambers.

"All rise for the honorable Judge Sherman," roared the Bailiff, opening Day 3 in the trial of *'The People of the State of California versus Reginald Washington.'*

The judge walked up the six steps to take his seat at the bench. He walked—not quite pompously, thought Eddie—but certainly with something more than pride.

By now, Eddie was becoming familiar with most of the bailiff and judge's routines—the swearing in of each witness, the reminders and admonishments before lunch, and at the end of each day.

Some of these reminders—no, most of them, are quite repetitive. Maybe that's by design. Will we really start accepting and believing this stuff as important if we hear it ten times a day?

At least superficially, the jurors seemed to be behaving in model fashion. Just a lot of mundane *'Hello, how are yous?'* and *'What did you do for lunch?'* dominated the jurors' downtime in the jury box and in their hallway conversations. On one such conversation, after lunch on Day 2, before the bailiff opened the courtroom doors, Eddie found himself standing next to a juror from another trial. Eddie did not recognize him from the Washington trial—seeing his juror's badge, assumed he was from the trial in the courtroom across the hall. Maybe five years younger than Eddie, he also appeared to be struggling to kill yet another chunk of the huge amount of time spent simply milling about while on jury duty. The young man walked up to Eddie and chose to inquire about the paperback book Eddie was reading. Noting how big it looked, his first question, rather than the title or name of the author, was the number of pages. The man looked surprised when Eddie said he didn't know. Curious himself, Eddie flipped to the back page.

"Let's see… 381."

"And you're just reading it for fun?"

"Sure," answered Eddie. "There's a lot of downtime around here."

"Wow," said the man, "I don't think I've ever read a book that long."

Eddie was certain his next question would be something along the lines of, *'So what's it about?'*

But instead, the man asked, "So what page are you on now?"

Eddie had always prided himself on his memory. He worked on it: little games and puzzles to keep sharp. One of these recurrent tests, encountered almost daily, was the challenge to commit to memory the page he was on of the novel he almost always had close at hand. He was proud of the fact that, since he was about eight years old, he never used a book mark. He also wouldn't dog-ear the pages to keep his place: he cringed when he saw people do this. Something about defacing the book by making those tiny triangular folds bothered him. He also hated thinking about, hated the distraction, when, especially with hard cover books, or library books, he couldn't help but wonder why a previous reader who dog-eared the page, had stopped right there. He never needed these tools, as, even if several days or weeks had gone by, he could always remember the page number of the last page he had read.

So Eddie looked up and said simply, "212."

The man appeared befuddled that Eddie didn't open the book to look, but quickly regurgitated this seemingly random number.

Eddie was a bit relieved when he saw the doors to his courtroom swing open—offering a welcome respite from the banal interaction.

The man said, "Guess duty calls! Nice talking to you."

Smiling awkwardly, Eddie was somehow able to suppress rolling his eyes.

Eddie was amazed that the lawyers simply assumed that the jurors could pick up right from where they left off after a long interruption. Himself, he was appreciative of the respect that assumption implied: that the jurors had the ability to follow the case and all the ramifications of the testimony or even the objections—without tediously rehashing everything after a break, or night off. He just wondered if the attorneys didn't sometimes give the jurors too much credit, or, if they didn't overly trust in the jurors' ability to follow the proceedings. He thought back on that one objection from yesterday by the defense—it could have referred to any one of several things...

Was it over some gang member named Leon's Boom box? An orange Datsun, or if some old lady was asleep? In fact it was never clarified. Obviously the defense thought it was important. Was it?

****

Levinthal, for the prosecution, took up where she left off yesterday.

"Good morning Officer Allen. Your patrol car was moving West on 126th Street as you first saw the defendant's car coming toward you. So his vehicle was heading East—is that right?"

"Well actually, when I first saw the defendant's vehicle, earlier in the evening, it was not moving, but, rather, it was parked, facing West on 128th Street," he corrected.

Damn. Here we go...

"So, if we refer to picture number 2—the picture showing the street in front of the building," she said, walking toward the easel, "depicted here in Exhibit 3... are you telling us that you saw the El Dorado parked here facing West?"

Eddie now began to get anxious.

If she mentions any direction, any direction at all—North, South, East or West—in combination with her stupid Exhibit— I'm going to write a note to the judge. I swear I'm gonna do it.

"Well, yes ma'am. I believe the Cadillac—the vehicle in question—made a U-turn at some point before the shooting and headed West."

"Excuse me officer, but don't you mean East?"

"Objection," said the defense, "asked and answered."

"Objection sustained," came the judge's reply.

That does it lady. Now you're confusing the judge, the witness and everybody... and they don't even know why!

He wrote quickly in his notepad, tore out the page, folded it, and held it in his lap for a moment. Eddie had been in a foul mood since the news his wife gave him earlier about the mishap with the cutting of the fabric at his business. He was mad at Renee for not telling him sooner. He was mad at Bella and his workers, especially John The Cutter and fabric spreaders.

They have too much experience to screw something up that badly!

He wanted to appear at his office, line up all of his employees, and vent. Simultaneously, he was mad at the district attorney. He wanted to jump out of the jury box and voice his not too subtle opinion in front of the whole courtroom. He found it was intensely frustrating to be a quiet spectator. He considered again the ramifications of what he was about to do, took a deep breath, and initiated his course of action; he held the folded piece of paper that he had ripped from his juror's notebook high over his head.

The bailiff's body language indicated that he immediately noticed Eddie, but the banter between Ms. Levinthal and Officer Allen continued.

On seeing this unusual act on the part of their fellow juror, several of the others soon stopped following the interplay between the judge, the attorneys, and the witness, turning their attention to Eddie. They couldn't help but be curious. Did they miss something? What did he see that they didn't?

Judge Sherman quickly saw that the raised hand by Juror Number 4 had become a distraction. He motioned for the bailiff to retrieve the note. Taking the folded piece of paper from Eddie, the large man winked.

What the hell was that? Could he know too?

The two lawyers were silent, watching with interest as the judge looked it over; the rare occurrence of a juror passing a note to a judge—especially during testimony—was invariably a source of anxiety for both parties.

Eddie felt the piercing glare of another set of eyes: those of the defendant. Reggie Washington also wondered what this juror wrote in his note to the judge.

Judge Sherman took a moment to clean his glasses before reading Eddie's note to himself:

> *The testimony in reference to the pictures in Exhibit 3 is meaningless, as the compass shown here is inaccurate.*
> *One compass cannot possibly describe the direction of all the photographs, as the vantage point varies.*

In order to fully understand recent testimony—
I suggest each of the pictures in this exhibit is
accompanied by its own accurate compass.

The judge took off his glasses to look across at the exhibit. He then put his glasses back on, and stared back at Eddie's note. He slowly separated some of the frayed scraps of paper generated by the row of torn holes from Eddie's spiral notebook page, and rolled them into little balls. Out of view of everyone in the courtroom, he flicked these miniscule untidy wads onto the floor.

Carefully weighing the risk of having a juror interfere with the proceedings, he decided to paraphrase Eddie.

"There seems to be some confusion as to the direction of the compass in these pictures. Ms. Levinthal, can you please clarify?"

"Yeah," Officer Allen interjected, "the picture you are referring to—East should be at the top—that would help."

Judge Sherman was simultaneously curious, and upset that the witness spoke, "Will the witness please refrain from speaking at this time."

"Sorry your honor, I..."

Like a traffic cop, rebuking a driver for encroaching into the intersection—Judge Sherman abruptly put his hand up to firmly cut him off.

Meanwhile, Sandra Levinthal had walked up to the exhibit, and crossed out the letters on the compass. She replaced them with E on top, W on bottom, S to the left, and N to the right.

"I'm sorry," she offered, "I wasn't a geography major. This should help."

"I don't think it helps," said the defense attorney. "I'm pretty sure North should be at the top."

"Well, for the purpose of this exhibit, North will be on the right," said Sandra innocently.

"But then," said the defense attorney, "you've got Century Boulevard running North-South. Like in picture number 4."

"Like I said, for the matter at hand, the street will just have to be North-South. Now I think we can move on," said Sandra.

"But," continued Defense Attorney Davis, "even in your own Exhibit—Exhibit 1 from yesterday, which we stipulated as being accurate—you had Century running East-West."

"Century Boulevard runs East-West, Ms. Levinthal," said the judge. "You can't change that."

"That's right," said the cop.

Judge Sherman pounded his gavel twice, raising his voice to an alarming level, "Mr. Allen, I'm not going to ask you again!"

The judge's usual calm demeanor, transitioning so abruptly, stunned a couple of jurors. Juror Number 6 looked across at Eddie, knowing full well that he was the cause of the uncomfortable situation.

Eddie quickly caught what he interpreted as a displeased glare, and immediately looked away, refusing to engage eye contact. Instead, he focused on the D.A. who now went to picture number 4 and drew another compass. This one had North at the top, but reversed East and West.

"But that makes the rest of the neighborhood off—as I understand it," said the defense attorney.

Hearing this, the district attorney then did a surprising thing: she rotated the exhibit 90 degrees on its' side. She smiled, not as if it were a joke, but as if she had just stumbled onto a brilliant solution to the problem.

"Now, we can still use the compass," Sandra explained, "Century Boulevard runs East-West, and North is at the top."

In the first two days of the trial, Eddie had become a fan of Sandra, thinking she was a fairly effective lawyer. But it was at this precise moment that he stopped.

Several more members of the jury were now looking at Eddie, thinking he would be the cause of them having to turn their necks to strain a look in attempting to understand the sideways pictures and labels.

The judge smacked his gavel again. "Will the prosecution please turn the exhibit back so that the photographs are all in their upright positions? The jury will have to figure out this issue of the compass, during deliberations, that is, if we ever get that far.

"Now does the prosecution have any more questions of this witness?"

Judge Sherman glanced at Eddie. But Eddie did not know how to interpret the look.

Was that a sign of appreciation that he acknowledged one of the jurors was paying such close attention? Or, perhaps a vote of confidence in my ability—was he in fact encouraging me to take charge of the clarification—and to convey that to the other jurors during deliberations? Was the judge admitting that he too was frustrated by the exhibit? Or just maybe there was another possibility—perhaps he's angry at me for bringing the glaring mistake and resulting perplexity front and center into his courtroom...

Eddie didn't know. He only knew that he wanted to scream.

****

If the district attorney had some salient facts to bring out of the witness, they were now lost on this jury. She tried in vain to simplify the logistics of what had actually transpired the night of the murder, but the jurors mirrored the impatience of the judge. She did manage to extract the final point from the arresting officer that Reggie was wearing a Kevlar bullet proof vest at the time of his arrest.

The defense attorney had only two questions for the arresting officer.

"Mr. Allen, at the time of the arrest, did you find a weapon in the Cadillac?"

"No," came the soft reply.

"Mr. Allen, to your knowledge, was any weapon linking the defendant to the shooting of Oliver Jefferson ever found?"

"No," he answered.

"Thank you. No further questions your honor."

****

Several other police officers gave their testimony. The prosecution also called up a couple of tenants, as well as The Palms on-site manager. The manager mostly repeated some of the same details offered up in earlier testimony by one of the cops. He relayed the layout of the apartment complex, the number of families that lived there and the racial makeup of the families—about 25% Latinos, but mainly black, with a few Koreans. He said he felt the layout depicted in Exhibit 1 was quite accurate. He also said he knew many of the gang members of the group that had gathered that night, especially on the North side of 128th Street, and reinforced that he saw Jimmy, Leon and Marcus out there, that he heard the screeching and skidding of the Cadillac, as well as the gunshots. However he testified that he did not see the shooting of Oliver Jefferson.

Eddie observed that throughout the testimony of the past five witnesses, he saw hardly anything being written in the notebooks by the jurors. Outside of the names and titles of each of these witnesses, Eddie himself wrote little, as he detected nothing poignant.

Sandra Levinthal called one final witness. He was a detective who explained that the tire marks on the curb in front of the Century Palms, as well as fresh skid marks on 128th Street, in front of the quad, were almost certainly made from the tires of the Cadillac El Dorado driven by Reggie Washington.

He also explained how his team had found two recently fired bullets. One was a 9 millimeter slug imbedded in the South wall of Building 4 of the apartment complex, as well as one of the same caliber lodged eight feet off the ground, in the bark of the lone eucalyptus tree standing in the center of the quad. Both of these bullets were entered into exhibits for The People.

Also entered as exhibits were enlarged pictures showing detailed rifling markings of the slugs. The detective testified that he was certain, and demonstrated from the marks, that both rounds were fired from the same gun, and that neither could have come from an S & W .38—the weapon that Jimmy used to shoot the basketball out of Marcus' hands on the night of the murder.

Furthermore, the ballistics, explained at length by the detective, indicated that due to the higher elevation on that end of Regent Park, across the street, it was deemed quite unlikely that either of the two shots could have come from the park, as, if there was a shooter standing near the fence at the North end of the park, he would have been up on the retaining wall, rendering the angle of a shot from there to the eucalyptus tree or Building 4 impossible. He explained his logic—given that Oliver stood 5'11" and the kill shot entered the area around his clavicle, approximately one foot lower, or 4'11" off the ground—a high-velocity bullet fired from the park above, would undoubtedly have passed through his body only to have been found in the surrounding grass by the metal detectors in the early morning hours following the murder. He also conveyed in detail how the angle of the impacted slugs, in combination with the distortion of the surrounding material of the stucco and the tree bark, meant that both shots originated from street level—more specifically—from the area of the street in front of the quad. Sandra got to use her exhibit again, referring to photographs 5, 6, 7, and 8. Photograph 5 showed a grey wall with a small pockmark, while Photograph 6 depicted a fresh scar in the bark of a tree. Photographs 7 and 8 were both super enlargements showing the bullets as they sat *in situ*, imbedded—before they were carefully carved out, from both the tree trunk and the stucco, and sent to the lab.

Sandra introduced into evidence two new photos, one being an enlargement of a tire skid, while the other clearly showed tire tread markings and fresh white scratches on the top and face of a cement curb. The detective explained how he found traces of light brown paint—paint that his lab matched up to the '67 Caddy—in the curb scratches. He confirmed that the small bag, held up by the D.A. as a new exhibit contained those same flakes of paint.

Eddie was impressed by this witness. He conjectured that his fellow jurors, along with countless jurors sitting on other trials, could naturally become overwhelmed with the tedious details such as angles and degrees and composition of various materials. He wondered the myriad details that an experienced lawyer would intentionally leave out, considering fully that the attention span of a juror could not possibly be infinite. He was fascinated with the detective's knowledge and ability to communicate difficult forensic concepts in simple terms. Eddie was beginning to think that Sandra Levinthal, in spite of that messy business with the compass, and her admitted non-proficiency in geography, had regained the momentum in this trial, as he observed a couple of the jurors resume writing diligently in their notepads.

Abruptly, the district attorney said, "No further questions your honor."

Eddie looked up mid-sentence from his spiral notebook. He wanted to call a timeout so he could write more. But the defense attorney was already approaching the witness stand.

"Just a quick question sir," said Ms. Davis. "Did you find any blood on the bullet from the eucalyptus tree, or on the bullet you retrieved from the stucco—the exterior of the apartment wall of Building 4 of The Palms?"

"Well we weren't..."

She interrupted him, raising her voice, "Did you or your partner or the lab find any blood on either of the bullets you found?"

"We know there were four shots fired. Five—if you count the earlier shot fired at the basketball. The quad, between the buildings at The Palms, opens up to Century Boulevard, which is a clear line of sight from the front of the apartments. Century has a lot of traffic—it's a busy street 24 hours a day. The traffic there means a bullet could—"

"I'm sorry detective, but it is imperative you give me a simple 'yes' or 'no' answer to this question. I'll ask again: to the best of your knowledge, did you, your partner, or your forensics team, the lab, or *anybody* find any trace of blood whatsoever on either of the two bullets you found that indicated they may have passed through the body of Oliver Jefferson?"

"No," he answered.

"Thank you detective," she said, with something more than a hint of condescension. "No further questions."

District attorney Levinthal got up and took another turn at the detective, in attempt to re-instill confidence in the minds of the jury as to what had transpired, asking him to expound on the fact that neither of the two bullets that had passed through Oliver Jefferson's body had been found. She asked him to clarify.

The detective began to explain, "It is possible that one or both of these high velocity rounds exited the deceased's body and ended up in a passing car on Century Boulevard."

"Objection!" shouted Davis. "Calls for speculation!"

"Objection sustained," ruled the judge.

The D.A. had no further questions of Officer Allen, so Judge Sherman excused the witness, and then looked up at the district attorney. "The People may call their next witness."

Sandra Levinthal stood. "The People rest your honor."

Without speaking, the judge turned toward the defense table. He stretched out his long black-robed arm, opening his upturned palm as if offering an invisible piece of candy to Ms. Davis.

She slid back her chair and stood. "The defense rests, your honor."

Eddie was in shock.

Is it over? This is too sudden. How can it be over so quickly? My god, the defense didn't even call a single one of their own witnesses! She just cross-examined whoever the prosecution put up there. Hell—she hardly asked more than one or two questions of anybody... Come to think of it, outside of that tiny yellow Post-It Note, and reading that stuff about the guards being required to do a few sit-ups, she didn't even enter a single one of her own exhibits! How many did the D.A. put up there? Eleven or twelve or more? Why didn't...

The judge interrupted Eddie's thought process, "It's nearly five o'clock. We'll adjourn for the day, and continue with closing arguments first thing in the morning. Please remember all of my previous admonishments to you. You are not to speak..."

Eddie knew the rest of the speech and stopped listening.

****

On the drive home from the Compton Courthouse, Eddie realized that he was disappointed his trial was coming to an end. He had become quite engrossed in the testimony, characters, and the detail of the crime scene. He could visualize the gritty neighborhood. He could feel the tension of the night of the murder: the security guards making their rounds; the gang members taunting them; the blaring rap music; the runs back and forth and confusion conveyed by Hernandez. Part of him wanted to drive by the Century Palms apartment complex—just to see it. He knew how to get there—it was only ten minutes from the courthouse, and he remembered the names of the streets—but he recalled something else he had read in the jurors' handbook, as well as one of the early admonishments by the judge. Something about *"...under no circumstances are you to perform your own detective work."*

He had just merged onto the 4th lane of the 91 Freeway, but now, as soon as he was in traffic, he battled the urge to exit. The Lakewood off-ramp was rapidly approaching. Could he resist the burning temptation to turn off? To take a quick detour, if even for a minute—just to see it—to drive by the site of the murder from his trial? He manufactured a fleeting thought: '*The Sirens of Compton.*' He congratulated himself on his witticism.

There's a seemingly incessant blaring of police sirens. And ambulances. Plus: the temptress. She's calling me to drive down to the city streets below. The seduction by this beautiful mythological sea nymph who wants to dash my boat onto the rocks. Am I being lured to destruction by the Sirens of Compton? Was that a pun? A double entendre?

He wasn't sure he knew the difference.

He realized he had been so engrossed in his thoughts that he was totally unaware of the song playing through the car stereo. It was the old Jefferson Airplane song '*White Rabbit.*' Three seconds to decide, two—the huge green off-ramp sign was directly overhead now.

The Sirens are calling me.

The synapses in his brain were firing and he had to make a decision. But instead of veering off the freeway, he commanded different actions to all four of his extremities. Eddie's right hand shot out, flipping the volume knob hard to the right. Guitars crescendoed. On vocals, Grace Slick screamed.

Was she the Siren?

Simultaneously, his left hand whipped the leather wrapped steering wheel to the left, as his left foot clutched. His right foot pressed down hard on the accelerator. The Corvette lurched away—into a faster lane—avoiding the beckoning call of the streets of Compton below him.

Eddie had a proud moment. He had faced the temptation, but exercised the will power to defeat it. He had risen above it—both figuratively and literally—for he was cruising on the freeway high above the odious surface streets—away from the treacherous rocks below.

But the pride was false. Eddie did not know it at the time, that, perhaps like Alice, in the song, he had already begun his descent down into the rabbit hole.

CHAPTER 9 - The Dream

October 20, 1993   PM
Palos Verdes, California

Eddie had real trouble falling asleep that night. He wasn't remotely tired. He certainly couldn't read, as his mind would not leave the trial. He heard Renee's breathing—looked over at the steady rise and fall of the quilt comforter. She was right there next to him, yet he felt alone. They never fought, but lately, there had been some mounting tension. He knew law-school was not her first choice in life—that she was suppressing her own dream of starting a family.

My mother-in-law certainly isn't helping matters. Her parents are small town folks, well, compared to L.A., anyway... They can't envision what it takes to build a company. To make it a force in the marketplace. Frank seems to get it, to some degree, but he's a factory man. Her mom has no idea. Her daughter and I have a chance to make something really special here... Don't you see that? We'll give you all the grandkids you want, soon enough. But let me lay the foundation. I don't need more pressure right now... Let me finish building this nice safe environment for them, so they can go to a great school. So they can have refrigerators and freezers stocked with food. So they will never have to worry about having a knife pulled on them...

Eyes wide open, he stared up at the ceiling. Rolling to his right, he looked out the dark window of their upstairs bedroom. He generally would have taken pleasure in the huge date palm, fronds backlit tonight by the perfect placement of the bright quarter moon. But he saw nothing. Nothing but the courtroom and the replay of witnesses and exhibits. How long he stared without blinking, he didn't know.

He remembered some of the many admonishments by Judge Sherman. He recalled warnings by the judge about jurors not being allowed to wonder why the defendant won't testify, or why this or that will or won't be talked about.

Hell! That's exactly what I am wondering! Why didn't the defense attorney put Reggie Washington on the stand? If he's innocent, let him tell us! Why weren't there any witnesses verifying his whereabouts as being somewhere else? What's his alibi? What about getting some expert—some guy from General Motors—to tell us that they never used that exact shade of brown paint found on the curb? And what about the Defense Attorney? On her cross examination of that last detective... that stuff about no traces of blood being found on the bullets... should there be, or shouldn't there be? How the hell are we supposed to know? Plus—is it possible that not one, but TWO bullets BOTH passed through Oliver Jefferson's body—only to wind up in car bumpers on Century Boulevard with both unsuspecting drivers now 100 miles away? The odds against that had to be a billion to one.

How can we NOT wonder about this stuff? If we're paying close attention like we're instructed to—then we are going to want to ask our own questions. The judge says 'don't conjecture.' He says we must base our thoughts and conclusions solely on the courtroom testimony and evidence.

I'm trying judge... I'm really trying to do a good job here. But I think you just might be asking the impossible...

The moon was long gone. It was nearly 4:00 AM before Eddie's racing mind and heavy eyelids finally shut for a bit. He drifted off into a dream...

He was diving—gliding through the cold kelp beds on the backside of Catalina Island, sixty feet underwater. It was dark, with only scattered rays of light angling through the golden rubbery leaves of seaweed. He was hunting. Searching for fish, but strangely, there were none. His oxygen was beginning to run low. He was down to 500 p.s.i. showing on his pressure gauge—or with relaxed breathing at that depth—about 10 minutes of air. The sea was absolutely calm, and visibility was perfect. But for some reason, the water felt colder to him than ever.

Out of the corner of his eye, off to his right, he saw a school of blue perch suddenly scatter. Then he saw the bubbles. He was able to barely make out a dark shape; another diver was there—partially hidden in the kelp. It was down in the depths—in the darkness below him, but it was moving up. The bubbles were getting bigger and closer.

The few rays that were able to permeate the depth of the seawater caught something. A reflection. A flash of light. It was the glint off of a silver spear tip. He could see the diver's eyes clearly now: it was Reggie. He wasn't wearing a neoprene wet-suit, but, rather—the same cheap brown suit that he had been wearing throughout the trial. Partly tucked into his facemask, covering his forehead, was a red bandanna. The loose corners of the bandanna, not held in place by the silicone straps of the mask were streaming behind him—almost like long red wavy contrails, or, Eddie mused, like blood leaking from a massive head wound. Reggie was approaching. Quickly. Eddie realized that he had never before seen anyone swim so fast. He noticed something else: Reggie had a huge disturbing Cheshire cat grin on his face. Big white perfect teeth. Then he saw someone, a lady, wearing a yellow dress. It was Alice; she was running away from the cat.

Is that Alice or my wife? Renee has that same yellow dress... But how was that possible? How could she be running underwater? It looks like Renee, but it can't be. She's pregnant.

What the fuck? Reggie has no regulator in his mouth!

Of course he has no regulator in his mouth! Otherwise I wouldn't see that big Cheshire smile. But, then, hey wait, then how could he breathe underwater? There are no hoses or gauges—nor is there a scuba tank on his back, yet he is still able to breathe underwater—I see all those bubbles!

How the hell is he swimming so fast! Mark Spitz couldn't swim this fast... it's like he's driving... driving a fast car. A big brown car.

Eddie tried to surface, but he couldn't move. His left flipper was caught in a twisted cable of seaweed. He started breathing harder, sucking at the precious air that remained. Now, 200 p.s.i. of air left in the tank. Reggie was closing; his finger curled around the trigger of the spear gun. Eddie was beginning to panic now. Fifty pounds of pressure. Reggie's grin turning to laughter—perverted silent laughter—the only sound Eddie could hear being his own labored breathing as he sucked on the regulator mouthpiece.

He tried holding his breath to conserve air. He regularly practiced holding his breath—all that practice with his wife, and their contests with the stopwatch. She always beat him, always pushing three minutes and beyond. Still, he could do two and a half minutes with ease. But now, he couldn't go five seconds. He started skip breathing to save air, but it only made him more anxious and he sucked harder.

Which breath will be my last?

Velcroed to his right calf was a dive knife. He ripped the straps open and pulled it out from its sheath. Hundreds of beautiful bright orange flakes of wood floated upward, surrounding him. Remnants of the pencil shavings from Renee's first navigation lesson. Strangely, his mind replayed a quick video—laughing with Renee at the neon pink handle of the blade—a gift from her for his 35th birthday.

But why did she stop laughing? Why is she running away?

He had seconds to cut himself free of the kelp or he wouldn't make it—but the knife slipped from his cold fingers—turning and flipping as it fell downward to the ocean floor in a sickening slow motion strobe—a flashing of alternating pink and chrome.

Was this what Oliver felt when that third bullet hit him in the arm and he dropped his pistol?

Reggie was twenty feet away now. Almost in range. Eddie saw him take aim with the grey spear gun—index finger of his right hand caressing the trigger. He glanced at the dial of his guage—eyes wide with disbelief on seeing the red needle pegged to the far left. He took a full breath. Then a half breath. Grasping the realization—the horror of the now empty tank— he sucked harder. Willing another breath, he thought if he just sucked harder he could extract just one more breath—one more moment of life. But he got nothing.

Why can't I at least get that pleasing sucking sound when the straw hits the bottom of the milk-shake?

Zero. These were going to be the final seconds of his life.

The tinted window is slowly rolling down. It's opening to reveal the driver of the Cadillac. But, how can that be? I've already been shot in the arm and it made me drop my gun. Or my knife. So the window should have already been down... Plus, I'm now 70 feet underwater! How can there be a car here? I need to run. I need to swim. But my feet are stuck... Stuck in the seaweed. It actually looks more like an umbilical cord tightening around me. I need the knife to cut the umbilical cord. Help me Renee! But she's running away from me. My pregnant wife is running...

He thrashed wildly at the kelp, becoming more entangled as the strong underwater vines were now wound around both ankles. The thick yellow tubed rubber bands were stretched tight on Reggie's cocked spear gun. The facemask magnified the awful intentions behind his bloodshot eyeballs. Those maniacal, asymmetrical eyeballs. Eddie spit the useless regulator out of his mouth, gasping, choking as he inhaled the cold water. The intense taste of the impossibly salty seawater. He thought of his dad, '...*potatoes need lots and lots of salt.*' Bitter and harsh as bile, the water trickled in. It jolted him— burning his throat and lungs. He took another futile final glance down at his tangled legs, and then another quick look up at Reggie, in time to see his finger squeeze the trigger. He focused on the deadly silver spear tip spiraling toward his own chest. The shocking seawater now pouring down—filling his lungs—inducing the violent gag reflex in such throes that he felt his ribs were cracking apart.

"Eddie! Eddie!"

"Wake up Eddie!" Renee screamed as she shook him.

Eddie thrashed back at his wife—trying to break loose from the blankets and the sheets—*the tangled seaweed.* Simultaneously, he thrust his arm up to block the oncoming spear—and elbowed her hard in the chin.

Choking, gasping, spitting—he opened his eyes.

CHAPTER 10 - Closing Arguments

October 21, 1993   AM
Compton, California

Walking slowly into the courtroom that morning, Eddie quietly took his seat in the jury box. He looked down, willing himself to avoid making eye-contact with the defendant. But he felt it. He felt the eyes on him. He looked up from his loafers, and across the short distance to where Reggie sat. He saw the same brown suit. The same bloodshot eyes staring back at him.

Was he actually smiling at me? Could he know what happened in the dream?

Eddie looked down again, away from the terrible eyes. But it wasn't a feeble disengagement from last night's assailant. He began carefully scanning the area beneath Reggie's chair— below the hanging tails of the brown suit—down to the tiled courtroom floor. But the floor was dry. There was no dripping seawater.

"Would *The People* care to present a closing argument?" Mercifully, Eddie's hallucination was broken by the familiar voice of Judge Sherman.

It seemed to Eddie that for the most part, the jurors appeared to have dressed a bit smarter this morning. Perhaps it was knowing they were about to hear closing arguments, and enter into deliberations, wherein, the focus of the trial would quickly shift away from the lawyers, judge, and witnesses, and toward themselves.

Eddie had become, not exactly complacent, but, comfortable with his position in the jury box during the past four days. He had after all, spent many hours watching and listening to the numerous players in this drama. He was able to assess, and even predict some of the reactions of the attorneys to various points of law and evidence that was presented. Once or twice he actually predicted an objection before one of the attorneys could voice it. He saw their strengths, and surprised himself, as, though he was a layman, was still able to recognize many of their faults and mistakes.

He thought back on how anxious he was during day one—especially during the voir dire—and how he had quickly become accustomed to the proceedings. However, his nerves returned upon realizing that this, the most critical stage of the trial—and in fact the very reason he had been mailed that summons—and all that it portended—was moments away. Eddie knew he had taken his call to jury duty seriously. In spite of the many reports he had heard of how boring it could be, or how the system was screwed up, or how it was unrealistic that he, one juror, on one trial, could have a meaningful impact, he felt compelled to prove it all wrong. He took pride in his many achievements: the money, the great house, the sailboat, the sports car—these were easy to list, but they were material things. His life, all that he had built, would take on yet another layer of meaning. Through his business, he gave people jobs, and certainly affected their lives in positive ways—gave them a chance to move on down the path toward realizing their dreams. His relationships, with Renee, with his parents, with numerous friends and business associates who respected him, were cherished. They were unique and special. He knew, as Renee wanted so badly, that someday, when the time was right, he would be a father. He also knew, as she often assured him, he'd be a terrific father, teaching his kid as many of the secrets of life as he possibly could. But this, the trial, was different; he could have another kind of impact on those around him. He might even be able to have a positive effect on hundreds, if not thousands of people in the city. People he almost certainly will never meet, just might, by a long complicated connection of circumstances, have their lives be microscopically better. He had made a commitment to focus on all of the testimony, and evidence he heard, using all of his skills at reasoning and logic, to arrive at the correct conclusion—the only possible conclusion: the truth. And that truth, he knew, would in no small part be arrived at by the role he played on this jury. He was a spear hunter again—aiming at a partially hidden target—the truth. He thought that if he could hit his mark, he would be instrumental in serving justice.

He brought forth the image of Harry, standing next to him that night a couple months ago, in the parking lot, after basketball and beers, recalling what he had said.

Was it tongue in cheek? 'You just want the chance to send a black man to jail.' Or was it something more…

Shit. Why did I just think about that? Not now! Well, if I think he's guilty, if I'm sure he's guilty, then, hell yes—I guess I'll have to do it…

Though he reluctantly admitted to himself that he had broken a couple of admonishments by the judge—in those short talks with Renee about the trial—he was able to rationalize it.

Those quick conversations were nothing. Were they violations? Yeah, I guess, but they were tiny infractions. Besides, I can't believe every juror sitting here next to me is not having similar conversations at home each night…

He defended it, in his head, and felt it ultimately only helped him think more clearly about the trial, so that he would indeed be able to deliver justice.

It appeared to him, that the other jurors were taking this seriously as well. Though he was the only one who was troubled with that issue of the compass, he was excited to think that this group of strangers was about to embark on an interesting and fantastic task—producing justice—in deciding the innocence or guilt of Reggie Washington.

And, if Reggie Washington was indeed a killer, wouldn't sending him to prison be better for every single person in all of Los Angeles? What better contribution to this city could I make than, I, as anonymous Juror Number 4, helped make the entire city just a bit safer…

A point of concern suddenly occurred to him: it was the eleven jurors who had surrounded him these past four days that he knew the least.

****

All eyes in the courtroom were on the district attorney, as she took a final glance down at her notes, and rose from her seat. Eddie had run the course in his feelings toward the prosecutor from respect, and admiration, to disappointment—even thinking at times that the she was incompetent and unprepared. Now, at this juncture in the trial, his opinion of

Sandra Levinthal lay somewhere in between. He did not think she was a great attorney—certainly not the inspiration behind a raging, brilliant prosecutor—the stuff of television and movies. He felt, however that she did an adequate job, and he wondered if Sandra was in fact representative of a typical D.A.

"Ladies and gentlemen of the jury," began Sandra, as she slowly walked toward the jury box, "throughout the past week you have heard numerous individuals testify in this courtroom. They have all helped paint a picture. We heard several people tell you that they saw the defendant in his car that night. The defense did not dispute this! We know his car made a wild U-turn—we even have paint shavings from the curb where he scraped his car. You saw pictures of tire skids that match the tires on his Cadillac. You saw evidence of the bullets that he fired from his gun. You heard that he was wearing a bullet proof vest.

"Oliver Jefferson's partner—Raul Hernandez—told you what happened that night. He ran for help when this man—the defendant, Reggie Washington—began threatening them from his car. In horror, Mr. Hernandez saw this man follow through on his threat.

"Though some of the evidence and forensics may have seemed a bit complicated at times, this is not a complex case, ladies and gentlemen. The picture you have seen painted before you this past week is tragically simple. It was late at night, and a good man, an innocent man, asked some gang kids to turn down their music for the benefit of the tenants who lived on the property. She pointed her tiny hand at Reggie. A coward, this guilty coward who you see seated right there, threatened Oliver Jefferson from across the street, started his car, made that U-turn, and then drove up and shot Oliver Jefferson in cold blood. The defense has not called a single witness! Except for a small yellow scrap of paper, they offered no evidence to counter the facts brought forth by the prosecution. They provided no exhibits or pictures for you to see. In fact, they do not dispute much at all of what you have heard this past week. Their case could not be any weaker. They are counting on a miracle to set this man free. They are relying on you, the jury, saying, 'So what? So another man was killed. Another daily, drive-by shooting. This is Compton—the 'hood.' That's life in L.A.

"Let's remember what we talked about back on the first day of this trial. Let's remember that we came here to perform a duty. And our duty is to let people know that a life matters. It does not matter if this courtroom is empty or full. It does not matter if there are television cameras and reporters or not. But—what does matter is the value of a human life. And if we find, beyond a reasonable doubt, who is responsible for taking that life—we need to provide the court the path for which to punish them. It is our obligation to punish them. We owe this to ourselves. We owe this to all of society. We owe this to Los Angeles—the community we live in. And perhaps most importantly, we owe this to Oliver Jefferson. We have a duty to find his murderer and punish him. So guess what, ladies and gentlemen of the jury? We found him. We found him two minutes later, driving away in his Cadillac. It was a complete act of cruelty—the act of taking Oliver's life away from all of us. We must do our duty to punish those—those like our Reginald Washington here—who feel they can take away a precious life, and then freely drive away into the night. Please think about this when you deliberate, and I'm sure you will return with a verdict of guilty. Thank you."

Sandra mirrored some of Eddie's thoughts in her closing statement. He had to admit he was feeling pretty strongly that Reginald Washington was indeed a murderer. To find him innocent, he thought to himself, he needed more evidence to the contrary. Any evidence to the contrary.

Hell, here I go again having these thoughts! But how can the defense not have a single witness? Is it really as simple as the district attorney says? Did I miss something?

He was eager to hear what the defense attorney had to say in her closing, as she rose from the defense table and walked forward. He was excited, and even conjectured as to what she would say to counter this strong summation just delivered by Sandra Levinthal for *The People*—her counterpart.

But Eddie was surprised. Almost immediately, Rosemary Davis seemed to lose her composure. It was bizarre, thought Eddie—up to this point, she had displayed a fairly professional and experienced air—even if her case was rather weak. Eddie recalled how she seemed to quickly grasp the erroneous compass of that early exhibit. In fact, he reflected, she just might have understood it better than anyone besides himself in that entire courtroom. He remembered her terrific performance with the wooden pointer, almost using it as if she were waiving the baton of an orchestra conductor, jabbing at the prosecution's exhibits—explaining the distances and turns of the Cadillac, using her adversary's pictures and diagrams while excitedly presenting an alternative and plausible timeline to the events on the night of the murder.

But now, after only a few sentences into her closing argument, the defense attorney appeared to be—ranting.

"How can the prosecution say the defense has no case?" she begged. "It's the prosecution who has no case."

Ms. Davis stormed up to the jury box, hands on her hips. Eddie felt a strange emotion: was this the same woman? Even her hair seemed somehow different. He was a little embarrassed for her—while simultaneously, ashamed at his own reaction to her voice—the way she now spoke: *kind of ghetto.*

It was almost—he searched for the right word—*'jive.'*

"The prosecution says they found bullets. But there's no *blood* on the *bullets!* They could have been shot into that wall or that tree that night, or—how about a year ago—during the riots? I'll bet most of us sitting in this court today were here in L.A. during the riots, and you know how much shooting there was and how many bullets were flying through the air. Did they find all of those bullets? I don't think so! And let's just think about this: we know for a fact that there was at least one other gun on the grounds that night. I'm sorry that Mr. Jefferson is dead, but we have to consider the possibility that the bullet that killed him was shot by somebody else. Like those kids on the side of the street who were shooting live ammunition at basketballs. We know for a fact that those kids were arguing with Oliver Jefferson. Maybe it's far more likely that one of *those* bullets killed Mr. Jefferson. One of those bullets went through his body and ended up in a car driving away on Century Boulevard. The po-lease never produced any bullets that shot any basketballs either—did they?

"Then, when the po-lease picked up the defendant..."

Wow—she is pronouncing the word much differently than earlier in the trial! It's now become a distinct two-syllable word—emphasizing 'po!'

"...they made a big deal about how my client was wearing a red bandanna, and a bullet proof vest. Now I ask you, ladies and gentlemen of the jury, is that relevant information? And what direction was he driving? Was it North? Was it South? Was it East, or maybe West?"

She was highly animated, exaggerating her movements with wild gesticulations in all directions.

"Do any of you know? Because I sure don't." She put her hands back on her hips, elbows angled out wide, like a gunslinger before a duel.

Eddie had of course remained in the same seat, in the front row of the jury box throughout the trial, and now, the defense attorney was standing directly in front of him, not five feet away. He was close enough to see dampened spots of the chiffon fabric under her armpits when she raised her arms and the sides of her blazer flew open. He was close enough to see a small portion of her satin cream colored bra-cup in the gap between two of the buttons on the blouse. He was close enough to see beads of sweat flowing freely from her shiny brown forehead. It was no coincidence that the attorney chose to stand this close to Eddie. Undoubtedly because of her just mentioned compass coordinates, she made unmistakable eye contact with him. Eddie stared back at her coldly, and she quickly—probably wisely—looked away to another juror.

Her rant continued, "I don't think the *po-lease* even know what direction Mr. Washington was driving his Cadillac! And you want to believe *them* that my client is a murderer?"

Eddie was outraged. He could not believe that anybody who had followed the trial for the past few days would swallow these spins—these spins put into the story by this emotional woman. She was clearly twisting the story—putting the emphasis on questioning the credibility of the cops.

"And let me ask you this, ladies and gentlemen of the jury," lifting both palms skyward, "did the *po-lease* find the gun? Where is it?

"So let's see: no bullets. No blood. And—oh yeah—no gun. Not exactly what we might think of as brilliant police work.

"Perhaps you would rather believe the story from the overweight security guard—the one who claims he is the world's fastest human—miraculously running up in time to see my client kill Mr. Jefferson."

Two jurors to Eddie's left chuckled.

"The prosecution, in her closing just now, spoke of a hoped for miracle by me. If I didn't have a job to do, an important job, in defending this innocent man," she had walked behind the defendant, and put a hand on Reggie's shoulder, "I'd be insulted." She stepped away from Reggie and walked slowly back toward the jury. "I'd be insulted as the real miracle is that negligent—heck—I'll say it: *obese security guard* breaking the world's record."

Eddie felt sick. He realized that Rosemary Davis was riling up the jury. She was acting, and it was working.

Could four days of sitting and listening to all of those excruciating facts come down to this woman playing to a couple of jurors' thoughts on Hernandez and the police?

Eddie could not help feeling that this was somehow dirty.

She couldn't prove that he didn't own a brown Cadillac, or a hand-gun, or never belonged to the Bloods. She couldn't prove that he was maybe at a movie that night—and could not have been at the Century Palms apartment complex. Not a single witness—not even a fellow gang member to lie for him! She resorted to playing to the jury's emotions. Their emotions—not surrounding the murder—but the emotions that seemed to run through the entire city of Los Angeles at the moment: the belief that the cops were racists. But the beauty of this unclean strategy! The beauty was she did not even need all of us—the whole jury—to buy it. She did not even need the majority of us to feel this way. The beauty was—she only needed one...

CHAPTER 11 - The Jury

October 21, 1993 PM
Compton, California

During a short recess ordered by the judge, Eddie found himself curiously rubbing his sore elbow. Then he recalled the bizarre scene in bed this morning in which he woke—flailing like a madman, and whacking his wife. He was dangerously close to being late in arriving at the courthouse, as he had overslept—having gone almost the entire night without sleep, only to finally succumb to that terrifying dream at dawn. He had looked at the clock and got dressed frantically without taking a shower.

Now, coupled with the grogginess from the restless night, he was also hungry from running out of the house without having eaten breakfast. He needed to settle his rumbling stomach with something quick from the cafeteria. But, more importantly, he needed to call Renee. If his own elbow was sore, he figured, she must really be hurting. He found a payphone but it was being used by a skinny white kid, perhaps 23 or 24, with torn jeans and a scraggly red beard. The boy was speaking loudly into the phone; as Eddie approached, he was able to overhear something to the effect of "… and that asshole wants to get me fired."

He looked around for other phones, but saw the hoards of people milling about the hallway on the ground floor of the courthouse. With nobody else waiting, he decided it best he stick by this one. Eddie tried not to listen, but it was impossible; he needed to stay in close proximity to make it obvious he was next in line.

"…dickhead manager thinks I stole two quarts of oil. Shit motherfucker! If I was gonna steal something, I'd steal some sparkplugs. They're smaller and much more valuable. Jack walked out last week with a fucking alternator!"

The young man turned and gave Eddie a little nod and a smile, putting an index finger up, to acknowledge he was aware he was waiting—that he would only be another minute. There were now two ladies lined up closely behind Eddie. The kid seemed oblivious to the fact that his conversation was audible to Eddie, as well as the others.

Eddie forced a smile back at the kid, who eventually ended his conversation with, "Fuck Pep Boys." He depressed the cradle with two fingers on his left hand while politely handing the receiver to Eddie, already digging into his pocket for a quarter. Eddie's mind replayed his morning exit: having bolted out of the house—he drove much faster than he should have—to barely make it to the courthouse on time. Feeling terrible that he hadn't been able to comfort his wife, having left her crying in bed, he dropped the coin into the slot. Noticing a curly rust colored hair on the mouth piece, he muttered an obscenity directed at the kid and quickly wiped the greasy receiver on his right sleeve. Listening anxiously to the rings, he prayed she would answer…

"Hey! It's a beautiful day so Eddie and Renee are out sailing. We don't know when we'll be back, but we'll call you then." Beep.

Shit.

Remembering she had a late morning presentation to give in one of her law classes, he fumbled for the words to leave on the tape machine, feeling awkward with the ladies standing so close.

"Hi... I hope you're OK. I love you. Uh, sorry about the chin."

Five minutes later he stood in silence in the cafeteria line, picturing her first presentation of the semester, in front of her professor, with a bruised face and an unflattering band-aid on her chin. Eddie shuddered at the uncomfortable explanations she would be asked to give multiple times throughout the day.

'Your husband hit you?'

He hated himself for putting her through this—hated himself for getting so excited about his summons to jury duty. Thinking back, he decided he was stupid not to let his basketball buddies talk him out of it. He hated the Compton Courthouse. But mostly he found himself hating Reggie Washington. He hated what he represented. It disturbed Eddie to realize that something, that a concept such as Reggie, even existed—an entity that challenged all that Eddie lived for. It wasn't just the obvious point that Reggie could murder somebody—an innocent man like Oliver Jefferson—it was even bigger than that. For years, Eddie had toiled: he thought he had built a safety net—an escape, from the uncertain and frightening world of his past—to build an exciting and promising future. And he thought he had succeeded. But now, it was apparent that Reggie—the force that created Reggie—was real. It was back, and it was a force that threatened the very dreams and all that made up Eddie's good life.

Reaching the front of the line, he perused a couple pieces of fruit. The apples had no shine to them. They looked old and the skin was beginning to form small wrinkles. The ratio of black spots to yellow patches on the banana peels was far too great; they were obviously bruised. He grabbed at, and began wolfing down a ridiculously sweet lemon swirl. The words *'pastry'* or *'fresh'* could not be applied, as the dough seemed to be there only as a vessel, to contain the disgusting yellow goo in the center. It was stale to the point of being hard, yet Eddie finished it before reaching the cashier.

Eddie walked briskly back to the courtroom; in the short recess, waiting in those two lines precluded any time to wash his hands. He picked up his notepad and pen, retaking his seat in the jury box. To his left, Juror Number 5 eyed him curiously as he tore out a couple of pages to use as napkins—fingers still sticky from the awful icing.

****

It took Judge Sherman nearly twenty minutes to read aloud to the jury, nineteen pages that included their instructions, as well as the numerous charges against Reggie Washington.

At 10:45 on the morning of the fourth day of the trial, the twelve jurors stood up from their seats and filed through a heavy brown door adjacent to the jury box, held open respectfully by Bailiff Ellis.

To the silent group now standing before him in the deliberation room, the Bailiff's huge frame seemed, almost intentionally, to block the exit. He explained the procedure for summoning him—pointing to an ominous red button inset into a metal light switch cover on the wall. He stoically wished them luck, closed the door, and was gone.

Eddie had the unpleasant sensation of being trapped—of being locked in. There were no windows. But in actuality—the irony was that the room was designed to lock the rest of the world out.

A thick air of tension and uncomfortable silence was broken by a middle aged black woman, who had been juror number ten, announcing, albeit a bit too loudly, "I don't know about ya'll, but I'm gonna sit down."

It enabled an immediate release of stress; several jurors giggled, a fifteen second game of musical chairs ensued. There were lots of little mundane movements and actions, shuffling of purses and jackets and magazines, as everyone sat. But the silence and tension returned. People positioned and repositioned their chairs. Some fidgeted with the proper placement of their new prized possession—their juror notepads. A few opened these spiral notebooks, pretending to adroitly synthesize a quick review of the case.

This time, it was juror number two, a young black man, who spoke, "I think we're supposed to elect a foreman."

"Yeah," confirmed another black man—juror number one, seated next to him, "I remember reading that in the juror's handbook. That's the first thing we do."

"Well don't look at me," said another, slightly younger, black woman who occupied seat five in the jury box during the trial, and now once again sat to Eddie's immediate left.

Nearly simultaneously, "Me neither!" and "No way!" announced two women, seated consecutively in seats numbered ten and eleven.

"Well," interjected juror eight, the one Caucasian female in the room, "I think maybe we're supposed to vote on it."

Number two spoke again, "We can't vote on it if nobody wants to do it. Does anybody want to be foreman?"

An Asian man in seat twelve frowned, shaking his head. Several others shook their heads in similar fashion, while the two women in seats ten and eleven each let out sarcastic grunts. Juror number five rewound and replayed her *'Don't look at me'* recording—this time, with a bit more volume.

Again, the room turned quiet, except for a few squeaks from nervous panelists swiveling in their seats a bit too aggressively.

"Anybody?" asked number two again.

"I went to college. I don't mind being foreman."

Eleven surprised sets of eyes turned toward Eddie.

"Does anybody have any objections?" asked number two.

Now it was Eddie's eyes that surveyed the large oval conference table. Mostly, he met with relieved nods.

"Sounds good to me," said juror number eight, as several others began speaking a bit more freely.

"You got it man," said juror number two, with a genuine smile.

"Yeah. We're already ahead of schedule. We don't have to even vote," said one juror.

"Cool, we can finish this and go home early," said another.

Eddie had been a summer camp counselor as a teenager, and had been in many discussion groups throughout his school days. Naturally, he also had experience driving the agenda of countless business meetings. He tried to quickly retrieve some of those numerous techniques for the effective leadership of a meeting, but at that precise moment, his mind was blank, save the one image that kept pounding at memory's door for the opening of a meeting in which the group was a bit uncomfortable, or nervous.

The memory was of a UCLA calculus professor, who, before a final exam, would have the anxious students clear their desks of calculators, bluebooks, and pencils. The professor then asked his students to sit on top of the desks, in the lotus position, close their eyes, and breathe deeply for two full minutes. To complete the effect, he even dimmed the lights. For Eddie, who was a master at cramming for exams throughout high school and college, this was a monstrous intrusion into his finely honed state of preparation, as his ability to immediately regurgitate concepts and formulas the moment a test began was greatly compromised.

Man, I hated that teacher! Was it Smith? Maybe Simpkins... I can't quite visualize the possibility of these 11 strangers acquiescing to me asking them to sit cross-legged up on the conference table for a brief meditation...

"I guess we've been thinking of each other the past week as Juror Number One, Juror Number Two, and so on... I know I myself have taken on a new identity as Juror Number Four. So why don't we go around the table and introduce ourselves.

"My name is Eddie," he said, looking to his left at the woman wearing a garish purple pant suit that contrasted loudly with her shocking pink nail polish.

"My name," she announced firmly, "is Lucille Franklin."

"Hi, I'm Ralph, juror number six."

"Jorge Ruiz." He made a slight wave of hello to the others in the room, and turned to his left with a smile.

"My name is Kate Richards. Nice to meet you."

"Hello, I'm Jeff Milch," said the other white male, who seemed to be about Eddie's age.

"Henrietta."

"Lottie."

Eddie noted that somehow, these two women—jurors ten and eleven—seemed to be a package deal.

"Juror number twelve—Mr. Wong."

"My name is Harold Williamson. Pleased to meet you."

"Juror number two—Darryl Rollins."

"My name is Annette Clarissa Rogers—juror number three. My friends call me Claire."

Sitting conspicuously, in the center of the table, an old wooden tray held the thick stack of papers with the jury instructions and charges. Eddie eyed the tray. In contrast to its stark surroundings in the clean, modern deliberation room, and especially as to the serious contents of the old tray, the fact that the wood was completely scarred by years of doodles in red, blue and black ink seemed almost whimsical. It was as if the tray was made from reclaimed wood—wood from the old fashioned desk of an innocent third grader.

Or did the doodles more accurately reflect years of nervous agony by past jury foremen?

Eddie stood and leaned forward. He slid the tray toward himself, as the rest of the group watched. Picking up the heavy stack of papers, he began skimming. Many thoughts raced through his mind, not the least of which was his cognizance of the scrutiny these people were putting him through. Nevertheless, he proceeded at his own comfortable pace. He found it particularly interesting, the several cross-outs by a heavy black marker. In addition, curiously, many words and sentence fragments had been inserted within the typed area by personal handwriting. He wondered for a moment if these changes were made by Judge Sherman, and then felt sure that they were. He was fascinated by the ramifications of the corrections—certain that each of them was critical in some esoteric way. He was hit with a desire to understand why some passages were blacked out completely—the judge being careful not to allow a single word of the original document to be read. Human nature, or at least *Eddie's* nature being what it was, he was more interested in the parts that were blacked out, than the stuff he could read.

Hell, if this is so critical, why don't they just type the whole thing over?

He made a mental note to ask his wife what she knew about the strange—user *unfriendly*—format of the instructions and all the censored portions.

My wife...

He flashed on belting Renee in the chin again, felt the soreness in his right elbow, felt the guilt. He thought about his lame phone message. He knew that by far, she got the worst of the deal. Blinking forcibly, Eddie was able to banish his mind's distraction from the task at hand, pondering for a moment whether or not it would be prudent to read the entire document aloud to the rest of the panel. His quick scan of the pages not only reinforced his memory, but also added another dimension to the same words read earlier by the judge. But he rejected the idea for two reasons. One, he recalled how tediously long the reading by the judge had seemed. He felt that the volume and wordiness of the charges could have been simplified—he recalled several fellow jurors shifting with bored body language when the charges were being read the first time—less than an hour ago. Secondly, he was anxious to start the discussions. He was overcome with curiosity. Did the rest of the jurors feel like he did? Did he miss something important during the trial? Or, was this simply a very clear cut case: no witnesses for the defense, plenty of witnesses for the prosecution, an abundance of evidence, and simply—short of a confession—the man on trial, Reggie Washington, was indeed the man who murdered Oliver Jefferson.

Part of Eddie wanted to take an immediate vote. Just for the hell of it. Maybe it would be unanimous, and they could get out of there in five minutes—setting a new world's record for quick jury deliberations. Also, he thought it would be interesting to take people's pulse at the very beginning—and then to see how far they evolved by the end. He thought of the classic old movie, *'Twelve Angry Men,'* and smiled to himself.

But once again, as far as the early vote, he rejected his own idea.

"I'm sure we all have many thoughts and questions about the case we have just heard. I can think of no better way to get started, since it's fresh on everyone's minds, than to jump right in. Let's talk about it. Now who would like to start?"

The first hand that shot up was from the woman to Eddie's right.

"It's Claire, right?" said Eddie, already pleased that during introductions, he had drawn a quick seating chart of the conference table with everybody's names. "Go right ahead Claire."

"Thank You. Does anybody else here think that the D.A.— the white woman—I mean, the lawyer for the prosecution— did a terrible job?"

"What the hell were all those cops talking about? I didn't understand them," said Harold Williamson from across the table, putting his hand down.

"My question is about the murder. They said the gun—"

Eddie was not even sure who said this, as the quick comments were now coming rapid-fire.

"I have a question about the last detective's testimony," said Jorge Ruiz. "When he was talking about the bullets in—"

Jorge was cut off by Juror eleven, Lottie. "What gang did they say he was in?"

Jeff Milch tried to answer, "I'm not sure that's relevant to the murder. He—"

Mr. Wong cut him off. He raised his hand and asked forcefully, "May I say something? May I say something?"

Darryl abruptly shouted, "How can we talk of murder already, how can you even use that word. Don't tell me that—"

Eddie had been following these frantic sentence fragments, stunned at some of the immediate implications.

"OK people, OK. Let's try to get some order established here." Thankfully, the outpouring came to an abrupt halt as Eddie spoke. "We have all the time we want to talk about this case, and nobody is going to rush us. But we can't have a meaningful discussion if everyone is talking at once. Let's listen to what each other has to say, because it might just be something that none of us has thought of before, and it could very well be rather important." Eddie paused, pleased that his idea appeared to take hold.

"So, back to Claire, you opened the discussion and I believe—"

"That's right," said Lucille.

Eddie continued, slightly miffed at the unnecessary affirmation, "—you said something about the district attorney doing a poor job. Do you want to talk about that, or do you have a question about something she did?"

"Well, I did not say she did a poor job. I said she did a terrible job. She was supposed to prove beyond a reasonable doubt. But I don't think she proved anything."

"Exactly," said Lucille. "She tried to confuse us with all that North, East, West, South stuff. But I wasn't confused."

She looked directly at Eddie. "I know *you* were confused."
Eddie's heartbeat quickened.

Darryl added, "I think that was just a trick—and I don't like being tricked. And it didn't fool me no-how."

Eddie held his tongue as Kate Richards spoke from the other end of the table. "I don't know how it could be a trick. It sure seemed to me like the district attorney was confused. I don't think she tried to trick us... in fact, I think she was a little embarrassed by that whole thing with the compass."

Jeff spoke as soon as Kate was finished. "How could anyone understand that stuff with the compass? Even the Judge said that the exhibit had the streets running the wrong way. I also remember him specifically saying that we should be able to figure it out during deliberations. So, no, I don't think she tried to trick us at all."

"Hey man," Darryl now addressed Eddie, "what exactly did you say in your note to the judge. I think you should tell us."

"Yeah," said Lottie, from across the table. "I think we have a right to know."

The discussion wasn't five minutes old, yet Eddie already regretted volunteering to be foreman. But he kept his composure, "I think we're jumping into an area... the issue with the compass didn't even happen until halfway through the trial. Let's not get ahead of ourselves so quickly. We'll talk about that soon enough... so let's see what we have here on a more basic level... A man has been accused of murder. What exactly do we all know about the defendant, Reginald Washington?"

"I think we can all agree he was a gang member," said Harold. "The *'Cimarron Avenue Bloods.'* Yeah, that's what I have written down here in my notes. And I don't think there was any doubt that he was the driver of that brown Cadillac."

Mr. Wong, seated next to Harold spoke in a heavy Korean accent, "I think that security guard, Henderson, was certain he saw the defendant. He was sure it was him from previous encounters in the neighborhood."

"Hernandez," Jorge corrected, emphasizing the proper Spanish accent.

"And," said Lucille, "they were hanging out across the street for a long time—listening to the music and drinking beer and all—but it don't make no sense to me that he would all of a sudden start the car and kill that man. I don't believe it."

Eddie spoke again, "Let's just try for a minute here to talk about what we're fairly sure happened—in relation to the defendant—what we know for certain about him. We can use the blackboard to try to list what we know—then later we can discuss what we feel it all means. Can somebody help write this down?"

Eddie looked at Juror number seven, Jorge, who was seated closest to the blackboard. He also liked the fact that, in addition to politely giving Wong the Henderson-Hernandez correction, Jorge also appeared to be paying close attention.

"Mr. Ruiz?"

"I don't think my spelling is so good," he said nervously.

"I'll do it," said Ralph, who was seated next to Jorge. "I'm a teacher—I'm used to getting chalk all over my hands and clothes."

He stood and wrote the defendant's name in large capital letters on top of the board. He appeared indeed to be familiar with the aggressive style of smacking chalk onto the board to command the attention of his students.

"So," said Eddie, "I think we all agree he was a gang member."

Ralph wrote: 1. Gang—Cimarron Ave. Bloods. On the next line he made a number "2" and then faced the group as if waiting for the correct answer from his class.

"He drove the Cadillac," said Wong, "and everyone knew him."

Ralph wrote 'Familiar in Neighborhood' adjacent to the number two, and 'Driver of Cadillac' on line three.

"He was drunk, and he was insulting the guards," said Darryl.

Quite defensively, as if she was the accused, Henrietta said, "Now just how do you know he was drunk?"

"Yeah," echoed Lottie.

"They never proved anybody was drunk. I don't remember any testimony about a breath test or urine test or anything," added Claire.

"I have to agree with Claire," concurred Eddie. "That's my recollection as well. Can we agree that he was drinking and yelling at the guards?"

"OK," said Darryl, slightly embarrassed as his was the first comment that people openly disagreed with, "but he was probably high on booze or drugs or both. And he definitely threw beer bottles at them."

This drew a loud protest from several sources in the room.

"Come on!"

"What are you talking about? They never mentioned drugs."

"Of course they mentioned drugs!"

"How do you know it was Washington who threw the bottles?"

"The detective said they found broken glass near the curb." Darryl defended.

"That whole street is probably full of broken glass," said Harold.

Eddie heard the fast clicking of chalk, and looked up at Ralph who began writing: 4. Partying 5. Insulting Guards. He approved of the teacher's quick simplification.

For the first time, Eddie was pleased with the way the discussion was going. He had to admit: it was exciting. "OK, what else do we know about Reginald Washington?"

Eddie looked at Juror nine, Jeff Milch, on Eddie's little chart.

Jeff, the only other white male besides Eddie, responded from across the table. "What strikes me as real incriminating—that Washington was a bad dude—is that he was wearing a bullet proof vest. I can't help but wonder why?"

"Are you saying he planned to kill the guard?" asked Claire, dismayed.

"Planned?" asked Harold.

"Hey," shouted Jorge, "they never said he was wearing the vest!"

"That's right!" confirmed Lucille, as Eddie's head whipped around the table to catch these quick snippets.

All eyes turned toward the big man at the blackboard as Ralph spoke, "I specifically remember they found him—the cops when they arrested him—wearing the vest. He was wearing the bullet proof vest the whole time he was sitting in the car."

"I remember that too," said Wong.

Several other voices joined in simultaneously, "That's right, that's exactly what they said."

"Uh huh."

"He definitely wore the vest the whole time."

"No way. You're wrong!" said Lucille with authority.

Claire now weakened her position, "Let's see, I remember them talking about the vest—I just don't remember for sure if they said he was wearing it when he was arrested."

"Forget about whether he had it on or not," said Jeff again, "why the heck did he have it in the car to begin with? Doesn't that prove his intentions?"

"I could be wearing a bathing suit," said Harold, "that doesn't prove I was at the beach."

"Oh come on! That's not nearly the same thing. You can't really equate a bathing suit with a bullet proof vest!" said Jeff.

Eddie happened to think Harold made a very valid point. Circumstantial evidence proved nothing, and that, the bathing suit comment, was probably the most succinct example of it he'd ever heard. However, Eddie felt he should restrain himself from airing his own opinions, in favor of acting in his role as foreman. Accepting that it was his job to preserve order, and in the interest of keeping the deliberations moving—he thought it best that he keep his thoughts on that to himself. At least for now.

"Please," Eddie interjected, "let's try to stick with listing the most obvious facts for now—we'll discuss what we feel they mean shortly. Perhaps the Kevlar vest will prove important, perhaps not. But let's see if we can at least agree where it was."

Jeff and Harold each were certain the other was dead wrong, but they, like Eddie, were able to temporarily belay their strong feelings.

"I know! I have the answer right here." It was Kate Richards, the lone white female on the jury, who spoke from the end of the conference table. All eyes were on her as the room had returned to calm after Eddie's brief speech. She fumbled with her bulky purse on the floor, pulling out something which at first looked like a small leather appointment book. She set it on the table in front of her and then flipped a switch.

It was a dictaphone. A slightly crackly, nasally, sound permeated the small room. It was powerful in its emanation from such a tiny device—not by its volume, but by the voice being instantly recognized as belonging to the district attorney, Sandra Levinthal.

"... fired four shots from a gun..."

"Wow, cool!" said Jorge who sat next to Kate.

"What a great—" began Lucille.

The slam of Eddie's hand directly in front of a frightened Lucille shook the heavy table. "Turn that thing off!"

"...brown El Dorado Cadillac..." continued the district attorney's voice from the small tape machine.

"Turn it off *now!*" shouted Eddie again, visibly startling several more of the jurors.

Kate's eyes widened from behind her thick glasses. Eddie could see grease spots and tiny flecks of dandruff suspended on the lenses as their eyes met. Her pride at having come up with a brilliant contribution to this jury—this group of strangers who she was so certain she would impress—was crushed after a mere five seconds.

Fumbling with the tiny silver switch, she clicked off the little device.

"Why can't we listen to the tape?" asked Darryl naively. "I think that's a great way to prove—"

Ralph had moved behind Kate. He flipped the white chalk a few inches in the air, and snatched it with a quick sweeping motion of his hand. In a baritone voice he asked, "Didn't you read the jurors' handbook?"

She didn't answer, staring instead down at her recorder.

"Hell," said Henrietta, "this is my fourth stint on jury duty, and I've never read that damn manual."

"Right on," chimed Lottie.

It was an early test of Eddie's patience. "There happens to be some very important information in there. Things we really should know before agreeing to participate as jurors."

Ralph spoke again, "It specifically says that we are not to use tape recorders. And there are some very good reasons for that."

Eddie was surprised to hear that several of these people were so freely admitting that they had not read the handbook that arrived in the mail. He was also rather thankful for the support from Ralph.

Finally, a wounded Kate, raised her head, "I don't see why we can't. Besides, I was only trying to help. Everybody seemed to be confused about the bullet proof vest and I thought—"

Eddie interrupted her, "I think we all appreciate what you were trying to do. But in the same way that the judge has been constantly admonishing us this past week—there are a lot of rules that we must follow. We can't—"

Lucille now interrupted Eddie, "Well most of those rules are stupid. And how many times does the judge have to tell us the same damn thing over and over? And another thing: I think we'd all appreciate it if you'd just speak plain English and use words we can all understand. Like 'ammonishing' or 'astonishing' or whatever the hell you just said."

"Right on girl," said Henrietta.

"I heard that!" affirmed Lottie, as Eddie suddenly realized that he abhorred every word that came out of this woman's mouth.

"Hey, like it or not, we gotta follow the rules," said Harold.

"I thought when we were locked in this room we could make our own rules," offered Darryl.

"I read the manual," said Claire. "I agree, most of it's junk. But I have to admit some of it is important. Like the stuff about tape recorders."

"That's right," said Jeff, catty-cornered across the table. "We can't just do whatever we want, Darryl—we've got to work within the framework of the guidelines they have set for us."

"The *'framework of the guidelines?'* Boy—what the hell does that mean?" asked Lucille.

In the last two minutes, this woman, Lucille, just attacked me and Jeff, the only two white males in the room... Is this a coincidence?

Ralph spoke up, thinking it would be better to leave Lucille's comments unaddressed.

"Hey—we shouldn't even be discussing this," explained Ralph as he pulled back his chair and took his seat. "It's not for us to decide what rules should or should not be followed. But the fact is—this juror here," he opened his palm toward Kate, "did break one of the rules. And we now need to figure out what should be done about it."

Mr. Wong announced nervously, "I think that's what we have alternates for."

Wong's comment froze the room. All eyes bore down on the humiliated Kate Richards.

"Like I said," she looked around, pleading, "I was only trying to help."

Eddie tried to quickly calculate the ramifications of buzzing the bailiff, bringing the court back in session, and going through whatever motions might be required in getting an alternate juror to take her place—and then starting deliberations over. He thought carefully, realizing, that for the most part, people seemed to be looking to him to lead.

"Ms. Richards," he began, "would you mind giving me the tape?"

She weakly nodded her head, as Eddie stood and walked over to her. She ejected the tape and reluctantly placed it in Eddie's palm.

Eddie held up the small clear plastic microcassette. "I personally did not hear anything on this tape that I did not hear before. Plus, I can say honestly that what I just heard in the few seconds that this tape was playing does not affect my feelings in any way about the evidence in this case..." He paused—catching the eyes of the sad woman, and thought of a way to possibly salvage the situation, "...nor do I have any ill feelings toward my fellow juror here, Ms. Richards, who I firmly believe was indeed trying in good faith to help."

Eddie considered for a fleeting moment gently resting his hand on Kate's shoulder, but rejected the idea. "I therefore see no reason why we can't proceed with our deliberations—proceed with the twelve of us seated right here. Does anybody feel differently?"

Lots of heads shook slowly from side to side. Jeff, sitting to Kate's left, gave her a gentle pat on the arm, at which she smiled. So did Eddie.

"What are you gonna do with the tape?" asked Claire.

Eddie was glad she asked. He held up the cassette, appearing to study it for a moment. He then began to pluck at the thin tape, pinching it with his right thumb and forefinger until he was able to get purchase on a small loop. He pulled it an inch out of the plastic cassette housing. Then, holding the little cassette with his left hand, he dramatically flung his right hand out to the side. The cassette's tiny geared wheels whizzed, as a long looping trail of brown celluloid flew through the air.

A couple of jurors' mouths dropped open, as Eddie kept repeating the motion—pulling and pulling at the tape—until he had a large brown tangled mess accumulated on the conference table. He yanked the tape free from the housing, and tossed the empty cassette into the corner, banking it off the wall and into the waste basket near the door, before walking back to his seat.

"I just want to say I'm sorry," said Kate. "I admit what I did was wrong. Thank you for not replacing me with an alternate."

"Thanks for saying that, Kate," said Eddie. "I hope we've all learned something here, and we can now move on. I do recommend that before we resume tomorrow, if you haven't done so already, that you each read your juror's handbooks that you should have received in the mail. If not, I'm sure you can get a copy downstairs in the—"

"Uh… " began Kate again, "I wasn't quite finished."

"That's OK—we accept your apology. Now we've got some serious work to do and—"

But she interrupted Eddie again, "That's not what I meant. What I'm trying to say is, as long as we're at it—that's only a 90 minute tape. I guess I should tell you about the others."

"Others?" asked Ralph.

Eyes bulged incredulously as she reached down and brought her large purse back up from the floor. She again swiveled the brass clasp and pulled out a gallon sized freezer zip-lock baggie. It contained eight additional tapes. She handed the bag to Jorge and motioned for him to pass it along to Eddie.

Jorge seemed almost afraid to touch the bag—as if it was somehow tainted. He quickly handed the baggie to the next juror. But Ralph didn't immediately pass the bag on to juror number five. With both hands, he held it up in front of his face, seemingly to examine the contents more closely. Strangely, he smiled. The yellow toothed smile of this huge man grew broader, spreading his moustache to the ends of his wide black face. He chuckled. Still holding the baggie aloft, he turned toward their foreman.

"You said your name was Eddie, right?"

"Yes sir."

"Well Eddie, that looked like a lot of fun—pulling all that tape out. In fact I've always wanted to try it." Ralph opened the zip lock bag and took out one of the cassettes. "May I?"

"Be my guest, Ralph," encouraged Eddie.

Ralph began pulling. The tiny gears whizzed again, and tape started spilling over the table—piling up in front of Ralph.

On either side of Ralph, Jorge and Lucille each grabbed a tape from the bag.

Kate, could now take some pride in her contribution to the jury deliberations. She stood up and reached back across the table, leaning across Jorge and Ralph. She grabbed the baggie and proceeded to dump out the remainder of her cassettes onto the table, grabbing one.

"I need one too. Toss me one," said Jeff.

"Get *me* a tape," said Claire, as, across the slick surface of the conference table, like a neat pass of a hockey puck across the ice, Ralph slid one of the cassettes to the left to Jeff, and then another to the right, to Claire.

Even Mr. Wong from the opposite end of the table spoke up, "I'd like to try one, please."

Eddie, at that moment recalled he had been in the same elevator with Kate, on one of their many rides up to the 6th floor, and had overheard her engaged in small talk with another lady about how she was born in Georgia. Obviously proud of her Southern roots, Kate now let out an authentic rebel yell, and tossed a cassette across the room to Mr. Wong who caught it with both hands.

By now, most of the jurors were getting into the act of spinning tape out of the cassettes. Ralph couldn't contain himself any longer. He let out a belly laugh. It started as a low bass rumble, and quickly crescendoed into a roar. It was like a Times Square ticker tape parade. Instead of the traditional horns and kazoos, a high pitched whirring of many miniscule gears shot out more and more tape as it spilled out over the table and onto the floor. As each 90 minute cassette held over 100 yards of tape, soon—almost a mile of plastic brown spaghetti filled the jury room. All twelve of the jurors, black, white, Mexican, Korean, male and female, were laughing. Some had tears in their eyes.

Eddie grabbed a couple of handfuls of the celluloid confetti to try and uncover the sacred wooden box that held the jury instructions. Rolling his seat back, he stood to address the group, "I think this might be a good time to call it a day."

CHAPTER 12 - Black Fingernails

October 22, 1993 AM
Compton, California

Bailiff Ellis held the door open for the jurors, as seemed to be the ritual. He said, 'Good morning,' twelve different times, there being zero discernable variation in any of the greetings. Eddie looked down, quickly noticing that the mounds of cassette tape had been removed, while the floor was freshly vacuumed. The waste basket had been emptied. The wooden box containing the jury instructions was perfectly placed in the center of the conference table as if it had never been touched. Each of the jurors notebooks had been collected by the bailiff as they walked out of the deliberation room yesterday afternoon; this morning, the books had all been put back on the table—placed neatly in front of the respective seats of their owners.

Eddie could not help but conjecture at the thoughts the Bailiff must have had upon entering this room last night—upon discovering the piles of brown tape.

Jesus! There's no way he ever saw anything like that before! How could he? He must be dying to ask somebody what the hell happened in here. Did he tell the judge about the mess, or about the tapes? Is he even allowed to tell the judge? On the other hand, it's hard to picture the Bailiff with a

220

vacuum; maybe some cleaning crew came in and made everything disappear—destroying the evidence.

Eddie's mind switched to thinking of how he would open discussions this morning. He took a quick look back over his shoulder at the big man in the doorway. Just as he turned to close the heavy door, and back out of the room, the bailiff made unmistakable eye contact with Eddie, paused, and winked.

Shit! That's the second time in this trial that this guy has winked at me! And both times it's been after something really strange... I think...

But Eddie's ruminating was unexpectedly broken by Lucille; she stood and made sure she had the attention of each of the jurors.

"I would like to share with all of you a bit of research I did last night. I assure you it is quite relevant and possibly even the answer to what we are all trying to do here."

"Excuse me, Ms. Franklin?" asked Eddie.

"I'm not finished yet sir," she blurted at Eddie—effectively starting the second day of deliberations off with a cannon blast.

"You cannot—" Eddie was cut off as the woman began loudly reciting a passage.

"If anyone kills a person, the manslayer may be executed only on the evidence of witnesses; the testimony of a single witness against a person shall not suffice for a sentence of death."

She scanned the room methodically. "It's here—in the Bible. The Book of Numbers, Chapter thirty-five, verse thirty."

"What's in the Bible?" asked Jorge.

"Uh oh. Somebody didn't read their juror's handbook last night," said Ralph.

"I don't understand," said Wong.

Lucille again made sweeping eye contact with each individual juror as she spoke. "It's very simple—we need at least two witnesses to prove anything. That's what the Bible says, and that's what I believe. I'll read all of you another passage..."

Quickly, she grabbed from her purse a small leather bound bible. It bore no markings—neither on the cover nor the spine—save for a large cross embossed in imitation gold leaf. Satin ribbons marked several places among the thin pages. She tugged on a blue ribbon and flipped open the well-worn edition. "On the evidence of two witnesses or three witnesses, he who is to die shall be put to death; he shall not be put to death..."

"Ms. Franklin! Please!" pleaded Eddie.

"Please *yourself* Mr. Jury Foreman! Don't you *ever* interrupt me when I am reading from this holy book—the very word of God." She read slowly and clearly, finishing the passage, "... a person shall be put to death only on the testimony of two or more witnesses; he must not be put to death on the testimony of a single witness.' Deuteronomy Seventeen, Verse Six."

"If it's written in the Bible, then so be it. Two witnesses." said Henrietta.

"God Damn right! Two witnesses!" parroted Lottie.

"Just who does he think he is?" said Lucille, this time pointing a finger at Eddie—today's nails being painted with a high-gloss black.

"Ladies!" It was Ralph again trying to be a voice of reason. "First of all—I don't believe our foreman, or anybody here is questioning the Bible in any way. It's a book with wonderful teachings for all of us. But, our Judge as far as this case is concerned—is Judge Sherman—and we must put the Bible aside for a moment."

Ralph continued, "Also, there were more than two witnesses, so I really don't get the point you are trying to make. Now—I happen to agree with our foreman again—we are not supposed to perform any outside research on our own. Didn't we discuss this very thing yesterday?"

What would I do without Ralph? And what will one of these women pull out of her purse next... a grenade?

Though it wasn't quite the self-flagellation exercise of many dark ages believers, Eddie opted to torture himself by sitting quietly—pleased that Ralph seemed to be as frustrated as he was—yet willing to engage Lucille.

Lucille stood again, "Are you telling me not to read the Bible in my own home? How dare you! You are worse than him!" She aimed the black dagger at Eddie again.

Ralph attempted reason, "Nobody is saying—"

"There really weren't two witnesses. Not if you don't count the cops." It was Harold who interrupted. "And as far as I'm concerned—"

"As far as I'm concerned," interjected Darryl, excited to share his first thought of the day, "all of the cops are lying. I learned that when I lived in Cleveland. And, the L.A.P.D. is even worse. They always lie. That's why we don't count the testimony of the cops."

"That's exactly right. That's exactly the point I've been trying to make this whole morning," said Lucille. "That's why I read from the Old Testament in the first place."

"Amen Lucille. The L.A.P.D. is a bunch of lying racists," said Henrietta.

"I heard that!" seconded Lottie. "In fact my husband said just the other day…"

Eddie tuned out the remainder of Lottie's sentence. His brain unleashed a thousand rapid fire thoughts. One that lasted long enough for him to grab hold of was: *Mistrial*.

"I have an idea," said Claire. "Why don't we take a vote?"

"You mean vote on whether or not we should be able to read from the Bible?" asked Kate with naivete.

"No, I mean vote as in Guilty or Not Guilty," answered Claire.

The room froze. "I mean," Claire continued, "that's the bottom line isn't it? Did Washington shoot the guard, or not? Let's see where everybody stands."

"Well, we haven't fully discussed many issues yet," said Jeff. "Perhaps we should wait until—"

"Wait nothing," said Darryl. "I tell you, if we were back in Cleveland—this wouldn't even be a discussion. It would be unanimous and we'd be outta here. So, what harm could it do?"

"Please," said Ralph with condescension, "enough of Cleveland. OK?" As if Darryl were one of his misbehaving students, Ralph gave Darryl a punishing look. "And—it could do a lot of harm. For starters, many of us need to discuss this case in a lot greater detail. We've barely touched on some of the real issues of this trial. Plus—"

But Darryl was obstinate. "So we can have a preliminary vote. People can always change their minds as we discuss more points of view," he interjected unconvincingly.

Eddie wanted to laugh. He already had the feeling there would not be much mind changing with this group.

Twelve Angry Men, hell. That was Hollywood. But, something needs to be done to refocus the energy of this panel. I know I'll regret not at least trying to get back on track with a meaningful discussion. A vote might be a great way to bring order back to this chaos...but, vote on what? There are several charges... do these people even realize that?

Eddie was further amused by this thought: the fact that several of them wanted to vote on something they could not possibly understand. But, he didn't care. He knew the outcome would not be unanimous, so the deliberations would go on.

"It's been suggested we take a preliminary vote," said Eddie, resuming his role as foreman. "Does anybody second that motion?"

Three separate voices quickly affirmed.

"OK, let's see. I believe a closed ballot would be the best way to do this. Let's each tear a single page out of our spiral notebooks. Write either: *'Guilty,' 'Not Guilty,'* or *'Abstain,'* and fold the paper. Does anybody have any questions?"

For a brief moment, the individual responsibility of the act of voting seemed to sober the group.

"Yes," said Wong. "I have a question: what are we voting on?"

Eddie was glad that he was paying attention. For a fleeting moment, he thought Wong's innocent question would force just one of these people—especially Darryl or a couple of the women—to pause and think about that question. But Wong's question was met with laughter.

"Well dude—maybe we're voting on whether Washington is guilty or not?" said Darryl sarcastically. "Could that be it?"

Eddie felt embarrassed for Wong. "Mr. Wong's question is actually a legitimate one as there are several charges."

"That's right," said Jeff, in agreement. "The judge read to us charges of assault, battery, reckless driving and several others in addition to murder."

"Oh quit stalling!" said Kate. "We're just taking a simple vote here on whether he's guilty or not. Can't we do that?"

"Yeah," added Lucille, "and it's been seconded by everybody. Besides—I've already voted."

"Me too," said Claire, tossing her ballot toward Eddie.

Worried about slipping backwards, Eddie knew he needed to follow through with the vote. He searched for the proper phrasing, but found it didn't exist.

"OK, let's get on with it. We're voting on whether or not Reginald Washington is guilty of murdering Oliver Jefferson."

Most of the votes were cast in remarkably quick fashion. Only two or three of the jurors even appeared to think before writing the critical words. Jorge erased something he had written, folded his paper twice, and tossed it into the center of the table.

Eddie began counting the folded pages. "One, two, three, four, ...ten, eleven, twelve." Leaning to his right, Eddie asked, "Claire, would you please help me verify the tally?"

"No thanks. I'm better at history than I am at math."

"Darryl?" Eddie asked.

Darryl got up from his chair and stood next to Eddie. "It'll be tough, but, I for one, believe I can manage counting to twelve," he said sarcastically.

Eddie drew three columns on a fresh page, and handed it to Darryl, making a mental note that Darryl had now insulted two of the jurors in as many minutes.

"I'll read, you tally..."

"Not Guilty. Not Guilty." Eddie unfolded a page which was obviously the ballot from Jorge. The word *'Not'* had been erased. "Guilty."

"Abstain. Not Guilty. Not Guilty. Not Guilty. Abstain. Abstain. Not Guilty. Guilty. Not Guilty. So the total is?"

"Let's see," said Darryl. "One, two, three..."

"Two Guilty, seven Not Guilty, and three Abstain," announced Ralph, before Darryl could tally his tick marks—intentionally dissing Darryl for embarrassing both Mr. Wong and Claire moments earlier. "I guess we're not ready to go home just yet."

"I think that's a fair statement," Eddie said with a smile. "All right, now Henrietta, you made a comment just before the vote about how you thought all the cops were lying. Do you care to explain to us just why you think that?"

The woman, shocked at becoming the focus of the group's attention, was unprepared for this affront. Body language revealing a moderate degree of unease, she blanked at thinking of something to say.

The woman fidgeted during the awkward silence, until Eddie prodded again, "Henrietta?"

Gaining some confidence, she boldly proclaimed, "I think it's time for lunch."

Eddie, who maintained his new pragmatic habit of not wearing his Rolex to the courthouse, looked down at the blue face of his much cheaper Seiko. It was a high school graduation present from his dad. "It's 10:10 in the morning."

"I didn't eat no breakfast," responded Henrietta. "I can't think when I'm hungry."

"Neither can I," retorted Eddie, "but we need to make progress, and we're not taking a break at this time." Eddie paused, before pressing Henrietta again. He looked directly at her. "Well? Would you like to back up your earlier statement?"

"Nope," she answered.

"How about you Lottie?"

Lottie shook her head. Eddie felt he was being borderline cruel by prodding these two women, yet he felt somehow compelled to do it.

"OK then, let's try something else. It has been mentioned by some of you that you felt there was only one witness. Let's talk about that. I assume you mean Raul Hernandez, the security guard of the Century Palms Apartments. He was of course Oliver Jefferson's partner. He was on the stand at length, for almost two entire days earlier in the week. Let's talk about that..."

"That guard was lying. That's all there is to it," said Harold. Up to this point in the deliberations, other than the bathing suit comment yesterday, Harold hadn't said much. But, he quickly made up for it now. "There's no way he saw the murder of Jefferson. I don't believe it."

He had the attention of all eleven of his peers in the deliberation room.

"Go on Harold," said Eddie.

"To me, the most compelling thing I saw, and I trust all of you did as well, was that stuff the defense explained with her pointer, yesterday, showing all those turns the Cadillac would have had to make in under two minutes for him to be telling the truth."

"Right on," said Henrietta.

"I heard that," Lottie affirmed predictably.

"Look, I ran track," Harold nodded at the two women, and resumed, "for four years of high school and two more in junior college. I'm strong and fast now. But that was 15 years ago. I was even stronger and faster then. And guess what? I never came close to what Carl Lewis did in the Olympics. A hundred yard dash in under 10 seconds?"

"It was meters," said Jeff.

"Yards, meters, same damn thing. No fu... uh... excuse my language. No freaking way did that obese guard do that!"

"Did you see the way his belly bulged out of his shirt?" asked Claire, her question being met with some laughter.

"I didn't quite follow all that stuff about the distances and turns and time and stuff," said Kate. "If the guard—"

"Neither did I," said Lucille, siding with Kate, while simultaneously interrupting her.

Kate continued, "but I agree with Harold. The guard was too fat to run anywhere."

This brought more chuckles from several of the jurors.

"If you are unable to comprehend it, or were not endowed with the ability to process the ramifications of those logistics," said Jeff, intentionally unleashing an uncensored onslaught of multi-syllable words at both Kate and Lucille, "then it is irrelevant whether he ran or jogged or walked or rode a skateboard, for that matter."

Kate did not possess the tools to respond.

Eddie was sure Lucille would make a snide comment about Jeff's vocabulary; he was surprised when she animatedly rolled her eyes in silence.

Jeff gave them a break by pausing, and then added, "Hernandez described it in pretty amazing detail—his partner getting shot."

The easels of the various exhibits had been moved into the deliberation room. Ralph walked over to Exhibit 1 and began looking it over fairly carefully. He had his back to the rest of the jurors. The discussion of Hernandez' weight and conjecturing as to whether he actually saw the defendant shoot Oliver Jefferson bounced around the table several times, from person to person. The repetition became obvious to Eddie, who eventually put his hand up. He was fairly surprised that the circular stream of comments immediately ceased. He looked across at Ralph, still studying the exhibit.

"What are you thinking, Ralph?" asked Eddie.

"Seems to me," Ralph answered without turning to face the people sitting behind him, "that Hernandez took the long way around."

"What do you mean?" asked Jeff, clearly on edge, and demonstrating an eagerness to renew his attack on a new player.

"Well, it's evident that there was construction here," he tapped Exhibit 1 with his pen, the area between Buildings 2 and 3. "But why didn't he run this way, around the other end of Building 3?"

"Because—there's a fence there. Remember?" said Jeff, again intertwining a hint of condescension.

Eddie was excited with this interaction. He had long before pegged these two, Jeff and Ralph, as the most intelligent and dynamic of the group of strangers before him.

"No, I don't remember anything about a fence. And if it's so important, why isn't it depicted in this Exhibit?"

"Raul Hernandez had to run exactly the way he did run," said Jeff. "It was the quickest way to get to the quad."

"I'll ask it again," said Ralph, "then shouldn't the Exhibit depict the fence?"

"It's impossible for an exhibit to show everything. It obviously doesn't label every blade of grass, nor the sidewalk nor every apartment unit number of the buildings, yet they talked about those things a lot as well," answered Jeff.

"I sure don't remember the stuff about the fence. It makes more sense that Hernandez should have run this way..." He drew a line on Exhibit 1 with his pen, from the guard bungalow, to the quad.

Since the cassette tape episode, Eddie thought, Kate seemed to have developed a newfound sensitivity for the rules.

"Are you allowed to mark on that?" she asked.

But her question dissipated into the air.

Eddie had garnered a lot of respect for Ralph, and was glad he was together with him in the deliberation room. But, Eddie also distinctly recalled brief mention of a fence in that area, at the end of Building 3. He was disappointed in himself, however, for not having written it down in his notes. Though the fence was not depicted on the exhibit, he thought Ralph was way off-base in his theory about the fence and Hernandez. He now had to wonder if Ralph, who up to this point had displayed a keen ability to follow the proceedings, and add rational input to the deliberations—simply didn't remember the part about the fence, or, more troubling, if he in fact was intentionally blowing smoke.

Maybe this is Ralph's way of introducing doubt as to whether he really believed that Raul saw the shot that killed Oliver...

"Does anybody have something about the fence written in their notes?" asked Eddie. Two or three jurors leafed through their notebooks, but most quietly shook their heads.

"I remember hearing about the fence." It was Claire. "I think it was from the apartment manager who lived on the property."

"Yeah, me too," said Darryl. "It was right after he was talking about how there were a few Chinese families who lived there."

"Korean," corrected Mr. Wong. "The manager didn't say anything about Chinese tenants. They were Korean."

Eddie was pleased that Mr. Wong was finally able to get back at Darryl.

"Is there a difference? Who cares?" Darryl was beginning to take on the style of the defense attorney in her closing argument: overly enunciating certain syllables in a higher than normal pitch. "Hernandez was just upset that somebody killed his partner. He wanted revenge. He would say anything."

"Can't say I blame him," said Harold, "but that doesn't make it the truth."

"You got that brother," said one of the twins. Eddie found himself not being able to discern who said what between those two women—Henrietta and Lottie. More importantly, he seemed to stop caring.

"If he," again Lucille pointed her black stiletto at Eddie, "didn't destroy the tapes—we could solve this whole thing!"

"That's exactly right!" yelled out Kate. "The stuff about the fence, I had it on tape! The stuff about the Chinese tenants—I had that on tape too…"

"They were Korean," said Jeff, as Mr. Wong buried his face in his hands.

"…but yesterday he made us destroy it all!" Kate announced.

So much for Kate's sensitivity…

"Let's please not discuss the tapes any more," said Ralph. "I thought we all learned that yesterday."

"I'll say it again: it don't matter," said Darryl, his voice yet another octave higher. "Chinese or Korean. Don't matter!" Darryl was squealing now. "It don't matter 'cause the cops are all lyin'!"

"Raul Hernandez was a security guard," said Jorge. "He wasn't a cop."

"Security guards, cops, detectives, L.A.P.D. They are all liars," announced Lucille.

"Damn right," said Darryl.

"No way would Hernandez be able to climb over a fence," said Harold.

"Not that fat Mexican!" said Darryl.

At this, several of the jurors laughed. Jorge was not one of them.

Jorge jumped up from his seat and leaned as far as he could over the large conference table—directing his disgust at Darryl, who was seated across from him, "Pinche pendejo maricón!"

"What the fuck did you just say to me?" asked Darryl.

"My Spanish is only so-so," said Claire, pleased at the chance to get in her own shot of retaliation at Darryl for the snide math comment earlier, "but I think he just said—*you like boys.*"

Eddie's Spanish happened to be much better than so-so. But he felt no burning desire to translate Jorge's curse. He also felt no burning desire to apply his duty as foreman, having lost that desire a bit earlier in the conversation.

The entire room erupted into a shouting and profanity laced tirade. Jeff got up and stood toe to toe with Ralph, who was now backed by Harold. Kate was yelling at Lottie and Henrietta. Jorge continued his angry Spanish slurs at both Darryl and Lucille. Mr. Wong was complaining to nobody in particular, while Claire grabbed the jury instructions and angrily started flipping through the pages. Jeff was forcefully pointing to the correct path, described by Hernandez on Exhibit 1, while both Ralph and Harold were defending the plausibility of the fence route. In all the poking by the three men, the art-board was knocked over, and for the second time in the trial of Reggie Washington, Exhibit 1 fell to the floor. Ralph then, in frustration, purposefully pushed over the easel. Harold stomped on the downed exhibit, leaving a footprint embedded over the tiny black 'x' that represented the dead body of Oliver.

Enraged bursts of *'cops, revenge, Koreans,'* and *'The L.A.P.D'*—intermingled with the words *'Cadillac, Kevlar vest, lost bullets and racists.'* The conversation to garble.

Eddie sat passively in his swivel seat. He was not taking part in the mayhem. That one word he thought of earlier inched to the forefront of his mind again. This time, Eddie said it out loud, but quietly. In all the noise, it was barely audible— even to himself, yet it was there: *"Mistrial."*

CHAPTER 13 - The Headphones

October 22, 1993 PM
Palos Verdes, California

The ten inch wide Goodyears shrieked as Eddie peeled out of the courthouse parking structure onto Acacia Avenue. It was as if he was escaping—making a getaway. Had a Compton policeman spotted him, the cop surely would have thought that he was after a criminal robbing a bank, or stealing a new Corvette.

The lunch break after the madness of that Friday morning's deliberations had not offered much relief; the afternoon session was not much better. For the most part, Eddie sat in silence, suffering through a debilitating migraine headache. He eyed the face of his Seiko more than the faces of the jurors—counting down the minutes until he could run to his car.

Eddie was sweating. He had experienced several anxiety attacks in his life, but the last one was five years ago. Now, he was in the throes of a bad one: he was nervous and his heart was pounding. Once he became aware of the banging in his chest, he knew from previous episodes, it was too late: the spiral had begun. It of course made him even more nervous and ratcheted up the cycle. He couldn't feel his hands. He kept taking deep breaths, but felt he wasn't getting enough air. His mind was racing, but he couldn't focus on a single thought—could not stop blinking. He mashed his teeth. His throat muscles seemed all jammed up and he couldn't swallow.

A horn blared from an old burgundy Cutlass; two young men cursed as they swerved radically to avoid broadsiding him at the intersection. It jolted Eddie from his stupor, as he realized he had just run a red light. He scared himself. Eddie made a quick left turn off of Acacia, onto Cypress, and then another left on the first street he saw. He pulled over to the side of the narrow street just a few blocks from the courthouse. Jumping from the car, he bent over, and vomited into the gutter.

Eddie was unaware of a group of kids building a fort out of old cardboard boxes on the driveway. They saw him and laughed.

"White boy can't handle his liquor!"

"That'll teach you to be drinking in the middle of the day!"

But Eddie just sat in the gutter—oblivious to their heckling.

He was too close. He was too close to touching the entire system—the race issues, and the impending doom that was sure to follow. He could not stop the string of painful images that fed the migraine, hammering at a precise point about two inches behind his right eyeball.

Rodney King. Reginald Denny. The riots. Los Angeles in flames. Mayors and Police chiefs who hate each other. Drive-by shootings. The L.A.P.D. The rantings of the defense attorney and the stupidity of these jurors—both black and white... Why do I keep seeing Reggie's eyes—even when my own are closed?

Strangely, he had it figured out, yet, he realized there was nothing that could be done.

He sat there with splatters of vomit on his shoes, and on his chin. He followed a particle of the foul matter—falling from the edge of the right front fender—inches in front of his face. He studied it, watching it make a trail by slowly dripping down the shiny chrome rim, picking up speed as it slid over the slick black surface of his freshly Armor-Alled tire, coming to rest in the middle of Mercury's winged shoe of the Goodyear logo.

He thought about the apocalypse.

That's it: the apocalypse is at hand. Am I the only one who sees it?

He thought about the Jefferson Airplane song from yesterday.

The Screaming Sirens. And Alice...

He was well into the rabbit hole now. He sat there in the gutter of this poor black neighborhood—*this ghetto*—pondering the full ramifications of his revelation.

****

Mercifully for Eddie, both the anxiety attack and migraine had slowly begun to subside. Several years ago, he had learned in a Psych class at UCLA that one of the defining attributes of a dream was being in a situation where you couldn't connect the dots. You were just in a place, or situation, with no trail, or no path leading you up to that situation. The timeline was incomplete, or broken. There was no waking up in the morning, getting dressed, eating breakfast, driving to the harbor, or airport, or train station. You were just *on* the boat, or *on* the plane, or *on* the train. Or running for your life.

There were gaps that could not be filled in, or explained.

How long have I been sitting here? Was I just in a car accident? Two black dudes were just screaming at me... What street am I on? I can't remember driving here, or getting out of the car... I've got gaps. I don't have my keys in my hand or in my pocket... Why is the engine running?

He wasn't sure. He steeled himself for the act of standing up. The big V8 engine was still running because Eddie hadn't turned off the ignition when he slammed the Vette into park and jumped out of the car. With that awful staccato breathing of the anxiety attack now gone, he took a much needed full deep breath. But the Santa Ana wind must have just shifted slightly to the South; the invisible carbon monoxide wafted toward him and he inhaled a lung-full of exhaust fumes. He puked again and moaned in agony.

Wiping his chin with his hands, he then wiped his hands on the curb, noticing, only a few inches away from where he sat, a few small ropes of fresh brown dog turds on the dead grass.

Whatever the hell is it that flys enjoy about warm dog shit?

He felt the nausea returning—but his stomach was empty and he could only gag.

For the first time, he became aware of the kids. They stopped their taunting as he turned to face them. They could see the rage in his eyes.

Eddie turned away from them—back toward the tire—studying the distorted reflection of his own face in the polished chrome wheel. Eddie wondered at the paths they would take, the kids, if they lived through their childhood—if they were able to make it out of these houses with the black iron bars on the windows and doors. Houses with tombstones of broken appliances littering the front lawns—lawns that had not been watered since the last rain six months ago. He grabbed the top of the fender to slowly pull himself up. Standing, he looked over the tan canvas roof of his car, toward the sun—beginning its descent into the Pacific in the West. He knew the ocean was out there somewhere, but he couldn't see it; his sunset view was occluded by several dark and imposing structures. They were silhouettes of the buildings of Compton High School right in front of him. The kids who had just mocked him would be entering this school in a few short years. He thought of a few of the characters in the trial...

Would they become the Reggie's and the Leon's and the Jimmy's of the future?

Eddie turned to look behind him—to check on the kids. But they were all gone.

****

It was a point that drove Renee crazy: how Eddie babied that car. During the day, at his office, he would meticulously fit a car cover over it to protect both the finish and the leather from the hot sun. At home, he parked inside the garage each night. In fact, even if he was going out again in a short time, he would pull all the way into the garage and hit the remote to close the door behind him. She thought of his explanation when they first met, *'It wasn't just those few minutes... it was ten minutes a day, every day for ten years that gradually yet surely cooked the life out of the upholstery and paint.'*

So, after her long and difficult day at school, as she pulled up to their house, Renee was surprised to see his Corvette sitting outside—in the driveway. She felt something was wrong, as it was definitely weird that the top was down. She *knew* something was wrong.

Her sensitive nose could smell the stale beer as soon as she walked in the door. There were green pieces of broken glass from a beer bottle on the granite countertop. A gold plastic and cork cap from a bottle of booze sat among a few pieces of glass—almost floating in a small puddle of yellow beer. Her pulse quickened when she noticed, down on the floor, several bunched up paper towels soaked with blood.

"Eddie?" she called out—voice cracking with fear. Other than the faint familiar hum of the Sub-Zero fridge, she couldn't detect a single sound. The house was silent. She took a few cautious steps out of the kitchen—stopped when she spotted more blood—a few small drops in the hallway. A bit further, there were a couple of bloody fingerprints on the wall. Heart racing, she grabbed an eight inch carving knife from the walnut knife block back in the kitchen, and resumed her anxious search.

"Eddie!"

The first thing she saw was one bare foot—angling up awkwardly above the end of the white leather couch. She had no time to enjoy any relief from the fear that had moments before engulfed her, as—upon finding him, and seeing a small movement from his foot—that fear instantly turned to anger.

He was sprawled out on the couch, a few steps down into the sunken living room. His head bobbed to a rhythm only he could hear, as he was wearing headphones. A crudely bandaged hand was propped up on a blood stained pillow. From the other hand dangled an open bottle of Chivas Regal.

"Eddie!" she yelled. "Eddie, what the hell is going on?"

But her shouts fell on deaf ears. His eyes were closed as he was lost in the music of an early Allman Brothers blues jam. Putting down the large knife, she shook him hard; he sat up clumsily, splashing her with a shot of the liquor.

"Eddie! God Dammit! What are you doing?"

"What?" he responded dumbly, as she yanked the headphones off of his head.

"What is going on here? Eddie! It's not even 4:00 in the afternoon. Are you drunk?"

"Well... I suppose... I am," he muttered.

"What are you doing home? What about the trial?"

"What trial?" he said with a smirk. "There never was a trial." He reached for the headphones, but she pulled them away. This time he doused himself with the Scotch, looked down at his wet shirt inquisitively, and took another slug directly from the bottle.

"What did you do to your hand?"

"Thought it was a twist-off," he slurred.

"How many beers have you had? Hell, how much bourbon have you had? Please talk to me!"

"It's Scotch."

"Don't be a jerk! What happened to your hand?"

"I told you: damn imported beers. They think they're being classy by not having twist-offs..."

He held up his right arm and tried flexing his fingers through the gauze. He rotated and inspected the hand almost as if he were a two-year-old, wondering what to do about the gloppy mess of peanut butter and jelly slowly oozing down his fingers.

He reached again for the headphones but Renee snatched them away.

"How's your chin?" he mumbled, reaching out to touch her band-aid, albeit not gently enough.

She winced and slapped his hand down. The distorted tinny sound emanating from the earflaps she was holding added to her confusion of the whole scene. She also hated the troubling lyrics: something about a whipping post. She followed the black cable from the headphones to Eddie's rack of stereo equipment. She didn't have much of an understanding of the components that made up Eddie's new high end system—all those knobs and LED lights and sliders and buttons—but, she thought defiantly, she could at least put an end to the racket by yanking the headphone jack out of the front panel.

Eddie saw what she was about to do and yelled out, "Don't! Renee... Please!"

But she thought he was just reminding her of one of his silly *'Edweirdo Rules,'* one of those ridiculous points he would make about not interrupting one of his top-ten favorite songs.

She was wrong.

Eddie yelled out again, imploring her, "You can't just... *No!"*

But it was too late. She received instantaneous punishment for her mistake. It felt as though she had been smacked on the head with a claw-hammer. She sank to her knees, cringing, as the thunderous volume of the 300 watt amplifier belted out its full force through the massive JBL speakers. Eddie jumped up from the couch, banged his left shin hard into the coffee table, and fell over. The volume level of the music was positively intolerable. He hit the floor with his full weight having transferred to his injured hand, as the Chivas bottle flew up and came down, on the edge of the table and exploded. It shattered—to the beat—in perfect time with a cymbal crash from the drummer. The pain in Gregg Allman's vocals, and Duane's slide guitar became his pain. And hers. She mashed the heels of her hands into the sides of her head, crushing her ears in a desperate attempt to blot out the sound. Now it was her turn to crumple to the floor—curling worthless—into a tight ball at the base of the stereo rack. He began crawling, over the glass shards, through the amber colored booze waterfall pouring off the coffee table and staining the white carpet. He crawled, like an enormous wounded garden spider scampering for cover, having just lost one of his legs to the rubber underside of a six-year-old boy's dirty sneaker.

He flailed his way over to the amp, bloody hand throbbing, bloody white gauze unraveling and leaving a trail behind him, while his cut from the beer bottle—as well as the fresh cuts on both knees from the broken Chivas bottle—stung and burned from the alcohol. His shin bled heavily—droplets mixing with the Scotch, forming beautiful Van Gogh-like swirls—warm shades of red and orange and gold on the white palette of their expensive new carpet.

The amp was only 18 feet away, but his crawl felt like the torture endured by a man dying of thirst facing 1,000 miles of the broiling Sahara Desert.

The singer increased his tortured wailing.

"Turn it off! Turn it *off*!" Renee increased her screaming.

Leaving blood in his wake, Eddie kept clawing and crawling. He was the only one who could do it: he felt he was charged with saving all three of them. He crawled like a madman, like that frantic spider in fear for his life—swimming on the carpet, through and over his huddled wife to get to his destination: the large black volume knob. He reached out and flipped it hard to the left, letting out a blood curdling primal scream—synching impeccably with both the timing and the anguish of the song.

"Fuck!"

At this, Renee took her hands away from her ears. She lifted her head, bewildered, looking up at this man, this beaten stranger who was heaped next to her. She stopped her own screaming.

She started sobbing.

CHAPTER 14 - The Last City

October 22, 1993 PM
Palos Verdes, California

"He's in the shower now," said Renee into the phone. "Harry, you've got to get over here."

"Tell me again what happened—I don't quite follow you."

"That's just it," she said, "I came home and he was drunk as a skunk. I've never seen him drinking alone."

"Well baby, most people don't get to see other people when they're alone."

"Oh come on Harry—don't try to be funny now, this is serious."

"Sorry, but I guess I've known him a bit longer than you."

"That's why I'm calling you. Harry—please! I think something happened at the trial."

"OK. Gimme thirty."

****

"So, let me get this straight, home-boy," began Harry, "you had a wonderful day in court. You made it through the first week of jury duty, you decided to celebrate by getting drunk, you tried to cut your finger off, you puked all over yourself, and then you took a shower. Did I leave out anything of importance?"

"I told you," answered Eddie, mustering a sarcastic grin, "I puked before I started drinking."

"Jesus Christ Eddie!" Renee said, her frustration unmistakable. "See Harry—this is what I'm dealing with! He—"

"Well then you are indeed a sick motherfucker old buddy."

"I guess I might be at that. You know, I never thought of myself as a racist," said Eddie, looking Harry in the eyes, "but, I guess deep down—I probably am."

"Just don't call me *boy*," Harry said. "That would be the proof."

"You know I'd never do that... boy."

"It's about time you came out of the closet," said Harry. "The truth will set you free."

"What are you talking about Eddie?" begged Renee. "I've never heard a derogatory word from your mouth until tonight. You've always hired African Americans. My God, you lived with Harry for years. Aren't you two best friends?"

"Well listen here baby girl," said Harry with a chuckle, "I think you're giving your man too much credit. My homey here has been taking money from us Negroes in card games and Backgammon for years. I'm fairly certain that is the real reason he tolerates hanging around people of color. You're just lucky he hasn't been winnin' lately, or there would surely be a payback lynching."

"Can you please be serious Harry? Do you want me to repeat what he said earlier?"

"It's your dime. By the way," he surveyed the broken bottles and pieces of different colored glass and the trail of blood leading from the couch to the stereo, "what the hell happened to your living room? Could be some rock-star's hotel room after a concert! Looks like a *hell* of a party! Was Keith

Moon here, with *The Who? Magic Bus, Baba O'Reilly, 5:15!*
Man—I dig those tunes. Why wasn't I invited?"

Without waiting for an answer to the rhetorical question,
he started singing—something about losing his mind on a
train...

"Damn you Harry!" she yelled. "Both of you! It's like
you're both roommates again in your 20's living back in the
good old days."

"OK, sorry girlfriend. I can see you're upset. I guess I
would be too if I came home and found Charlie Manson's first
stop after escaping from Corcoran prison would be coming
over to my house and appearing in my living room dripping a
bloody axe on my white carpet."

"I'm warning you..."

"Well, it's not often you see a big sharp carving knife in
some white people's nice living room."

Eddie scrunched up his brow on noticing the knife for the
first time. He turned up both palms in disbelief as he faced
Renee, but neither of them said a word.

Harry continued, "It's just that I'm having a little trouble
following the story. We left off when Eddie was on the couch.
Go on. I'm all ears."

"Tell him Eddie," she demanded, but saw that his eyes
were closed and he had begun humming that *Who* song.

"Oh hell, I'll tell you myself. He said after today's
deliberations, he felt like running up the stairs to the roof of the
Compton Courthouse and taking aim with a high-powered rifle
on the people in the ghetto below."

"Oh Eddie. You *are* a racist! I knew that about you the day
we met—that someday you would crack like that guy who
took rifles with scopes on them up into the bell tower in
Oklahoma—shooting all of those innocent people below."

"Texas," Eddie corrected.

"Really? That was in Texas?"

"Yep."

"No matter. Texas, Oklahoma. Same thing. Both cracker states. Full of goddamn red-neck crackers. But the point is, speaking of crackers—I knew you'd crack…"

"See that honey? Even Harry knew I'd crack. Now it's here. So let's all go down to the sporting goods store and buy some ammo. I think BIG 5 is still open."

"Stop this bullshit right now!"

"Renee, listen..." Harry held up one enormous hand, huge crooked fingers spread wide, the remnants of many fistfights as well as countless intense basketball games. "You're a nice Midwest girl. You're not from L.A. You didn't grow up around here, Eddie and I did. Remember last year, during the riots—when people went up to their rooftops to protect their property—with rifles?"

"Yeah…"

"Well, sometimes I myself feel like shooting all the stupid black people in this city. I just can't comprehend their ignorance. I can't fathom—and I can't tolerate—their sheepish, Southern Baptist, Hallelujah spouting, dumb amen parroting, non-thinking for themselves, uneducated, high school dropout, Holy rollin,' jump on the band wagon, do whatever their preacher tells them to do, bastard, fatherless, gang joinin,' riot startin,' flying leap off the cliff, loot and burn down the neighborhood mother fucking mentality."

Seeing her jaw drop, eyes bulging to the point of bursting, he gave her a break by pausing.

"But... on the other hand, I often feel like putting white folks out of their misery too."

He had been holding up that iconic scarred-knuckled hand the whole time, and finally put it down.

"Now, it sounds like, from hearing Eddie's side of the story, that this gang-banger on trial was indeed the dude that killed that guard. It also sounds like the defense had no case. And I'm gonna be so bold as to say I don't even need to hear the other side of the story."

"But how can you—" interrupted Renee.

"You wanted me to be serious, OK, I'm being serious." Up again went the hand. "Kindly stop me now if you can't handle it. I can just leave now and be on my merry way," he waived his hand over the sunken living room. "I should leave you two lovebirds alone to get back to your little party…"

"No," she said, scanning again for herself, in disbelief, the scene—the knife, glass, blood, wads of paper towels and trail of gauze below. "Don't leave. Please go on."

"OK then, look…," he lowered the hand, "I've known Eddie about as long as I've known anybody. If he says it happened—then it happened. I don't need a court, and a trial and lawyers and witnesses and a judge. I just know it's the truth. You're his wife, and you know as well as I do what I'm sayin'."

"Yes, Harry, I do know what you're saying. But I'm talking about you being a black man, and him white and—"

"Exactly! On one level—the level of truth—it doesn't matter if he's white and I'm black or both green. It's just pure and simple truth. Man murders another man. He's guilty. That's the truth of it and the bottom line should be pretty simple. Give his murdering ass the injection or the electric chair, or send him to San Quentin forever. Or, how about they tie him up and put him in a room with the parents or wife or kids of the dead guard—they can go to work on him for five minutes with a garden shears and a Louisville Slugger. I don't care. But the point is, it's simple, and it's pure, and I'm cool with it.

"The thing here, what makes this foggy—real fucking foggy—is that this isn't just a man who is accused of murder. This is a *black* man and this is *1993 Los Angeles!* Now that simple distinction—that combination of facts—sure opens up a hell of a lotta skeletons from the closet of the old ballgame."

"See how Harry mixes his metaphors when he gets excited honey?" said Eddie. It was a little problem he had himself, of which she continually reminded him.

"Shut up Eddie," she said.

"Yeah, shut up Eddie," said Harry.

"Black people," continued Harry, "and white people are not the same. Now that fact is pretty obvious to anybody who is three months old with a set of working eyeballs. But... black people and white people are *really* different where the law or the L.A.P.D. is concerned. Now I know if that fact hurts you— Miss second-year-law-school-student—you—"

"You're damn right it hurts. You can't tell me—" Renee attempted, but Harry cut her off.

"Now listen—are you interrupting me because you disagree, or is it because you can't handle what I'm saying? There is a difference you know. Like I said earlier, if you can't handle it, then I'll gladly stop, because I know this might get a little heavy."

"I think it's already gotten a little heavy," said Eddie.

"Shut the fuck up Eddie!" they both said in unison.

"No—don't stop," said Renee. "I really want to hear what you've got to say. She turned to give her husband a sour look.

"So," she said, "1993 Los Angeles. Continue…"

"Look, I love both of you guys. You could be black, you could be white. I don't give a shit. But it seems to me, that Eddie here got a little too close today. In this trial, he's gotten too close to the vortex of where black meets white. Where black *intersects* white. Now, *black*—or *white*—should not matter in the eyes of the police or the jury. Guilt should matter. Again, skin color should not matter in the eyes of the law or the court, but it does. Now let's just stop and think for a second..."

Harry turned to look at Eddie, "I'm assuming there is at least one black woman on your jury—right? How many?"

"Four."

"Four? You're shittin' me!"

"Nope. Claire, Henrietta, Lottie and Lucille. Four."

"Oh—you poor bastard!"

"I'm not following," said Renee.

"What do you mean you're not following? I thought you were a smart college girl. That's four times the poison!"

"Dammit Harry!"

"OK, just hear me out. And Eddie, I'm assuming—I'm going to go way out on a limb here—I bet you have a pretty strong feeling that these women are all voting *Not Guilty,* correct?"

"That appears to be the case, yes."

But she was too frustrated, too upset to put it together.

"Harry, how could you have known what those women on the jury…"

Again, up went the hand. "Just listen for a second. OK?"

"Sorry, go on…"

"So, can you imagine the husband of a black woman on the jury after the trial is over—sittin' around over dinner at their kitchen table in Inglewood, or Hawthorne, or Lawndale, or L.A. or Watts, or wherever, and they're eatin' their bucket of Church's Fried Chicken, and he's asking her how she voted? Can you imagine his reaction to her saying she voted *guilty*— to send a black man to jail?"

Renee squinted, afraid of the implications of what he was saying.

"Imagine this exact discussion we're having now. It would be happening in several other homes around the city—homes of some of the eleven other people who are on Eddie's jury. I guarantee you it would be happening in the homes of those four women. Now let's just say this wasn't a hung jury, as Eddie sure thinks it will be. Let's just pretend that they all voted—and voted unanimously that this dude—Washington—you said his name was, right?"

"Right," confirmed Eddie, impressed that Harry had remembered the guy's name.

"OK. So in our scenario, it was unanimous and they voted that Washington was guilty. Then it would be happening right now—this instant—as we are sitting here.

"Listen?" Now he put that big hand up to his ear.

"Maybe you can hear it… oh… wait, it's not a discussion any longer. The drumsticks and chicken wings just got thrown off the table and onto the floor! Ouch, what was that? Can you hear it? She's screaming now. The black husband is beating the crap out of his wife for sending his black brother to jail!

"Is it that hard to imagine? Is it?"

Renee was disturbed now. Eyes wide. She was visibly shaken.

"The fact is," said Eddie, softly, "is that it's frighteningly easy to imagine."

"I just don't understand," said Renee.

Eddie stood from the leather chair. He walked over to the French doors and peeked outside. He saw his convertible in the driveway, considered running down to pull it into the garage, but decided it could wait. With his back to his wife and Harry, he began talking in a slow voice.

"I did not meet a black person until I was in the 5th grade. Would you believe that? Growing up in Inglewood, and I was ten years old and up to that point all my friends had always been white. Every single one of them. The school was lily white. Sure I saw them on the street sometimes, and I knew they were around... you'd see them driving by in cars, or at the stores once in a while. But I never met one. Then one day, in the middle of the semester, this new kid shows up in school. The first black kid. It was a little after the Watts riots—so it must have been 1965 or '66. But—it was pretty soon after the riots, so the kids were afraid to talk to him. Hell, nobody wanted to sit near him. I think it was his third or fourth day—I was captain of the kickball team during lunch. He was standing there with his brown fingers hooked through the chain link backstop. I could see that he obviously wanted to play. I was out in front with the other captain, and we were picking players. So after a few picks when all of the top guys were taken, and I'm scanning the remainder to fill out my team, I made eye contact with this kid. I can still see those big white eyeballs looking out from behind the fence. I couldn't look away. I pointed my finger at him, and picked him. He hurriedly ran out from behind the backstop to stand right next to me. Almost like he was reporting for duty or something. It was weird, I could see it: he didn't just *look* different from the other kids—he *moved* different.

"His name was Michael. Michael Sams. He kicked the hell out of the ball his first time up. And he ran like the wind! I mean at the time, I was one of the fastest runners. But he was faster than me. He was faster than any other kid in the whole school—by a mile. I told Sid, my dad, about him—about how strong and fast he was—so my dad drafted him to be on our Little League team.

"Michael was like the Jackie Robinson of our Little League. In our second game he crushed a pitch—over the left field scoreboard. My dad said it was harder and farther than any ball he'd ever seen any kid hit on that field. What a great season we had: The Owlcats! But here's the thing—he was also such a nice guy—he was smart too. And funny! We became best friends, and spent a bunch of time together the next couple of years.

"Then came the late sixties. The demographics of the neighborhood started changing. It was the time of the 'great white flight' for a lot of my friends and their families. The families who had money moved to the beaches, or to Orange County. Anywhere—just get the hell out of Inglewood. But my parents wanted to stay put. This was the house my dad bought with his G.I. loan, when he got out of the army. It was the house my mom and dad got married in. I was born in that house. My brother was born in that house.

"They talked—and taught—about not being prejudiced and about treating all people fairly and equally. People, neighbors, would talk to my dad about real estate values falling, and that was of course lost on me. All I knew was that in school, things were changing. Changing fast. The tough black guys would regularly relieve me of my lunch money. Sometimes they'd come up and ask for a quarter. Then, three or four guys would start going through my pockets—just like that—they'd stick their hands in your pockets. *'You're in the lunch line white boy. We know you got some money...'"*

"So please mom, don't ever give me a paper dollar for lunch. Ever. That was like a flag. I remember it became a rule with the white kids: *'Don't take a dollar bill out of your pocket—it's like waiving the Stars and Bars in Harlem.'* God I remember pleading with my parents—trying to make them understand—*'Please don't give me anything bigger than a quarter!'* Can you imagine trying to make them understand? Especially, when just a year or two before that—we'd beg them for a dollar bill or even a five-spot because it made the kid who held it such a player!

"Now, we were forced to develop all these new survival rules. Different ways to make it through the day in a mixed neighborhood. Pretty scary stuff when you're ten or eleven or twelve years old. A few times I got punched pretty hard. Or even beat up. Michael tried to step in a couple of times—he absolutely saved my ass once, but of course it was tough on him jumping in the middle. More on that in a second... by then, you see, the school was mostly black. It was crazy—in the period of three years from 1965 to 1968 the neighborhood and the school completely changed. The day Martin Luther King got shot there were riots at my junior high school: Henry Clay Jr. High. A teacher got stabbed. Remember—in those days guns were unheard of; only the police, and kids' fathers who were into hunting had guns. That was it. So, a stabbing was a pretty big deal. At one point in the pandemonium, they were yelling and screaming—at the school—that all white people were to share in the blame for the King assassination. About five real bad kids, from the toughest bunch, got a hold of me; I even remember one of their names: Delano. He was the worst. And I *knew* he always carried a knife! I'd seen him pull out that awful switchblade a couple of times, and it scared the hell out of me. I remember an old black and white documentary on TV on World War I. It was an interview with some infantry soldiers and they were talking about trench warfare. They said they feared a bayonet in the back, or in the belly, much more than they feared a bullet. Kinda weird, but it always stayed with me. And I thought of that bayonet in the belly thing when Delano had me! They had me pinned up against a wall and were starting to slug me. Pretty soon there were about twelve of them. And do you know what? Michael sees it and starts throwing guys off. I saw him yank Delano by his afro and pull him away. He just jumped in the middle and, well, it was like he was making an announcement. Or a proclamation. He said to the semi-circle of shocked black kids that were surrounding the two of us, *'If any of you niggers touches this white boy,'* and he actually patted the top of my head twice, *'they're gonna answer to me.'*

"So they left me, and ran off to beat the hell out of all of my white friends. When I came home that afternoon—after King was killed—with bruises all over my arms and shoulders and my shirt ripped with blood on it—that was the last straw. I remember, the phone was ringing all night as parents of my friends were calling and comparing notes about what the hell happened at Henry Clay Junior High that day. My folks yanked me out of school the next day. I mean—I didn't go back. Not even to clear out my locker. They put the house up for sale and we moved out of Inglewood to a safe white neighborhood.

"I never saw Michael again. Shit, I didn't even have his phone number, and we never drove back to the old neighborhood to look for him.

"I always thought I'd see him on T.V. playing wide receiver for the Green Bay Packers or something."

"Do you blame your parents for moving away?" asked Harry.

"Hell no. I don't blame them for anything. They learned that the school was unsafe. That's got to be their first concern. See, I never told them how bad it was getting—didn't want to be a pussy, plus, all these friends—who I'd grown up with—I was afraid we'd move away like a lot of the other kids when the shit started. I remember how the remaining kids used to talk about the pussies who moved away. I mean—we'd never see them again. They would never return to the old neighborhood. Never.

"But, finally, after the riots, the first riots—just a couple years earlier—in Watts—and now the King Riots... Hey, I just realized there were two sets of King riots: Martin & Rodney!"

"Jesus dude," said Harry, "I hadn't thought about that either. So you can truly say, living in L.A. your whole life, you've now been through *three* different race riots!"

"I don't even want to think about it..."

After a quiet moment, Eddie continued. "Funny that you mentioned Charles Manson earlier. *'Helter Skelter'*—the Beatles song—remember? It was Manson's mantra—and his phrase for 'Apocalyptic Race War.' Holy shit! I bet you: Charlie has got to be loving some of the things that are going on today."

"Yeah," said Harry, "sick mofo has a swastika tattooed on his forehead. But now that you mention it—absolutely—he would dig all these race riots and the racial tension we're talking about."

"Sure would. And he thought the best place to start the crazy shit would be right here in L.A."

"Seems like the crazy shit always starts right here in L.A," said Harry.

"There's no place like home," Eddie said.

"Aren't you two guys just a big barrel of fun to hang out with on a Friday night!" said Renee.

"Hey baby, you called me to come over, remember?" said Harry. "So, OK, Edweirdo—continue with your story... you were talking about your school..."

"Right, so there was no hiding it from them—my parents, I mean. Shit, that school was rough. I wouldn't want my kid going to a school like that. Forget about classes and learning and books and blah blah blah... it was just plain dangerous!

"So, I don't know how they did it, but I started going to another school in another area—before they were even able to sell the house. Maybe for all I knew—my dad was tennis buddies with the other principal—anyway—it was an all white school. It was all white for a semester anyway. Then, guess what? Integration. Bussing. Man! So two or three yellow busses started pulling up to school with these black faces peering out of all the windows. They were just as scared as us, if not more so. At first, it was weird all right, but they didn't really make a dent in the overall school population—maybe one or two black kids in each class. So then some genius politicians decided that the experiment was working, so *bam!* Here they come! Now dozens of busses were pulling up every morning. And hundreds of black kids are pouring out. Think about it: it wasn't possible to become good friends with any of them. You couldn't say, 'Hey man—come on over to my house after school—we'll shoot some hoops.' You couldn't invite anybody over, or they would miss their bus home! We were afraid of them and they sure as shit didn't want to go through the humiliation—so it was both sides with an attitude from the get-go."

"One of those scared black faces on one of those yellow busses belonged to me," said Harry.

"Are you kidding me?" asked Renee. "You were bussed away from your home? For forced integration?"

"Uh huh."

"It was a weird time man," said Eddie. "Anyway, like I said, my parents finally cracked and moved to an all white neighborhood with no bussing. So no, I don't blame them a bit. Yep, it was a weird time."

"Apparently, no weirder than today," said Harry.

"You got that right buddy," said Eddie. "In fact, I'll go so far as to say that those days seem pretty tame compared to what we've got now. From what I've seen this past week, on my little vacation to Compton, we're all dead meat. Black people and white people are at war. They will always be at war. That's all there is to it. It's taken me 25 years but I've just figured it out."

"Jesus, Eddie!" chimed in Renee. "You make it seem so hopeless."

"The cops in South Central are outgunned by 16 year old kids in gangs. What do you call it?"

"We still can't give up. The alternative is unthinkable," said Renee.

"The unthinkable might be upon us, sister," said Harry. "Lincoln freed the slaves over a hundred years ago, remember? 'Forty acres and a mule.' And maybe even a little hope. Now my mule died a few years back, and I sure as shit don't own no forty acres. The hope part—well, I've held onto that a long time. There's been a lot of progress. That's for sure. We've come a long ways from tar and feathers and colored drinking fountains. Hell, for a long time I've thought L.A. was about as civilized and evolved as you could get. You know, the last city. But I gotta be honest with you. We are teetering on the edge. People are on edge. It won't take much to set the whole thing off. It might be one crazy trial. Or one weird verdict. Or one random bullet. This place is about to crack off and fall into the ocean, and it won't be because of no damn earthquake. We sure as shit came close last year. Tanks rolling down Century Boulevard. I know you guys remember that night—when you got in from your little sailing adventure—shit, that whole week! It sounded like The Fourth of July every night. But those weren't firecrackers. And that might have been just an appetizer. Like my boy, Eddie here, has just figured out—the unthinkable might indeed be close at hand."

The three of them sat in silence for a full minute. They were exhausted.

"So what's the answer, Harry?" Renee asked.

Harry thought for a long second. "The answer? I'll start with a question: can a brother get a drink—or did this drunk bastard spill out all of the bourbon?"

"Scotch," they both said simultaneously.

CHAPTER 15 - Now What?

October 25, 1993 AM
Compton, California

Once Harry left their house, very late on Friday night, Eddie had a rather uneventful weekend. Being virtually alone, as Renee was consumed by her studies, he spent most of the time down at the marina.

Her taking of the State Bar exam was a little over a year away, but she was already beginning to feel the pressure. It was a widely known fact that the California Bar was the most difficult law exam to pass in the entire country. In California, two out of every three students who took the test failed. Many were the exasperated students, whose hopes, following three years' sacrifice in the form of all-consuming work, combined with the massive expense in preparation to be a California lawyer, were dashed. They now had to begin studying all over again, hoping to pass the test the next time it was given—six months down the road. Most decided at that point that they needed to reconsider their career choice of being an attorney—or to at least weigh the option of moving out of California.

Renee was quite aware of these facts, and had no qualms about making sure that Eddie fully understood them as well. He could not fathom the increasing stress she would be under—and chose wisely to give her a wide berth, the solitude to work, especially in light of last night's lost study time.

If she would have only let me sleep it off on the couch, and hadn't pulled the damn headphones off my head, none of this would have happened... But I have a feeling that it wouldn't be wise to tell her that. Something bad always happens when you stop one of those songs...

I'd better spend the weekend working on the boat; maybe I'll even sleep on the boat, so as not to disturb her...

Fortunately, his various cuts from the glass weren't too deep, so with a few well-placed bandages and kneepads, he was able to do a little mindless sanding and varnishing on some of the woodwork on the sailboat. Mindless, except for Eddie's inability to think of much else besides his ongoing stint on jury duty.

As Eddie had long before acquiesced to, and as Harry had rightfully surmised, it would indeed be a hung jury. There was simply no other possibility. Dreading going back to that jury room on Monday morning, he kept bouncing back and forth as to if he should make any attempt whatsoever to resume reasonable discussions; the entire fiasco had become a gigantic emotional drain, as well as a colossal waste of time. He realized it had been days since he even checked in with his company. What he didn't realize, was that he had completely forgotten to write a check to the IRS. He owed a quarterly estimated payment of $34,000. The late penalty would be substantial. Eddie had always been a master of organization— but now—things were falling through the cracks. The trial was taking a toll on him.

Wasn't it just a week ago, dinner last Sunday night, when she said to me 'Don't do anything stupid like volunteer to be foreman.' I should have listened. Do I have some sort of additional responsibility, as acting foreman?

He thought of the multi-colored ink doodles on the wooden jury room instruction tray. He thought of the defendant's ill-fitting brown suit, even tried recalling the different ties Reggie wore each day. He was bombarded by a multitude of minutia—details from the trial—mostly trivial and meaningless details. But nonetheless, they kept coming at him.

Where does it end? Are any of the other jurors thinking about this as much as I am? Ralph, Jeff. Maybe Claire...

He couldn't focus. He needed this trial to be over. He fought with himself, but couldn't come up with the answer, waffling between the choice of quitting as foreman, or giving it one more day.

Maybe, I'll just sit in the deliberation room and say nothing, until it's over...

The sun was out in the Marina. He popped open a cold bottle of Dos Equis; after just two sips, his mind slipped away from the trial. He thought back to Harry's comment last night about those great *Who* songs, and smiled at the image of Keith Moon & Pete Townshend smashing guitars on the furniture in his living room. He slapped a cassette of *Quadrophenia* into the tape deck. The beer must have helped enable a laugh, as a tightly rolled $100 bill fell out of the cassette case and onto the floorboards. He turned the volume higher, eventually losing himself in the sanding and pleasant smell of laquer that mingled with the fresh salt air blowing through the rigging of his yacht.

****

High pitched sounds of squeaky little Nintendo beeps pierced through his ears and into his brain like shish-kebob skewers.

"Excuse me—please!" said Eddie. "Juror number ten—Henrietta—can you kindly put that away so we can concentrate on the discussion?"

The woman did not even look up from her game. Eddie was incredulous. It was a terrible way to start Monday morning—the sixth day of the trial—the third of deliberations. In spite of the days last week of utter frustration in being part of this jury, he drove to Compton this morning, still holding on to a shred of optimism. It was a shred that disappeared in the first five minutes.

"I am concentratin' man!" said Henrietta. "I just passed 40,000 points!"

"All right—now! Get him! Get that green guy!" said Lottie, grabbing for the game.

"Come on ladies," said Harold, "you can finish your game at the break."

"OK, but he...," pointing a finger at Eddie, "can't tell me what to do."

"Thank you Henrietta," said Eddie with more than a modicum of restraint. "Now let's talk for a minute about one of the charges here: *assault*. Does everybody know what *'assault'* means?"

"Yeah sure man," answered Darryl, with a snicker, 'assault,' like pass the ah-salt and the ah-pepper!"

The two clones Henrietta and Lottie shrieked with laughter.

In his thick Asian accent, Mr. Wong spoke for the first time that day, "People please. A man's life is at stake. Can we please take this seriously?"

"Tell that to the cops, dude," said Darryl. "Ask them to take this seriously—Mr. Wrong."

The clones laughed again, "Mr. Wrong. I like that," said Henrietta.

"My name Wong. Please do not insult me again." He was visibly upset. His English grammar and pronunciation had been excellent the first few days, but now, under the pressure and the attack, it seemed to have waned. "I come to America eight years ago from Korea. I think it honor to serve on great U.S.A. court system. But this—this no honor. This bad joke—this jury. This disgrace. You... Lady Number Ten... you play child's game. You... Number Two," pointing at Darryl, "you no care about facts. You no listen to judge. I no want to be part of this jury."

Rolling his seat back from the conference table, Wong stood. He walked toward the intercom. "I tell judge I quit jury."

Eddie quickly rose. Being closer, he beat Wong to the door. With his right hand he covered the intercom button.

"Mr. Wong, please. You can't quit the jury. The judge can order you to remain on the panel. He can hold you in contempt."

Wong looked down at the floor. "I am ashamed to be part of this jury."

Eddie took his hand off the red button and gently placed it on Wong's shoulder. "I also thought it would be different. I thought people cared. That's why we all decided to be here in the first place. We agreed to listen to the facts. We *swore* we would. We swore we would try to set our prejudices aside—even if only for a few days. We each took an oath to perform this duty. We all could have been excused from jury duty quite easily. We each knew what those questions the judge asked us during *voir dire*—the jury selection—implied. The attorneys were accepting or rejecting us based on our answers. We all understood that.

"Getting excused from jury duty is the easiest thing in the world. But... none of us wanted to be excused. We wanted to be *chosen*! We wanted to be believed by the lawyers and the judge as if *we* were the ones on trial! All any of us had to say was 'I don't believe white people,' or 'all cops lie,' or 'I have seen the way gang members act in Cleveland,' or 'the entire L.A.P.D. is corrupt.' If we said any of those things we would have been excused. All we had to say to be excused was any of the very same things we have been saying here the past few days in this room.

"But we all lied a little. We lied a little to get accepted to be on the panel. Because now *we* are in power. We in this room are more powerful than the judge or the lawyers or the cops. Now *they* have to listen to *us*! And they must *obey* us. They must obey what *we* decide! It's exciting to have this power isn't it? We can set a man free. We can send him to prison.

"Robert Alton Harris—remember him? He murdered those two kids in San Diego. Just last year, he was the first man to be executed in California in 25 years. He was sent to the gas chamber. Are we in this room really prepared to set *those* wheels in motion?" Eddie paused and looked around the room. Most of the jurors looked down, not wanting to engage eye contact with him.

Eddie continued, "Is this power that much fun? Is it that exciting of a game? Let's all think about that... I personally am exhausted from having this power. I am terrified of having it.

"I too was excited when they chose me. I didn't want to be rejected—to have to go back into that jury pool—back down into that room of five hundred schmucks waiting for their names to be called so *they* could go on trial before the judge and the darn lawyers. My gosh—even the *defendant* had the power to excuse us! I remember... he kept whispering in the defense attorney's ear... I remember hoping he wasn't telling her anything about me...

"No, we didn't want to go back into that pool of losers. We each wanted to be selected into the elite group of the lucky twelve. The privileged twelve. For us, the choice was easy: do we go back to that crammed room with the hard benches and watch soap operas and play scrabble and read magazines all day? Or... do we get involved in an actual real life exciting murder trial?

"Let's ask ourselves: did we lie to get selected?"

"What was your lie Eddie?" asked Ralph.

"Me? I think each of us has our own prejudices. It is impossible to put them completely aside—even for ten days. They are built both consciously and subconsciously through our experiences over the years. How can we possibly close our minds to a lifetime of experiences? It's an impossible task... but we have to try."

"That was well said, Eddie. What's more, I happen to agree with you. But you didn't answer my question. I asked you how you lied."

"Well, I sure wanted to hear the defendant testify. I thought maybe I could figure out if he was a murderer by hearing him speak. I know the judge asked us the question: 'Will it make a difference to any of you in deciding guilt or innocence if the defendant does not take the stand?' I remember, I thought about it, that I just might judge him unfavorably, but didn't raise my hand. So, I wasn't quite being truthful about that. I thought I would be able to tell if he was lying on the witness stand, or, that maybe he would just break down and confess. So our decision would be pretty easy. Maybe that's Hollywood. So—me personally—I would have liked to hear what Reggie had to say for himself."

"I sure would have liked to hear that too, man!" shot out Claire.

"Yeah." A half dozen affirmations and an 'amen' were mumbled.

"Well," Eddie continued, "I guess the point is—most of us here kept some pretty strong feelings inside. We were not completely straight with the judge."

"Speak for yourself dude," interjected Darryl.

"I think I just spoke for myself, Darryl. Perhaps you'd like to tell us now how you left all of your prejudices outside the door of this courtroom?"

"Hey man—I was eight years old when I watched two white cops gun down my older brother. I can still see my mother kneeling in Donnie's blood—begging the cops to help—while we were waiting for the ambulance. But they just sat in their car sippin' on their Cokes and eatin' their doughnuts. Fuck those police man. And fuck these police."

"I don't remember you telling the judge that story Darryl. I guess you too were hiding something."

"Yeah—I guess I was Mr. Jury Foreman. So now what?"

Now what indeed…

Eddie thought to himself. He flashed back to those first five minutes of deliberations, when he felt he had a strong understanding of the trial and the elements of the charges. He felt he could lead a meaningful discussion—a discussion containing an intelligent and thorough analysis of the testimony, evidence and attorneys' arguments. Volunteering to be foreman; he felt actual excitement—that he could participate in an instrumental way—to perform his duty in helping to uncover the truth. To arrive at a verdict. He wanted—no—he *needed* to do his part in dealing out justice.

But all of that, in just a few days, evolved. It evolved into something very different than what he had envisioned at the outset. It morphed into something he could not quite understand. He could not drive these discussions; he could not lead this group, the people in this small enclosed room. He failed. He failed in his attempt to impart reason—admittedly—it was his, Eddie's own reason, but it was a reason he had always done exceedingly well with both in business and in life. A reason he trusted implicitly. He failed to be able to convey that reason, or more in line with the requirement of the task at hand, as he was charged by this court—to arrive at a conclusion—to decide guilt or innocence beyond a reasonable doubt.

Now what?

He had no good answer.

CHAPTER 16 - The Palms

October 25, 1993 PM
Compton, California

Along with his passion for playing basketball, it was also Eddie's favorite spectator sport. He loved the NBA Playoffs, and kept a large library of tapes to enjoy during the off season. Tonight, he popped an old tape of a game he had never seen into his VCR. Sitting back in his comfortable leather chair, he savored a couple of cold Coronas. It was a much needed respite from the trial, offered up by the combination of the game and the beers. Thankful for the distraction, he eventually lost himself in the high level action and hard fought battle between the Knicks and the Bulls.

"...the hundred and twenty seventh consecutive sellout here in Chicago. Michael Jordan with the ball. The Bulls trail by one. They'd surrender home court advantage in this best-of-seven series with a loss tonight. Twelve seconds left. Eleven. Ten. Jordan dribbles to the top of the key. Pippen posting up under the basket. Patrick Ewing shifts over to double-up on Pippen. Jordan drives the lane. Seven seconds. Six..."

Abruptly, Eddie jumped out of his chair, clicking off the remote.

He vaulted up the stairs to the bedroom, and rifled through the oak dresser. The stopwatch. Something had gnawed at him constantly, both during the defense's grueling cross of Hernandez, and in the jury room.

"Babe, I'm running out a minute."

"Eddie, what are you doing?" shouted Renee, from the study. "It's after ten! Where are you going this late?"

"Don't worry. Be back in a bit."

"Eddie! *Eddie!*" The heavy door to the garage slammed, cutting her off.

Pulling out of the driveway, he smiled to himself, realizing he was driving somewhere he had never been, yet, knew exactly where he was going.

Haven't I heard all the street names fifty times so far during testimony? Plus, I've seen them all plastered over several of the exhibits by the D.A. in six inch block letters. I'm sure I can find the place...

That tape he had just been watching: Jordan dribbling the ball with ten seconds left, and the clock counting down, did it. With the game on the line, the Chicago Bulls' announcer tried to convey the intensity. In fact, he was quite good at achieving it, but Eddie's brain processed that information and that intensity in a different way than what the announcer had intended. Eddie transferred that intensity—he transferred that pure energy and brought it up—accessing it from a subconscious drawer of his mind. That special holding place in his brain overpowered his enjoyment of the basketball game he had been watching for over an hour. It bubbled up, rendering it unimportant that there were mere seconds left in the game. Instead, he thought of the ten seconds Hernandez had in order to have seen Oliver go down. It didn't matter to Eddie what Michael Jordan did. What mattered were the ten seconds.

Compton is only twelve miles from my house... It's just down the hill...

How could the world change so much in twelve miles?

He frightened himself, speculating that he was possibly beginning to know the answer.

An eerie feeling of *déjà vu* hit him as he pulled up in front of the dimly lit apartments of the Century Palms. It had been one year and ten days since the murder. He looked at his watch. 10:32. In fact it was almost exactly this time of night, recalling clearly the Post-It-Note with the time stamp '223500' in red ink, 10:35 PM. Eddie thought again how odd it was, being the one and only piece of evidence presented by the defense...

Eddie parked his car across the street from the apartments, on the South side of 128th. Getting out of the car, he locked the door with the key, instead of the remote, to avoid making that little beep sound that activated the alarm; he needed to be as quiet as possible. Save for one sporadically flickering amber streetlight, Regent Park was dark. Except for the faint garble of a few radios or T.V. sets from the apartments across the street, and an occasional car a couple blocks away on Century Boulevard, it was silent; the neighborhood was still. The typical late October night air was damp; a sheen of dew covered the grass of the quad. A pleasant smell of jacaranda hung in the air. Eddie couldn't see these trees, but assumed they were somewhere in the park behind him.

Halfway across the street, he paused mid-stride, as if held by an invisible hand. The lone streetlight illuminated the surrounding asphalt of the silver grey street. Understandably, Eddie's heart was already beating a bit faster than normal, but when he looked down and saw the skid marks, his pulse quickened further. Quite ominously, almost purposely, any refraction of light from the streetlamp was absent from the black skid marks. Like a black hole which refused to allow light to escape—the skid marks formed a barrier—causing Eddie, standing there, in the middle of 128th Street, to pause and reconsider his mission.

What am I doing? I'm on the jury! I'm not a freaking detective! This isn't the neighborhood I want to be poking around in at night... This just might be the dumbest thing I've ever done... I think I'll just forget this idea and drive home. I can always tell Renee I ran out for some ice cream... Especially if I bring back her favorite—Haagen Daz Chocolate Chip Cookie Dough...

He turned to look back at his Corvette, and for the second time in a week, mentally berated himself for not having driven his wife's Mazda; the fervid nature of Eddie's decision to run out of the house and drive to this place did not accommodate that rational thought. It struck him that he had parked within a few feet of where, a year ago, Reggie had been sitting, parked in his El Dorado. Eddie's shoulders twitched, recalling some of the testimony about all the gang members who were hanging out, surrounding the car. He imagined the beer bottles and crack pipe being passed around. He saw Reggie's familiar face through the car window.

Or is that the horrible face from my dream?

He knew that face and those eyes. He was well aware that during most of the trial, Reggie was watching him, and he hated the fact that now, in order to carry out his plan, it would be necessary for him to turn his back on those terrible eyes.

Breaking out of the momentary trance, he turned around and forced another step. Adrenaline kicking in, he crossed over the year old signature of black rubber left by the old brown Cadillac. The stopwatch in Eddie's left hand was slippery with sweat. A ghostly bluish light from two second story televisions found its way down through the broken screens and security bars on the old windows to help light his path to the guards' bungalow. Praying the office would be vacant, he then recalled from somebody's testimony that the landlord of the apartment complex had been unable to find a replacement for Jefferson. Shortly after the murder, Hernandez had quit, as did the other team of security guards.

So was The Palms now operating without full-time security? Is that a good thing or a bad thing tonight?

Eddie wondered... He had to admit the enormous rush he was getting, although the excitement that had been consuming him for a solid week now, in his desire to experience this place, was very nearly trumped by his fear.

Strangely, he thought about Jerry Takeyama, his CPA and financial advisor. He'd known Jerry since high school—the first of his friends to become a multi-millionaire. Eddie often asked him for advice on how much money to put into different investments and stock purchases. *'Greed versus fear,'* would be Jerry's boilerplate answer.

"Come on Jerry, you know the numbers," Eddie would plead, "don't be an asshole. Just tell me how much to buy!"

But Jerry would just calmly and methodically repeat, "Greed versus fear."

He feared it: the loss and the waste. A hung jury and a mistrial. It drove him, as he detested waste and failure. He couldn't leave it alone; he was consumed—compelled to get at

the answer. The greed: Eddie's desire to solve the problem—
the hunt to get at the truth.

I've got so much time and energy into this trial, but the whole damn thing turned South. South... hey, there's that compass reference again! When Reggie was driving away, right after he shot Oliver, didn't he turn South? Does that mean something? What's that expression about a 'moral compass?' Maybe I should be holding a compass in my hand instead of this stopwatch...

Damn right Takeyama. It ALWAYS comes down to greed versus fear...

At least Eddie's apprehension of having to explain his late-night affairs to a Century Palms security guard were unfounded, so he was now free to proceed with his solitary experiment.

Eddie slowly walked up the six steps to the guard bungalow door. He put his right hand on the knob, held it there for a moment, and carefully looked around. He was alone.

On the exhale of a deep breath, he whispered, "Ten seconds."

Jordan with the ball...

Ten critical, impossible seconds. The defense presented a case, such that Hernandez would have had to run from this exact door to the quad in ten seconds that night a year ago, to see his partner's murder. I can see some of the detailed explanation of the defense by Davis... The wild gesticulations with her pointer, re-creating all the stops and turns the Cadillac had to make in the streets of Compton, working backwards to the point where Hernandez had a mere ten seconds to have made it from here to where he could witness Reggie shoot Oliver.

I can hear Raul Hernandez from the Day 1 testimony, 'I was on the phone with the Compton Sheriff when I heard two quick shots...'

Eddie cupped his hand between his forehead and the rough screen of the old swinging door. He could smell, almost taste, the rust. It was dark inside, yet he was able to barely make out some of the contents of the interior.

The Guard's Bungalow. I first saw it depicted in Exhibit 1. Here it is—attached to Building 6. Just like the Exhibit. I remember what I wrote in my notes: '6 Buildings, 6 steps to the Bungalow by Building 6.'

He had written '666' and circled it.

666: The Reckoning. The Devil's number.

Sitting in the jury box, feeling at the time that it might be important, he even made a diagram, complete with all those positions—those stickers—placed by Raul. He had copied as accurately as possible, drawing Exhibit 1 on a page of his juror's notepad. Now he was standing at the real thing. He peered inside.

Could that be? The actual phone Hernandez was on when he was talking to the Compton Sheriff and heard the first two shots? And there's the time clock, right next to the phone on the desk... 'I have a habit of punching the time clock...'

Heart racing wildly now, in this seesaw battle, the fear was beginning to overtake the excitement—the greed.

I need to do this: I need to time myself! But is it an ill-advised experiment? Shit. The better path, the better run— would probably be to run back to my car to get the hell out of here...

He heard the rumble of a car rolling down 128th Street.

Oh my God... Reggie must have just started his Cadillac! In a few moments he'll be speeding East on 128th to begin making that wild U-Turn!

Taking another deep breath, he said out loud, "Fuck it." Eddie paused. Then, even louder, "Bang. Bang."

He clicked the big button on top of the stopwatch. The merciless ticking began. Of all the many times he had used it, he did not recall the sound of the ticks being this loud. He bounded down the wooden steps, only touching half of them, almost losing his balance as he hit the ground. Pivoting for the radical right turn, and flailing his arms wildly, he regained control. He picked up speed nearing the end of Building 6. Glancing to his left, down the corridor formed between Buildings 2 and 3, he noted the still incomplete construction and the ditch that was mentioned during the defense attorney's cross. Four seconds gone. He was flying through the night— between the buildings of The Palms. He passed a couple of overgrown oleander bushes.

Weird, I'm familiar with everything, except these bushes. That must be because they were never mentioned in the trial, nor were they depicted on any exhibits. It's like the problem

*with the fence—it was not shown on any exhibit, yet became a
point of contention during deliberations...*

He pushed the thought out of his mind and concentrated on
his running. Ahead, he could see the lone eucalyptus tree—
which he distinctly remembered being shown in the center of
the quad in that now infamous Exhibit 1, presented by the D.A.
He saw flashes of shadow and light as the pistons of his legs
pounded the changing terrain interspersed with grass and
pavement. A synapse in his brain sparked, bringing forth the
image of flying through the kelp, underwater, in a chilly cove
off of Catalina Island. Sun rays, shadows. He had his spear; he
was a hunter again, hunting for the truth. This led to the
thought of Reggie—making the appearance in his dream the
other night—but he pushed that out of his mind as well.

*Just keep running. I'm back at Henry Clay Junior High,
racing the fastest kid in school... Michael Sams.*
Faster! Reggie is taking aim at Oliver...

A quick glance at the stopwatch: seven seconds. He was
getting close. He could see the end of Buildings 2 and 5. He
could see the quad and the near corner of Building 4, which he
knew to be across the quad. He needed to make it to the end of
Building 2 in ten seconds, so he could look quickly to the left,
to the street, to see Reggie's Cadillac, and Oliver—the same as
Raul would have done. Somewhere in here, on any one of
these strides he was now taking, occurred shot number 3—the
shot that hit Oliver Jefferson in the arm. He could see the
eucalyptus tree, growing closer. Larger. He needed to run
faster, so he could turn and look left.

Where Oliver would still be standing, alive, NOT already laid out on the ground.

He was just a few strides away now. Heart thumping, he felt he was actually running to save Oliver. The same thought Hernandez must have had. One year ago. Right here.

Jordan with the Ball. Four Seconds. Three... Ewing reaches up to block...

Reggie pulls the trigger on the 9-millimeter for the third time. Oliver drops his own gun, eyeing his bloody right arm quizzically.

Hernandez running. Oliver looks up at Reggie... terrified. He's out of air.

Eddie was running faster than he'd ever run. He could see the finish line, the corner of Building 2—where he would make the turn and punch the stopwatch.

He did not however, see the garden hose. Eddie's trailing foot caught the black hose at the instep, catapulting him through the air. He must have flown eight feet, parallel to the ground. The heel of his right hand touched down first, ripping off a layer of flesh, as it scraped the sidewalk for ten inches—until it found a seam where the sidewalk turned into grass. The crystal face of the stopwatch fractured on impact, and then acted like a tiny ski—propelling his body even faster. When his right knee crashed down, he came to a halt.

Eddie was face down—nose stuffed into the wet grass. He lay there for a moment to catch his breath. He tried to lift his head slowly, apprehensive of the body parts that would not be working, and rolled onto his back.

What is this? The second—no, the third time in three days I've found myself under crummy circumstances sprawled on the ground? Crawling through glass and blood and Scotch, sitting in a gutter amongst flies and dog crap and vomit... And now this?

Whatever happened to spending my days with my feet up on my big mahogany desk, in my nice air-conditioned office, buzzing people in to bring me a sales report, or a cold Coke?

Or opening envelopes with nice checks in them...

Son of a bitch—my hands hurt like hell. And if I bang this knee one more time...

"Mister, are you a cop?" The voice was high and squeaky—certainly unlike any he had heard recently.

"No, I'm not," he responded to the small black boy who couldn't have been more than eight years old.

The kid was holding a basketball.

"Yes you are. I can tell a cop when I see one."

"Is that right?" asked Eddie, forcing a smile.

The kid nodded. Eddie grimaced in pain.

"Are you OK, Mister?"

No—I'm quite a long way from OK.

Eddie looked down at the stopwatch. He moaned again, partly because the crystal was cracked, but mostly—in fact ironically—because it was still working. The second hand was still ticking. It was way beyond ten seconds.

"I've been better."

"It looks like your watch got broke," said the kid.

"Looks like it."

I wonder if my wrist also got broke...

"I was by my bedroom window. I finished all my homework. It was my bedtime. I always like to sleep with it open. Marcus always closes it cuz it's closed each morning when I wake up. I think he comes in and closes it after I'm asleep. So when I was opening the window, I saw you running and then fall. So I came out here."

"What's your name young man?" inquired Eddie.

"My name is Lamont. What's yours?"

"Eddie."

"Are you here about Oliver, Mr. Eddie? I know you're here about Oliver. He was my friend. He used to shoot hoops with me when he got off duty. We'd play catch with a baseball too. He could name all the Dodger opening day starting lineups since they moved to Los Angeles. I think that was in 1959."

"Actually it was '58," Eddie gently corrected, moderately pleased that at least one body part seemed to be functioning on a basic level. "'59 was when they won their first World Series in L.A."

"Oh, right. My bad."

"No biggie. You were close."

"Are you a Dodger fan, Mr. Eddie?"

"Yes I am."

"Did you ever see Koufax pitch?" Lamont had learned to leave out the 'L.'

"As a matter of fact I did, one time. I was a little kid— about as old as you are now."

"Wow. I heard he was the best."

"Wow is right. He *was* the best. My dad took me to see him shut out the Twins in the 1965 World Series."

"I sure hope I can go to a World Series game one day. But I ain't got no daddy."

To this, Eddie couldn't respond.

"Did you catch the guy who killed Oliver? Is he in jail?"

Eddie was amazed at this kid's ability to change subjects so fast.

Homework. Window. Koufax.

He was even more amazed to be hearing Oliver's name.

"Not exactly."

"My brother Marcus told me never to talk to cops. But you don't seem so bad."

The kid looked off into the direction of the quad, seemingly to think for a second. Or maybe it was to check to see if they were alone. He went into the back pocket of his Levi's, pulled something out, and put his balled fist a few inches under Eddie's face. Then, he slowly opened the small fingers.

Eddie leaned forward, propping himself up on one aching elbow. At first he thought he was looking at two small jelly beans the kid was offering him. Or rocks. But no—they were a little shiny. The kid held two bullets in his left hand. They appeared to have slightly different shapes and even different colors. One was a bit disfigured at the tip. The larger one was cleaner. They both were sort of a dull metallic bronze color, but one had a kind of greenish cast to it. That one, slightly smaller and more distorted than the other, was stained with a tiny speck of what Eddie first discerned to be grease, or rust.

It was clotted blood.

"I found that one in my basketball they popped. My brother Marcus called it a 'hollow point.' Marcus bought me this new ball," said Lamont, proudly holding up the new leather Spalding, in his right hand.

"That other one—the green one—came through my bedroom window that night."

"Where do you live, Lamont?" asked Eddie.

"Right over there." He curled the basketball up under his armpit, turned and pointed.

Eddie followed the trajectory of the little finger. He was pointing upstairs, to the corner unit of Building 4.

Eddie's mind was racing at an impossible pace. The kid was changing gears too fast—throwing too much at him.

The basketball. The Dodgers in the World Series. The bullets. He lived in Building 4! Oh my God! Exhibit 1! The Cadillac, the X on the sidewalk, the eucalyptus tree... didn't one of the bullets lodge into that tree trunk? But another bullet making it through the branches and leaves... That would have put his bedroom right in line...

"I guess I was lucky, or I could have got broken glass falling into my room."

No, he's lucky he wasn't standing by the window in his bedroom! Just like he was tonight when he looked out and saw me! He's lucky he wasn't shot and killed by one of Reggie's bullets! The same bullet that killed Oliver—could have also killed this kid!

Lamont went on, "It was funny 'cause it stuck right in the end of my math book up on the shelf. I kept it to remind me of Oliver."

CHAPTER 17 - Chalk & Onions

October 26, 1993
Compton, California

Fortunately for Eddie, Renee was sound asleep when he slipped into bed after his impetuous decision to make that late night drive to Compton. He found an empty wineglass on her nightstand, and took it correctly as a sign she was down for the count.

I don't want to explain—at least not until morning. It can wait until then. She's been mad enough at me as it is, mad as hell, in fact, with the blood on the carpet and walls, and her losing a whole night of studying. Plus of course the chin episode—she hasn't quite forgiven me for that one, and I can't say I blame her. God, I hope her chin heals before we fly to Ohio for Thanksgiving. The last thing I need is to have to explain hitting her to her mother... Dream or no dream, the truth is I really whacked her. It will be a long time before we can look back at that little incident and laugh about it.

Christ—my ankle hurts—where I nailed that fucking garden hose. My knees and elbows hurt—again! My right wrist aches. And what do I tell her about the damn stopwatch? 'Sorry about the cracked watch, honey. I know it was the first Valentine's present you ever bought me... I was timing myself to see how fast I could do the dishes—and I, uh, dropped it.' Bullshit. She'll know it's bullshit. She was already alarmed, as

*early as seven days ago—when I forgot the Rolex. Hey, two
dumb things involving watches in a week—are they related?*
God I need to sleep. I'm tired. Close your eyes...

But he could not keep them closed. Reaching across the
bed, he gently touched her shoulder. But it wasn't to be
affectionate. It wasn't that first romantic touch of an evening—
it was more of a check—to make sure she was still asleep.

*I want to tell her everything. I really do. But I fear she
might not find me the modern day version of Sherlock Holmes.
Truthfully, the opposite is much more likely. She just might
think I was coming unglued. Would she be wrong? Driving
alone to Compton—to a gang infested neighborhood late at
night? Into the heart of the Bloods' turf! In a new Corvette?
God that was moronic! I could have at least taken her car...
Compton—at night—where people are being gunned down in
the streets for no reason! Doing my own detective work?
Violating some very specific admonitions? Right. I need to
bury this—at least for now. I certainly couldn't share my little
story about the bullets with the rest of the jury.*
Could I?

****

Stepping into the bathroom, he was pleased to see her in
the shower. Pleased to gaze on her incredible naked body. She
was slender, strong and sexy. He loved the way the lather of
white shampoo bubbles oozed down, through her dark hair and
over her spectacular curves. But mostly he was pleased—
thinking he could shower downstairs, grab a quick blueberry
muffin and get out of the house without having to engage in a
conversation.

She had her back to him, but must have spotted something—perhaps a reflection in the glass or in the brushed nickel fixtures. She turned abruptly to face him, and spoke loudly to be heard over the rushing water.

"Where the heck did you go last night? What was that all about?"

Though the view was fantastic, he forced himself to turn away.

"Oh nothing," he answered, wondering if the guilt was obvious.

"Don't *'nothing'* me, Eddie! Where did you go?"

After a barely perceptible hesitation, he said, "I spoke with Bella from a payphone yesterday on our lunch break—I had forgotten all about it with the trial craziness."

"So you went to your office? At 10:00 at night? You *never* do that."

"I know," he lied. The second lie flowed a bit easier, as did the third. "She said I needed to help solve some computer problem, as they were having trouble printing invoices."

She's slightly squinting—trying to keep the soap out of her eyes—so she's probably not getting a good look at my face. I can't look at her… she knows me too well…

"I wish you would have told me that. The way you ran out—and the way you've been caught up in this damn thing—I was afraid you might be running out…"

Oh God, please don't say, '…to the apartments in the trial.' Please don't…

She had a big smile on her face now, so, to his relief, he knew she was kidding, "...like you said the other night—to buy some ammunition—to get some bullets."

That *relief* lasted three seconds. His heart almost jumped out of his chest, upon her mentioning the word *'bullets.'*

For the wrong reason, she was astonishingly close...

I've got to try a deflection—maybe a little humor. That usually works with her...

"I did stop by BIG 5. But they were closed. So I decided to go to my office instead."

"God Eddie—for being the smartest guy I know—you truly are an idiot."

Now it was his turn to smile, although his was fake.

She'll know something's wrong if she gets a good look at my eyes. I've got to get out of here. I can't hide it much longer. I can't lie to her again...

The bullets. The bullets...

She turned to grab another squirt of conditioner. "Now get your butt in this shower and help me wash my back."

****

Driving to the courthouse that morning, it wasn't quite the thrill he normally got from his terrific ride—his new convertible with the killer sound system. He had the guilties—had them bad. He felt guilty about violating the oath he had taken—with the joyride to The Palms last night.

Didn't I swear at the outset of the trial I wouldn't do anything like that?

He felt guilty lying about it to his amazing wife. Now he would have to consider creating some sort of cover-up at work so Bella actually thought he was there, in the office last night, tinkering with the printer.

He felt guilty that he had honestly wanted to go downstairs to take a shower, rather than what he did, which was to jump in with his hot wife for what ordinarily would have been some delectable, slippery, soapy morning pleasure. He knew full well that *not* immediately peeling off his boxer shorts and joining her in the shower would have been tantamount to a signed confession.

****

Will any of the other jurors notice?

The stinging had subsided, but his eyes were still red. He had intentionally splashed a dose of her shampoo into both of his own eyes. It was a genius answer to his anticipated problem of her making close eye contact after they'd made love in the shower. But Eddie was miles away from being able to enjoy his brilliant shampoo solution, as, the guilt overshadowed all.

Throwing soap in my own eyes? Self flagellation again?
She might have been making love. I'm not quite sure how to define what it was that I was doing...

It was somehow fitting, noted Eddie, that the deliberations instantly turned to a discussion of guilt and lies. Eddie didn't say much, feeling exhausted from the repetitive points and strong opinions held by most of the people in that room—intractable opinions—that all the cops were lying. He was exhausted from yet another night of no sleep. And he was exhausted from the incessant pounding in his head—the squeezing of this newfound secret he was desperately trying to keep inside.

Was it possible that Ralph could see that Eddie was a bit out of sorts this morning? As, mercifully, it was Ralph who was able to break the non-productive stream of babble by raising his hand—somehow manifesting a pause in the noise. He stood, walked over to the huge blackboard, and grabbed a long new stick of white chalk.

"I'd like to try something a little different, if I may." He looked across to Eddie, ostensibly not to seek permission from the jury foreman, but, rather, as if he *knew* something. Something that needed Eddie's acquiescence.

Intrigued by this fresh creative tack by the man, Eddie thought of the eye contact communication he often relied on to be an effective point guard in basketball; he nodded back at Ralph without saying a word.

Ralph began smacking chalk on the board, geometry teacher style, like he was excited to prove the world changing Pythagorean Theorem to a class of high school sophomores. He drew two long parallel lines—perhaps eight inches apart. Then he drew six fairly neat rectangles above the parallel lines.

The six apartment buildings of The Palms.

It was clear to Eddie that Ralph was trying to recreate People's Exhibit One.

The noisy room had instantly changed: silent, except for the hitting of the chalk. There was little doubt—after just a few seconds of aggressive smacks and clicks—he had commanded everyone's attention. This was not lost on Ralph, as he was keenly aware of the effect his demonstration was having on these people. He was hitting the board so hard, that at one point the chalk stick broke, half of it falling and clanking off the aluminum tray chalk holder that protruded a couple of perpendicular inches out of the board, before flying off to his left and onto the carpet. But Ralph didn't miss a beat, keeping up his deliberate drawing.

He seemed to intentionally leave off several of the familiar details of Exhibit One, such as the construction area, and eucalyptus tree, but he did include a rectangle inside the lines, and lastly, in the area that defined the quad of The Palms, he placed a small 'x'.

Turning sideways to address the curious group, he began, "OK, let's say this rectangle represents Reggie's Cadillac." Ralph quickly made some zig-zags and chalked in a good deal of the small rectangle. "It's parked here on the side of 128th Street facing this way." He drew a small arrow.

"And let's say this little 'x' represents where Oliver Jefferson was standing."

"Is everybody with me?"

All of the jurors nodded at Ralph. For the first time in days, observed Eddie, there was unanimous assent. In fact, he thought, the last time these people seemed to be on the same page on anything was that little cassette tape party on the first day of deliberations. So far, he liked where this was going.

"So let's see…" said Ralph, scanning all the faces of the quiet room.

But Eddie perceived something fishy. It was really subtle, yet it was there: almost like he was overly animated. Like this could possibly be some sort of an act. Eddie was following along quite intently, as were the others, but he detected something; he could not help feeling that Ralph—in his animated scanning of the onlookers—was feigning randomness.

"Lucille, can you come over here to help me please?"

Much to Eddie's surprise, without hesitation, she rolled her seat back and stood to walk over to Ralph. Ralph had already begun opening a new box—a box that had been sitting untouched all week on the blackboard tray—that contained multiple pastel colored chalk sticks. His thick brown fingers were already covered with a good deal of residue from the white chalk, but he didn't seem to mind.

He offered Lucille the box; Eddie thought it looked almost as if he were offering her a cigarette in a noisy bar from an old classic movie.

"Go ahead Lucille," said Ralph, "pick any color but white."

Or perhaps, maybe not a pack of cigarettes from an old movie. Maybe more like a magician, about to perform a magic trick. 'Pick a card—any card.'

"Sure," she plucked one out, adding with a slight chuckle, "orange is my favorite color."

"Orange is perfect," said Ralph.

"I've seen that you have taken a strong interest in this case, and I trust that you've been paying close attention."

"I have indeed," was her confident response.

"Great. Then will you please, to the best of your ability and recollection of what you understand happened that night—please draw with that orange chalk—the path you think the

Cadillac drove… starting from where it was parked here…"

Ralph tapped the center of the chalked in Cadillac.

At this point, Ralph stepped back from the board, opening his palm, in invitation for her to proceed.

She turned back to look at the ten seated jurors. Eddie had a fleeting thought, a moment of apprehension, that she would excuse herself, reconsidering the request for Ralph's purported help. Not unlike when Claire had said a couple of days ago that she wasn't good with math, or when Jorge confessed that his spelling wasn't great, Eddie thought it more likely than not, Lucille would bail, claiming she couldn't draw. It was one of those rare times when Eddie was glad he was wrong; she quickly spun around and began putting the orange chalk to the blackboard.

Lucille narrated as carefully as she drew. "The Cadillac first drove off this way," she drew a long orange line between Ralph's two parallel white lines, "and when it got to about here, it made a U-Turn, and came back down 128th Street this way."

Again, Eddie's eyes met Ralph's. She had specifically intersected the white and orange chalk lines at the end of the U-Turn, in the exact spot where the detective had said they found tire tread markings and paint shavings from the car's bumper and fender scraping against the curb. Eddie blinked forcibly at Ralph, who returned the subtle non-verbal communication by slightly raising one eyebrow.

"The car kept going, and I believe it stopped about here." She ended her orange line at a point near the straight white chalk line that represented the curb—directly in front of the small white 'x.'

She turned to Ralph, "Do you want me to keep going?"

Ralph stepped forward and gently took the orange chalk from her, "No, no—that's fine. You did great."

Feeling quite proud of herself, she walked back to her seat, while making a show of dramatically brushing the orange powder from her hands.

Ralph began speaking again as he replaced the chalk back into the box.

"Does everybody agree with Lucille here? Do you think this is an accurate depiction of the path that the defendant's El Dorado took that night?"

"Sure man," said Darryl.

"Looks right to me," said Kate.

"Good job Lucille!" shouted out Henrietta, albeit a bit too loudly.

"Right on girl," came the now-expected affirmation by Lottie.

"I wouldn't change anything," said Jeff, actually smiling at Lucille.

"Well, let's put it another way," said Ralph, "does anybody think there is anything wrong with this drawing? Can we all agree that we feel strongly that this is the path Reggie drove his Cadillac on the night Oliver Jefferson was killed?"

Everybody nodded their heads in concordance.

"Nobody disagrees?" asked Ralph being careful to confirm.

Eddie was intrigued. Ralph definitely had his attention, and he was beginning to get excited as to the ramifications. Eddie also noticed that Ralph had been flipping the eraser up and catching it in one hand. Ralph then returned to his seat. For some strange reason, he took the eraser with him. This act was not lost on Eddie, but Eddie couldn't figure out why.

Kinda weird.

Remember that Mediterranean trip—those old men in Greece? They were constantly fingering their worry beads. Or how about Captain Queeg from the Caine Mutiny? He was always clicking those steel balls together. Another Captain: Ahab, daily hanging from the same shroud—pegleg anchored in a worn out hollow in the deck—scanning the horizon for a whale spout.

Maybe this eraser thing was just a nervous habit Ralph developed while teaching...

Ralph continued, "Not to beat a dead horse, but can we have a show of hands?" Ralph raised his own hand. "Who thinks Lucille portrayed an accurate picture with that orange chalk line she drew just now?"

Within seconds, all 12 jurors had their hands held high.

"This is very interesting as," he spoke slowly, meticulously enunciating every single word, "it appears, after all, that each of us here in fact believes very much of what the police had to say during this trial."

Brilliant! Ralph knew! As a black man, he had a chance at pulling this off. He hand-picked Lucille—knowing she might respond to him—If this was my idea, there is no way she would have freely taken the chalk from me!

"What the hell?" said Darryl, but he brought his hand only half-way down. "Whose side are you on man?"

"I'm not on anybody's side," answered Ralph. "I just wanted to prove that we all in fact really believe the police."

Silently, Jeff mouthed one word: *'Wow.'*

"But the cops lied," said Henrietta.

"They always lie," dittoed Lottie.

Incredibly, they still had their hands raised.

"What about you, Lucille? You have been saying repeatedly these past few days that the cops were lying. In fact I believe it was you who said the cops, detectives, and security guards are all the same—that they're all liars—" Ralph increased his volume level, while keeping the deliberate pronunciation, "—but you just showed everybody that you truly believe a great deal of what the police had to say."

Lucille was visibly fuming now. She was the first to take her hand down. Seven other jurors quickly followed suit.

"That chalk line you tricked me into drawing doesn't prove a Goddam thing!" Her voice was a couple octaves higher than normal. It was piercing.

Eddie thought of the Bible reading offered up by Lucille on the morning of Day 2. He felt like displaying his own knowledge of the Ten Commandments by quoting, '*Thou shall not take the Lord's name in vain! Exodus 20: Verse 7!*' But in the interest of not interrupting the flow Ralph had going, restrained himself.

"Oh yes it does," insisted Ralph. "It proves plenty. The path the Cadillac took that night was only spoken about by the police—the police and the detectives. They are the only ones who testified about that. Where else would you gather that information to be able to draw that orange line, complete with that radical U-Turn? You even, very accurately, I might add, depicted where Reggie's Cadillac ran into the curb. Where else did you hear that—if not from the police?" Ralph was hammering home his point with her, and it was clear to all that she was incapable of defending herself.

The room started getting loud again. Loud and unruly. Lucille stood and walked defiantly back up to the chalkboard. She looked around frantically for a piece of chalk, but Ralph had tucked all the pieces neatly back into the pack, even closing up the Cellophane. Fidgeting excitedly with the box, she became frustrated, as those long fake fingernails would not allow her the dexterity to open it. Recalling the broken half-stick that had fallen earlier, she looked down on the floor, until she realized she had just crushed the piece under her shoe. She looked at the bottom of her shoe as if she had just stepped in dog shit. She scoured the tray again—confounded that she could not find the big eraser that had always been there.

Oh my God! Could Ralph possibly be the greatest chess-player in the world? The ability to think that far ahead! That skill would even strike fear in the minds of Garry Kasparov or Bobby Fischer! Could he have foreseen this entire scenario? Can Ralph be that much of a genius to have actually gone back to his seat—knowingly taking the one eraser with him?

Eddie raised his own hand even higher.

The pride Lucille felt just moments earlier vanished. Her pride in being able to demonstrate something—to make a contribution so important that all of these people, black, white, Asian or Latino, would have to rely on—instantly crumbled. It crumbled—not unlike the chalk dog shit she now had on her shoes. She had become a caged animal, and now acted with animal instinct.

What happened next astounded all eleven of her fellow jurors—even the ones who were holding tightly to the *'cops lying'* theory as being the essence of Reggie's defense. Lifting her left palm to within inches of her face, she spit in it. She did the same with her right. Not just little dry poofs containing mostly air, but big globs of wet saliva. She then began scrubbing her orange chalk line, frantically wiping and rotating her wrists as if she was a worker at a car-wash, waxing a customer's car, in the hopes of receiving a bigger tip. The white chalk mixed with the orange which mixed with the saliva. The heavy white chalked in area, drawn by Ralph, that was Reggie's El Dorado—obliterated. She turned it into a chalky paste. Blackboard shaking, she smeared her orange chalk line U-Turn, in attempt to expunge it as well.

She needed to purge the line she drew. She needed to purge it from the blackboard, and, even more importantly, if at all possible, to purge her self-incriminating actions from the memory of these people. Ralph's neat drawing, his time-consuming, methodical depiction of the apartment buildings and street of Exhibit One, decomposed; it evolved into something more closely representing a preschool kid's finger painting. She kept smearing and swirling until there was no discernable trace of her carefully drawn orange line, nor Reggie's Cadillac, nor the little white 'x' that represented Oliver.

She walked away from the blackboard, eyes fixed coldly on Ralph. She then switched her gaze across the table, directing the same poisoned laser-like focus at Eddie. But, she made a rather large faux pas, as, while being fully engaged in her curse infused staring, issuing unspoken profanities at these two horrible men—she was not aware of her hands, other than that they felt dirty. Lucille was so caught up in her will to send these men to eternal damnation, that she did not realize something: she had begun wiping her hands on her purple pant-suit.

It was the same garish purple pant-suit she had worn last week, back on the first day of deliberations. Eddie mustered an incongruous thought, thinking it was the same color purple as the Lakers' road uniforms. As she kept wiping, with each inch of her shameful journey back to her seat, the hand prints became more and more prominently visible. The orange chalk, the white chalk and the spittle mixed, creating a Jackson Pollack splatter of hands on her purple outfit. The hands went up and down the sides of her blazer, and her very ample hips. One seemed to caress her right breast. Another perfect orange hand appeared to be grabbing at her bright purple crotch.

Neither Lottie nor Henrietta could stifle their giggles.

"Oh girl," said Lottie, "you really ought to get yourself to the ladies' room."

****

The jurors had just filed back in after their lunch break to resume Day 7 deliberations in the trial of '*The State of California vs. Reginald Washington.*' As soon as the last juror was seated at the table, Eddie spoke.

"I think maybe it's time for another vote."

"Yeah, maybe it'll be unanimous and we can all go home!" said Darryl enthusiastically.

To which, Harold said, "Fat chance."

"So do we vote to see if we should vote?" asked Kate.

Eddie thought she was possibly attempting humor—but by the confused expressions on the faces of a few jurors—he was uncertain.

"The heck with it," said Darryl. "Let's just do it."

"OK," said Eddie, "we'll make this a closed ballot. Everybody tear out a sheet from your notepads. Think for a minute, and then clearly write either: "Guilty, Not Guilty, or Undecided—"

"Hell, I don't need no minute for that!" snipped Lottie.

"—fold your page," continued Eddie, glaring at Juror 11, "and place it in the tray here in the center of the table."

A few folded sheets of the pastel green paper were tossed into the tray within seconds. The rest of the jurors stared at their blank ballots; some thought hard while others pretended concentration. Jorge looked at Eddie as if he needed to hear the instructions again, yet abruptly wrote something.

In under two minutes, all twelve ballots were cast.

"OK, let's see if we feel that Mr. Washington is guilty beyond a reasonable doubt," said Eddie, reaching for the wooden tray. He gently mixed up a few of the sheets, not unlike a pastor, milking the excitement of his congregation, by repeatedly running his hands into the hopper at the church fundraiser before announcing the lucky raffle winner.

Eddie grabbed a single sheet, and unfolded it. It happened to be his own ballot. Without looking up from the paper he read boldly, "Guilty."

Six different jurors quickly made their own score pads in their spiral notebooks.

The seats were spaced comfortably, nearly three feet apart from each other, around the oval conference table. Upon hearing the reading of the first vote, Lucille, on Eddie's immediate left, sharply slid back on her seat casters. Fortunately for her, during lunch, she did a fairly good job of removing most of the chalk from her clothes. She stood and took two quick strides to position herself behind Eddie. Hunching over him, she reached for the first ballot which was still in Eddie's hands.

Eddie's first thought was his own self-criticism at not having had the foresight to ask for someone to aid in his tabulation of the ballots. But, quickly, it became clear. He realized the true meaning of Lucille's rush to his back: she simply did not trust him to read the results truthfully.

His nostrils flared slightly at the detection of an unpleasant mix of foul fumes from her earlier lunch, coupled with a copious quantity of bad perfume. At the lunch break, she must have splashed a healthy dose of the stuff on herself in what had to have been a manic attempt to clean up the self-inflicted sexual harassment and unwanted touching in the form of those chalky hands and fingers poking into very private areas of her purple pant-suit.

She was way too close to him. It was an absolute violation of his personal space.

Who the hell was this miserable woman?

Eddie recalled a quote from Harry, years ago, during a very heated extra-inning softball game out in the San Fernando Valley. *'Don't ever walk up on anybody. Don't get in their space. If you do, you must look at their hands. Look only at their hands, not their eyes. A fist will be coming your way. You must expect that, and be ready with your own fists.'*

He thought about Harry's scarred knuckles.

I have little doubt, from what I've learned this past week that there must have been jury room deliberations that morphed rapidly from words to fists.

But... has a white man ever punched a black woman?

He felt, no, he *tasted*, the warm air of her breath containing the sour residue of pickles and onions. It shocked him. But it didn't shock him as much as what happened next: she firmly yanked that first ballot from his fingers, while, when leaning forward, her hair brushed against his shirt collar, neck and left cheek. A few strands of course hair grazed the left corner of his mouth. He cringed. But, Eddie, as foreman, somehow found the will to stay on task; he proceeded to unfold the next ballot.

"Not Guilty."

The third: "Not Guilty."

The fourth: "Not Guilty."

Lucille smiled and backed off a couple of inches. Eddie opened the next ballot—folded many times so that it was down to business card size, figured correctly that it was from Jorge, and read, "Undecided."

In two seconds, he felt it: her hot breath returned. It overwhelmed him, like a mushroom cloud, consuming his oxygen. The onions, her onions, the reconstituted onions from *her* tongue and *her* esophagus burned his eyes. He felt like he was eating the same sandwich she must have had for lunch just 30 minutes earlier.

He was going to retch.

For, what is this now, the second or third time in a few days? I haven't felt like puking this much since... that UCLA dorm room... that stomach virus back in college that practically wiped out Rieber Hall...

He moved faster, unfolding and reading in rapid succession. He had to read faster, or he was going to vomit on the conference table, right into the tray holding the precious instructions from the judge.

"Not Guilty. Not Guilty. Guilty. Abstain. Not Guilty. Not Guilty."

He abruptly jerked his seat back on his own set of casters, purposefully startling Lucille. Unfortunately for her, those same shoes that crushed that piece of white chalk earlier in the day, were open-toed. Her toe-nails sported five little spots of the shocking pink nail polish that matched the fingernail polish she wore on Day 1 of the deliberations. One of the heavy casters from Eddie's seat caught her, rolling over the baby toe of Lucille's right foot. She let out a guttural shriek, and limped back in pain.

Eddie acted surprised. "Oh, sorry, I didn't see you there." But his words were something less than heartfelt.

He then stood and read the last ballot, "Guilty."

Grimacing, Lucille hopped into the corner behind him. She clenched her teeth in attempt to push back the pain, while muttering unintelligible sounds. It was almost as if she was speaking in tongues. Meeting her eyes for a millisecond, Eddie turned toward the jurors' restroom, pushed open the door, and quickly locked it behind him. He stood in front of the porcelain sink, confronting the urge to barf. For a full twenty seconds he faced the mirror, unsure of the owner of those eyes belonging to that stranger who stared back at him. The red bloodshot eyes. They were no longer red from Renee's shampoo. Nor were they red from sleep deprivation. They were red with rage. He needed to wash his face. He needed to scrub with soap where her hair had touched his cheek and mouth. He could still smell those rancid onions.

His mind brought forth the image of the fires. The rage the blacks of Los Angeles must have been feeling, last year, in the riots. Their justified rage at hearing that the cops who beat Rodney King were exonerated. He wondered if it felt anything like this—what he felt now. In a low voice, he mouthed to himself a handful of words that Harry had said the other night—something about how close they were to a meltdown of society with one weird verdict, or one random bullet.

Though the nausea was gone, he now wanted to stick his fingers down his own throat to purge himself of the experience. Thinking ahead, he actually scanned the restroom for a shower, but of course there wasn't one.

He imagined the pain that woman must be feeling. She just had a heavy chair and the full weight of a 190 pound man roll over her baby toe. He empathized. He had played years of basketball and once broke a toe. Lifting weights, somebody once dropped a barbell on his foot. After one varsity football practice, in high school, a 300 pound offensive tackle went into the showers wearing nothing but his enormous helmet. Somehow, in the locker room silliness that ensued, the heavy helmet ended up crashing down on Eddie's big toe. He understood her pain, and he felt bad. Felt bad, that is, because it wasn't enough. He wanted to burst out of the juror's hermetically pristine restroom—back into the deliberation room. He hoped Lucille was still hopping around in the corner like a clown. So he could corner her.

He wanted to dig his fingers into her throat.

CHAPTER 18 - The Red Button

October 27, 1993
Compton, California

Arriving home, Eddie badly needed to talk with Renee—needed to share some of what had transpired the past couple of days. He wasn't comfortable with his own thoughts. Disturbing thoughts. It upset him to find a note from her at the top of the stairs; she left a napkin saying she'd be out with her study group until at least 2 AM—*'Don't wait up.'* He called his parents, but couldn't focus, his mom spending most of the conversation trying to get Eddie to answer the question of whether he would be going to Ohio every Thanksgiving for the rest of their lives. He called Harry, but hung up upon hearing his answering machine. He made himself a quick peanut butter and jelly sandwich for dinner, and then, for only the second time in his life, took two sleeping pills. Within half an hour, worries of burning buildings, Lucille, ruined fabric, babies, or bullets, turned into a light fog.

****

He arrived at the courthouse a few minutes early to start the morning of Day 5 deliberations. Outside the elevator on the 6th floor, he spotted a copy of the Juror's handbook lying on a bench, and, for some reason, picked it up. While waiting for his fellow jurors to settle into their seats, he began to leaf through the small green pamphlet. But he couldn't get beyond page one, where in the third sentence he read:

> 'While jury service may cause you financial
> loss or personal inconvenience, the opportunity
> to participate in the administration of justice
> should be a rewarding experience.'

Let's just think about that… By now—with the fabric fuckup along with other various items that surely have fallen through the cracks in my absence—the financial loss to the company is already well into five figures. No big deal—I'm making four bucks a day! I've got a $28 check coming from the County of Los Angeles when this is over!

Hmmm… the 'personal inconvenience' part… a few bandages for my elbows and knees and for my wife's chin. A new carpet if the bloodstains don't come out with a deep cleaning. Christ. I wonder if I can find that exact same stopwatch so she'll never know I broke it? And then, maybe there's a trip to a marriage counselor in the near future…

Hell, I lied to her. I've never done that before. Is a visit with a divorce attorney much more likely?

He re-read the sentence from the handbook.

Now, as for 'administration of justice' and 'a rewarding experience?' Justice? For who? For Oliver Jefferson? For Reggie Washington? Are you freaking kidding me? A rewarding experience? Was this even written this century? Who comes up with this nonsense? Bullshit and even more bullshit!

Lucille trumpeted loudly as she blew her nose. Pulling the dusty pink Kleenex away from her face, she examined the contents of her production, as a narrow glistening string of snot snapped back into her left nostril.

Eddie was disgusted.

He wanted out. The original excitement that had engulfed him seven days earlier was gone. He reflected for a fleeting moment on his energy and enthusiasm upon walking through those courtroom room doors for the first time. The respect and awe he held for this place—that feeling was what the author of the pamphlet he still held in his hand probably had in mind—especially with the lofty sentence that caught Eddie's attention on page one. But now, he was disgusted at himself for having had those thoughts, while simultaneously, he was disgusted at his fellow jurors for not having those same thoughts.

Out of the corner of his eye, he saw Lucille fumbling through her orange plastic purse. *'Orange is my favorite color,'* he recalled her saying yesterday—right before the chalk incident. He cringed, realizing she was digging for a fresh tissue.

What is it with these women and their purses? What other hidden horrors did they conceal?

Weary from being in the same room with these people, Eddie looked at his watch—9:45. He could not spend another day in this room. He wanted his life back—wanted to go back to his office—back to where he could control so much of the goings on of his day. Each day, people asked him a full range, from simple to complex questions. *'All the fashion mags say Turquoise will be big this spring, so how many blouses should we sew in style 306, Eddie?' 'Should we buy 500 yards of white cotton at 2.90 per yard, or commit to 2,000 yards at*

2.50?' Rarely was he annoyed. On the contrary, he appreciated that they would come to him—to have them trust and respect his judgement. The sum of all his experiences, coupled with his profound ability to assess the likely outcome to many business scenarios, had earned him this. He was generally able to give quick and accurate answers to their queries. He wanted to go back to his warehouse, to the perfect environment that he had built—that efficient, well-oiled machine—back to where there were people who listened and acted on his thoughts and decisions. He longed to be back in control, surrounded by people, good people of varying races and backgrounds, wherein he never gave a second thought as to whether it was a black woman, or a white man who said or did something.

On his payroll, he had 8 Caucasians, 6 African Americans, 14 Latinos, and 11 Vietnamese. Race was never an issue. He didn't ever need to consider it, as problems related to race simply never arose. His secretary for the last seven years was black. His bookkeeper was black; Eddie gave him the money for the down payment on a new car after the old one was destroyed in last year's riots. His top designer was black. They had all been to Eddie's home numerous times for various events—holiday parties, major heavyweight fights, and the annual Super Bowl party he threw. They were always invited. He knew their families. There were many cultural differences, but they were a far cry from problematic. On the contrary, it added an interesting and even fun element to the atmosphere in his company. Besides the African Americans, the Vietnamese had different holidays; Eddie's favorite had to be *'Tet,'* the Vietnamese New Year. The date changed from year to year, due to reliance on the lunar calendar, but the fun factor was often described as 'Christmas, New Year's and your birthday all rolled into one.' He also had a couple of Jewish employees. The Jews had several of their own special days, Passover,

Rosh Ha Shanna and Yom Kippur being the biggies. On Passover, Jews celebrated their freedom from slavery in Egypt—acting like kings—and being required to drink four glasses of wine. How could anyone not love that? Cinco de Mayo was celebrated as much by the non-Mexicans, if not more so. To the delight of all, pitchers of margaritas often magically appeared in the lunchroom at the end of the day whenever May 5th fell on a weekday.

His staff and employees got along with each other beautifully, so—as far as problems with religion or race? Never.

Now, being a member of this jury, he thought back on that moment after closing arguments—that moment when he realized that it was the eleven people sitting with him in the jury box that he knew the least. He didn't comprehend it at the time, but that apprehensiveness was well-founded, as they quickly sank into an area in which race played a critical role in nearly every topic in the deliberations, and quite nearly every statement made by the jurors. He thought back to the first minutes in this room—the opening of the all-important deliberations. He did not want to be foreman. He did not want the responsibility, or the pressure. He was perfectly willing to sit and listen to somebody else drive the discussions—to respect and follow somebody else's lead. But in those first few minutes, it was obvious that nobody was going to step forward.

The frustration of his current situation was mounting; he was not in charge of these people, but rather, he was almost at their mercy. The fact was—they were indeed his peers as far as ending the trial and coming to a fair and just conclusion—and that fact overwhelmed him. Because the bottom line was: these people, this jury, was deadlocked. There was no logic, or reason or persuasiveness that could change the reality of this stalemate. It was hell.

He noticed that, much like the magical disappearance of those piles of cassette tape from Day 1, the blackboard was perfectly clean. He looked down at the floor, thinking of what to say to begin the morning. The crushed stick of chalk had been completely vacuumed up. Just a few feet away, to his left, he couldn't help observing that Lucille had worn much sturdier shoes today. It also seemed she was sitting slightly farther away from him than every other day this past week.

He looked up, across the table, where his eyes met Ralph.

"I think we should all go home," said Eddie.

Silence permeated, until Henrietta spoke, "What? We just got here."

Ironically, it was nearly an exact reversal of the same interaction between Eddie and Henrietta from last Friday.

"We can't go home," said Kate. "It's not even 10:00 in the morning. We've got all day. Besides, we haven't reached a decision yet."

"Really? Is there anybody here who hasn't reached a decision?" asked Eddie. "Is there anybody in this room who just needs to hear a little more discussion because they're sitting on the fence and can go either way at this point?"

Silence again.

Eddie continued, "I have a hunch that there's at least one of us who feels that Washington is innocent. Is that true?"

"Well hell yes he's innocent," said Darryl. "Like I knew all along, he was framed."

"Damn straight," agreed Henrietta, as the now expected affirmation from Lottie, as well as several others followed.

"Framed? Are you serious?" asked Harold. "Wouldn't the police have produced a gun if he was framed?"

Jeff spoke up, "Or how about bullets with Jefferson's blood on them? The cops certainly would not have just said, *'Oh well, BOTH bullets that hit and passed through the body of Oliver Jefferson must have ended up in cars driving down Century Boulevard. And BOTH of those cars just drove away—into the night—never to be seen again.'*

Jeff summarized firmly, "It's ridiculous! Ridiculous and impossible!"

"If the cops lied, Reggie should walk," said Darryl. "That's all there is to it. And they lied about everything."

"Right on," said Lottie.

"Oh really?" responded Harold. "They lied about *everything*? Even their names? They lied about not being able to find a single bullet with traces of Jefferson's blood? How idiotic is that? To me, that's telling the truth."

"Dude, are you calling me an idiot?" asked Darryl.

Eddie found himself hoping big Harold would give him an honest answer, but the question just hung in the air.

"Whatever, man. All I know is Reggie should walk."

Incredulous, Harold repeated Darryl's statement as a question, "Reggie should *walk*?"

"That's what I said. If they are from the L.A.P.D.—then they are dirty. Plain and simple, they cannot be trusted, they plant evidence all the time, they are racist and they are liars," answered Darryl. "They need to lie so they can get away with their police brutality."

Ralph spoke up, "Police brutality is not one of the issues of this trial. I think we just showed yesterday, that they told the truth, at least to the degree that we all believed the critical aspects of the exhibits and testimony. Plus, you just said, *'they plant evidence all the time?'* Jeff is right. If they *wanted* to plant evidence, as you suggest, they certainly could have done that. Oliver Jefferson's body was laid out on a slab in the morgue for days; the cops had access to it. How tough would it have been to get just one or two tiny drops of his blood and dab a trace on one or both of those bullets they dug out of the stucco or the tree? They could have planted blood wherever they wanted! But they didn't. And, more importantly, Darryl, the L.A.P.D. is not on trial here. Reginald Washington is."

"Well if the L.A.P.D. is not on trial—they oughtta be!"

The room began rumbling again. Two or three separate arguments quickly escalated in intensity. Somebody started shouting about the Rodney King beating. Claire was spouting facts about the makeup of the Simi Valley jury from the King trial. Somebody else wanted to tell one of her own stories about bigoted cops. Darryl reprised his intimate knowledge of the way the police force operated in Cleveland, while Kate began sharing an experience in Georgia.

But somehow, Eddie's words were heard by all—above the din. "Well that's my point—let's just all go home. I think he's guilty. No, let me rephrase that: I'm sure he's guilty."

To Eddie's own surprise, he was not interrupted. "Not one of you has given me a single reason to think otherwise in almost a week. Reggie Washington wasn't in a fight with the guards—with Oliver Jefferson or Raul Hernandez. There was no heated pushing and shoving. It was not self-defense. It was cold-blooded murder."

Eddie waited again for the interruption, but it didn't come. He continued. "And reasonable doubt? Forget it. There is no reasonable doubt. There is zero doubt. Washington was able to ditch the gun, and it was never found. That does not make him innocent. Right after shooting Oliver, he easily could have tossed it out the car window to one of his underling Bloods, some other gang member, who never made it to the trial, who ran off with it, and made it disappear. It's in a sewer or garbage dump somewhere, or maybe even tossed off the Santa Monica

Pier. It's not even a big stretch of the imagination: Reggie's gun is gone. Period."

At this point, Eddie mulled over the idea of talking about the bullets. It was positively infuriating not to. Incredibly, three of these jurors, Ralph, Harold and Jeff, just mentioned the bullets, so it was clearly on their minds. He had kept his enormous secret about his trip to The Palms bottled up inside for a day and a half now. It was like a vigorously shaken can of Coke—just ready to blow when somebody pulled the tab.

He knew he did something absolutely against the rules— probably cause for him to be held in contempt, or to have some huge fine or penalty imposed on him by the judge. It was blatant juror misconduct. A different fragment from the Juror's Handbook bubbled to the surface of his memory. This one, he had memorized; it was from page seven and he had read it many times—over and over:

> 'As a juror, you must not become an amateur
> detective. For instance, you must not visit the
> scene of an accident or an alleged crime.'

Shit! That's exactly what I did! There's nothing ambiguous about it. Could I go to jail over this? An amateur detective— going to the scene of the crime. What I did was way worse than Kate's recorded tapes. It's way worse than Lucille's reading from the Bible about needing two witnesses or her trying to take back her orange chalk line!
Still....

He thought to himself and was torn. The intensity of his dilemma was borderline overwhelming. He struggled with telling these 11 people about his discovery…

...the one bullet, shot by Jimmy that ended up in the basketball, eliminates any possibility that it was the bullet from Jimmy's gun that killed Oliver. The other, the greenish bullet that I saw in Lamont's hand, was the proof of the whole thing! All that forensics—those detectives and metal detectors couldn't find it. But this 8-year old kid had it all along. Hell: he's carried it around for over a year! And simply because his brother, Marcus, told him not to talk to cops—and because Marcus closed his little brother's window AFTER the bullet had gone into the math book on the shelf—it remained a secret—the cops didn't see a broken window, or glass on the ground outside Building 4, so they had no reason to search inside—in Lamont's bedroom. Jesus! It remained a secret for a whole year, until I found myself sprawled out on the wet grass of the Century Palms two nights ago...

No. He would have to keep all of this to himself. Besides, he was absolutely certain it would make no difference. So Eddie choked down the knowledge, continuing without revealing the most critically important piece of evidence in the entire trial.

"Some of you think the cops are lying. You feel that they are lying because the defendant is black, or because they are white, or because they are from the L.A.P.D. If you want to believe that, you will have to live with that—but it does not change the fact that Reggie murdered Oliver. You might not like the point that Raul Hernandez was overweight, or that he was the only real witness to the shooting. Let me rephrase that: he was the only witness who *testified* to have seen the shooting! As I understand it, there were more like 20 witnesses to the shooting. There were tenants on the property, and gang members in the street. But they were Jimmy's faction, or Reggie's gang, and they conveniently disappeared as soon as they saw Oliver go down. When Hernandez reappeared on the scene in the quad, he was alone... Why did they disappear? To me, it's obvious—*none* of them was willing to go up against Reggie Washington. Would you?"

Eddie scanned each juror seated around the conference table. "Well? Any of you?" But they were all quiet.

"He is one of the higher ranking Bloods in all of Compton—hell, possibly in all of L.A. Who in their right mind would want to testify against Reggie?

"Remember that guy, the very first witness to testify in the trial?" Eddie quickly looked to the first page of his notes, "Yes, Enrique Chavez. Remember him? The night and morning after the shooting, he gave all those details of what he witnessed to the police. And then, at the trial, conveniently forgot everything. He did not testify that he *didn't* see it—Reggie shooting Oliver—he testified that he didn't *remember!* 'No recuerdo.' Oliver had a bone sticking out of his throat! Well, if I had ever seen anything like that, I can tell you—it would have made an impression on me that would have been impossible to forget."

Eddie paused to look at each individual face again. "What would somebody's life expectancy be if they did testify against him?" Silence again. "The security guard, Hernandez—he was obviously nervous as hell. I would be too!"

Eddie continued, "For God's sake: Reggie shot and killed a man for absolutely no reason. What would he do to somebody who testified against him?

"So, no, I don't foresee changing my mind. Like I said, let's push the button and call in the bailiff. It's a mistrial. We've all done our great civic duty and we can be quite proud of ourselves." Eddie's sarcasm was losing its subtlety. He decided it was the perfect time to quote from the handbook, "The opportunity to participate in the administration of justice has been a rewarding one," and added, "…it was so nice to spend time getting to know each of you."

Eddie intentionally blurred his vision. He wouldn't focus on a single individual around the table as he stood and walked in silence back into his only sanctuary, into the restroom.

"What do we do now?" asked one voice.

"What a waste of time," said another.

"We can't just—"

"I want to go home too." It was Wong.

Mr. Wong had probably said the least of any of the 12 jurors during deliberations. In fact, the few times he spoke, he was largely ignored. But he certainly had everybody's attention now. "I'm going to push red button. Please don't try to stop me this time."

Nobody did.

CHAPTER 19 - The Foreman

October 27, 1993
Compton, California

"Ladies and gentlemen of the jury, this court would like to hear if you have reached a verdict on the charges in the criminal matter of *The People of the State of California versus Reginald Washington.*"

Judge Sherman was calm. He spoke with no discernable emotion. "Juror Number Four, Mr. Curtain, I understand you have acted as foreman throughout these deliberations?"

Eddie's heart, which was already beating faster than normal, now began to pound.

Hell—I didn't realize I'd be singled out at this point. Let me think, Perry Mason, Ironside, L.A. Law... How many hundreds of courtroom television shows and movies have I watched? Were they authentic depictions? Somehow this, the real thing, feels quite different. Should I stand up? I think the jury foreman always stood... What about for a hung jury? I can't recall a movie where the climax resulted in a hung jury. It was always some amazing, wild surprise verdict, where the courtroom went nuts with the judge screaming about 'order in the court,' banging his gavel as flashbulbs from a dozen cameras started popping and that black and white newspaper banner headline started spinning... I don't think we're gonna see much of that today. Not from this trial...

So, do I stand? What do I say? I stopped wearing a tie on Day 2... should I have worn one today? Are there official words, or will I have to explain what happened during deliberations this past week? Shit. Why isn't there something written that I can just read. There certainly wasn't anything about this in the Juror's Handbook.

Please don't make me explain anything, judge... Please don't make me explain why we failed. Why I failed...

Eddie stood. He swallowed hard—another anxiety attack knocking at the door.

I need a drink of water...

All eyes were on him now. "Yes sir, your honor. That is correct sir—I am the foreman.*"*

He had experienced failure very few times in his life—he was certainly not used to it. Sweeping across their stares, he spent a moment thinking of some of the key players in this drama.

The Bailiff, Cedric Ellis. Quick eye contact with the imposing man. Eddie thought of Melville's Queequeg again, wondering if his chest and back were covered with three-masted clipper ships, or anchors, or whaling tattoos. Or if he kept a harpoon handy when guarding the judge's chambers.

Why do I keep having thoughts of Moby Dick? Is it because, like Ahab, I'm compelled? Compelled to reveal the truth that Reggie is guilty? Is that my White Whale?

Mercifully, this time, the Bailiff did not wink at Eddie. Had that occurred, he might have lost it; he might not have been able to defeat the panic attack.

The district attorney was sitting, not twenty feet away from him. Today the red-headed Sandra Levinthal wore a tailored pant suit, in yet another shade of green. As if keeping time with a metronome, she tapped a long yellow No. 2 pencil against her small palm. Eddie figured she had to be nervous at this critical moment, obviously apprehensive about what he was about to say.

Rosemary Davis, Reggie's court appointed defense attorney, was a different story. To Eddie, she looked almost smug. Cocky. Eddie recalled his own reaction—how impressed he was with her after what he assessed was a bloody cross-examination of Hernandez. All her prancing around the easels, smacking and poking at the exhibits with the wooden pointer—like it was a sword—impaling the fat security guard. She had spouted so many details: facts, distances and times without once consulting her notes. But Eddie was now stuck after doing a one-eighty—not unlike the U-turn Reggie executed driving the El Dorado. He hated the way she riled up the jury with her closing arguments. He saw how that carried over into the thinking of many of the jurors during deliberations. He found himself detesting her. He wished hard that he could make a 'Guilty' announcement—envisioning the melting of that smug, arrogant, expression.

Eddie looked out and saw Oliver's partner, Raul Hernandez, in the very last row of the courtroom gallery.

As much as Raul dreaded returning to the courthouse, he felt he owed it to Oliver. Tanya Jefferson, Oliver's wife, had been calling Sandra Levinthal almost daily. Shortly after the shooting, she had moved away from Los Angeles, back to her family in St. Louis. With the D.A. being fairly tight-lipped about the proceedings, Tanya began calling Raul, pressing him for any sign of encouraging news that would lead to a conviction for the man who had murdered her husband.

I don't think there's any doubt about the verdict you want to hear today, Raul! I'm sorry I failed you as well...

His scan of the courtroom players stopped at Reggie.

My gosh, the horror in those eyes! The one weird eyeball, adding to the perversion—to the twisted horror. What led to the twists and turns and linear connection of dots that eventually created Reggie? Didn't he once build cardboard forts in his yard like the black kids on the street just a few blocks from this courthouse? Didn't he spend his summers enjoying the simple boyish pleasure of throwing a baseball? Or didn't he ever beam with excitement and pride at owning a new basketball, like little Lamont?

Maybe he once proudly wore an L.A. Raiders cap that showed his support for the team that recently won the Super Bowl. When did that same black and silver Raiders cap evolve, away from football, to become some horrific symbol of sociopathic gang activity? Were these some of the same forces at play that yielded the Cimarron Avenue Bloods' leader, Reggie Washington?

Those eyes revealed the horror that Oliver must have seen through the glass, through the windshield of the Cadillac on that night—his final night—a year ago.

It was also the same horror that I saw magnified through different glass—through the facemask in my dream. The wavy wet contrails of the red bandana coming out of that mask... I want it to be blood streaming out of the back of your head, you bastard! But this time, Reggie, it's ME with the spear!

I'm Ahab with the harpoon!

I don't know for certain if Raul made it to that corner of Building 2 in ten seconds. I don't know if he really witnessed you pulling the trigger… which means… of all the people in this room, including the judge—there are only two of us who know the absolute truth! You and me, Reggie! I saw the bullets! My God—I touched the fucking bullet that went through Oliver's throat! I didn't realize it until just now, but you must have touched that same bullet when you loaded your gun!

At this last thought, Eddie shivered. His right index finger felt numb, almost buzzing. He felt unclean.

His mind kept machine-gunning thoughts, short-circuiting the incessant firing of the synapses in his brain. It was just as he was overloaded with the rapid-fire data that was thrown at him by that kid, Lamont, two nights ago.

All the time and effort that went into this trial. The People of the State of California vs. Reginald Washington—all the evidence and hours of testimony will not be enough to send Reggie to prison. Like Mr. Wong said: 'this joke of a jury.' Deadlocked. Hung. A Mistrial. The trial will be over, and Reggie probably will be set free when the district attorney realizes that there is nothing that could have prevented this outcome. Not a new witness, or a better witness. Not another exhibit, or better mounted color pictures. Or an accurate compass. Nothing will make the outcome of a new trial any different than this one. So, in all likelihood, in just 60 days, Reggie will be released from custody. The handcuffs will come off yet again. He'll return to his role as leader of the Cimarron Avenue Bloods. He'll be free to resume cruising the streets of Los Angeles in his Cadillac.

He will be free while Oliver was in his grave.

When Judge Sherman spoke again, Eddie was uncertain as to whether a millisecond had gone by since his last query about him being the foreman, or if the judge had been repeating this same new question to him over and over for the past ten minutes.

"Has the jury reached a verdict?"
Though he felt all eyes in that huge room bearing down on him, he refused to look at anyone seated next to or behind him in the jury box. They were not part of his just completed perusal of the bailiff, the attorneys and the accused—not a single one of them. He hated being with these people—his 'fellow jurors.' He certainly hated speaking for them. He felt ashamed.

I guess I made somewhat of a connection with Ralph, and Jeff, respecting and in fact agreeing with almost everything they had to say, yet, I won't miss them. But Darryl? Shit. Jorge was right—'pendejo.' Even though she voted 'Not Guilty,' Claire seemed to have put some thought and reason into the things she said... But the white woman, Kate—what was her IQ? 70? And the other women? The clones Henrietta and Lottie? And, of course Lucille? How could these people have been allowed to enter my life to this degree? I want them all gone!

Eddie felt at this moment as though he was the defendant, not the jury foreman. He recalled having a similar feeling during *voir dire*, but this was worse.
He steeled himself, locking eyes with Reggie again. Although this time, it was not out of weakness, as when he was checking for seawater on the morning after that horrible dream. Then he saw it. He saw Reggie blink.

Could this be the first time in the past seven days that I actually saw you blink? It was you! I know it was you! You murdered Oliver Jefferson, you son of a bitch!

Eddie wanted to scream out for all to hear. The Coke can was shaken, bulging, ready to explode... but for Eddie, instinct and desire took a back seat to reality. He snapped his gaze away from Reggie, paused, and turned directly toward the judge.

"No, we have not, your honor."

****

The judge asked several more questions of Eddie, in essence inquiring if there was any chance that further time spent deliberating could eventually lead to a unanimous verdict. He asked if Eddie felt there was some testimony that could be read back to add clarity to their discussions. He asked if there was an exhibit, or piece of evidence that was of particular concern to the jurors that might possibly change some of their feelings if it were presented again with a different or simpler explanation. He asked if there was anything in his instructions or in the charges brought by the State that required clarification, or if a re-read of either of these might facilitate movement in feelings on the part of the deadlocked jury.

No Judge. If you only saw half of what I saw in the jury room this past week, you'd stop asking me these questions! You would realize that more time spent deliberating would be a complete waste.

Eddie understood that the judge had the power to force them—he could order the jury back into their miserable little room for further deliberations.

Please don't do that judge. Don't do that unless you are prepared for the outcome, as—it just might lead to a couple of brand new murder trials for your courtroom.
Please accept the words I'm about to say...

"I'm certain that additional time won't help, your honor."
Eddie took it upon himself to sit down.

Judge Sherman had been dealing with his own anxiety and apprehension over the trial. The floor around his feet was littered with more than two dozen crumpled up tiny wads of paper. He also somehow managed concealing from all of the people in his courtroom this past week, his predilection for eating pistachios whenever he felt a trial began taking a turn for the worse. These bright pink shells did not make it onto the floor, however, as the judge dropped them neatly into his top drawer. A hung jury was nothing for a judge to be proud of, especially when he was fairly certain of what an accurate and just verdict should be. In spite of many of the shortcomings of the prosecution, and the inevitable hitches with exhibits and evidence and witnesses, combined with the many intangibles of the jury, ultimately, he had to consider his own failure.

He abhorred the current state of gang activity in Los Angeles. Yet, he had perfected the ability to hide the scorn he felt for defendants—defendants like Reginald Washington sitting now in front of him.

He gently grazed his thumb over the butt of the Glock, nestled under his left armpit in the leather shoulder holster he had concealed beneath his robe. The Judge hesitated, moving his hand up to adjust the way his glasses rested on the bridge of his nose.

He scrutinized Eddie. He then methodically swept over the other eleven faces in the jury, but eventually circled back to the foreman.

Eddie was uncertain if it would help or hurt his case to engage the judge's stare. He tried hard to manufacture, to present, an absolute blank expression, but even this seemingly mundane effort was exhausting.

The sound of Judge Sherman clearing his throat was louder than the words that followed, "This court would like to express our sincere appreciation for your service. You have spent eight long days on this case, and it is obvious from the time you took during your deliberations, that you took this very seriously, following my instructions, and that you carefully considered all of the evidence that was presented in this courtroom. There were many facts and details presented to you—some of them moderately complex. It is clear to me that you pored over these details, and discussed these points at great length. Again, I would like to thank you. At this time, ladies and gentlemen of the jury, you are dismissed."

****

It was as if Eddie was driving on a rail. Like one of those rides at Disneyland, where the rider can pretend to be steering, but the rocket or boat or train or flying elephant just goes where it's supposed to regardless of which way the wheel is turned. And, like a movie unfolding before the rider, the scenery is just taken in passively. But, this ride was not one of those thrilling Magic Kingdom views of dinosaurs from a train through the Grand Canyon or a river cruise up the Amazon. This ride home was a rather unamusing amusement park ride. This ride took him through a tunnel of garbage. The garbage of the inner city—the cars, streets and buildings. A fake backdrop, a movie set, it wasn't real to him. It wasn't so much that he felt above this—not that he felt more worldly or superior or more intelligent or had another comma or two in his bank account passbook. It was something much more basic: he felt as though he didn't belong here. This was not his home. He didn't understand how these people, this multitude of lives actually functioned and survived on these streets. The fact was, that many of them, like Oliver, did not survive.

He felt that he tried—at the beginning—he really tried. He thought back to those first painfully boring hours in the jury pool room down on the first floor. Room 102. He wanted to get into conversations. He wanted to play checkers. He wanted to have interactions—as he thrived on new, on different. From the time he was young, he learned and grew and took energy from these interactions. His entire life, he had always embraced interacting with strangers from different states, or foreign countries thousands of miles away or across oceans. But these strangers were from his own city—only twelve miles from his house. Yet, they were the strangest of all. He thought of the kids playing in their cardboard fort—when he was barfing in the gutter. Mostly, he thought of the little black kid from the Century Palms—Lamont. The eight year-old kid who ultimately—by simply opening his small hand to reveal those two bullets—solved everything. He wanted to take the kid out of Compton. He wanted to take Lamont home with him—hell, maybe even bring him to a World Series game one day. Would that give him a better chance to survive? Or would Lamont be unable to handle being Eddie's kid, growing up in Eddie's world? Would that experiment be doomed to failure? It might be like jumping off a boat to begin a dive—but with no air in the tank. It would be the stuff of dreams—like Reggie, from his dream, being able to breathe underwater with no tanks, and that, be it dream or reality—eventually turned terrifying. Was there something, anything, he could do to improve the chance that Lamont would not become Reggie? He wondered. He was disturbed at the thought that the possible outcome of his efforts might destroy him. Maybe both of them.

Didn't Ahab's quest to kill the White Whale end in something that more closely resembled suicide?

He longed for the end of the ride—back to reality—back to *his* reality of a gated community. Just one big gate with a guard sitting at a computer checking all cars going in and out of the neighborhood.

Where a big brown Cadillac would not be allowed in.

There would be a smiling guard who knew his name.

'Nice to see you Mr. Curtain. Great wax job on the 'Vette.'

He wanted to go back to his safe neighborhood, something very different from a place like The Century Palms. His house that had no iron bars on any of the windows. A house with landscaping. And a gardener. A house with a fountain and a bird-bath and fruit trees. Back to his house on the hill.

CHAPTER 20 - City of Angels

October 28, 1993
Marina Del Rey, California

It was Friday afternoon—two full days since the trial ended. Remarkably, they had no chance to talk about it, as they hardly saw each other. Renee was dialed in with her studies, the clock ticking on her intense preparation for the bar exam. Eddie spent long hours at his business, putting out the usual fires, but additionally, he needed to attempt more than a little damage control for the mistakes that occurred in the eight days he missed. The cutting of the fabric—that fiasco—was already spoken of in code—a three letter acronym among his employees; "OFF" was the term that would hence forth refer to that infamous Orange Fabric Fuckup. He even went in to the office last night, when Renee was out with her study group, partly because he was playing so much catch-up at the office, but, there was a piece of him that had to address something else—something fairly underhanded. He needed to try to sell his lie from the other morning, when she was in the shower. He was not at all comfortable with this task, hating the fact that he needed to spend one iota of energy thinking in such a dishonest fashion. But he judged it necessary, at least for now. He figured if Renee believed that he went in, at night, a second time, she might never bring the subject up again. He would then be off the hook, as far as it being necessary to spin a broader web of fiction. He thought perhaps—he *knew*—that someday, he would come clean with her, as to his Tuesday night drive to Compton. It was way too big for Eddie to keep to himself; thus far he was maintaining, but the secret was taking a toll on him. It was nearly impossible to bear it alone—to keep it pushed just barely below the surface of nearly every thought in every waking moment. It had to be shared—maybe not with the judge, or attorneys or the jury—but absolutely, he had to share it with her.

The dimly lit street, the buildings of The Palms, the run from the guard bungalow, the stopwatch, the little black kid, the open window, the closed window... the bullets! The proof of the murder! I've got to tell her...
Someday soon...

He stayed late at his office, until after 1 AM, knowing she would be asleep if he got home that late. She'd be dead tired—exhausted from all her reading. He also knew that she had to wake up quite early to do some work down at the law library. So then, when she left the house, it would be his turn to be asleep—especially if he took another sleeping pill. Almost by Eddie's design, they were perfectly out of synch.

So, before he drove back to his office, he left a note on the kitchen counter that read simply: "Sunset sail tomorrow?"

Returning late, walking into the dark house, he found a flickering half-melted candle illuminating the note on the kitchen granite. She wrote nothing, but the answer to his question was conveyed, his three words encircled with a pink heart, drawn from one of her pink highlighters.

Perhaps it was that thought he had driving home from the last day of the trial—he was concerned about the future of those kids playing in the poor neighborhood. He never thought about kids—they had always been invisible to him. Yet now, he also found himself thinking about Lamont. But it was more than Lamont—it was the concept of having a son. Going to ball games. Teaching him things.

What did he say to me? 'I ain't got no daddy.'
Someday soon... Maybe I should stop saying that...

It was the first time in his life Eddie ever felt like being a father. His business and all his other interests precluded that concept. He had achieved nearly every goal he ever set for himself, large and small. But his proudest moment had come when he was able, two years ago, to buy his mom and dad a house. He fulfilled a promise he had made to himself when they lived in that tiny house in the rough neighborhood back in Inglewood. No camera could capture the look on his mother's face when he led her into that sparkling new kitchen for the first time and she saw the enormous bowl overflowing with fresh fruit. Remembering the immense joy his parents got from their son, now, he wondered if he would ever experience something like that. He knew Renee wanted to start a family—wanted it more than anything. He knew that her commitment to become a lawyer was big. It drove her. But he also knew that it paled in comparison to her true desire: to be a mother.

****

Once they arrived at the dock, it was all business. Unclasping the blue canvas wheel and boom covers, positioning blocks and winch handles, running sheets and guys and readying halyards to hoist the main and jib. Through all of these tasks, there was almost zero non-boat talk. And with their journey into the insanity that had become their lives these past few days—that was probably for the best.

The sky had turned a deeper blue, enabled by the sun sinking lower. After they had sailed about two miles offshore, sitting together, in the cockpit, the tape in the cassette player came to the end. It had just finished one of their mutually agreed upon feel good albums—'*Legend*,' the classic Reggae album by Marley. But now—the quiet was as good as the music. They enjoyed the steady, soothing rhythm of the rise and fall of the sharp bow—pointing like a spear, first impaling, then obliterating, and finally withdrawing, to reveal that magnificent orange orb of the sun. That wonderful hypnotic motion of *Lazy Lightning*, their boat, was somehow made easier to savor when the music was off.

He looked down at the compass—that instrument of perfection that commanded his attention for so many hundreds of glorious hours while at sea. Now, he wondered if it would forever be a haunting reminder of his week on the jury. Eddie's heart began beating more rapidly.

How about now? Do I tell her now how I think I might be ready to be a father?

Renee turned back to look toward the receding beach, where she saw the first lights in the city beginning to come on. The silence of their joint meditation was broken by her voice. She sort of mumbled, more than spoke, "The last city."

Eddie, immediately detecting the pensive mood, leaned closer, catching her whispering something else.

"One random bullet…"

It was a replay of Harry's words from the other night—incredibly–the same words Eddie used when he was alone in front of the mirror in the jurors' restroom three days ago.

He wasn't quite sure that she even intended him to hear it.

"What did you say?"

His question hung in the air for a few seconds.

"Some day we're going to burn it down," she said, without looking at him.

Eddie looked astern, trying to see what she had seen. "You mean the city?"

"Uh huh."

"Burn it down and start over?" he asked.

"I don't know if we'll be able to start over. I just know Los Angeles is going to burn down."

She was probably the most positive—maybe the most optimistic person he had ever met. He hadn't seen this look on her face since the night on an early date when she first shared the story of her childhood friend, Leslie, who drowned. It was pretty unusual for her to come up with a thought as depressing as this.

Eddie waited for a moment before speaking. His mind spinning with ways to engage her, to comfort her, to be her soul mate, in this rare display of doom and darkness. He realized she had also suffered plenty through his week of jury duty, picturing her curled up in that tight little ball on the floor in front of the stereo the other night. She was weak, defenseless, holding her hands over her ears, while sobbing in wounded misery. The image disturbed him.

Maybe this is not the time to tell her I want to be a daddy.

"What's the compass course to Bora Bora?" he asked.

****

Since they had rounded the rocks of the Marina Del Rey breakwater, leaving it to starboard, Renee had been steering the entire time. She executed two flawless tacks, Eddie manning the winches on both the jib and lazy sheets. It was a picture postcard Southern California night: a balmy 74 degrees, wind 12 knots out of the North-West, sun growing, flattening, and turning more crimson every second as it slid toward the golden shimmering strobes of water below the horizon line. Just a few thin cirrus clouds in the distance would add to the majesty of the sunset. Eddie had heard that there was some meteorological phenomenon rendering October sunsets the best—wherein the lovely wisps of color in the cloud formations seemed to hold the intensity of those fiery coral and orange streaks long after the sun dissolved.

Without a word, Renee tapped Eddie's right hand and gently placed it at 12 o'clock, on top of the large wheel, before stepping away from the helm. It was warm from where her hand had been. She grabbed the teak handrail and nimbly climbed down the four steps of the companionway, disappearing below into the cabin. Eddie was left alone, topside, for a few minutes. Curling a couple fingers of his left hand around one of the cold spokes of the stainless wheel, he looked up at the wind indicator at the top of the mast, and then at the telltales—the two pieces of red yarn tied to the shrouds. He turned his face directly into the wind coming off the starboard bow. Smiling to himself, he took pleasure in the fact that he did not need to alter her course—not even two degrees—as she had been accurately sailing the trim of the jib.

Eddie didn't know—maybe she went below to grab a sweatshirt for the oncoming cooler night air. Or, maybe it was to open a bottle of the good rum, and fix a couple of her perfect

Cuba Libres to enjoy in the final moments of the sunset. Perhaps she was going to sit at the nav-station to see if she could actually plot a course to Tahiti.

Small tears began to form in his eyes. Were they tears of joy, upon acknowledging his fortune in having found her for his wife? Or, perhaps they were tears from way over at the other end of the continuum—the dark end. It's possible these were tears of despair, as thoughts in the wake of the trial had caused him to consider impending doom himself several times this past week.

'Burn it down,' she had said.

Who was it who spoke about L.A. being the last outpost—the pinnacle of Western Civilization? It was settled last, even after San Francisco. The Gold Rush, the Sutter's Mill prospectors, the pioneers and the settlers—they all moved West. They had hit the Pacific, this Pacific, exactly where we are sailing now—they hit the sea and could go no further. And now, the dream of the Promised Land of the West had become the Wild West once again. Gangs and indiscriminate killings, and so much racial tension. Outlaws like Reggie Washington running free. Truth—like she told me about in the quote from that law professor, is no longer valued. So, is it inevitable that a cleansing by fire is the next logical step?

Were Eddie's tears, tears of sadness at not knowing Oliver Jefferson in life, but only in death? Eddie only knew him as the murdered security guard. In fact, he realized that he had no idea what Oliver even looked like, other than that he was a 5'11" black man. To Eddie, he had no face. It was an awful—a disturbing—truth, that Eddie would forever have to live with the image of that terrible distorted face, the unbalanced eyes of Reginald Washington burned into his brain, while Oliver

Jefferson had no face—no eyes. Not a single picture of Oliver was shown throughout the entire trial. But, to make matters worse, he recalled from the one piece of evidence, the one time Oliver was represented, that was in Exhibit 1—there, for all to see—he was depicted on the large white board, hanging on the easel, with an almost obscene simplicity, as a tiny black 'x.' And later, during deliberations, cruelly, he again was shown the same way: as another small 'x,' this time drawn with white chalk. Like the same chalk the cops use to outline a dead body.

It's also possible that there was a much simpler explanation for the tears in Eddie's eyes. They could have been from simply staring too long directly into the fresh ocean breeze. *'Just another one of life's great paradoxes,'* Eddie once explained, to the delight of Renee, on one of those early dates, *'the wind simultaneously created, yet dried your tears.'*

Eddie did not know Oliver. But, they shared something in common that Eddie could not possibly have known. Like Oliver, Eddie too, on occasion, would intentionally blur his vision to create various visual effects.

Like an owl, Eddie rotated his gaze away from the bow, back to the stern wake behind him, where he enjoyed the lovely legs of an isosceles triangle, formed of white tipped waves continuously growing longer, as the boat sliced through the dark water. The two angles of these receding, yet simultaneously evolving lines of water, seemed, almost like giant outstretched arms. The arms held, or rather, *offered* for his pleasure, everything that lay in his field of vision in front of him. The far base of the triangle, four miles away now, opposite the vortex of his rudder, was the line of rocks which composed the long breakwater. He could see, above the low rocks which defined the horizon line of his vision, hills and buildings and silhouettes of impossibly tall palms; the offering was his city, his home, L.A.

The masterpiece of the cirrus clouds had faded, as the last bit of color had melted into the Pacific behind him in the West. But he could now see millions of points of new light appearing from the city before him. Twinkling amber, red, green and white. To Eddie, they became gold, and rubies, and emeralds and diamonds. Like so many jewels—Los Angeles draped in treasure—in flickering diamonds. He had tried to describe it to his Midwest and East Coast friends or to business associates who had not experienced it—the viewing of the sunset and subsequent birthing of the lights of L.A.—when seen from a small boat a few miles off-shore, was something every human being should experience. He likened it to one of the required bucket list items, on par with El Capitan in Yosemite, or Sunrise at Haleakla Crater in Hawaii, or Iguazu Falls from the Argentina side.

What did they call it? People who lived high on the cliffs of Palos Verdes to his South, looking down on the lights? That wonderful arc of lights separating the vast black ocean from the twinkling sprawl of L.A? Yes: 'The Queen's Necklace.' Perfect.

He looked below and called out to her, "Renee, can you come back up—there's something I want to tell you..."

Like Oliver used to do as a child, Eddie played the same trick, blurring his own teary eyes. He saw the perfect lasers and lines of color shooting off into the night in all directions. Shooting out into infinity, emanating from L.A.—The City of Angels. He saw the rays of light. The rays of hope.

It was beautiful.